What readers have to say about *The Boy with no Boots*

'Stunning. Beautifully written, with an exquisitely poetic narrative'

'One of those rare books that stays with you long after you've finished reading it'

'The most heart-warming book I have read in a long time. I did not want it to end'

'Fabulous read'

'One of the best books I have read. I couldn't put it down'

'Brilliant'

'The prose is simply superb. When the sheer beauty of words can evoke tears, that's the sign of a gifted writer'

'Of all the books I have bought, this is the best'

'I thought all the characters were brilliant'

'A book to touch your heart'

'Every page was a pleasure to read'

'This novel is sweet and insightful and shows a good understanding of human emotions'

'Spellbinding'

'I thoroughly enjoyed it and the insight into the afterlife was so interesting'

'Sheila Jeffries is an amazing storyteller'

'A truly unique book, one that I would highly recommend. I can't wait for her next'

'Deep insight and understanding into the pain and fear many people live with. I heartily recommend this book to everyone who is tired of the violence and anger in so many books now'

Also by Sheila Jeffries

Solomon's Tale
Solomon's Kitten
The Boy with no Boots
Timba Comes Home

SHEILA JEFFRIES

The Girl by the River

**SIMON &
SCHUSTER**

London · New York · Sydney · Toronto · New Delhi

A CBS COMPANY

First published in Great Britain by Simon & Schuster UK Ltd, 2016
A CBS company

1 3 5 7 9 10 8 6 4 2

Simon & Schuster UK Ltd
1st Floor
222 Gray's Inn Road
London WC1X 8HB

www.simonandschuster.co.uk

Simon & Schuster Australia, Sydney
Simon & Schuster India, New Delhi

A CIP catalogue record for this book is available from the British Library

Paperback ISBN: 978-1-4711-7682-1
eBook ISBN: 978-1-4711-5493-5

Typeset in Bembo by Hewer Text UK Ltd, Edinburgh
Printed and bound in Great Britain by CPI Group (UK) Ltd, Croydon, CR0 4YY

Simon & Schuster UK Ltd are committed to sourcing paper that is made
from wood grown in sustainable forests and supports the Forest Stewardship
Council, the leading international forest certification organisation. Our
books displaying the FSC logo are printed on FSC certified paper.

To the Earth Angels, with gratitude.

The Girl
by the River

Prologue

1960

Three o'clock. The chimes of the Hilbegut church clock cut through the heat haze that shimmered in the air. Above the village, on a south-facing hillside, the girl with the chestnut hair was watching the sunlight glint on a wafer-thin Gillette razorblade she held between finger and thumb. It winked and flashed, triumphantly, she thought: the sharp silver blade that was to bring her hated life to a glorious end.

Her chestnut hair rippled around the girl's bare shoulders. Red flowers burned in the grass, scarlet pimpernel and sheep sorrel. Red, red, soon to be joined by the red of her blood. She would lie down, and place her cut wrist on the springy turf, and let her life soak away into the earth she loved. Even the cushions of birds-foot-trefoil had flecks of red in their yellow petals. She wouldn't look at her blood draining into the wiry grass. She'd turn her head away, and wait for sleep.

A blue scabious flower nodded intrusively at her. She picked it and stared at the blaze of blue with a core of violet.

It reminded her of her father's eyes. Those eyes. They knew everything. Even stuff she didn't want them to know. Just thinking about those eyes brought her father's face before her, one of his unexpectedly wise remarks bobbing to the surface. 'It's not the big things that break us,' Freddie had said to his youngest daughter, 'it's the little things.'

The pain in his eyes, the memory of it, made her tighten her grip on the Gillette razorblade she had taken from his bathroom cupboard. She dropped the scabious flower and examined her wrist, the blue veins of it like rivers in the sand. One cut, one sleep, and it would be over, there on the blood-soaked hillside.

The sudden, raw, stinging pain of the cut was shocking. Nauseous and trembling, she threw the red razorblade onto a patch of pink thyme. Light as a butterfly, it pitched there in the sun. Gasping with fear, she pressed her slashed wrist into the turf, and turned her head away. She'd done it. The burn of triumphant anger drained away, transmuted into a ringing silence. Regret dawned, fiercely, like the midsummer sun. The girl's eyes gazed out across the land she loved, over the velvet greens of the Somerset Levels to the distant silk of the sea, the magic islands of the Bristol Channel and the Welsh mountains beyond. With love too bright and hate too dark, her mind cracked open like broken china. She let go, and let the waves of giddiness take her floating, the waves of her chestnut hair a drifting cloak of comfort.

The butterfly arrived just as her eyes began to close. It was the last thing she saw as it pitched on her hand. She felt its delicate legs clinging to her skin. It sat attentively, its red and purple wings fanned out, its antennae glistening stiffly, its tiny pointed face watching her with blue-black eyes. Questioning her. Why?

How had it come to this?

PART ONE

1945

Chapter One

1945

'Why is Mummy screaming?'

Freddie looked deep into the questioning eyes of the child on his lap. Then he looked away, gazing at the autumn sky outside the window. He tensed, watching a sparrowhawk hovering against wine-dark clouds. It came closer until he could see its cream throat and the beat of its brindled wings. The red of the rising sun glinted on its sharp claws. Level with the window, it glared in at Freddie, a clear, yellow chill of intention in its eye.

'Daddy? Daddy, why is Mummy screaming?' Three-year-old Lucy pinched the tweed sleeve of his jacket in her chubby hand. Freddie stroked the child's white-blonde hair, letting a strand curl around his finger and marvelling at the rose fresh-ness of her, the purity of her eyes in the dawn. He didn't know how to answer her question. There was only the truth. And truth could hurt and frighten a young child.

He had a go at distracting her. 'Look at the big bird. A spar-rowhawk. See it? Down it goes – look!' The sparrowhawk dived like a stone falling, and flew up, satisfied, with a tiny, rumpled sparrow cheeping in its claws.

'Bad bird!' said Lucy and turned her frightened eyes to look into his face. They both froze, and clung together, as the longest scream rang through the walls. It went on and on, and Freddie could hardly bear the way it echoed through his heart. He picked up Lucy and walked about with her, his feet tramping the brown lino floor, his voice whispering an assortment of desperate prayers to a God he wasn't comfortable with. 'Please, please, don't let her die – please God – I need my Kate – I need her.'

He was grateful for the way Lucy wound her soft little arms around his neck and clung to him until the screaming stopped and sunlight swept across the garden and through the square panes of the eastern windows. The silence was a moment when the colour of fear became an intense gold. Then the sky darkened over Monterose and a new cry soared above everything, like the sparrowhawk, a cry of challenge and anger.

The cry pierced Freddie's calm. In a moment of clarity he heard a message encrypted in that wild cry, and it said, 'I'm BACK,' and even as he raced up the stairs there was dread tangled with hope in his heart. What he had seen in a vision, years ago, in the eyes of a drowning woman. Pale blue eyes with a core of gold, like the sparrowhawk.

'You can come in now, Freddie.'

Dykie, the midwife, met him at the bedroom door, her wrinkled face looking up at him brightly, her papery cheeks flushed and smiling.

'Is – is Kate all right?' Freddie asked.

Dykie searched his concerned eyes, shuffling the responses in her mind. 'She's tired – but she'll get over it. It was –' Dykie hesitated, then beamed reassuringly, 'And you have a little girl, Freddie – another one – a sister for Lucy. How about that?'

Secretly, Freddie had hoped for a boy, and he knew Kate had too. They'd chosen a name – Robert Levi. It had a ring to it – Robert Levi Barcussy. 'Well,' said Freddie. 'Two little girls – I hope to God they don't grow up to be nurses and school teachers.'

Dykie laughed. 'Come on – in you go – I'll go down and tell Lucy she's got a little sister.'

Freddie pushed the bedroom door open a crack and peered in nervously. Kate was waiting for him with a radiant smile. As always, he was caught off guard by her beauty – the way her skin seemed luminous like the top of a church candle. The flame in her eyes drew him into the bedroom, their love nest with the red tasselled curtains, the colourful rag rugs Kate had made, and the picture of two Shire horses pulling a loaded hay cart against the sunset. On the deep window sill stood the stone angel with her sweet face and praying hands, Freddie's first ever stone carving.

'Don't look so worried, dear,' Kate beamed at him. 'We've got a beautiful baby girl – and she's big and healthy. I'm sorry I made all that fuss, dear. You must have been pacing the floor.' She patted the damask bedspread which Dykie had smoothed and straightened to bring some order into the room. 'It's all right, dear, you can sit on the bed.' Kate reached out and took his hand. She pulled it to her face and leaned her hot cheek against it. 'I do love you, Freddie, more than anyone on earth. And I'll soon be up and about again, cooking dinner and bossing you about.'

Freddie wanted to smile, but his face felt rigid with the hours of anxiety. 'Let's look at the baby then,' he said. He hadn't told Kate how afraid he was that another baby would distract her from loving him with all her heart.

He leaned over her to see the baby who was tightly wrapped in a shawl his mother had made. They both gazed at the tiny, crumpled face. 'She's sleeping,' Kate said fondly, touching the baby's brow with a caring finger, trying to smooth away the delicate furrow of a frown. 'She's already had a suck, and she's really strong. We're so blessed, Freddie. Two healthy little girls. Well . . . say something!'

'Who does she look like?' Freddie asked, and the baby girl opened her eyes right on cue and stared up at him. His blood ran cold. Pale blue eyes with a core of gold. He looked at Kate, and they both spoke at once. 'Ethie!'

There was a silence.

Mesmerised by the baby's gaze, Freddie offered a long calloused finger, ingrained with oil and stone dust. The baby grasped it and clung. It took Freddie's breath away. This tiny being had claimed him. She had him forever. And she looked like Ethie.

He remembered his vision of Ethie, years ago, long before she had been swept to her death by the Severn Bore. He'd seen her floating on her back in the speeding brown water, her hair twisting with the creamy curl of the foam, her eyes glaring a last glare, her blue lips forming words, 'I'll be back – I'll be back.'

'Penny for them?' said Kate. Freddie's silences were like green apples. They took a long time on the tree to get ripe, and when they did, the result was usually amazing, or funny or prophetic.

'Well,' Freddie hesitated, still feeling the powerful grip of that small fist around his finger. He looked into Kate's amber brown eyes and saw the sunlight which was always in there like the view of a cottage garden from the stone archways of his fear. 'I hope she won't turn out like Ethie.'

Kate looked determined. 'Well, if she does, dear, then we must love her and support her. Ethie was a tormented soul. None of us understood what made her so difficult, but she had good in her too. She was clever, and deep – too deep for her own good, really. You'll be a wonderful father, Freddie. You're so good with Lucy.'

'Ah. Maybe.' Freddie felt a smile twitching at the corners of his mouth. He tried to forget the sparrowhawk, and its menace. He knew it was gloomy thinking, like his mother. Fearful and negative. He didn't want to be like that. Or like his father.

''Tis powerful,' he said, 'what we inherit from our parents. My old dad – he had a terrible temper – he'd smash every plate in the kitchen, and cry with shame. I vowed I would never be like him.'

'And you aren't,' Kate said firmly.

'I'm all right – with you in my life.' Freddie put his other hand gently over Kate's brow. Her hair felt damp, her skin hot.

'Ooh, that's lovely, lovely and cold,' she said, and closed her eyes, soaking up the healing energy that came from Freddie's large hand. He wouldn't say so, but she knew what he was doing – sending her strength and peace in a way that came naturally to him. 'You're making me better.'

Freddie glanced at the mound of Kate's body under the quilt. 'Is – is everything all right – down there?' he asked. 'You know what I mean.'

'Yes, dear. Everything's all right,' Kate beamed at him and her smile flooded his world with light. Those words – 'everything's all right', the way Kate said them with such assurance, had rescued him countless times from the maelstrom of anxiety that swirled around in his soul, dragging him into itself.

Gently extracting his finger from the baby's fist, Freddie went to the window. The sparrowhawk had gone, and cockerels were crowing all over Monterose. The smell of steam drifted through the open window from the station, and the sounds of shunting engines, shouting men, and people whistling as they rode down the street on creaking bicycles. One particular bicycle with high handlebars and a basket on the front was moving fast under the vigorously pedalling feet of a small, square woman who was riding it towards the house, her face shining like an apple.

'Here's your mother!' said Freddie, and just stopped himself from reminding Kate that Sally, her mother, had been hoping for a boy.

'She'll be thrilled.' Kate looked down fondly at the new baby girl. 'You're going to meet your granny.'

'I gotta get to work,' said Freddie.

'Oh, stay for a minute, won't you?' implored Kate. 'We must choose a name. And Lucy must see her little sister.'

Dykie put her head round the door. 'Lucy won't come upstairs,' she said. 'I didn't want to force her. She seems a bit upset. I think she wants her daddy.'

Freddie ran downstairs, the money jingling in his pockets. He paused by the kitchen door, startled by the conversation going on between Lucy and Sally.

'Mummy doesn't like my baby sister,' Lucy announced.

'Course she does. All mummies love their babies,' said Sally briskly.

'But not THIS baby. She's a bad baby.'

'Oh, don't be silly, Lucy. She can't be a bad baby when she's only just been born. There's no such thing as a bad baby.'

'I'm not being silly, Granny.'

'Don't you stamp your foot at me, young lady,' said Sally. 'Now come on. You come upstairs with Gran and we'll see what we think of the new baby. You might like her!'

'I won't,' Lucy muttered. She looked up and saw Freddie in the doorway. 'I want Mummy. I want Mummy to come downstairs. I don't want a baby sister. Baby sisters are bad.'

13

Freddie nodded at Sally. ''Tis a girl,' he said. 'Strong as an ox, she is. You go up. I'll take Lucy out in the garden.'

'Is Kate all right?' Sally asked.

'Seems to be – yes – but . . .'

'But?'

Freddie hesitated. 'It was – she had a bad time – worn her out.'

Sally nodded. 'She'll get over it. You know Kate, always looking on the bright side.'

Freddie picked up Lucy, who was clinging to his legs, and together they watched Sally bustling up the stairs proudly carrying a tiny yellow and white matinee set she had knitted for her new grandchild.

Lucy rarely cried, but she did now, snuggled against Freddie's shoulder. Freddie maintained a calming silence, his eyes waiting for the moment when Lucy would look up at him. Then he would send her his love, wordlessly, his big hand patting and stroking the child's small, indignant back.

'Where's Granny Annie?' sobbed Lucy, looking at the Bakery Cottage next door.

'She's still asleep,' Freddie said quietly. 'See, the curtains are closed. It's early in the morning. Granny Annie can see the new baby later.' He was glad he hadn't woken Annie. She would have been worrying twice as much as he was, about the birth.

A late red rose was hanging over the wall. He sniffed its fragrance, and immediately sensed the presence of a bright spirit. A blaze of light. A smile. A scent of honeysuckle. A pair of wise, familiar eyes. Granny Barcussy! His beloved Gran who had died when he was a child. Freddie looked at Lucy, wondering if she had seen her too, but he was pretty sure she hadn't.

'Let the flowers do the talking,' said Granny Barcussy, and he felt her touch his arm. Then she vanished into the light, leaving him a feeling of warm acceptance. Had she led him towards that red rose?

He put Lucy down and looked into her eyes. 'You pick Mummy some flowers.' He took a penknife from his pocket, opened it and neatly cut the red rose. 'No – wait a minute,' he said, as Lucy held out her hand for it. 'Let Daddy trim the prickles off.'

Smiling now, Lucy waited while he neatly shaved the prickles from the stem, and gave her the rose. Freddie watched her staring at it and he sensed that the vibrant life in the flower was radiating love and warmth. Lucy darted all over the garden, picking Michaelmas daisies, sprigs of mint and rosemary. She arranged them round the red rose and brought him the posy. 'Some string, Daddy?'

'Ah – string.' Freddie rummaged in the depths of his jacket pocket and found a grubby curl of white string. 'That do?'

Lucy nodded, beaming. 'You tie it, Daddy,' and she put the posy down on the broad back of the lion he had carved from Bath stone.

'This is a reef knot,' he told her as he tied the stems together. 'Left over right and right over left. It's strong, see?'

15

'You are clever, Daddy,' Lucy looked at him adoringly, her eyes shining now. Freddie felt energised by her joy. He fished in his pockets again, wanting to see Lucy's eyes shine even brighter.

'There you are – a silver sixpence for the baby, and a silver shilling for you. Don't lose it now.'

Lucy gasped. 'Thank you, Daddy!' She flashed him a smile and ran into the house, clutching the flowers and the coins. Freddie strode after her, pleased to see her white-blonde curls bouncing as she ran. He couldn't describe the magic of making Lucy happy. It was a blessing in his life.

He followed her upstairs, smiling as he listened to Kate's cheerful voice. Lucy was on the bed, curled against her mother, and she had dumped the posy on Kate's heart. Sally was walking around with the new baby in her arms.

'We've got to choose a name,' she said, looking down at the baby with her eyes full of tears. *Old tears*, thought Freddie. *Tears for Ethie!*

'Who is she like?' he asked.

Sally didn't hesitate. 'Ethie,' she said. 'I saw it straight away. It's like – like she IS Ethie, reborn. Ethie was exactly like this, and a difficult birth. So why not call her Ethie? It's short for Etheldra.'

'No,' said Freddie and Kate together, and Freddie bit back the comment that burned on his tongue. He felt the name Ethie would be a curse on the new little baby.

'What do you think, dear?' Kate asked him, and he noticed that her face was suddenly pale, her eyes half closed.

'Something plain and simple,' Freddie said. He watched the tiny baby who was staring at him over Sally's shoulder, her pale blue eyes burning with intensity. 'Tessa,' he said. 'How about that?'

'Hmm. Tessa. We haven't got a Tessa in the family,' Sally said. 'We could call her Tessie for short.'

'What do you think, Kate? – KATE!' Freddie turned to look at Kate, shocked to see her eyes closed, her face drained of colour, her eyelids blue, her sweet lips unmoving. He took her hand. It was limp. 'KATE! Something's wrong. Call Dykie up.'

'Mummy's asleep,' said Lucy firmly.

Everything happened quickly. Dykie came running up the stairs. 'You take Lucy downstairs, Sally – and the baby – for now. And you, Freddie – best leave the room,' she said, but Freddie stayed close, holding Kate's limp hand, his thumb fondling the plain gold wedding ring and the diamond engagement ring she wore so proudly.

'Don't look,' said Dykie, and she rolled the quilt back over Kate's body. Freddie caught a glimpse of blood-stained sheets.

'Oh my goodness!' Dykie's eyes flashed up at him, dark and afraid. 'She must go to hospital. Immediately. No time to telephone—'

'I'll take her in the lorry. You hold the doors open – and find some towels, will you please?' Freddie wrapped an old tartan rug around Kate's shoulders, flung the sheets back and lifted her. 'Never mind the blood,' he said, and, unexpectedly, tears ran down his cheeks and dripped from his chin. In

17

a daze, he carried her down the stairs with Dykie running ahead, and Sally white-faced in the kitchen doorway, the baby screaming in her arms. 'Get some cushions for her – and you get in the back with her.'

Sally came running with two brown cushions from the sofa. Between them they bundled Kate into the back of the lorry which was half full of stones from the quarry. A trail of blood was left along the garden path and into the road.

'You look after the children – please,' Freddie said to the distraught Sally who was close to panic, 'and keep calm.'

'My girl. Please, please God, don't take my girl.' Sally was openly weeping and staring at the sky. 'Don't take our Kate – she's all we've got – please God.'

Dykie climbed into the back of the lorry with Kate, her navy blue skirt getting covered in stone dust. 'The baby will have to go with her,' she called to Sally. 'See if you can get someone to help – then bring her up in the pram.'

Freddie didn't usually swear at his lorry, but he did now. 'Start, you bugger. Bloody well start.' The engine spluttered into life and he put his foot down and roared up the hill to Monterose Hospital where Kate had worked as a nurse in the years before Lucy was born. 'All that love she gave,' he muttered as he drove furiously. 'Now it's gotta come back to her – oh God – if I lost her . . .' His whole body was shaking uncontrollably as he turned into the hospital drive. He braked carefully, not wanting to jolt his precious cargo, and Dykie leapt down and ran into the hospital.

Shaking and terrified, Freddie managed to lift Kate down from the lorry. She opened her eyes and looked up at him. 'My baby?' she said. 'Where's my baby girl?'

'Your mother's got her. Don't try to talk, Kate – my love. You lie quiet.'

The doors of the hospital burst open and two nurses in starched hats, and a burly porter rushed towards them with a trolley. Freddie stood, mesmerised, with Kate in his arms, and he didn't want to let her go. He pulled the tartan rug tightly round her. 'That was Ethie's blanket,' she said, in a voice like a dry leaf. Freddie felt her trembling in his arms, and the morning sun lit her pale cheeks. Her skin looked grey, like the face of the stone angel.

'Put her on here.' The porter helped Freddie to gently lie Kate on the high trolley. He smiled confidently. 'Don't you worry, sir – we'll take good care of her.'

Freddie nodded. Miserably, with his heart thumping, he followed the trolley inside, and Dykie took his hand as if he was a child. 'There's nothing we can do now, Freddie. Except pray.'

They stood watching the doors close on Kate's dark head as she was wheeled away. NO ADMITTANCE was stamped in red letters on the doors. It looked very final.

'You're shaking, Freddie,' said Dyke looking up at him like an enquiring robin. 'You should sit down.'

'Ah. Sit here and wait, I suppose.' Freddie sat obediently on one of the hard metal chairs against a wall. A bleak and cheerless place. He found hospitals intimidating.

'I'll wait with you,' said Dyke.

'Thanks.' Freddie stared around at the peeling paint on the walls, the exposed pipes and brown linoleum floor. He looked at the stains of Kate's blood on his shirt; he could smell it and it terrified him. Kate's life draining away. Wrong. It was wrong. It shouldn't be happening. And was it his fault? Their love-making had been beautiful, a warm and blessed secret that meant the world to Freddie. 'Kate was my only love,' he said to Dykie. 'I never looked at another woman. I loved Kate since I were nine years old. Loved her. And she wanted this baby so much – we wanted a boy, but she'd love anything, Kate would. If she gave birth to a blimin' frog, she'd love it – that's the way she is. Heart of gold.'

'Don't torment yourself, Freddie,' said Dykie kindly, but Freddie needed to talk. He felt nauseous and giddy with shock, and the talking distracted him from the question of whether he was going to pass out, fall on the floor and disgrace himself as he'd done many times in his childhood. He didn't tell Dykie that. He was the man. Had to be strong.

'Last time I came in here was four years ago, before Lucy was born,' he said. 'And my mother came. We came here to a presentation ceremony, and Kate had the "Nurse of the Year" award. We were so proud of her. But she laughed it off. Fancy me getting that, she said, I haven't done anything special. Always laughing, she is. Always laughing. The house rings with it.'

'And she will be again,' Dykie assured him. 'We got her here just in time, thanks to your wonderful lorry.'

Freddie wasn't convinced. He found himself once more on the descent into gloomy thinking. He looked into Dykie's birdlike eyes. 'Tell me honestly, will you – could she die?' he asked.

Dykie wagged a skinny finger at him. 'Now what would Kate say if she heard you saying that?'

The corners of Freddie's mouth twitched as the possibility of a smile drifted through his being. 'She'd call me a – a prophet of doom. Don't be a prophet of doom, dear, she'd say.' A negative thought rushed in, wiping the smile before it happened. *That's what I've become*, he thought gloomily, *a prophet of doom.*

And hard upon that thought came another one. *That baby*, he thought, *she's brought bad luck.*

Chapter Two

MADAME ELTURA

Sally's cheeks were crimson with worry and frustration as she marched into the hospital with baby Tessa screaming in her arms.

'Any news?' she asked breathlessly.

'No. Nothing. They took her through there,' said Freddie, raising his voice above the screaming baby.

Sally handed Tessa to Dykie. 'She's never stopped crying all the way up here,' she said, 'and I found the pram but I couldn't drag it out from under all that wood. I did try. But in the end I put her in my bicycle basket, tied her in with string and rode up here, pedalled up that hill with her bawling. Turned a few heads, it did. It's a cold day but I'm hot as ten fires.'

'Poor little mite's hungry,' said Dykie. 'She ought to be with her mother.'

Sally struggled out of her heavy bottle-green serge coat and hung it over a chair.

'You're breathless,' Freddie observed. 'Come on, you sit quiet and get your breath back.'

Sally looked at him gratefully. Sensing she was on the edge of tears, Freddie looked into her worried eyes, and thought about what he was going to say. Words came through to him in a bright stream, words that didn't come from him but from a shining spirit person who had befriended him long ago when he was a child. 'Kate's going to be all right. She's a strong woman, full of life, and she won't let go. She loves being a mother. It's important to her. She'll be all right, you'll see.'

Watching the calming effect of his words settling around Sally like a soft cloak, Freddie felt empowered. 'Let me hold the baby,' he said to Dykie. 'You go and find someone – tell them we've got her and she should be with her mother.'

'I should think the whole hospital knows she's here.' Dykie eased the howling infant into Freddie's arms, and something magical happened. He looked down at the baby's tiny scrunched-up face and saw it smooth itself out like a flower in the sun. In wondrous silence, baby Tessa gazed up at him, her clear inquisitive gaze piercing his heart. Freddie talked to her in the language of silence, and he listened to the flow of her thoughts.

'She's going to be a daddy's girl!' said Sally.

'You just got yourself a job, Freddie,' Dykie said.

Freddie hardly heard them. Tessa's stare completely absorbed and unnerved him. She WAS like Ethie, but he could also see Kate in her, and his mother, and – a startling thought – *She's like me.*

Freddie walked to the window and showed Tessa the sky over Monterose. Silver and ivory clouds bubbled over the distant hills, and thousands of elm trees dotted the landscape like splashes of chromium yellow, and along the hedges the hawthorns hung heavy with scarlet berries. Far out across the Levels, the starlings made immense towers of black specks, swerving and shifting. 'A million birds with one mind,' Freddie told Tessa and saw a spark of recognition in her pale blue eyes as if she knew everything about the world she had entered. Her unwavering gaze stripped away the layers of knowledge he'd worked so hard to accumulate, stripped his soul bare. In an instant, the clever hardworking mechanic had fallen away like a black shell, and the creative artist with the gift of prophecy stood there in the sun, hand in hand with this new little being who had burst through the gates of pain and arrived, with nothing.

The squeak of shoes and a whoosh of Dettol-scented air brought him back to reality. The door marked NO ADMITTANCE was open, and two white-coated doctors stood there with grim expressions.

'Mr Barcussy?'

'That's me.' Freddie's heart began to thump again, he could feel it pulsing against the layers of thick crocheted shawl wrapped around baby Tessa.

'And I'm Kate's mother,' Sally stood up, her eyes on fire with anxiety, 'and Miss Dykes – Dykie – is the midwife.'

'Come this way.'

Again, the nausea and the fear whirled through Freddie's head as his feet followed the two doctors into a small room with dark oak chairs and a desk topped in olive green leather. On the walls were yellowing charts of people's insides, horribly fascinating but not exactly calming. A skeleton dangled in the corner, chillingly cheerful, with a tobacco-factory grin. Freddie turned his back on it, not wanting the baby to see it.

'Your wife has lost a lot of blood, Mr Barcussy. We've managed to stop the haemorrhage. But she's very weak. We need your permission to give her a blood transfusion.'

'And what's that?' asked Freddie. His skin felt cold and sweaty. He wished he hadn't asked. He didn't want to know about Kate having someone else's blood in her veins. 'Anything,' he said, interrupting, 'I'll sign anything to get her better.'

'It will help her recover very quickly – otherwise it's touch and go, and six weeks of complete rest. I imagine that's not an option?'

'I want – what's best for Kate,' Freddie said, and he signed the papers with a cold, sweaty hand. 'And where is she? I'd like to see her please.'

'And the baby,' said Sally. 'She's newly born – and hungry.'

The corridor was long and squeaky, full of ominous doors. They walked in silence and above his heavy footsteps Freddie heard the sudden roar of rain on the roof and the harsh cry of a heron as it passed overhead on its way to the river.

'Wait here while we set up the blood transfusion. It's ready to go. Then you can come in, and we'll see if the baby will feed.'

Again, the three of them waited, this time standing up, in a corridor where nurses bustled to and fro with trays and trolleys. Beyond the double doors marked MATERNITY there were babies crying. It set Tessa off, crying again.

'Give her to me,' said Freddie and, with tender pride, he scooped Tessa into his arms. He could calm her down, and show Kate he had bonded with their new daughter. Freddie wanted to be the one to put Tessa back where she belonged, in her mother's arms.

The ward sister had an intimidating starched hat and an even more starchy expression. She eyed Freddie up and down, her eyes pausing on his boots which were covered in oil and stone dust. 'We don't usually allow MEN in the maternity ward,' she said. 'Shall I take the baby?'

'I'm coming in.' The steel in Freddie's blue eyes made her step aside.

'Just ten minutes then. And strictly with the curtains round.'

Still carrying his daughter, Freddie followed the starched hat into a long ward full of women. The knitting needles stopped and twenty pairs of eyes stared at him. He ducked through the cream curtains, and there was Kate, not lying half dead as he'd expected, but sitting up, dazzling them all with the love that shone from her bright brown eyes.

'That's the best thing I've seen today!' she declared. 'My wonderful Freddie.'

Speechless, he leaned over and kissed her tenderly, his eyes searching hers. Then he tucked baby Tessa into her arm. 'My baby,' she breathed. She unbuttoned her nightie and exposed a breast that was full and throbbing.

'We don't usually let men . . .' began the starched hat but one quiet power stare from Freddie silenced her.

Tessa began to suck noisily, her eyes gazing steadily at Kate. 'Bless 'er little heart,' said Sally. 'Thank goodness!'

Freddie propped himself on the bed, his arm round Kate, his mind already creating a stone carving. A mother and child. In alabaster. He'd use the beautiful pink alabaster boulder he'd found in the quarry, and he saw himself carving it out in the sunshine, with chisels and sandpaper, and running water to make it smooth as marble. It would express his gratitude and awe at the way Kate looked so ripe and peaceful, and the baby utterly contented. Beyond the wonder of it was the statement his carving would make about priorities and wordless love.

Freddie bristled when he saw the vicar's long black robe and pristine shoes coming through the hospital entrance just as he was leaving with Sally and Dykie. So far, he'd managed to keep his mouth shut and not get into confrontational arguments with vicars. He found this one, the Reverend Reminsy, particularly patronising, and right now he felt vulnerable and nervous after the stressful morning. He wanted his family together under one roof, private and safe.

The Reverend Reminsy reminded Freddie of a heron inspecting an estuary – a yellowy-grey pointed face with black eyes that didn't allow any glimpses of who was actually in there behind the ecclesiastical smile. Irritated, he stood back and let Sally butter him up. He half expected her to curtsy. Instead, she took the vicar's hands and gazed into his face. 'How kind of you to come,' she gushed.

'I was told you'd had some kind of crisis,' the Reverend Reminsy said. 'What's happened?'

'Everything's all right now,' Sally said joyfully. 'Our Kate is in good hands. She's having a blood transfusion – and we have a beautiful little granddaughter – another one.'

'Oh, what a blessing.' The Reverend Reminsy grinned like a wizard. 'Congratulations, Freddie. You'll be having her christened, of course.'

'Ah,' said Freddie, not wanting to agree or disagree. He'd have to go along with traditions, he thought, for the sake of peace. And if he saw an angel in the church, he'd have to keep quiet about it. Long ago in his childhood his parents had drummed that into him as if they were padlocking his soul. 'Even if you do see spirit people,' his father had thundered, 'you don't talk about it. I forbid you to mention it, ever again, to anyone. Especially not Doctor Stewart.' And Annie, his mother, had added, 'Nor the vicar.'

At the funeral of his father, Levi, Freddie had been a rebellious lad of fourteen. He'd sat on the steps at the back of the church and refused to sing, and as he stared at the coffin and the backs of people's heads, he'd seen an angel. She had filled the church with an immense cone of light stretching from floor to ceiling, her luminous robe covering the entire congregation, her light gilding the black hats and the stiff shoulders. Her radiance fizzed and sparkled as if it shone on a rainstorm, turning each drop into a twinkling star.

Freddie had sat transfixed, letting the reassuring, joyful light fill his miserable being until he felt on fire and empowered. He'd wanted to crack the hard shells of protocol that encased the assembled family and he wanted to assert himself now that his father was gone. He'd picked his moment, waited until the last verse of *Rock of Ages* had died away. Then he'd stood up and told them he'd seen an angel.

When the dust had settled, his brother, George, had frog-marched him outside and slammed him against the stone wall. 'Don't you bring shame on the Barcussy family,' he'd hissed furiously. 'I'm the head of this family now, and you'll do as you're told – boy.'

It still hurt thinking about it. A bitter lesson, but the radiance of the angel hadn't faded. It stayed in his heart, strong and bright, sustaining his spirit through the dark years of the war when he and Kate had worked so hard, and had so little. Another of his prophetic visions had come true in the war years. He'd been called up to use his skills as a mechanic, working on Spitfires at Yeovilton. Long ago, as a schoolboy, he'd seen himself standing on the airfield in a blue overall, a spanner in his hand as he watched the brave little planes taking off into the dawn. He'd felt proud, and glad not to be fighting, glad to go home to Kate at the end of the long day.

'Have you given the baby a name?' The Reverend Reminsy's question brought Freddie back into the gloomy foyer of the hospital.

'Tessa,' he said, and added, 'Tessa Francis, after my old granny. She was Francis.'

'Oh yes, and a real character she was, old Mrs Barcussy. I remember her well.' The Reverend Reminsy stood looking up at Freddie with an unnerving expectancy in his eyes. *Something close to mockery*, Freddie thought, and he felt the vicar was deviously trying to make him talk about his very private ability to see spirit people.

'I gotta go.' Freddie put on his tweed cap and resisted the temptation to outstare those keen little eyes. But in his heart he wanted to tell this holy man about the sparrowhawk, about Ethie. He wanted to ask if curses were real, and if they were, what did God think he was doing? The question burned on his tongue.

'You go on to work, Freddie. I'll talk to the Reverend Reminsy. Then I'll fetch Lucy and . . .' Sally's words were cut short as the roar of an engine rattled the doors of the hospital.

Freddie stiffened. There weren't many lorries in Monterose. Most of the tradesmen still had horses and carts. Freddie's Scammell lorry was his pride and joy, and he knew the particular sound of that engine. Who had started it, out there in the hospital car park? Frowning, he crossed the foyer in long strides, only to see his precious lorry lurching out of the car park, a strange young man at the wheel, the whites of his eyes gleaming as he revved the engine, his eager hands wrenching the steering wheel.

'Oy!' Freddie ran forward, the money jingling in his pockets. 'What d'you think you're doing?'

The way the young man grinned at him ignited a hot rage in Freddie. It burned from the depth of his being, up into his arms, into his throat and over his cheeks. 'Bring that BACK!' he roared. 'That's my lorry. I worked my back off to get that.'

Devastated, Freddie ran after it, never close enough to touch it, but choked by exhaust smoke and dust as his lorry hurtled through the wide gates and down the road, away from Monterose. He ran until his lungs were on fire and he was crying with fury. Gasping, he collapsed against a farm gate, his breathing louder than the fading sound of his lorry disappearing into the distance.

The cows crowded up to the gate to look at him with motherly eyes. 'My lorry's gone. Stolen,' he informed them, 'and I had to stand there and watch him take it.' He felt the cows soaking up his anger, their dark eyes calming, caring, offering him silence and stillness. 'What am I gonna do?' he sobbed, and immediately the words came through to him.

'You get a hold of yourself, lad, and get it back.' His father's voice was very close, but Freddie was too shattered to see him. 'Don't ever be like me,' Levi said, and momentarily Freddie felt the warmth of a hand on his shoulder. He took some deep breaths, trying to calm his shaking body, and remembered his father's destructive rages which had wrecked his childhood. He remembered the owl he had made from the smashed pieces of china, and how good it felt to make something beautiful out of a disaster.

Calmer, he stood in the lane, listening, making a plan of action. He had to figure out who had taken his lorry, and he had to work out how far it would go on the fuel left in the tank. He was too upset to go back to the hospital. He found himself walking towards the stonemason's yard. Herbie would be there, and Herbie would help him.

Without his lorry, he had nothing. No way of earning to keep his growing family. The bright eyes of baby Tessa sparkled in his mind. Ethie's eyes. Had she come back through this tiny new being? Had she sent the sparrowhawk? Was it a curse? A curse encrypted long ago from the white hot metal of jealousy, a curse carried across time by an embittered, angry woman, Kate's sister, Ethie, drowned in the Severn River. She was dead. But it wasn't over.

Freddie had hypersensitive hearing. Years of listening to the deeper sounds of the countryside had given him a unique ability to detect secret dramas in the natural world. He could stand close to a hedge and hear the crack of an eggshell as a baby bird hatched. The language of the wind in the trees was clear to him; each tree had a different voice, and there were conversations between them, the ripple of poplar and the roar of oak, the whisper of beech and the singing of pine. In spring, he could even put his ear against a tree and hear the sap whistling up inside the heartwood.

So now, instead of heading down the road to Herbie, Freddie found himself listening again. He was sure he could hear his lorry, far away, parked, with the engine throbbing.

And voices around it, arguing. A fast high-pitched, scolding voice that was firing questions, and between the questions was a monosyllabic grunt in reply.

Freddie turned around and followed the tyre marks, glad that the wheels had been muddy from his recent trip to the alabaster quarry. With the road covered in mud and horse manure, it wasn't difficult to follow the curve of his lorry's tracks, down a narrow lane that led through woodland and on towards the Levels and the river. He knew the lane well and strode down it, still shaking inside, spooked by what he might find round the next bend, the sound of the lorry's engine growing louder and closer with the quiet thud of his footsteps.

At the bottom of the hill two scraggy dogs charged at him barking. Dogs didn't faze Freddie. He saw their fear and how it turned up as fierce barking. 'Now you quieten down,' he said in his quietest voice. 'What's all that fuss about? Eh?' He'd discovered long ago that if you asked a dog a question it would usually stop barking and sidle up to you, its tail flipping apologetically. And it worked with these two. Once they'd smelled his hand and accepted a gentle stroke, they trotted dutifully beside him. As the lane narrowed into a sharp bend, Freddie felt like a dog himself, his hackles rising, knowing that whoever was round there had heard his voice and fallen silent, awaiting his approach. A smell of wood smoke and soup hung in the air.

His lorry was there, awkwardly parked with its nose in the hedge, the driver's door flung open, and no one inside. 'Now you calm down.' Again the voice whispered to him, and strength steadied his mind. In slow deliberate strides, Freddie reached inside the cab and turned the engine off. He took the can of distilled water from the back, opened the bonnet and sensed the state of the engine. It was too hot to touch, and it had a sooty smell, like a steam train. With his hanky wrapped around his hand, he unscrewed the water tank and poured some in, the hiss of steam clouding his glasses. The glug of the water going in was oddly comforting as the thirsty engine creaked gratefully.

Only then did he turn to face the two pairs of eyes watching him. The young man, now staring sulkily at his boots, was sitting on the steps of a brightly painted gypsy wagon parked on a wide grassy layby, the skewbald horse tethered and munching at the grass and bramble leaves.

Standing over him was a tiny, birdlike woman with a frown clenched into her brow, two spots of crimson on her cheeks. 'Say you're sorry to the gentleman!' She aimed a slap at the young man's hunched shoulders, knocking him sideways, her wine-red shawl flying.

'Sorry,' he mumbled, and she gave him another clout, this time on his ear.

'Sorry what?' she demanded.

'Sorry – sir.'

Freddie stayed silent, standing guard in front of his lorry. He tried to see the eyes of the young man who had dared to steal it, but they were downcast.

'He's only a lad. Fourteen he is, and just lost his father.' The gypsy woman's eyes glittered with a feeling Freddie knew only too well. Grief. How it felt to lose your father at fourteen, as he had done. 'And his mother,' she went on. 'Died giving birth in the pea fields when he was only eight. But 'tis no excuse.' She raised her bony hand and the boy cringed. 'You get back down the farm, get on with the hedge-laying – that's what you're supposed to be doing. Not stealing lorries.'

Freddie's silent appraisal seemed to spook her. She hobbled up to him, a curious fire in her eyes as they searched his face for understanding. He gazed back, reminded of his granny. Words floated through his consciousness, but none of them would do so he maintained the silence. He thought it might coax the truth out of the boy and his feisty granny. But he was unprepared for what happened next.

A change came over the gypsy woman. The deep frown disappeared, eclipsed by a beguiling look of genuine surprise. 'Don't you worry – your lorry's safe now, and there's no harm done,' she said, and she took one of Freddie's large roughened hands between hers.

Startled, he let her unfold his palm, her touch like hazel twigs, a bright glow in the air between them. She studied his palm as if it were a map.

'I've got nothing to give you, sir, only a box of clothes pegs,' she said, pointing to a basket piled high with freshly made pegs whittled from the insides of sticks. 'But I'll tell your future for you – for free – as compensation.' She looked directly into his eyes, seeing him hesitate. 'And believe me, sir, you need to hear it. No one else will ever tell you what I can see. I'm a Romany Gypsy, sir, and proud of it, and my gift has been handed down through five generations. Seers, that's what we are.' She leaned closer, her voice husky. 'And I'm telling you now, sir, whether you're listening or not – you're one of us. You've got the gift of prophecy and you don't use it. You know you've got it – and it's been beaten out of you. You need to use it, because you've got trouble in your life, and today is only the beginning.'

Freddie felt a ripple of shock through his whole body. He stared at the gypsy woman's face and saw she was deadly serious. Immediately, the eyes of baby Tessa bobbed into his consciousness, not young eyes, but old eyes that harboured a sinister darkness under the bright gaze of a newborn. He felt himself crumpling inside, all his defences crashing as he meekly followed the gypsy woman into the painted caravan, eyeing the garish red and yellow promises splashed over its flaking surface: 'Madame Eltura, the one and only true fortune-teller'.

He still hadn't spoken, and the multiple shocks of the day were gathering in his bones, making him tremble.

'Sit down there.' She drew him inside and he manoeuvred himself onto a tiny, rickety chair, his long legs hunched awkwardly. Threadbare purple curtains festooned the cubicle, with gold and silver stars stitched into them in tarnished sequins. A cloth of heavy black velvet hung over a round table, and in the middle was a crystal ball.

What am I doing here? Freddie thought, alarmed, and his father's angry words came bounding back at him like long ago dogs barking through the halls of his life. 'I don't want no fortune-telling or mumbo jumbo in this family!' Levi had thundered.

'Don't touch that!'

Freddie's finger sprang back from the crystal ball. He'd wanted to touch the cold gleam of its mirrored surface.

'Is that – real rock crystal?' he asked, speaking for the first time since his arrival.

'Pure as the sun and moon, good sir.' Madame Eltura wrapped her twig-like hands around the orb of crystal and closed her eyes. Freddie thought fleetingly of Kate. If Kate had been there she would have giggled. He thought how cold and cheerless his life would be without her bright spirit of fun.

The eyes flickered open again and fixed him with a gimlet glare. 'Now don't interrupt me, sir. It's a trance, you see. But listen, listen for your life – and remember – forever.'

She started to talk in a different voice, a voice beautiful and spellbinding. Freddie sat, mesmerised, his eyes widening, his heart pounding with the revelations that poured from her woody old lips. How could she know these things? Yet he believed her. Deep in his eternal soul, he knew beyond any shadow of doubt. She was right. It was true. It would be true.

And he, Freddie Barcussy, would have to deal with it.

Stunned, he waited until she had finished. Then he asked, 'Have you got a piece of paper?' She gave him a page, torn from a red memo notebook. 'I'm not leaving until I've written this down,' Freddie said. He took a stub of pencil from his pocket and quickly covered the paper, both sides, with his copperplate script. Then he folded it into four, tucked it into his breast pocket, and extracted his legs from the cramped space.

Without another word, he started his lorry, backed it out of the hedge, and drove home. He strode through the kitchen, past the surprised faces of Dykie and Lucy. 'I got a job to do upstairs. Won't be long,' he said.

'You look shaken, Freddie,' Dykie called. 'I'll put the kettle on.'

Freddie took an envelope from his bureau and put the folded piece of paper inside. Then he found a stick of red sealing wax and a box of matches, took it into the bathroom and locked the door. He sat down on the edge of the bath, drew out the piece of paper, and read the gypsy's prophetic words one more time.

His heart was heavy as he replaced it in the blue Basildon Bond envelope, lit a match and dropped a blob of melted red sealing was over the flap. He let it cool and wrote his name and the date.

He took it back into the bedroom, and sat on the edge of Kate's side of the bed, tapping the envelope and making a silent vow. Never, never, would he disclose its chilling words, to Kate, or anyone in his family. He alone would carry in his heart the power of the gypsy's prophecy – unless – unless . . . Freddie opened a concealed drawer in his bureau and picked out a small brass key. He unhooked a picture from the wall. It was a watercolour he'd done of Monterose Church. Behind the picture was a little wooden door with a brass keyhole. He unlocked it and put the sealed envelope in the hidden cubbyhole, rested his hand on it in a moment of silent prayer, and locked it in.

Never to be opened, he vowed.

Chapter Three

TESSA

'I wish I could open the window and throw you out!' Kate gently lowered the screaming baby into the green painted cot. She turned her back and stood at the window, her hands over her ears to block the extra sound baby Tessa was creating by kicking her tiny red feet, making the shabby old cot rattle like a tambourine. 'Never in my life have I been so exasperated,' Kate said, talking to herself, 'and so TIRED.'

Lucy sidled up to her, wide-eyed. 'Don't cry, Mummy,' she said, wrapping her arms around Kate's legs. 'Tessa's a BAD baby. I told Daddy.'

'You're so sweet, Lucy. Bless you.' Kate picked the child up, glad of her angelic three-year-old's hug and her placid temperament. She carried Lucy out of the room, and shut the door on the screaming baby. That's what they'd all told her to do. Put her safely in the cot, walk out and shut the door. Leave her to scream. She'll soon learn, everyone said. But it didn't work with Tessa. Nothing worked with Tessa. She would cry for hours, the crying building into howls of fury.

No matter how much Kate tried to rock her and sing to her, no matter how often she was fed and changed, Tessa would ball her fists and fling her blankets off. It was impossible to keep her warm in the cold bedroom. Lucy was so upset by Tessa's behaviour that they had moved her bed into the spare bedroom.

Annie had come into their kitchen and was standing at the table, thoughtfully arranging a bunch of daffodils and willow catkins in a blue glass vase. 'I brought some flowers to cheer you up, Kate,' she said. 'I heard all the screaming – where is she now? In her cot?'

'Yes – and still crying,' Kate said, 'and she's trying to kick the cot to bits. She seems such an angry baby.'

'Wearing you out, isn't she?' Annie said. 'You stick to your guns. Leave her there. She'll cry herself out.'

'That'll be the day.' Kate sniffed at the white narcissus flower in Annie's hand. 'Isn't that beautiful? It's kind of you to bring them in.'

'Well, I don't know how else to help you. I can see you're having a hard time, Kate, and I expect you miss your mum, don't you? Pity she lives so far away.'

'I do miss her,' Kate said. 'But she's with family, and she wants to stay close to where Ethie died. She's never got over it. When the children are old enough we'll take them up to see her.'

'I wouldn't go all the way up there,' Annie said. 'Gloucester-shire! I've never been beyond Yeovil in my life. Never seen the sea. I could have gone on a day trip, on a charabanc,

41

but I couldn't do that. Terrified, I'd be. I just like to stay home.'

'Good for you, Annie,' Kate said, and listened as a fresh volley of screams came from upstairs. 'I'd better get back to her.'

'No – you leave her – little madam!' Annie said, and frowned, 'or she's gonna be trouble when she's older.'

'I'm not trouble am I, Granny?' asked Lucy.

'No, you're a good girl.' Annie patted Lucy's shining head. 'But that Tessa – she's wearing your mother out.'

'It would help me if you had Tessa for an hour,' Kate said, 'then I could take Lucy for a walk.'

Annie shook her head. 'No, I'm too old to cope with Tessa. No one helped me with my children – mind you, they were all well behaved. None of them ever screamed like she's doing. They wouldn't have dared! Children should be seen and not heard, as they say.'

The only person who could silence Tessa was Freddie. When he walked in that evening, tired and grubby, he found Kate exhausted and frustrated, nothing like the radiant girl he had married. She blamed Tessa. 'Lucy was never like this,' she ranted, and Freddie held out his arms and took the hot-faced bundle of screaming baby. And Tessa was quiet, her eyes gazing raptly into his soul. Freddie carried her outside and let her feel the breeze on her cheeks. It was April, and the sky was piled high with extravagant palaces of cloud. A raindrop sparkling on a leaf held Tessa's attention and Freddie let her study it, sensing she was seeing something invisible to him. He let her reach out and touch it; the wetness on her finger made her squeal with surprise. He stooped and picked a dandelion clock, held its perfect sphere against the sky and blew it for her. 'One o'clock, two o'clock . . .' By the time he got to six, Tessa was chuckling with delight.

There's nothing wrong with you, Freddie thought. *You're like me – happier outside in the sunshine.* So why did people keep saying there was something wrong with Tessa? He wanted to understand.

Freddie sat down on one of the wooden garden chairs he'd made for Kate, and rocked Tessa in a slow, soothing rhythm. He talked to her with his thoughts, and was rewarded with a quizzical stare and an appealing little cry that told him she didn't want to be rocked. She wanted stillness. So he sat motionless with her, almost holding his breath as he sent her his silent thoughts. He told her how she was beautiful. He told her he loved her. And something magical happened to the baby in his arms; a light shone from within her, her skin luminous, her eyes ablaze with the spirit of who she was. In that moment, Freddie visualised her as a young woman, a goddess with tendrils of chestnut hair winding around the drapes of satin enfolding her young body. *A gift*, he thought. *A gift to this world.*

For the first time, Freddie felt Tessa was actually there, fully present as the beautiful person she was. In the perfect silence, he asked her 'Why do you cry so much?' His question was greeted with a tiny frown and an intense gaze. The reply came to him by telepathy, like the sound from inside a seashell.

'I don't want to be here. I don't want to be in this baby's body.'

'Why's that?' he asked kindly.

'It's not who I am,' she replied, 'and I don't think I can stay in it.'

The conversation was telepathic, but Freddie took it seriously. He and Kate had brought Tessa into the world in a sacred act of love. They wanted her. But Tessa Barcussy, or whoever she really was, didn't want to be here. A sobering thought. A suicidal adult was bad enough, but a baby! A tiny baby who didn't want to live? And she'd only been with them for a few months. What had gone wrong?

Tessa was looking at him expectantly, wanting a reaction. Freddie prayed for some words, but none came. She must have trusted him a lot, he figured, to send him that thought. Had it been spoken, Kate would have fired it straight back with a 'Don't be so silly' approach. *Acceptance*, Freddie thought, *acceptance is all I can offer Tessa. And hope – maybe.*

'LISTEN!' he hissed, and froze, his eyes watching the garden. In the electric atmosphere he seemed to have created, a blackbird started to warble in the cherry tree, hidden in the coppery leaves which were unfolding around the dangling blossom. He and baby Tessa listened together in a shared moment of enchantment.

The words he needed tumbled from the blackbird's song.

'It's spring,' he said, aloud, 'and everything's growing, Tessa. You're growing, every day. It will get easier, and when you're bigger you can run around with Lucy. You stay put. For Daddy.'

He bounced her on his lap, and let her feel how her legs wanted to stand up. And suddenly Tessa smiled, a gummy grin of pure joy, and squealed as Freddie smiled back.

'She's pretty when she smiles,' said Kate who had felt drawn out into the ambience of the garden. 'Now why don't I bring our tea outside on a tray?'

'Tessa's happier outside,' said Freddie, and he debated whether to tell Kate about the telepathic conversation. He looked at Tessa's eyes and sensed anxiety. It was a secret between them. Not to be shared. Like the secret he'd kept with his mother, Annie, when he was seven years old. Annie suffered from agoraphobia and Freddie had felt responsible for her. He'd been her lifeline, not only because he ran errands for her, but in the way he'd calmed her down and coaxed her home if she'd ventured out and panicked. He understood her fear of confiding her problem to a doctor. She feared being labelled 'mad' and sent to an asylum.

Annie lived quietly now, next door in the old bakery, tending her garden and selling posies of flowers and herbs at the gate. She adored three-year-old Lucy, but so far she'd avoided helping out with Tessa. 'Something's wrong with that child,' she'd declared. 'I hope she don't turn out like me!'

★   ★   ★

Freddie's silent work with Tessa led him ever deeper into the child's mysterious eyes. At first, he'd felt malevolence from her, but now he sensed anxiety beyond that steady pale blue gaze. Little flecks of gold clustered around the dark pupils but they seemed masklike and superfluous, glistening like reeds around a deep pool. Freddie felt he'd been given a new task in his life – the task of caring for the rare spirit that was Tessa.

'You're so good with her, Freddie,' said Kate, putting the wooden tray on the garden table. It was laden with fresh ham sandwiches, tomatoes, and an enormous curly lettuce. There was a jar of homemade apple chutney, one of Sally's home-made cheeses, and a plate of jam tarts Kate had made with Lucy.

'Ah,' said Freddie, 'I wish I had more time to spend with her.' He looked at Kate's tired face in concern. 'I can see she's wearing you out.'

Kate's bright brown eyes shone as she treated him to one of her reassuring smiles. As always, it made his heart turn over. Her radiance had made him fall in love with her, the light from some inextinguishable inner flame. To him Kate was like a garden in the sun, always a new flower opening – for him! – a new ripe apple or a plum. One smile and he was aroused, awakened and energised. Sitting there with baby Tessa in his arms, he would have liked to roll in the lawn with Kate, and feel their love-making pulsing into the earth. But, with their busy lives, love-making was now slotted into the night, between the starched sheets and the tiredness. *Better than nothing*, he thought.

'Don't look so worried, Freddie,' Kate said. 'Here we are on a lovely evening with two beautiful little girls.' She handed him a plate with a thick sandwich and a dollop of chutney. 'Put Tessa down on the rug.'

Freddie felt instant resistance from the baby in the crook of his arm. He looked at her eyes. 'Do you want to stay with Daddy?' She leaned her plump cheek against his tweed jacket, and clung to a handful of his shirt with her tiny fist. 'She understands everything you say,' he said, and hung on to Tessa, while he ate his tea with one hand and watched the butterflies flitting over the aubrietia flowers. There were orange-tips, yellow brimstones, and tortoiseshells fluttering like flakes of colour over the spring garden. Along the fence was a mass of white flowers on tall stems with lush green leaves. Freddie watched Lucy pick one and bring it over to him.

'What's this, Daddy?'

'Ah – that's Jack by the Hedge,' he said, 'garlic mustard. The butterflies love that.'

'Why?' Lucy asked.

'You watch,' Freddie said as an orange-tip butterfly came to the flower Lucy was holding.

The child's eyes glistened with curiosity. 'It's putting a black stick inside the middle of the flower,' she reported.

'That's not a stick,' said Freddie, 'that's like a drinking straw, a thin one.'

'Is it drinking milk out of the flower?'

'No. Nectar!' Freddie's eyes lit with the reflection of Lucy's joy. 'It's like honey.'

'Oooh – honey!' Lucy's smile was heart-stopping. Like Kate. It swept the darkness from his soul.

The darkness wasn't something he wanted. Freddie had thought about it a lot, but never taken the risk of telling anyone. He hadn't been born with it, he knew that. Freddie had been a child of light, like Lucy. He felt the darkness had been imposed on him; not just imposed but planted deeply in his subconscious where it had grown tenacious roots reaching into his mind. He knew what the ingredients were. Fear was number one, and it wasn't a rational fear. His childhood of grinding poverty, his mother's terror of going out, his father's violent temper, the barking voice of Harry Price who had been his one and only teacher from the age of five to when he was twelve. The negativity, the criticism, the siren-like ringing of endless warnings about what would happen if he didn't conform to the norm. Deeper still, and more cosmic, were the accusations and the condemnation of the most precious essence of his soul, his gift of prophecy.

That evening, Freddie decided to risk telling Kate. It would help him so much to share his feelings. Surely the woman he trusted and adored would understand. Telling her would open a door inside his mind and let the light flood in.

He chose a rare moment of peace when Tessa was asleep and Lucy tucked up in bed. Kate was at the kitchen table, making butter, beating and beating the creamy milk in an earthenware basin. He wanted her to sit out in the garden with him and listen to the thrushes and the baby lambs, and watch the sunset paint the sky over Monterose.

'I can't leave this,' Kate said. 'If I do, it will be wasted. You sit at the table and talk to me.' She went on beating, not looking at him. Freddie wished she would keep still for a minute, but she never wanted to. He sat down at the scrubbed wooden table, his fingers smoothing the wood, touching the knots that had been branches, wondering whether the wood was still alive, still holding a memory of the tree it had once been. Did it feel resentment at being a kitchen table? Did it long for leaves and sap and the tingle of a chaffinch nesting in its branches?

'You look thoughtful,' Kate said. 'Penny for them?'

'I sometimes think you're full of light,' Freddie said. 'And me – I'm full of darkness.'

He was deadly serious, but Kate laughed. 'Oh don't be so MORBID,' she scolded. She scooped the crumbly lump of freshly made butter onto one of the wooden pats and began to tease it to and fro between them, each time squeezing out pearls of moisture. 'You wait 'til you taste this. It'll fill you up with good country sunshine.'

Freddie couldn't help smiling. Kate had a way of deftly changing the subject, as if she'd turned him around and pushed him into the light, even if he didn't want to go. He took the breadknife and sawed the crust from a loaf of bread, sniffed it, and handed it to Kate. 'Nothing nicer than the smell of fresh bread.'

Kate spread some of the crumbly butter thickly over the crust, broke off a corner for herself and gave the rest to Freddie. They sat at the table munching the satisfying snack, and an extra sparkle came into Kate's eyes. 'AND . . .' she announced, 'I've got something exciting to tell you.'

'What's that?' Freddie asked.

'Well – Susan Jarvis popped in to see me, and she's getting married in June.'

'About time too,' Freddie said. Susan Jarvis had been to school with Kate, and worked with her as a nurse through the wartime.

'Well, at least it'll stop her making eyes at you,' teased Kate. 'I'm glad I got to you first!'

'She's never forgotten me helping her over the station bridge when she was little,' said Freddie, remembering the blonde plaits, and the look of terror in Susan's eyes. 'She was scared stiff of walking over the cracks between the planks. So who's taking her on then?'

Kate still seemed to be hanging on to a secret, her eyes bright like a magician pulling surprises out of a box. 'Well – who do you think?' she announced. 'She met him at Cheltenham Races. They've been courting for a year now, and he's buying a place down here, that farm with all the stables out on the Taunton Road – and he'll be bringing his racehorses down.'

'Who? Who is he?' Freddie didn't like the sound of that. He didn't want Kate getting mixed up with Susan and her racehorses. Suddenly he felt pressure rising in his head.

'Well, you'll remember him,' Kate said. 'Ian Tillerman.'

'Ian Tillerman!' Freddie felt the colour rush to his cheeks, his temples throbbing. A shadow crept over his life like a storm cloud across the sun. Words gathered in his mind, words of anger and fear, words that flew up like a flock of black starlings. He felt himself go into lockdown mode. Silence was his retreat place. It held the key to his happy life, his peaceful marriage. Kate did the talking, and he did the silence. Most of the time.

Kate chattered on about racehorses and weddings and he hardly heard her. He felt a gulf opening between them, as if the sound of Ian Tillerman's name had cut a chasm through everything he treasured, everything he'd worked for.

She delivered the final blow with a radiant smile. 'The wedding is going to be here, at Monterose Church. It will be a big society wedding, and, oh I'm so thrilled, Freddie. We are invited! I told Susan we'd come, and she wants Lucy to be a bridesmaid.'

'I'm not going,' said Freddie in a loud voice he hardly recognised as his own.

Kate looked startled. Her eyes searched his face, but Freddie couldn't look at her. He couldn't bear to see the disappointment on her face. Hurting Kate was hurting himself. But this!

'I told you. I'm not going.' He stood up. 'I need some fresh air.'

'You haven't finished your supper,' Kate said caringly, but Freddie took his cap from its peg and walked out into the April evening.

★　　★　　★

There was only one person Freddie hated and it was Ian Tillerman. Ian had once tried to take Kate away from him, and the shock had caused him to lose his cool. In a rare moment of furious anger, Freddie had crashed his motorbike into the canal. Far from home on a bitterly cold winter day, he had lain on the bank in a coma until he was hospitalised for weeks, disastrous weeks of being unable to work and earn, a time of deep depression. He believed he'd lost Kate for ever to this ruthless toff who had everything Kate wanted. Horses, money, a big home in the country. All the things Freddie couldn't offer her. It had made the diamond ring he'd had in his pocket seem totally inadequate.

Yet Kate had come back to him, and when he asked her about Ian Tillerman she'd said flippantly, 'Oh him. I told him to go to Putney on a pig.' Freddie felt confident that Kate loved, adored and needed him, especially after the happy years of marriage. Their love had burned steadily through the dark years of the war, through the hard times of living next door to Annie, and the arrival of Lucy and Tessa. It was strong. It had already stood the test. So why did the mere mention of Ian Tillerman's name set alarm bells clanging in his mind?

Ian had been safely out of the way in Gloucestershire. But now, he'd got the brass neck to come down here and invade his patch. Worse, he was marrying one of Kate's friends. It wasn't going to be possible for Freddie to avoid seeing him. Susan's mother, Joan Jarvis, had been a friend and mentor to him and to Annie. Things were going to get complicated.

Freddie walked in long strides, for once not hearing the song thrushes or seeing the elm trees along the street. His feet took him down to the stonemason's yard.

'What's up wi' you?' Herbie was inside his office, which was made of black corrugated tin. Inside, it was festooned with cobwebs covered in stone dust and piles of flimsy receipts stacked onto metal spikes. Old tobacco-yellowed calendars swung from the walls along with a patchwork of dog-eared postcards, each one pinned up with a single brass drawing pin. Herbie was sitting on a battered dining chair which was tied together with baler twine.

'Have you got a fag?' Freddie asked.

'Sure. 'elp yerself.'

Herbie studied him with a penetrating stare while he lit one of the Players Navy Cut cigarettes. 'Don't bottle it up, Freddie,' he advised. 'That's what killed your father. Like a time bomb he was.'

'Ah,' Freddie said, agreeing. He drew a deep lungful of smoke and blew it towards the ceiling. He played with the end of the fag, jerking it to make little smoke rings. But he didn't talk. He wanted to tell Herbie everything. His concerns about Tessa, the relentless struggle to feed and clothe his family, the stress of living next door to Annie, and, top of the list, was Ian Tillerman. He shook his head, but he still didn't talk. The two men sat in companionable silence with only the sound of a tap dripping into the Belfast sink. Freddie appreciated Herbie's quiet acceptance of his need just to sit and .calm down. The stone angels watched them from the yard, blushing pink in the sunset, the stacks of stone blocks somehow calming, grounding. *Ian Tillerman couldn't carve a stone angel*, Freddie thought.

'Women?' said Herbie eventually.

'Ah – women.'

'And babies,' Herbie said. 'I couldn't stand my lot when they were babies. Love 'em now. But I think babies are an abomination. If I have to carve anymore cherubs holding birdbaths, I'll throw me chisels in the river.'

'Ah – babies.' Freddie finished the cigarette and ground the stub into the overloaded glass ashtray Herbie had filched from the pub. He stood up. 'I'll see you tomorrow.'

'Where are you going now? Home?'

'No,' Freddie said. 'Down the woods. Listening to owls.'

'You ought to take your shotgun,' Herbie advised. 'Good gun that. Never use it, do you? I'd be shooting rabbits if it were mine. Pity, leaving it stuck in that cupboard.'

'I don't like shooting. If you look a rabbit in the eye, really look I mean, you wouldn't shoot 'im.'

'Get on – ya old softie. Here ya' are, take another fag with you.'

'Ta.' Freddie nodded at Herbie and walked off, blowing curls of blue smoke into the late sunlight. As he headed for the woods, he was glad not to be carrying a gun. He liked to stand in the moonlight, motionless against a tree and become part of the woods, hardly breathing, just watching, waiting, knowing that birds and animals would come close to him, accepting him as part of their world. The gun had belonged to Kate's father, Bertie, and she'd insisted on giving it to Freddie. He'd never used it. But now, as he struggled with his feelings, he could think of one very good use for that gun. Ian Tillerman.

The woods stretched for miles along the southern slopes of the Polden Hills, broken only by the alabaster quarry, the railway, and the road to Hilbegut. Freddie wanted to go to a part of the wood where lime trees grew. He wanted the calm of their cool canopy. He wanted the old secrets Granny Barcussy had taught him. 'Take your anger into the lime wood at twilight,' she would say, 'and let the tree spirits turn it into toadstools.' Then she would cackle with laughter. 'That'll stop you eating poisonous fungi!' It was part of the folklore he'd grown up with. Freddie had puzzled over it, but discovered there was truth beyond the words, a truth that did heal his anger, a truth that was nameless and mysterious.

He walked on, through birdsong and fragrant hedges. He climbed a field gate and headed up towards the wood where the lime trees grew. Halfway up, a spring gushed out of the hillside, from under a clump of elder bushes, their creamy flowers richly perfumed. Freddie paused to look at the water glinting in the sunset, and to listen to its gurgling music. Something made him stand very still. His skin suddenly had goosebumps.

At the source of the stream was a shimmering light. He watched and waited, hardly daring to breathe. It was how he felt when he had a vision. Unearthly.

And then he saw her.

A young woman, with chestnut hair. She had unusual clothes, such as he'd never seen a woman wearing. Light blue flared jeans, a light blue jacket with silver studs. Beads and ribbons gleamed in the long curly tresses of her hair and it rippled with life. She was beautiful. Just beautiful. But what took Freddie's breath away was the radiance of her face, and the colour of her eyes as she looked at him. Pale blue eyes with a core of gold.

'Tessa.'

As soon as he whispered her name, the vision flickered and began to sink back into the shimmering light like a reflection glimmering in a lake of gold. He saw a rose in her hand, a peace rose, and she threw it with graceful fingers into the stream. He thought she blew him a kiss before she vanished and became a memory, an invisible sweetness on the breeze like the perfume of the elderflower.

A vision of the future. He had seen his daughter, waiting for him, somewhere beyond the present time. Beyond his reasoning mind.

The ordinary colours of earth filtered back into his consciousness. The grass, the cuckoo flowers and speedwell on the banks of the stream. Reed warblers and blackbirds singing. The apple green leaves of the woods.

Freddie walked on, into the lime wood, holding the vision in his heart. As the last spark of the sun went down over the distant Quantock Hills, he found his favourite lime tree. It was ancient, and the trunk had a little alcove where he could sit. He leaned his head back, looking up into the canopy.

The vision of Tessa had been a gift, a pearl to tuck away in his heart. Another, less welcome vision was waiting. A shadow loomed over the lime wood, something that shook the earth and made the foliage jingle like bells. He saw birds and animals fleeing from their homes, and the bees searching hopelessly for nectar in a barren wasteland of ashes and dead wood. He opened his hands and watched the seeds of an impossible dream fall into them like jewels.

Clearly, he and Tessa had work to do in the far distant future. Ian Tillerman was just one of the obstacles. The others were fear, poverty, and self-doubt.

Freddie walked home in long strides through the honey-scented dusk. He lingered in the garden, below the bedroom window, and smiled at the sound of Kate reading Lucy a bedtime story. Lucy would be listening, wide-eyed, as Kate put deep sorrow into her voice.

'. . . down came a basket all over Ping and he could see no more of the boy, or the boat, or the sky, or the beautiful yellow water of the Yangtze River.'

Thinking he shouldn't break the spell, Freddie went over to his workshop, a low stone outbuilding with a sagging roof and no glass in the window. The air inside was beautifully cool, and there were swallows' nests in the rafters. He switched on the light and saw a row of baby swallows peeping over the rim of one of the nests.

He chose the block of Bath stone he wanted, and imagined the carving he would do of the girl by the stream. The waves of her hair, the grace of her hands.

But first – he picked up a piece of pink and white alabaster, and began to carve a rose.

Chapter Four

'SHE'S A BRAT!'

On the day of the Tillerman wedding, Tessa had her worst
ever tantrum. At eight months, she was crawling and into
everything.

'She was putting stones in her mouth,' Annie shouted to
make herself heard above Tessa's enraged howling. 'I had to
bring her inside.' She groaned with the effort and put the
grubby infant down on the sofa. 'You stay there, madam.'

Kate stood at the top of the stairs in her white satin petticoat, her feet bare, and her make-up half done. She'd been
unrolling a brand new pair of nylon stockings with fancy seams
when she'd heard the commotion. Her one concern on this
exciting day was that she had to leave Tessa with Annie.

'Can you come down and deal with her?' Annie shouted,
her face dark with an unhealthy flush as she tried to hold the
thrashing child on the sofa.

Kate ran downstairs. 'Stop that noise,' she said in her
'I-must-be-obeyed' voice. Her eyes glittered imperiously at
Tessa. 'Do you want a smack?'

Tessa squinted at her through shiny tears, her pale blue eyes drowning in a whirlpool of fear and fury. She held out her arms to Kate.

'Don't give in to her,' Annie said.

Kate ignored her and sat down on the sofa next to Tessa. Her hand tingled with the desire to smack her hard, but the need to understand was stronger. She'd watched and learned from Freddie. 'Let her cry,' he'd said, so often, 'no matter how much you want her to stop. She's gotta cry all of her tears, not half of them.'

'There you are! Spoil her,' Annie said contemptuously. 'I wash my hands of her. I never spoilt MY children. There – look at her – she's getting worse. Today of all days,' she added, as Kate tried to hold Tessa close and the furious child struggled even more violently, kicking and pushing her mother away, her hands smearing mud on the clean white petticoat.

'Look at the MESS,' said Annie, and Kate suddenly wanted to scream herself. Caught between Tessa's extreme distress and Annie's avaricious judgements, her head rang with the conflict. And now Lucy was at the top of the stairs, wailing, in her yellow organza bridesmaid's dress, the sash trailing on the floor. 'Mummy, I can't do my bow. I want you to do it.'

'Will you help Lucy, please?' Kate said directly, looking into Annie's hovering eyes. She took a deep breath, the way she'd done in her years of nursing, and held on to calm as if it were a real rock in a torrent. She was glad to see Annie hauling herself up the stairs, the ageing banister creaking under her weight. Kate didn't care about the mud on her petticoat. No one was going to see it, she figured. She didn't care what Annie thought. Priority was to understand what was causing the intense distress in her child.

'Are you worried about Daddy?' she asked, and Tessa actually looked at her for an instant before the crying started again. Kate tried to pick her up but she arched her back and went rigid, holding her breath then coughing alarmingly. 'I'm worried about Daddy too,' Kate said in a quiet voice. She leaned her cheek on the top of Tessa's head, stroking the downy chestnut curls in a moment of sadness. Was baby Tessa picking up on Freddie's strong feelings that day?

Freddie had gone out early. He'd kissed her goodbye and given her one of those long questioning looks. Usually he went out in the morning whistling, but today he was silent and withdrawn, his cheek twitching a little as it did when he was stressed.

Kate was bitterly disappointed. She'd tried and tried to reason with him, but Freddie's mind was set in stone. He was NOT going to the Tillerman wedding, and he was NOT going to be manipulated. Kate had shown him her outfit, his favourite slinky red dress with the black lace sleeves and plunging neckline showing off her curvy figure. She'd shown him her hat, wide-brimmed and elegant, and trimmed with red roses. It wasn't new. Kate had found it in a jumble sale at the town hall, and pounced on it. 'My sixpenny hat!' she called it proudly, and she looked stunning in it. She'd let Lucy put on her yellow organza dress that Susan's mother,

Joan, had made for her, and Lucy's eyes had sparkled with joy when she paraded and twirled for her daddy.

Kate had taken Freddie's suit out of its mothballs, ironed his white shirt and tie, and hung it up, hopefully, next to her dress. She'd polished his best black shoes until they shone like mirrors, and even put a beautifully ironed white hanky in the top pocket of his jacket.

It was an act of love, and hope.

Freddie was hauling loads of timber fence posts that morning. His heart was heavy with anger as he drove through the town on his way to the station. When he saw the array of expensive motorcars parked along the kerb outside Joan Jarvis's house, he put his foot down and roared past, with the timber thundering in the back of the lorry. His hands burned with splinters, and his mouth felt parched. Normally he called in at home for a cup of tea, but not today. He had to stay out, keep his head down and lie low until the dreaded wedding was over.

The road to Tarbuts Timber wound upwards into the wooded hills. Shaded by tall conifers, the narrow road was always covered in pigeons and rabbits who weren't used to the speed and sound of a motor vehicle. Freddie usually took it slowly, blowing his horn to scare them away. But today the conflict in his mind had made him reckless, watching the wild creatures of the wood scattering before him.

The sickening thud of a young rabbit's soft furry body hitting the front bumper sent a shockwave through

Freddie. He had killed a wild creature. A creature who hadn't harmed him but had simply been sitting there in its own environment.

Devastated, Freddie stopped the lorry, turned the engine off, and got out. The complex silences of the woods sank into his consciousness, fizzing through him like an aspirin in a glass of water. A line from Oscar Wilde unfurled and flew like a flag in his mind.

'Each man kills the thing he loves . . .'

On heavy feet he walked round the front of the lorry and found the young rabbit stretched out in the bright grass. Its eyes were wide open, and it was breathing. Freddie sat down and picked it up with tenderness and sorrow. Under the velvet fur he could feel its heartbeat. 'Stunned,' he whispered, 'you're only stunned – and I'm sorry – I'm so sorry.' He stroked the rabbit's long ears, so delicate, like pink paper. It trembled under his hands and it seemed to Freddie that the trembling was getting stronger. Was it recovering? Should he put it in a cardboard box and take it home? The rabbit looked up at him with eyes that clearly said, 'I have a right to live – and a right to be free.'

He opened his hands and, in a pulse of energy, the rabbit leapt out of his arms and disappeared into the woods with a flick of its white tail.

Freddie drew a great breath from the silence of the wood. He remembered what he'd said to Herbie. 'If you look a rabbit in the eye, I mean, really look, you wouldn't shoot it.' These words, coaxed out of him by Herbie's quiet acceptance, were tucked in the inner pocket of his mind, like a key. A key he'd need one day. The key to a peaceful world.

He had to look Ian Tillerman in the eye.

He looked at his watch. Was there time?

The sense of peace and quiet felt like a benediction to Kate. She lowered the sleeping child into her cot and stood watching Tessa's magical transformation into an angelic-looking cherub, her eyes closed, and the beautifully curved chestnut lashes fringing her cheeks. She was pale now. She had burned herself out. 'Sweet dreams, my little one,' Kate said kindly. 'Mummy will be back later.' She tiptoed out and peeped over the banister at Annie, now in her favourite chair with Lucy on her lap. Annie was reading a Beatrix Potter book in a slow thoughtful voice, just like Freddie, and Lucy was loving it, her eyes wide, her yellow dress fanned out over Annie's knees like a dandelion.

Kate was proud of Lucy. She'd taken her to the church on the previous day for a rehearsal, and Lucy had behaved impeccably. She quickly understood exactly what to do and how slowly she had to walk down the aisle in front of the bride. 'She's perfect!' Susan had said in delight. 'What a wonderful little girl you've raised, Kate. You'll have to give us some tips on child rearing when the time comes.'

Kate had given Susan a hug. 'I'm so happy for you.'

'I'm scared stiff, Kate!' Susan had confided in a whisper.

'Oh, you'll be fine – we'll be there to help you – won't we, Lucy?'

Lucy nodded. 'And my daddy.'

'Cross fingers,' Kate said, and on the way home she tried to explain to the excited Lucy that Freddie might not be there.

'He WILL be there,' Lucy insisted confidently. 'I told him he had to come and watch me be Susan's bridesmaid.'

Kate felt sad as she slipped the red dress over her head and rolled the new nylon stockings up each leg, clipping them carefully onto the suspenders. She brushed her hair and put on her red shoes with the high heels, the ones that Freddie loved so much. She laid her hat and long gloves on the bed, and looked at the clock. Half an hour before they must set off down the road to the church. With a rare slot of time to herself, Kate sat down on the edge of the bed and looked at the photograph of her father, Bertie, who had died in the wartime after years of illness. 'I'm still your golden bird, Daddy,' Kate said, and felt an overwhelming need to weep the tears of grief that she'd never allowed. 'I hope I am,' she whispered. Her father had named her Oriole Kate, after a rare golden oriole had appeared in the garden on the day she was born. Just before he died, her parents had hoped to move back home to Hilbegut, into a lovely cottage close to the farm where Kate and Ethie had grown up. Sally had been devastated and had chosen to stay in Gloucestershire to be close to Bertie and Ethie's graves. *I wish Mum was at Hilbegut,* Kate thought sadly. *I could go on the bus, and take Lucy. She'd love to walk down through the copper beeches with me, and see the old court.* More sadness. The magnificent Hilbegut Court was now an abandoned ruin.

Stop it! Kate thought. *Stop being morbid on the day of Susan's wedding!*

The truth was that any romantic occasion triggered the tears in Kate. Tears she'd never permitted herself to cry. It was happening now, that huge ache in her throat. Could she really stand in church and watch Susan pledging her life to Ian Tillerman? When she knew only too well what Ian was like. Susan was sweet and vulnerable. She'd kowtow to Ian and pretty soon those stars in her eyes would go out, probably for ever.

Kate stood up and looked at herself in the mirror. She saw a curvy young woman with wavy black hair and bright brown eyes. 'You get a hold of yourself, girl,' she told herself, and pasted a smile on her face. The smile said, 'I am in control of my life. I can manage Tessa. I can cope with Annie. And I'm going to enjoy Susan's wedding. Even if I am the only woman there without her husband.' She smoothed Freddie's suit with her hand, and gave it a hug.

Moments later, the ache of tears surged in her throat yet again when she glanced out of the window and saw Freddie getting out of his lorry. Kate flew down the stairs.

Worn out and covered in sawdust, Freddie looked sombre and nervous. But all Kate saw were his blue eyes coming in the door, lighting up with love as he saw her in her red dress. His eyes said everything. They said he wanted to peel that dress off her and take her to bed with tenderness and passion. They said he'd come home from the war, the war within his mind, the Ian Tillerman war. But his mouth said, 'I hit a rabbit up on the road to Tarbuts.'

'Did you dear?' Kate looked puzzled. She waited.

'It – made me think – I ought to go with you.'

Kate's mood lifted. 'You'll have to be quick then, Freddie.' Giggling, she bundled him upstairs and pushed him into the bathroom. 'You need a wash.'

'Me hands are full of splinters,' Freddie said, 'and oily. I can't shake hands with anyone.'

Freddie felt proud as he walked down the road in the hot sunshine with Kate swanning along beside him. He thought she looked like a film star in her 'sixpenny hat'. 'Don't you dare tell anyone where I got it,' she'd said, and her eyes flashed up at him mischievously. 'Let them think I've been up to London and bought it from Harrods.'

His first glimpse of Ian Tillerman was a surprise. Standing in the front pew, Ian looked smaller than Freddie's image of him. He was slightly tubby and had a bald patch at the back of his head.

When the music started, the heads turned to watch four-year-old Lucy in her yellow dress parading ahead of the bride, her little face radiant and confident. She glanced up at Freddie with a beguiling smile, so like Kate, heart-stopping. The air shimmered around her and around Susan in her rustling taffeta dress and veil, a bunch of cream lilies and the pinkest of roses in her hand. Mesmerised, Freddie stared at the golden light around them and realised he was seeing his daughter's beautiful aura. It stirred a memory of the spiritual visions he'd had in his youth. Would they come again? He gazed around the church, half expecting to see an angel, a real one. It was there, camouflaged in the sunlight pouring through the stained-glass windows, he was sure. The immensity of it lived in his memory. The angel he'd seen had been a massive being of light. It would have made Ian Tillerman look no bigger than a fly. Was the angel talking to him now? Into his mind in secret? Telling him to follow his dreams – and dream big – and not be afraid.

Kate was nudging him, and Freddie realised he was supposed to be singing. He looked at the hymn book she was sharing with him. '*Love divine . . .*' He heard Kate's sweet voice singing it next to him. Love divine! That wasn't what Ian Tillerman was going to get with Susan, he thought.

By the time the moment of eye contact arrived, Freddie felt powerful. He felt full of light and gratitude. With Kate staunchly beside him, he looked down at Ian Tillerman in the porch, after the photographs had been taken. Susan's mother, Joan Jarvis, came up to him in a whirl of ostrich feathers and scarlet lipstick. 'You MUST meet Freddie and Kate,' she gushed, and dragged him towards Ian and Susan. 'Well, you know Kate already. But look, Ian, Freddie is so clever. He carved this statue of St Peter. Isn't it marvellous?' She waved her arm at the statue on the stone shelf inside the porch, of St Peter with the 'keys to the kingdom'. It had been Freddie's first commission.

Ian didn't know whether to look at Freddie or at the statue. He looked overwhelmed. So he blurted, 'Excellent, my man. Excellent!'

His eyes shifted to and fro, avoiding Freddie's steady gaze. Then they came to a halt on Kate, sweeping over her with blatantly lustful approval. 'You should see the new horses we've got now, Kate,' he said. 'When we move down here, anytime you fancy a ride – you're welcome.'

Freddie tensed. He felt Kate squeeze his hand reassuringly, and, as always, she knew exactly what to say. 'Well, thank you, Ian,' she said, with her back very straight, 'but I'm sure you'll be too busy looking after your wonderful new wife.' She beamed at Susan, who fluttered her eyes nervously. 'And I'm a busy mum with two beautiful little girls,' Kate added, looking fondly at Lucy who was leaning adoringly against the cool taffeta of Susan's dress.

Right on cue the happy atmosphere with the ringing voices and posh hats was ripped apart by the sound of a child screaming. Freddie and Kate looked at each other in disbelief.

'Who on earth is that?'

The crowd of wedding guests parted as an old woman struggled up the church path pushing a battered pram with a squeaky wheel. It was Annie, her face puckered with fury, her grey hair stuck to her brow with sweat, her feet in moth-eaten carpet slippers. She saw Freddie and Kate in the porch with the Tillermans and made a beeline for them. She was emanating such anger that people were leaping out of her way. All conversations stopped, and shocked faces watched the invasion of earthy rage. There was only the squeak of the pram wheel and the roar of the baby inside.

'Annie!' Joan Jarvis was first to speak. 'My dear! What's happened?'

Annie brushed her aside. She shoved the pram at Kate. 'I've FINISHED with this child,' she ranted. 'She does nothing but cry and she won't let me change her. She fights like a wild cat. I'm not looking after her, Kate. She's a BRAT and that's the truth. I'm at the end of my tether. I'm leaving her here, wedding or no wedding.'

'Annie!'

'Don't touch me!' Annie shook Joan off as if she was a wasp. She took her ebony walking stick from the pram, straightened her back and limped away down the path. Again, people jumped out of her way and someone whispered, 'WHO is that angry old woman?'

'You should go after her, Freddie – take her home,' Kate said, concerned. But Freddie leaned over the pram and looked at Tessa, sad to see her little face swollen with crying. She was too big for the pram now and Annie had strapped the covers down to keep her in there. Tessa was crying, and hiccupping, and coughing, and she had made herself sick. She looked up at Freddie like a drowning cat. 'Now then – what's all this about? Eh?' Freddie undid the straps and picked up the distraught child with his quiet hands. 'There. Daddy's got you. Now you quieten down.'

'I'm so sorry.' Kate was obviously burning with embarrassment. She tried to see the funny side of it. 'So much for my beautiful daughter,' she joked. But no one laughed.

'Don't you worry, Kate. I'll see Annie home,' said Joan. 'It must have been a huge effort for her to come up here.' She trotted after the retreating figure of Annie who was somehow managing to make even the back of her head look angry.

Freddie carried Tessa through the crowd, across the churchyard and under the whispering shade of the elm trees. He felt her simmering down as she listened to his slow heartbeat, his rumbly voice, and the soothing rhythm of his footsteps.

'Now I'm gonna tell you something,' he said, sitting down on a bench made from railway sleepers. He watched Tessa's eyes opening wider, brightening as she started back at him, quiet now, her breathing settling. 'I love you,' Freddie told her. 'A lot. And I love these elm trees; they're my favourite trees. They've been here for hundreds and hundreds of years, and my old Granny Barcussy used to tell me elm trees were the guardians of the spirit. They shelter us from the wind and the hot sun, and they make deeper, cooler shade than any other tree. They're the tallest trees in England, and lots of wild creatures live in them.' He paused and saw that Tessa was listening intently to his story, her pale blue eyes slowly filling with light. He showed her a tortoiseshell butterfly. 'That butterfly – see? – she lays her eggs in an elm tree – and way up there in the branches there are birds' nests, and a hole where the woodpecker lives. And . . .' he lowered his voice to a whisper, 'it's said that the elves live in elm trees – and they're magic.'

Tessa was smiling now, and to Freddie it was an immensely satisfying time for him, sharing magic with this little person who was gazing at him raptly, hungry for every word. 'Now if you come here at night,' he continued, 'and sit under an elm tree with a torch, you can see the elves' eyes shining like stars, they say – but I know different – it's the eyes of moths that are shining, and some of them are orange – like your orange juice, see?' Tessa squealed in delight. Freddie touched her face and her skin was cool again, the way it should be.

Kate was walking over to him with Lucy skipping beside her.

'Thank you, Freddie. I'm so grateful,' she said. 'It was embarrassing, wasn't it? Humiliating.'

Freddie shook his head. 'Not to me,' he said. 'I'd rather be here, under an elm tree, with our little Tessa than at any posh wedding. My church is out here, under the elm trees, if you can understand that, Kate.'

'Oh – I can.'

'And – I know you want to go to the reception – so you go with Lucy. Just bring me a slice of cake. I'll take Tessa home when we've finished looking at the elm trees.'

'I don't know how you calm her down,' Kate said, 'it's like magic.'

''Tis simple,' Freddie said. 'I talk to her as if she's grown up – and she will be. In a few years, she'll be a beautiful little girl like Lucy. We've just got to believe in her, Kate.'

★   ★   ★

72

A few weeks later, Freddie came home for his mid-morning cup of tea, and was not best pleased to see Ian Tillerman's Daimler parked outside. He debated whether or not to get back in his lorry and drive on, but a strong territorial instinct sent him into the kitchen where Ian Tillerman was sprawled in the best chair, his beefy legs clad in breeches and brown leather riding boots. Clipped around the heel of each boot was a highly polished silver spur. Freddie looked at them and winced. Did the man really dig those cruel spurs into the flanks of a horse? His eyes travelled up the legs to the blue Aertex shirt, the expensive smooth tweed hacking jacket, the hairy wrist flaunting a chunky gold watch. *What a toff*, he thought. Then he got to the eyes. *Piggy little eyes*, he thought. *Shifty*.

'Hello, Freddie,' Ian said, and Freddie just nodded at him. He didn't intend to speak.

Kate got up and gave Freddie a hug. 'Ian was telling me about the place he's buying,' she said, pouring him some strong tea in the earthenware mug he liked. 'Susan's here too and she's taken Lucy for a walk down to the shop. Tessa's asleep.'

Freddie sat down. He didn't feel like talking to Ian. He wanted him to go.

'Darkwater Farm – out on the Taunton Road,' Ian said. 'We can't move in until next year – there's so much work to be done before the horses can come down. Do you know the place?'

'Ah – I do,' Freddie said. 'Have you actually paid for it?'

'Well – no – but I'm going to make an offer.'

'Then you're a fool,' Freddie said bluntly, and Kate gave him a little kick under the table.

Ian frowned. 'Why?'

'You can't keep horses down there,' said Freddie. 'Anyone would tell you that.'

'Why not?'

"Cause it's under water for most of the winter. That part of the Levels floods every year.'

Ian laughed. 'I don't take any notice of local folklore.'

'Freddie is right,' Kate said. 'Didn't they tell you that when you viewed it?'

'No.'

'I'll bet they didn't,' said Freddie. 'And it's not folklore. I've lived here all my life, and when I were a boy we used to row a boat over the flooded fields from Langport to Taunton.'

'I'm sure it can be fixed with a bit of intelligent drainage,' Ian said.

Kate and Freddie looked at each other. 'I'm surprised Joan didn't warn you,' Kate said.

'She did have a go,' Ian said, 'but I don't take any notice of women's scaremongering. I've had a lot of experience in preparing equestrian property, and my men will have the paddocks fenced and the gallop circuit built before the winter. Once the stables are renovated, we can move down.'

'You're buying trouble,' Freddie said. 'You mark my words.'

The two men eyeballed one another across the table.

'Well, let's not come to blows over it,' Kate said pleasantly, 'not in my kitchen!'

When Ian had gone, Freddie stayed at the table drinking a second cup of tea. 'I don't want him in here,' he told Kate.

'He's not doing any harm,' she replied, startled at the brooding anger emanating from Freddie. 'And Susan is my friend. You can't invite Susan and not him. We must put our likes and dislikes aside.'

'Ah – 'tis deeper than that. I'm telling you, Kate, I don't want him here.'

'But when they have children it will be good for Lucy and Tessa to have friends to play with,' said Kate. 'AND they might get invited to play, and to ride one day. Susan's planning to have ponies for her children.'

'I don't want Lucy and Tessa down there.'

'Well – we'll see,' Kate said pleasantly and Freddie thought that 'we'll see' usually meant that she hadn't given up on the idea, and further manipulation was to follow when Kate deemed it safe to try again.

'He won't last five minutes down here – that Ian Tillerman,' he said. ''Tis no good him coming down here lording it about. Money don't talk as loud as he thinks it does. He's got to have some sense and listen to local people, not scoff at them – he's going to come unstuck in a minute, Daimler or no Daimler.'

'You're usually right,' Kate said. 'We'll see what happens – but at least you've met him now, Freddie, and broken the ice.'

'Ice?' Freddie said. ''Tis a mile thick at the North Pole. Herbie told me that. And that's how thick the ice is between me and "Lord Tillerman". I'm never gonna like the man – but I'll try and keep the peace, Kate, for your sake. Just don't ask me to play cards with the bugger.'

He reached across the table and took Kate's hand between his rough palms. Immediately a spark flared between them and her eyes gleamed enticingly at him. She loved him, and wanted him, and to Freddie that was a gift more precious than gold.

Chapter Five

THE ROMANY GYPSIES

The Romany Gypsies rolled into Monterose on a Saturday morning in May. Freddie was in the garden hoeing the carrot bed when he heard the eerie sound of the elder flutes and the jingle of tambourines starting up at the edge of town. He went to the gate and listened, his hoe in his hand as he looked up and down the street.

'What is it, Daddy?' Three-year-old Tessa appeared beside him, a daisy chain around her neck, her chestnut curls shining in the sun. Her clear pale blue eyes looked up at him enquiringly.

''Tis the Romany Gypsies,' Freddie said, and even saying the words sent a chill of apprehension up his spine. Would she be there? Madame Eltura? Would she see him there, with Tessa?

He propped his hoe against the wall and together they watched the convoy turn into the street. The smell of horses and old canvas, the hot fragrance of dried herbs, the tang of new paint and polish. 'You go and get Lucy – and Mummy,' Freddie said. 'Tell them to be quick.'

Once they were all there, he lifted the two girls up on the wall. 'You sit there and watch. Don't you go running round the vardos,' Freddie said, feeling in his pockets for money. He fished out a handful of coins and gave them to Kate. 'You get whatever you want – clothes pegs or whatever they've got.'

'They've got tistie-tosties!' shouted Lucy. 'In a big basket.'

'Don't shout, dear. If you're good girls, you can have one each,' Kate said. 'So stay up on the wall. I won't have you running round – but I might take you to stroke one of the horses, if they stop.'

Freddie went into the kitchen and opened the cutlery drawer. He took out the long bread knife and put it in a cardboard box. Then he added all the other knives he could find, carried the box outside and put it down behind the wall.

He stood with his arm round Kate, a strange feeling of unease in his stomach. The Romany Gypsies had never bothered him before; they'd been part of his rural life, and he wanted the children to see the wonder of the painted vardos.

The sun blazed on the gleaming paintwork as the lofty horse-drawn vardos came majestically up the sloping street, each horse plodding obediently, some with jingling brasses, some with their long manes plaited and tied with raffia. Bunches of green elder leaves were stuck in their bridles to keep the flies away.

Most of the vardos were painted in two colours, red and yellow, blue and yellow, or cream and emerald. Some had carvings on the doors of horses, birds or roses, decorated in gold leaf. Freddie glanced at Tessa's face and saw that she was spellbound, taking it all in, drinking the energy from the vibrant colours. Lucy was giving a running commentary. 'That one's got red wheels! That one's got pretty curtains with tassels. That one's got a golden bird on the door.'

'Like you,' Freddie looked down at Kate and gave her a squeeze. 'A golden bird.'

Kate gave him one of her radiant smiles and his heart lifted. He looked into her eyes and felt reassured that nothing could possibly go wrong. His children were healthy and strong, sitting happily on the wall kicking the heels of their sandals against the weathered blue-lias stone. Tessa was calmer most of the time, especially in the garden. She didn't talk much, but her eyes were expressive, the eyes of a dreamer, Freddie thought. But many times he saw fear in her eyes, and it manifested as anger – just like Annie – and if Tessa hurt herself, she was terrified and would run away and hide in the most unlikely places. No one was allowed to touch or even look at any wounds she had, not even Kate with her nursing experience. 'I'll do it BY MYSELF,' Tessa would yell, and it was the same when she was learning something new. She wouldn't accept help.

'Heaven help her when she starts school,' Kate often said.

The convoy of nine vardos with their domed green canvas roofs came to a halt, parked along the level end of the street, filling it with colour and noise. Annie hobbled out of her gate and stood with the family, watching the gypsy women climb down from the vardos and unload willow baskets full of clothes pegs, paper roses, elder flutes, bunches of herbs and handmade lace. With a basket on each arm, they began their journey down the road in their flowing skirts and coloured shawls, knocking on every door.

'Will they come to us?' Lucy asked.

'Ah, they'll come,' Freddie said, his eyes watching the last vardo which was smaller than the rest and decorated in red and purple. He tried to see the lettering on the side. No one had emerged from it, and the door stayed firmly shut. *It had to be her*, he thought uneasily.

Kate went into the cottage and came out with a bucket of water. She carried it over to the nearest horse, a bay cob with a shaggy black mane trailing almost to the floor. She put the grey metal bucket down and the horse drank noisily. Along the street neighbours appeared with buckets and took them to the horses.

'Thank you kindly, ma'am.' The dark-eyed gypsy lad gave Kate a smile and a nod.

'Can I bring my children over to stroke your horse?' she asked.

'Yer welcome, lady. I can see you love horses.'

'I do,' Kate beamed at him. 'What's his name?'

'Prince.'

'He's wonderful. So GOOD, aren't you, Prince?' Kate gave the horse a kiss on his soft muzzle. She ran to fetch the girls who were waiting with eager faces. She lifted Tessa down from the wall.

'You hang on to her, Kate,' Freddie said anxiously. 'Don't let her get under his feet.'

Kate could feel Tessa trembling with excitement when she put her down next to Prince. The horse lowered his head graciously to the two children, blowing hot air out of his velvety nostrils. Tessa gasped and turned big eyes to look at Kate. 'He's like a DRAGON,' she whispered.

'A dragon?' Kate laughed in delight. 'Why's that?'

''Cause his breath is on fire,' Tessa said. She reached out and ran her soft fingers through Prince's mane, entranced by its heavy, wiry fronds. The sun glistened through it in ripples of silver and tinges of blue.

Then she did something unexpected, something that took Kate's breath away. Tessa parted the festoons of mane as if they were curtains, crept through them and sat down between the horse's front legs. She reached up and touched the soft-ness of the horse's belly hair. And Prince never moved a muscle.

'Mummy!' hissed Lucy. 'Tessa's being naughty.'

Kate trusted horses. She knew better than to reach in and drag Tessa out. 'Leave her alone. She's all right,' she said. She felt Tessa was having a magical experience and to break it would be sacrilege. Even so, she was relieved when Tessa emerged, her face radiant.

'Prince loves me,' the child whispered, 'and I felt his heart beating ever so slowly under his fur.'

Kate picked Tessa up. 'Stroke him here,' she said, rubbing Prince's neck just behind his ear. 'He likes that.' She had a

81

lump in her throat, remembering Daisy, the huge Shire horse she had loved as a child. She felt it was an important experience for Tessa, a moment of trust and bonding, and finding unconditional love, the kind of love which Tessa might not find in humans. A child like Tessa was going to have a hard, hard journey in her search for love.

Predictably, Annie was not happy and neither was Freddie.

'Fancy letting her do that!' Annie was ranting. 'A three-year-old child. She could have been killed. I've never been so frightened in my life, Freddie. My old heart is thumping.'

'Calm down, mother. She's all right.'

'THAT KATE,' Annie glared at him. 'Just because she's a farmer's daughter, she thinks she knows it all. Will you say something to her, Freddie? You've gotta take her in hand. Lay the law down.'

'I'll talk to her later,' Freddie said, to appease his mother. Laying the law down wouldn't work with Kate, and he shared her conviction that rare moments of happiness were precious for Tessa. 'And I won't hear a word against Kate,' he added, raising his voice just enough to silence his mother.

Sensing the animosity, Kate steered Lucy and Tessa away from Annie. She took them to meet two gypsy women who had baskets burgeoning with paper roses and tistie-tosties which were irresistible golden yellow pom-poms made from freshly gathered cowslips. She bought two for a penny, and gave one each to Lucy and Tessa who buried their faces in the fragrance and brushed their small fingers through the pillow-soft blooms. Soon Lucy was teaching

Tessa the old rhyme as she threw her ball of cowslips up in the air:

'*Tistie-tostie, tell me true*

Who shall I be married to . . .'

Kate stood looking at the paper roses in amazement. 'How do you make these? They look so real!'

'They're made from stretchy crepe paper,' the gypsy woman told her. 'We cut 'em out, roll 'em up and curl the petals with scissors. Then we dip 'em in 'ot wax. You can 'ave five for threepence, lady.'

Kate was tempted to buy some for Annie, but she guessed what the response would be. 'I don't like artificial flowers,' Annie would say haughtily. *Do without them*, Kate thought, and moved on to buy clothes pegs, ten for sixpence. Freddie had given her five shillings, so she parted with one of them, and piled the twenty wooden clothes pegs into the pocket of her flowery apron.

Freddie took his box of knives down the length of the convoy until he came to the knife grinder's barrow, beautifully painted with elaborate scrolls and pictures of birds pecking at bunches of grapes. A man who looked like Grumpy in the seven dwarves was sitting on the seat, pedalling vigorously as he held a knife against the spinning grindstone. He glanced into Freddie's box. 'Sixpence,' he said, 'for that lot. Take me about ten minutes.'

'I'll come back for them.' Freddie handed him a silver sixpence and walked on towards the end vardo. He caught a glimpse of sequins twinkling on the curtains, and now he could read the lettering – 'Madame Eltura, the one and only true fortune-teller'. The vardo looked closed and rather dilapidated. He wondered if she had died. The horse, different from the one he remembered, was dozing, its eyes closed and one hind leg resting.

Freddie didn't want to be obviously looking, so he sat down on the low stone wall outside the bank and lit a fag, watching the vardo without appearing to do so. He didn't feel conspicuous with people milling around in front of him. He was stubbing the end of his fag out on the pavement when the door of the vardo opened. A young woman with tresses of wavy dark hair stepped out, a basket over her arm laden with sprigs of white heather, her eyes surveying the crowded street. She looked up at the sky which was now overcast by a looming cloud, a cloud with a silver lining as it billowed over the sun.

The young woman turned and helped a small wizened figure with a crooked walking stick to climb down to the road. Freddie tensed. *Time to go home*, he thought. *What am I doing here?* The truth was that he didn't know. He'd felt compelled to come, even if he didn't speak to her. Something in his heart was smouldering with a feeling of impending change. So he waited, wanting it and not wanting it, thinking he would sit there and be invisible. He'd let the young woman and her elderly granny go on down the street with their basket of white heather.

He froze in disbelief when Madame Eltura's piercing eyes found him instantly and stared across the street, right into his soul. She nudged the younger woman, pointed directly at him, and the two of them made a beeline for Freddie.

Madame Eltura was tiny, and bent almost double, clutching the crooked stick, her ancient hand bedecked with rings that glittered as fiercely as her eyes.

There was no escape. He hoped no one he knew would see him there, especially not Annie.

'I remember you, good sir.' Madame Eltura's eyes pinned him to the wall. 'You cross my palm with silver, because I've got something new to tell you, sir, something very important. I didn't pick you out of the crowd for nothing. I was compelled to come over to you – compelled – and I'm a Romany Gypsy, sir, I see only the truth.'

She used the word 'compelled' the way he'd felt it. An unseen magnetic force. Directing his life!

'Don't ask me any questions, sir, and don't tell me anything,' she continued, 'and whether you cross my palm with silver or not, I'm going to tell you – because I have to.' She moved closer. 'That little girl in your life, her name begins with a T, and she's got a special destiny, and you are her guardian, her spiritual guardian. There's something you must do – today – this very minute, to help her . . .'

Freddie waited, hardly breathing. He felt as if he and Madame Eltura were inside a private bubble of light that excluded everything and everybody.

'There's something you've been thinking about,' she said, 'and you must do it – today. It's a place you have to go to, and it's on the road out of this town, the road that leads to the hills. You will know it by the three big pine trees, and you will know it from the angels. They sent you up there, and you've been procrastinating, sir, believe me, I know because those same angels sent me over here to talk to you. You must go there, today, and make up your mind – courageously. You have nothing to fear, and everything to gain.'

Madame Eltura shut her mouth firmly. She nudged the young woman who gave Freddie a sprig of white heather. He took it and tucked it into his breast pocket. He gave the old lady a shilling, doffed his cap to her, and walked away without speaking.

How did she know? How could she possibly know what was in his mind? That place with the three tall pine trees. How could she know he had been there more than once? It was his secret. He'd told no one. He'd tried to forget about it. But it haunted him, it followed him wherever he went, like the rising moon bobbing along the dark hedges, beaming between the elm trees like an eternal, invincible face. Madame Eltura was uncannily right. Her words became footsteps as he walked. 'Make up your mind – courageously. You have nothing to fear – nothing to fear.'

The sky was darkening to a translucent grey as Freddie picked up his box of sharpened knives and headed home, no longer seeing the Romany Gypsies. He paused only to speak to Kate. 'I've got a job to do.'

'On a Saturday?' Kate said, surprised. He wasn't good at keeping secrets from Kate. Once she sensed a mystery she would ferret and ferret until she found out. So he added, 'It won't take long.'

'All right, dear.' Kate looked puzzled. She stared after Freddie.

'He's up to something,' Annie said. 'I know that look.'

Freddie went upstairs two steps at a time. He dragged the rug from under the bed, pushed the bed sideways, and used the newly sharpened bread knife to lift one of the floorboards. Dust rose from the dark space, and the smell of mice and mould. Freddie lay down and reached his arm in there until his hand touched cold metal. He withdrew a square red Oxo tin with a lid. Working quickly, with one ear listening for anyone coming up the stairs, he prised the lid off the tin. Inside were three fat rolls of bank notes. He crammed them into the inside pocket of his jacket, and quickly replaced the floorboard, the rug, and the bed.

When he left the cottage, the gypsy convoy was moving on and it was spotting with rain. Annie, Kate and the children were on their way home, with Annie carrying the tistie-tosties and Lucy and Tessa contentedly licking a shiny brown toffee apple each.

Freddie hesitated, his hand on the door of his lorry. Make up your mind – courageously.

'Can you come with me, Kate?' he asked her.

'Where to?'

''Tis a secret,' Freddie said, his eyes twinkling.

'Ooh – I love secrets! How exciting. Can we all come?'

'No – just you – please,' Freddie said. 'Mother will have the children, won't you? Just for an hour.'

'Can't you take Tessa with you?' Annie said. 'I don't mind Lucy.'

'No, I can't take Tessa – please, Mother, just for once, will you try and manage?'

'Don't look as if I've got a choice,' Annie said resentfully. She brushed the sleeve of his jacket. 'Look at you – covered in dust. What have you been doing?' She patted the bulge of bank notes stashed in his jacket pocket. 'What's that? A lump of lardy cake?'

Freddie shook her off. 'Please, Mother – just look after the children.'

Annie crouched under the table, her arms and legs quivering with terror. She sat awkwardly, her short legs splayed out, her head jammed against the dusty underside of the scullery table. She'd dragged Lucy under there with her, and the child's puzzled eyes were staring into hers with disarming honesty. 'What are you frightened of, Granny?' she asked.

'Thunder,' Annie said, and as she spoke, the interior of the old bakery cottage was illuminated by a jagged artery of lightning from the coppery gloom of the afternoon sky. The window panes rattled and the china on the dresser rang with the thunder, a deafening, earthy growl that rolled down the streets like a horde of escaping cider barrels. Annie pressed her hands over her ears and moaned with fear. 'It's a curse upon us all,' she said, and scowled at the rain-flecked window.

'What's a curse, Granny?'

''Tis bad. Bad like your sister,' Annie said, and immediately regretted her words as Lucy's eyes widened. Freddie wouldn't like what she'd said. She wasn't sure she liked it herself. Sometimes Annie's extreme fear emerged from her lips as anger. But then – anger was more acceptable than fear, she reasoned.

The next roll of thunder broke overhead, like tumbling bricks. Annie shuddered and so did the walls of the cottage. A scream was lurking deep in her chest, but she held it back. It wouldn't do to scream in front of Lucy. A mad woman, that's what they'd say. Mad women screamed. So she held it in.

Then there was Tessa.

She listened fearfully. Three-year-old Tessa was somewhere in the cottage. Not on the dresser, Annie prayed. Please, please not on the dresser. Where was she? Between thunderclaps the silences were ominous.

'Tessa!' she called, sternly from under the table.

Silence. A sigh of rain on the scullery roof. A gurgling from the drainpipes. But no Tessa.

'Shall I go and get her?' Lucy asked.

'NO.' Annie grabbed Lucy's cardigan and held on to it as another bolt of lightning vividly lit the walls with their copper pans hanging. 'You stay here, Lucy – just in case – we'll be safe under this strong table if the house falls down.'

Lucy's bottom lip quivered. 'I'm frightened. I don't like it.'

'Cuddle up to me then,' said Annie.

'But you're frightened, Granny,' Lucy said. 'I want Daddy to come home, and Mummy.'

'They'll be back soon, I hope.' Annie frowned. *Freddie and Kate should never have gone off and left her in charge of Tessa*, she thought resentfully. *Today of all days.* Freddie wouldn't tell her where they were going. A mysterious sparkle had danced in his eyes. It was a secret, he'd said. Even Kate didn't know. She'd climbed trustingly into the lorry, her face bright with anticipation.

'We won't be more than an hour,' Freddie had promised. Minutes after they'd driven off, the storm broke over Monterose.

Lucy squirmed out of Annie's arms and ran to the window.

'No, Lucy. You'll get struck by lightning.' Annie felt her heart lurch into a different gear. Her chest hurt with the hammering, and her back ached from sitting on the hard floor. What if she had a heart attack?

'Tessa's in the garden,' Lucy reported, 'and she's taken her dress off.'

Annie groaned and began to rock herself to and fro, her hands clutched around her chest. Suddenly she couldn't breathe. 'I'm gonna die,' she moaned, 'here under the table. And they'll have to drag me out by my feet.' She pulled her navy blue dress down to cover her knees. Sweat trickled out of her hair and glazed her ice-cold skin. The room darkened, and Lucy's voice was distant.

'Granny, Tessa's dancing in the rain.'

Annie didn't care. Well, she did care, and she didn't. She hated herself for being in a panic. She hated what fear did to her. Was it the fear, or was it real? She couldn't tell. Either way it was humiliating.

'Tessa's standing in a puddle and it's up to her ankles,' Lucy shouted. 'I banged on the window but she won't take any notice. And the lightning is like a broken tree flashing in the sky.'

'Tessa is an impossible child,' Annie said, rocking harder. 'Serve her right if she gets struck. And serve her mother right for bringing such a brat into the family . . .' She gave in and let a stream of vitriol pour through her, not caring that Lucy was listening. Annie had tried to like Kate, but her own sense of inadequacy and powerlessness had got in the way. Everything had been going along nicely, she thought, until THAT TESSA had been born. Now the little hussy was out there dancing naked in the rain, in HER garden. The shame of it. The shame.

The storm wilted into a dripping silence. The rooftops of Monterose glistened and the wet leaves sparkled with a sense of satisfaction. The streets gurgled with rivulets of sooty, oily, muddy water, all heading down to the station yard. Annie stayed under the table, feeling her heart slowing down, beat by shameful beat.

Kate's bright voice and Freddie's reassuring footsteps brought Annie's guilt and humiliation into sharp focus. Jealousy was there too, stabbing at her heart. Kate was in the garden – laughing – and it seemed to Annie that the laughter was ringing through the street like the church bells.

Kate came into the kitchen, radiant, with Tessa in her arms and Lucy clinging round her skirts. 'Ooh, you are a pickle!' Kate said to Tessa. 'Did you enjoy the rain?'

Tessa nodded, her pale blue eyes shining with joy. 'I danced,' she whispered, 'and now I've got stars on my skin.'

Kate laughed even louder. 'You mean raindrops! Stars indeed. Anyone would think you'd been sprinkled with fairy dust.' Her laugh seemed to energise the whole cottage.

'Tessa's wicked,' Lucy said. 'I didn't take MY dress off. Granny said Tessa was a curse.'

Kate frowned. 'Don't talk so silly,' she said. 'It's not wicked to enjoy the rain. Come on, madam, into the bath with you.'

'But Granny's under the table,' said Lucy, and the moment Annie dreaded had arrived. She couldn't get up from the floor on her own, especially not from under the table. If Kate laughed, it would be the last straw. The thought of that ringing laugh added another spike of anger to Annie's overloaded emotions. Hot tears zigzagged through the wrinkles on her cheeks.

Kate swung round to look at her, but Tessa got there first. Her pale blue eyes stared under the table just as Annie was wiping her face with the corner of her flowery apron.

'Don't cry, Granny.' Tessa dived under the table and put her bare wet arms round Annie's shoulders. Annie only saw the splodges Tessa's wet feet were leaving on the floor. She saw her wet navy blue knickers and the splashes of mud over her legs and socks. In her fury, Annie didn't see the compassion and the love the child was offering her.

'You bad, wicked girl.' Annie pushed Tessa away. 'Look at the state of you. Filthy dirty. I don't want you near me.' She glared out at Kate. 'I told her not to go outside, and she did. She should be made to do her own washing – look at the state of her – and – and she was DANCING in the front garden in the pouring rain where the whole neighbourhood could see her. Out there in her knickers. Aren't you ashamed of her, Kate? Oh – that's right – CRY!' she added as two silent tears ran down Tessa's face. 'I'll give you something to cry about. Wicked child.'

Kate saw the light drain from Tessa's eyes. 'No,' she said firmly. 'That's not fair. I won't have her treated like that, Annie. Tessa was trying to be kind to you. Fancy pushing her away like that. I'm not having it.'

Annie snorted. 'Well, are you going to help me out of here?' she demanded. 'I'm an old woman and I can't get up.'

Kate wanted to tell Annie that as far as she was concerned, she could stay there. *But I'm here to love*, she thought. *I'm here to keep the peace, keep everyone happy.* So she reached under the table, gave Annie her hand, and spoke to her kindly. 'You'll feel better in a minute. Don't upset yourself.'

She pulled the trembling Annie to her feet and looked at her caringly. 'Come on, it's all right now. We're home and everything's all right.'

Disarmed by the kindness, Annie allowed Kate to guide her to her favourite chair and tuck a blanket round her. 'I can't help it,' she said. 'It was the thunder. I tried to keep the children safe – I tried – but that Tessa . . .'

'Now you just sit here quietly,' Kate said. 'Freddie's on his way in. Everything's all right, Annie. I'm going to sort out this wet child, and then we'll have tea and toast. AND – we've got a surprise.'

'I don't like surprises,' Annie warned. 'A surprise can be a shock for an old woman like me. Bad for my heart.'

'Leave it to me, Kate,' Freddie said later. 'I'll tell Mother – she'll take it better from me. You go and put the girls to bed.'

He walked Annie back to her own cottage next door, thinking it best to have this particular conversation away from the girls. He knew Annie was upset, but he needed to tell her what he'd done. She'd take it hard, but he'd talk her round.

Freddie sat down in his father's old chair, his fingers smoothing the brass studs that held it together. Half of him was listening to Annie ranting on about thunderstorms and the other half was still in a happy haze from the secret hour he'd spent with Kate. Her reaction to his surprise had been everything he'd dreamed of, the way she'd flung her arms around him and danced around with such enthusiasm. Danced! Yes, she made him dance, and he'd loved it. His face still ached from smiling. He couldn't wait to take her to bed that night, the memory of the passionate kiss they'd shared and the way he'd felt so wanted and so appreciated. Telling his mother seemed like an ordinary duty, nothing he couldn't handle.

'I've got something to tell you, Mother,' he began, and Annie stiffened. What she'd dreaded was about to happen.

'What's that?' she asked.

Freddie looked at her with his level, steady gaze. 'I bought a house.'

Annie's voice dwindled to a whisper. 'A house?' she said, as if a house was a disease worse than the plague.

Freddie took a paper from his inside pocket, unfolded it and handed it to her. 'There. You take a look. It's a beauty. Brand new, with an acre of garden. Half a mile out of town on the road to Hilbegut. Built with red brick.'

'Bricks?' Annie gasped. 'I don't like those things. Vulgar.'

Freddie winced. He was glad Kate wasn't there. He waited, watching the expression on his mother's face as the news sank in. An unhealthy lilac tinge crept up her cheeks, her eyes narrowed and her lips set in a purple line. He was reminded of the times he had coaxed her out of the panic attacks when he was seven years old, walking backwards in front of her, his small hands hurting with the tightness of her grip, his feet blistered raw from wearing wooden clogs, his only footwear. She'd been dependent on him.

'You BOUGHT it, you say?'

'Yes.'

'How much money? How much?'

'Seven hundred pounds.'

'Seven hundred pounds! I've never seen that much money in my life. Where did you get it?'

'I've been saving, Mother, all through the wartime, and every single haulage job with the lorry. Ever since our wedding. I want to give Kate the home she deserves.'

'She's got a perfectly good home here, and so have you.'

Freddie was silent. He waited. The last thing he wanted was a confrontation with his mother.

'So – what are you going to do with this brick-built house?' Annie asked. She picked up her ebony walking stick which lay beside the chair, and put it on the floor, leaning on it as if to anchor herself. The stick began to shake harder and harder.

'Kate and I are going to live in it. With Lucy and Tessa,' Freddie said as gently as he could.

Bitterness cut into Annie's eyes. She nodded. 'I thought that was coming.' Her voice shook. 'What about me?'

'What about you? You're all right here, aren't you?'

'I'm your MOTHER,' she spat. 'You can't LEAVE me. I'm old now.'

Freddie leaned forward and took both her hands in his. 'I know, I know 'tis hard. But we're not abandoning you. We'll look out for you, and bring the children.'

Annie snatched her hands away and screamed at him in a high, thin voice, her mouth foaming, her eyes erupting with tears. 'Don't do this,' she begged, 'don't leave me, Freddie. Don't leave me here to die on my own.'

Freddie was shocked. He never remembered his mother crying, even when his father had died. She'd been stoical and silent, frightened, but never like this. She was working herself into a frenzy.

'I'll never let you go. Never,' she cried. 'You leave this place over my dead body.'

Chapter Six

IN SEARCH OF FOREVER

> *'And out again I curve and flow*
> *to join the brimming river.*
> *For men may come and men may go,*
> *but I go on forever.'*
>
> 'The Brook'
> by Alfred Lord Tennyson

'Do you like that poem?'

The teacher's question was followed by an elastic silence, tension stretched into snapping point.

'Tessa?'

Seven-year-old Tessa froze, her anxious eyes locked with the demanding stare of her teacher. Miss O'Grady had a knack of dropping one of these questions into the middle of her daydream where it sat like a granite pebble, an obstacle that sparkled mockingly. There had to be a word, Tessa thought desperately, a 'yes' or a 'no' to deflect the question, but she didn't trust words. Words got you into trouble when you spoke them. But words could suck you into multi-coloured dream worlds, and that's where Tessa was when Miss O'Grady asked her the question.

Tessa had been pondering the word 'forever', and the concept of a stream flowing into eternity. Forever was where you went when you died, she thought. It was where her grandad had gone. Gone, into the 'silent land', the forever place where no one would ask you questions. In her mind Tessa had gone to the banks of the millstream, taken off her Clarks sandals and her school socks, and waded into the silver water. She'd always wondered where the stream was going in such a hurry. Now she knew. The stream was going to 'forever'. And if she followed it, she could go there too. She could see Grandad, and live in peace in this 'forever' place.

Why wait? Tessa thought, and the idea looped around her like a hug of joy. She leapt to her feet, overturned her chair, and ran to the classroom door. She clutched the round brass doorknob and turned it with both hands.

'Tessa!'

She heard the creak of Miss O'Grady's chair, the clop of sensible black lace-up shoes, the thud of a book falling to the floor. She struggled with the doorknob, wrenching at it until it turned. The heavy door swung open, and Tessa fled down the polished corridor, her new Clarks sandals clap-clapping like Kate's butter pats.

'You NAUGHTY GIRL.' The words bounded after her like a farm dog, but Tessa didn't care. She was out. Out, out, OUT under the vast blue-silver skies, under the whispers of mighty elm trees, over the pitted asphalt of the playground, through the clang of the wrought-iron gate. She seized a stick and ran it along the iron railings, playing a tune of freedom, a wild tune, an escaping tune.

With her chestnut plaits flying, she headed over the water meadows towards the millstream. She would follow it on its babbling journey until it joined 'the brimming river'. Tessa let those enticing words into her mouth, turning them over, sucking the sugar from them. The brimming river. The brimming river. She so wanted to see it, swim in it like a duck, drink its crystal water and follow it – to forever.

Kate took the two halves of her freshly baked Victoria sponge to the kitchen table. She spread the lower half with home-made raspberry jam, and the top half with rich, creamy butter icing, then carefully sandwiched them together, and put the cake on a paper doily. Singing happily, she set the table with the best willow-patterned china and silver cutlery. She peeped under the crisp navy and white tea cloths to check the cucumber sandwiches made from a wondrous new product – sliced bread. She checked the egg mayonnaise ones, and the ham. They looked fresh and moist. Gingerly she plugged in her new electric kettle, and spooned tealeaves into her favourite teapot which looked like a cottage.

It was going to be fine, she told herself firmly. Kate was proud of her lovely red brick house with its big garden and the three tall pine trees. It had elm trees too, all along the hedge bordering the lane. Freddie had made a long path with blue-lias flagstones, bordered by his vegetable garden and a magnificent lawn. His stone carvings stood proudly around the edges, and he'd made a swing for the children from two old telegraph poles, a thick rope and a seat made from the lid of an oak chest he'd found in the hedge.

The garden had magical places too, for it had once been a much loved cottage garden before the cottage had been demolished and the new brick house built in its place. There was a hollow where the Anderson shelter had been, now overgrown with lilac and buddleia, a place of secrets where Lucy and Tessa loved to play.

That morning, Kate had sent them to school in clean cotton dresses, with new ribbons in their hair, white ankle socks and stiff new Clarks sandals. 'Keep nice and clean today,' she'd said. 'We're having a tea party when you come home from school. Auntie Susan and her two children, and Auntie Lexi will be here, and Granny. Mind you be good – on BEST behaviour. Then you can have a slice of my Victoria sponge.' Two pairs of eyes had shone back at her, reflecting her smile.

But, as always, Tessa had pouted. 'I don't like Auntie Lexi.'

'Well – grin and bear it, dear,' Kate said, briskly. She tightened the blue satin bow on one of Tessa's gleaming chestnut plaits. The anxiety in the child's eyes annoyed her. 'Try and be more like Lucy,' she advised. 'Lucy gets on with everybody, and she smiles.' But Tessa gave her a mutinous, chilling glare. Kate bit back the angry response that danced in her throat. She'd already had one confrontation with Tessa that morning, over the new sandals. Tessa refused to wear them and it had ended in tears and a slap. The mark of Kate's furious hand was still there like an accusing red flame on Tessa's firm little thigh.

Watching the two girls set off for school on the summer morning, Kate had breathed a sigh of relief. Impressing Susan and Lexi was important to her, mostly because they had horses. Lexi was a riding instructor, and Freddie called her 'Ian Tillerman's leather-bottomed sister'. Susan's children, Fiona and Michael, were already riding and winning rosettes on two feisty little ponies. Kate wanted Lexi to be so captivated by her well behaved, courageous daughters that she would offer to teach them to ride. It was the one thing she and Freddie disagreed about.

'I know you love horses,' he'd said. 'You grew up with them, Kate. But I've always been wary of them, see? I don't want you going riding racehorses like you used to, with that – that Ian Tillerman. He is a TOFF.'

'Yes – he is,' Kate agreed, 'but he can't help it. And not all horsey people are toffs.'

'Well, I don't want our girls turning into two leather-bottomed toffs,' declared Freddie, 'and it's not only that – riding is a dangerous sport.'

'Ooh, I love a bit of danger!' Kate said, her eyes lighting up at the memory of galloping with the wind in her hair. 'It's character forming.'

Freddie looked at her sadly. 'Our two little girls are precious to me, Kate, really precious, and I'm happy just to see them run to me at the end of the day, with their eyes shining like stars. I don't want no sadness or struggle for them, like I had. Let them simply live and be happy. Don't drive them.' He put his cap on, and kissed Kate tenderly on the lips. 'I gotta go to work now, dear. And you remember that, will you? Don't drive them.'

In her deepest heart, Kate knew that Freddie was right. But she felt driven by her own sense of adventure. She missed the farm life and the loving animals she'd grown up with. Freddie's life seemed dominated by engines which he talked to as if they were dogs. He worked for hours into the night on some oily lump of black metal, whistling and singing out in his workshop. Increasingly, people were asking him to fix anything mechanical from lawnmowers to lorries. Freddie was even talking about buying a garage and setting up in business. He'd succeed, Kate was sure, but she dreaded it. She didn't want her children to grow up in a smelly, oily garage in the middle of town.

To get what she wanted for her girls, she would have to be manipulative, Kate thought, relishing the challenge. And today's tea party was a step in the right direction.

A dramatic clatter of hooves sent Kate rushing to the front door. She gazed up the lane as a smart, high-stepping hackney pony sped into view, with Lexi, red-cheeked and rake thin, sitting high on the seat of a carriage, holding tightly to the long reins, the muscles glinting in her leathery arms. Thrilled with the energy and the polished black coat of the pony, Kate stood at the garden gate, waving. Susan sat on the back seat with Fiona and Michael on each side of her.

'Whoa!' Lexi brought the pony to a halt, its bridle jingling. 'Whoa, Tarquin.'

'Ooh, how lovely! What an arrival!' Kate felt the heat from the pony. She sensed the pain in his neck from being too tightly arched, and she immediately gave the hyped-up creature a hug, rubbing his ears and mane as the reins eased. 'There. Good boy, Tarquin. You HAVE done well,' she soothed, 'and you've come to see Kate. Well, I might find you a carrot.' She nipped into the garden and pulled one of the carrots Freddie had grown.

'Good grief!' Lexi exclaimed. 'What an extraordinary carrot.'

'Some of them are two foot long,' Kate said, brushing off the red Somerset clay and feeding the orange carrot into the pony's velvet lips. The sound of crunching teeth echoed down the lane.

'By the way, we are here too, Kate,' Lexi said, swinging her lean brown-booted legs down from the carriage.

'I know you are, and a warm welcome,' Kate beamed at Lexi and Susan. Both wore Aertex polo shirts open at the neck, breeches and boots, and silk headscarves with horses on them, tied under their chins.

Michael, six, and Fiona, five, looked confident and disciplined. They sat still in the carriage and waited for Lexi to tell them to get down. Susan looked intimidated as always, Kate thought, feeling sorry for her. She'd been a good nurse and had enjoyed the camaraderie of working in the hospital. She and Kate had laughed and cried together through the wartime. But now Susan had gone back into her shell, especially since marrying into Ian's managerial family. She seemed totally overshadowed by Lexi, as she had been by her mother.

'What's for tea, Kate?' Lexi asked. 'I'm starving.' She deftly unhitched the pony from the carriage. 'Bring him into the garden, Sue,' she commanded. 'Tie him up to that ring in the workshop wall. Freddie won't mind, will he Kate? Then we can have tea in peace. Where are the children? Don't let them go running round behind Tarquin. He kicks, especially if he doesn't know someone.'

'They'll be back from school any minute.' Kate glanced down the lane, thinking Lucy and Tessa were later than usual.

'I hope they're well-behaved children,' Lexi said in her ringing voice. 'I can't stand brats.'

'Don't worry, they know what's expected of them,' Kate said. 'You've met them before, haven't you?'

'Course we have,' said Lexi. 'Now Lucy, I could pick her up and take her home. She's a charming little thing – but the other one, Tessa, she's a different kettle of fish. I've never seen her smile, and she won't answer when you talk to her. Always in a bad mood.'

Kate felt a tiny bubble of anger rising, but she smiled disarmingly at Lexi's challenging eyes. 'Wait 'til she sees my Victoria sponge,' she beamed. 'It's their favourite tea.'

'We found Tessa surly and difficult.' Lexi was in for the kill. She stared demandingly at Susan. 'Didn't we, Sue?'

Susan looked appealingly at Kate as if she was a guiding light. 'Maybe – a bit,' she mumbled and looked at the floor. Disagreeing with Lexi was a risk she wasn't going to take.

'Children come in all shapes and sizes,' Kate said brightly. 'I try and treat our two the same. What one has, the other has – and Freddie adores them. I wouldn't change them for the world. Is this Tarquin's hay net?' she asked, unhooking the sweet-smelling bundle from the back of the carriage. She put her arm round the pony's sleek neck. 'Come on, you come with Kate and we'll find you a drink of water, and tie you up in the shade. Ooh, you are beautiful.'

Tarquin gave Kate an affectionate push with his nose. She missed horses so much. She led him over to the stone water trough and let him drink. Watching the lane for a sign of Lucy and Tessa returning, she was surprised to see Miss O'Grady herself come into view, striding along with Lucy beside her. For once Lucy looked serious, her small back importantly straight as she walked beside her teacher. Where was Tessa? *Something's wrong*, Kate thought. Not today, of all days – with Lexi and Sue here.

At the same time, Annie was struggling down the garden path in her best navy blue dress, her eyes bright at the prospect of a tea party, a plate of scones in her hand. She walked awkwardly now, her wide hips seesawing, her ankles turned inward. She'd put on a lot of weight that year from sedentary living and unaccustomed plenty.

There was no escape. They all met in the lane outside the garden gate. Annie, Lexi and Susan with her two obedient children, and Miss O'Grady and Lucy. Kate tied Tarquin up quickly and bustled over there, the beat of her heart quickening with anxiety.

'Don't CRY,' snapped Miss O'Grady as Lucy's face crumpled. 'Your mother doesn't need any MORE trouble. Hold your head up and don't be silly.'

Bewildered, Lucy glanced dubiously at Lexi and Susan. She went straight to her mother. Kate could feel the sobs shaking Lucy's little body as she leaned against her. 'Lucy!' she crooned. 'This isn't like you.' She gave Miss O'Grady a searching stare. 'Don't tell her not to cry. Something's obviously wrong. What is it? Where's Tessa?'

'Tessa just upped sticks and ran out of the classroom. Little madam.' Miss O'Grady pursed her thin lips and a forklike frown dissected her face. 'In the middle of a poetry lesson, if you please.'

'There – I told you, didn't I?' said Annie triumphantly. 'I always said there was something wrong with that child.'

'Nothing a good slap wouldn't cure,' said Lexi.

Humiliated, Kate tried to shoo them away. 'Why don't you go in and start tea?' she suggested. 'I can sort this out. Go on Lucy – you take Lexi and Susan into the dining room and show them where to sit. I won't be long.'

It got worse. Lucy clung to her, the sobs still shaking her slim body. Miss O'Grady's next remark was a shock. The words exploded from her thin lips like gunfire. 'I have to tell you, Mrs Barcussy, that I'm sorry but I cannot have your daughter at our school any longer. She is sullen and disruptive. And – and unmanageable.'

A hungry silence opened its jaws between them standing there in the lane with Miss O'Grady glaring at Kate.

Kate's cheeks went crimson. She tossed her glossy black hair, and glared back. 'No, you can't do that, Miss O'Grady. Tessa's only seven. We can sort it out if we sit down and talk it over. I won't have it. Don't think you can expel my daughter, Miss O'Grady, because I won't let you. Why did she run away? And where is she now? I'd like to know, please.'

Annie was looking admiringly at Kate. She took Lucy. 'Come on, you come inside with Gran, and you two. We'll start tea. You carry that plate.' She gave Lucy the plate of scones and marched her inside. After a curt thumb jerk from Lexi, Michael and Fiona scrambled down from the cart and floated after them like two ghost children.

But Lexi stood there, her riding boots planted squarely in the grass, her lean face concerned as Kate and Miss O'Grady eyeballed one another. Clearly, Kate was going to win.

'Where is Tessa?' Kate asked again, and the answer made her go cold all over.

'We don't know. She's not in the school building. I expected her to be here.' Miss O'Grady went pale. 'Isn't she?'

'No. So where is she? What time did she run away?'

'About half past ten. I assumed she'd run home.'

'Half past TEN? That's hours ago. Surely someone could have looked for her? Couldn't you have telephoned me?'

A blend of panic and fury was driving Kate. She struggled to remain courteous. 'We do have a telephone, you know. Don't you know how to use one?'

'Most families in Monterose don't have such a luxury as a telephone. It's not normal practice for our school to be spending time and money telephoning parents who can't – who don't . . .' The words died on Miss O'Grady's wiry lips as she caught the glint in Kate's eyes. She took a deep breath and looked at her watch. 'You realise my school day actually ended half an hour ago? I brought Lucy home, and that's it. You must find Tessa yourself, Mrs Barcussy. I wash my hands of her.'

Kate gasped in disbelief, and felt a restraining hand on her arm. 'I suggest you go home then,' Lexi said, acidly. 'You're beneath contempt. Go on. Buzz off.'

Kate was shaking as they watched the thin figure stalking away from them. She leaned on the field gate opposite the house, trying to stay calm, her brown eyes scanning the miles of wild flower meadows and the thickly blossomed hedges. She stared down at the river valley. A rich haze of buttercups and red sorrel. A sliver of light on the water. The river! A crippling memory made her clasp her hands to her temples so tightly she wanted to crush her own skull.

Ethie!

When they lived in Gloucestershire, Ethie had gone to the river. Ethie, like Tessa, had been obsessed with water. And Ethie had never come back. Missing, presumed drowned. Until, one terrible day, a sheep farmer had found her body, miles upstream, a victim of the Severn Bore.

Surely it couldn't happen again? Could it?

Despite the child's difficult personality, Kate loved Tessa fiercely and unconditionally, the way she'd loved Ethie. The difference was that Kate needed Tessa. With both her children, the mother love had overwhelmed her. It was an unexpected, awesome power, a demanding power which hadn't made her a better, wiser parent. It had made her vulnerable, and Kate had never felt vulnerable. She'd always been confident and in charge of her life. Until Lucy and Tessa had taken it over, taken her heart and most of her energy. Even her fine private education, her hard nursing training and the frugal, nerve-wracking wartime years had not prepared Kate for the maternal savagery that engulfed her life now. It was a different kind of love. A savage, protective love that didn't gel with behaving like a nice girl from a nice family.

'Kate!' Susan was beside her, quietly supportive, her arm around Kate's shoulders. 'Don't worry – she's bound to be somewhere nearby. Lexi and I will help you find Tessa.'

'But it's FIVE HOURS she's been missing! With no lunch and no coat,' Kate said desperately. 'Where did she go? Why – oh why didn't she come home?'

'One more load, Freddie. All right?' Herbie shouted over the roar of the lorry's engine.

'Yeah, all right. She's got just enough petrol,' Freddie said. He looked at Herbie's eyes shining blue in his dust-covered face. The whole man was covered in stone dust and might have been a stone carving of a gargoyle. 'I'd do anything for you.' Freddie's eyes twinkled as he nodded at Herbie and drove away, enjoying the shudder of the engine and the way it responded to his touch. One more load of blue-lias stone, then he could go home to Kate and his two little girls. It was their anniversary, but Freddie was glad to be missing out on the tea party. It was women's stuff. He felt awkward, especially around Lexi and Susan.

Following the winding road over the Poldens through the green twilight of the woods, Freddie remembered the happy picnics he'd shared with Kate, and the games they'd played with the children. He longed to stop and rest on the ridgeway, to walk up there on springy turf and see the butterflies, especially the large blues which appeared in June. He wished Kate had arranged a picnic, just for the four of them, not a tea party dominated by disapproving aunties and his mother's indefatigable negativity.

Life was good at The Pines, and he'd never regretted buying it. But detaching from his mother hadn't worked out and, after months of stress and arguments, she'd finally agreed to move in with them, into her own downstairs apartment and a square of garden. She had electricity and a bathroom with hot water, luxuries Annie had never experienced.

Earlier that day, Freddie had bought Kate a bouquet of a dozen fragrant red roses. It was sitting in a jar of water in Herbie's office, and the two men had joked about not letting a single speck of stone dust spoil those precious roses. Freddie was looking forward to going home and seeing Kate's radiant smile when he gave them to her.

He allowed himself one brief stop on the best viewpoint high on the hills. He lit a fag and sat gazing across the Levels. Far below, a silver ribbon of water wound its way through the water meadows. And it was then that he heard a cry. The cry of a child.

His skin began to prickle. His pulse quickened in the way it had done years ago in his youth, always just before he saw or heard something he wasn't allowed to talk about. Forbidden fruit. Fruit of the spirit. Don't talk about it, boy. You're a liar. A liar.

The air shimmered, and Freddie inhaled a lungful of smoke from the last of his fag. He stubbed it into the dashboard ashtray which was so crammed with dog ends that it wouldn't close. He wound the window down and got out, suddenly needing the reassuring turfy fragrance of the hillside. He walked a few strides over the grass, stepping between the ant hills, looking down at the pink mats of wild thyme, scarlet pimpernel and blue scabious. Butterflies flitted over the flowers, bobbing like Lucy's blonde curls did when she ran.

Freddie knew he should be working, but something drew him up to the skyline, to a spot where he and Kate had often sat. He tried to ignore the insistent cry in his heart, the relentless shimmering of the air that announced the unseen presence of a spirit who wanted to talk to him.

He sat down on the skyline, and lit a second fag, the nicotine dulling his senses. He listened intently to the skylarks and the linnets, and the clack-clack of a hay-baler far below in the fields, the sound of hammering from the village, the drone of a tiny aeroplane. He closed his eyes and put his hands over his ears. All the sounds in the world could not block this insistent voice. He felt the touch of a hand, like a tulip brushing his shoulder. He smelled her perfume, honeysuckle and lavender. And she was there, clear as a painting, Granny Barcussy with her radiant, two-toothed smile. In his difficult childhood she'd been his only friend. So why was he trying so hard to ignore her, while she was trying so hard to speak to him, to wrap him in the feel of a hug that swung around his tired shoulders like soft velvet?

'I gotta work,' he said aloud. 'Have to fetch another load from the quarry.'

He stood up, and allowed himself a final gaze at the blue-green landscape. Again that glint of water caught his eye. The cry came again. Tessa. It was Tessa. Those pale aqua eyes, appealing to him, needing him. He knew beyond doubt that Tessa was in trouble. But then, Tessa was always in trouble. So why was it different today?

Freddie got back into the lorry, turned it round and headed down the winding hill, away from the quarry, and he drove more and more recklessly, the words of the gypsy haunting his thoughts, 'I see a girl, a girl with pale blue eyes . . .'

Chapter Seven

DOGS WITH RED EYES

'Don't you DARE take those sandals off,' Kate had said to Tessa in her 'I must be obeyed' voice. So when Tessa had reached the mill stream that morning and realised the only way to follow it was to paddle in it, she had kept her sandals on. For a long time she stood in the water, watching it crinkling in the light, making nets of gold flicker across the clay bed. The clay was different colours, ochre yellow in some places, grey in others, but mostly it was a pinky red, embedded with pebbles that made the water babble and gurgle. Mesmerised, Tessa watched it turning her white socks into grubby dishrags, striped with skeins of green weed. Her new sandals filled with water like two sauce boats, her small feet sloshing around in them. She had a blister on each heel from the hard new leather, and the ice cool water healed the fiery soreness. When she lifted her foot out of the water, a shoe-shaped cascade poured out, glistening like crystal. Stamping was even more fun, raising shoe-shaped splashes of lemon-white spray.

Tessa had never been so ecstatically happy as she was now, by herself in the glittering mill stream. She felt the water was talking to her, and so were the creatures of the stream who stared at her with the brightest, friendly eyes: the gold-skinned frog who hopped ahead of her, and lingered in the grass, staring at her, waiting for her to catch up; the dragonflies, visions of turquoise, escorted her on wings like golden glass, flying ahead, pausing, watching her with complex eyes; the indigo scissor-like glint of the swallows who flew low over the water in front of her, snatching a drink. They were leading her. All the magic creatures. Leading her into their world as if she were a giant they had befriended.

The way the creatures of the stream looked at her with undisguised curiosity and friendliness was nurturing to Tessa. It gave her a sense of belonging, a sense of unconditional acceptance. People didn't look at Tessa like that. Their eyes were accusing, puzzled or angry. Only her beloved dad, Freddie, looked at her with peaceful eyes, loving her, no matter what kind of mood she was in.

The stream was leaving the water meadows now, winding into a copse of willow and poplar, the banks sculpted into mounds and hollows with carpets of cowslips and starry white stitchwort. Tessa climbed out and picked a bunch of cowslips. She sat in a patch of sunshine, holding their fat pink stems and burying her face in the extravagant fragrance and velvet of the yellow and sage-green blooms. *Friends*, she thought, *these flowers love me, they don't tell me what to do.*

She felt inclined to stay there and go to sleep with her face covered in flowers. Once her mum had told her about an auntie, Auntie Ethie who had drowned in the Severn River – and how her family had gone out in a boat and thrown flowers on the water in her memory. The flowers were to say they loved her.

Tessa stood up. She breathed in the perfume of the cowslips one last time, then threw them, one at a time, into the water and watched them twirling away like ballerinas. Little moments of stillness, then wild dancing on the polished water. 'In memory of Auntie Ethie,' she said, and tears poured down her cheeks. It didn't matter, because there was no one there to tell her not to cry.

When the stream reached the road, it plunged into a stone tunnel, too low for Tessa to walk through. She dropped to her knees in the water, wetting the edge of her dress and the ends of her plaits. In the cold of the tunnel she almost panicked when a pair of heavy Shire horses clopped over-head, pulling a hay cart that rumbled like thunder. She touched the stone ceiling and felt it vibrating under her fingers.

It was a water vole with merry black eyes who led her through to the other side, his wiggling body trailing a wake of minute bubbles. She watched him swim out into the mysterious garden of the mill, his back glistening as he swam across the deep dark pool.

Tessa hesitated. She wanted to find 'the brimming river' out there in the sunlight, leading to 'forever'. Instead, confronting her was the polished black surface of the mill pool. She watched some willow leaves floating with a few rose petals and one of her cowslips. At first they twirled slowly on the black surface, then vanished at speed over the roar of the weir.

Ivor Stape was a reclusive old man with a secret even darker than the mill pool. His wife, it was rumoured, had left him long ago, and he ran the water mill on his own, employing young boys who were too desperate for work to stand up to his bullying ways. No boy ever stayed longer than a month or so before leaving under a shadow of silence. He was fanatical about his garden and kept a pair of basset hounds to patrol the property. Their bark was a fearsome sonorous baying, guaranteed to spook the most intrepid intruders.

Such a bark was intimidating but when magnified inside a tunnel it became heart-stoppingly loud, especially to a sensitive soul like Tessa. Now soaking wet, she had crawled to the exit where the stream poured with the silence of oil into the black pool, and the few sparkles on the surface reflected in an oscillating lattice on the roof of the tunnel. She crouched in the water, peering into a gloomy garden of heavy evergreens and sloping lawns. In her mind, Tessa was trying to guess the depth of the pool. She couldn't swim. But maybe she could wade around the edge and get onto the lawn. The garden was full of good hiding places. An eerie, birdless quiet hung there, punctuated only by the chug and whoosh of the great water wheel turning at the side wall of a house swathed in Virginia creeper.

The howling bark of the dogs turned Tessa to stone. They charged along the bank of the pool to the tunnel and looked in at her. There was a moment when they both saw her there in the water and the barking turned into a frenzy, echoing down the tunnel, a terrifying sound to a seven-year-old child. Tessa stared in horror at their eyes and thought they were red. Dogs with red eyes! Like the dog with three heads in her fairy-tale book. Red eyes. Red jaws. Red like blood. A colour that terrified Tessa. It went right back to the moment she'd been born into a world of screaming women and blood-soaked sheets.

She turned round and scrabbled to get back to the tranquillity of the water meadows. Her heartbeat shook her right to the core, so fast, so urgent she thought she was going to die. The bed of the stream was slippery in the tunnel and now she was going against the current. The water rushed and swirled towards her, filling her cotton dress, her knickers and socks. In her panic, she even swallowed some of it, gasping, breathing it in and coughing it out again. Shivering from the chill of the sunless tunnel, she paused to look back at the dogs, and saw they had gone. Where were they? She listened and heard the scuffle of their paws as they raced across the road above. They had anticipated her planned escape, and seconds later they were both at the other end of the tunnel, barking furiously and bouncing up and down.

Tessa heard herself screaming at them. Her hands clawed at stones embedded in the stream bed, hurling them out at the dogs, the stones ricocheting off the walls. 'Get off me,' she howled. 'Leave me alone.'

Returning to the black mill pool seemed to be her only option. Shivering violently, she turned round again.

And there, leering at her from the bank of the pool, was a man who looked like a troll.

'Well, well, well,' muttered Ivor Stape. 'God has sent me a water baby.' And he rubbed his fleshy red hands together and smiled.

As the sun mellowed towards evening and bars of saffron light stretched across the water meadows, the search for Tessa became ominous. The people of Monterose gathered at the iron gates of the school, grim-faced, a few helmeted policemen among them. Some carried torches or had dogs on leads, the women in dresses and wellies, the men in caps and work-worn jackets. They set off in silence, fanning out across the fields and woods, their eyes searching the ground, as instructed by the police, for any small sign of Tessa; a piece of ribbon, or a hanky, or a footstep, or a thread ripped from the blue and white cotton dress she'd been wearing.

Annie had never seen Kate in such a state, her lovely rosy face pale as marble and covered in tears. Kate and Lexi had walked miles through the woods and fields, searching hay barns and hedges, and places where Tessa and Lucy had played. The railway embankment was a favourite haunt of theirs, a wonderland of wild strawberries and tall pink fireweed growing in the beds of cinder from years of steam trains.

Kate had told them never to go on the railway lines, and she believed they wouldn't. Yet this afternoon she and Lexi had climbed up there and stood looking hopelessly at the long cold curve of the rails. It was too awful to contemplate.

Neither of them had a watch, but relied on the chimes of the church clock. When it struck six, Kate felt they should go home. They'd no way of knowing if Tessa had been found. She might be there, waiting for her mum. With that thought, Kate had hurried home through the hot afternoon, feeling giddy and light-headed. She'd had nothing to eat or drink for hours and her delicious tea was untouched on the table. Lexi had turned out to be a good and sensible friend in a time of trouble. She'd sent Susan and the children home with Tarquin to sort out the horses. Lexi had insisted on staying. She'd stuck with Kate, searching and shouting Tessa's name, trying to reassure her that all would be well. 'She'll be there waiting for us, you'll see,' she'd said repeatedly.

The worst moment had been arriving home and finding no Tessa, and no Freddie either. Kate was surprised. She knew Freddie wanted to avoid the tea party, but he hadn't said anything about working late. She clung to the idea that Tessa might have gone to find her daddy. Even now he might be bringing her home.

It was Lexi who insisted on telling the police. They came to the house and interviewed the distraught Kate. It was horribly familiar. The police interview. The beginning of the search. The aching, empty hours of waiting. Just as it had been when Ethie went missing.

'You MUST remain here, Mrs Barcussy,' the police had insisted. 'It's important for Tessa. When she is found – and we WILL find her – she'll want her mum waiting at home.'

So Kate stood in the garden in the rose-scented evening, watching the road until the welcome sight of Freddie's lorry came into view. She watched him swing his long legs down from the cab. Then he turned and reached inside, backing out again with a bouquet of red roses. He came to her smiling, his blue eyes twinkling. 'Happy anniversary, dear.'

'Oh Freddie –' Kate collapsed into his arms and wept. She couldn't speak.

Shocked, Freddie held her tightly, stroking her hair. It felt hot and sweaty, and she was trembling. 'Whatever's the matter?' he asked, but Kate just shook her head and cried against the steady beat of his heart. 'Don't cry on our anniversary,' he said, taking her over to the wooden garden seat. 'Come on, you sit down, sit quiet with me and tell me what's wrong. Kate – I've never seen you like this,' he added in alarm as her face looked up at him with desperate eyes.

'It – it's Tessa,' she whispered in a voice hoarse and defeated.

'Tessa?' Freddie stiffened. The cry. He'd heard it. And he hadn't listened. He had a terrible feeling of impending doom.

'She – she ran away from school at half past ten this morning and – and –' Kate blurted out the whole story, her words tumbling in an avalanche of pain. 'The police and – and half the village are out there searching for her. Where is she, Freddie? Where's my little girl?' A fresh burst of crying overwhelmed her. 'I'm sorry, Freddie,' she sobbed, trying to get a hold on herself. 'I'm sorry to make such a fuss.'

Kate was grateful for Freddie's quiet strength. But when she looked at him he was staring rigidly into the distance, his mouth twitching a little as it did when he was deep in thought. They were both glad to see Lucy come running into the garden. Annie stood at the door. 'Any news?' she asked.

Kate shook her head. For once she was glad of Annie's solid presence. She held out her arms to Lucy, but as usual Lucy wanted her daddy at this time of day. She climbed onto his lap, her clear eyes shining, 'Where's Tessa?' she asked.

'Oh she'll be back soon,' Kate said in her bright, everything's all right voice.

'Tessa was naughty,' Lucy told Freddie. 'She ran away when Miss O'Grady asked her a question.'

'What was the question?' Freddie asked.

'About – if she liked a poem.'

'And what poem was that?'

'It was 'The Brook' by Alfred Lord Tennyson,' said Lucy clearly.

'Ah – I know it,' Freddie said. 'I used to learn that in school.'

'So what did Tessa say?' asked Kate.

'She didn't answer. She just ran away.'

Annie was standing there, looking worried. 'Tell Daddy what happened before that,' she prompted.

'Well,' Lucy sat up straight and waved her fingers

expressively. Her eyes sparkled, enjoying the attention. 'Miss O'Grady called Tessa a liar. She was really cross with her.'

'A liar?' Freddie's heart gave a jolt. 'Why? What did Tessa say?'

'Well,' Lucy said in her musical voice, 'Miss O'Grady showed us a picture of Alfred Lord Tennyson, and Tessa said he was there in the classroom. She said he was standing by the blackboard.'

Annie and Freddie looked at one another, both remembering something they'd tried to forget.

'And then . . .' continued Lucy dramatically, 'Tessa answered back and said she wasn't a liar and said she could see Alfred Lord Tennyson and that he'd got a book in his hand. And Miss O'Grady dragged Tessa out to the front and made her stand on a chair and told everyone she was a liar. Well —' Lucy rolled her eyes, 'you KNOW what Tessa's like. She won't stand on a chair because she gets giddy. So I told Miss O'Grady that and she let her get down, and she called her a liar again and said she was nothing but trouble.' Lucy's eyes widened as she looked up at Freddie. 'Miss O'Grady hates Tessa.'

'Serve her right,' said Annie. 'Petulant little madam.'

'You WOULD say that,' Kate glared at Annie.

'Well 'tis time.' Annie lifted her imperious bust and glared back at Kate. 'That child . . .'

'Mother!' said Freddie in a warning voice. 'Hold your tongue, will you.'

Annie snorted. Kate didn't usually confront her, and

Freddie was mostly tolerant of what he called her 'doom and gloom'. Privately, Annie thought Tessa should be sent away to one of those 'reform schools'. Well, perhaps it would happen now, she thought, satisfied. 'I'll get Lucy to bed,' she said. ''Tis a good thing you've got one decent child.'

Kate couldn't sit still. She needed to be watching the road for a sign that Tessa had been found. So she and Freddie sat up on the blue-lias wall under the three pine trees.

'It's getting dark,' Kate said desperately. 'What if they don't find her?'

The question hung in the air. A peach-coloured moon was rising over the hills. Barn owls glided low over the meadows and from the distant woods came the first unearthly bark of a vixen.

Freddie jumped down from the wall. 'You promise me you'll stay here,' he said. 'Don't you go off searching in the dark. But I'm going, Kate. I think – I know where our Tessa might be.'

'Where?'

Freddie wouldn't tell her. Kate knew better than to fuss. She trusted Freddie, and he knew the landscape like the back of his hand, he often said. She let him go, watching his rangy silhouette padding down the street in the moonlight. She stood up on the wall to see which way he would go, and caught the gleam of moonlight on his cap as he climbed the stile and headed down the footpath towards the mill.

Kate could see the lights down at the station and the puffs of white steam from the late train coming in, its windows glowing with light. She heard the doors slamming and the footsteps of people on their way home from work in Taunton. Then the guard's whistle and the shunting of the engine as it set off through the cutting, over the viaduct and away into the hills. She remembered how hard Freddie had worked as a child, carrying luggage at the station, how he had saved every penny tied up in old socks and hankies and hidden them under a floorboard in his bedroom. On his sixteenth birthday, he had spent his savings on a lorry and started his own haulage business. He'd taught himself stone carving and was soon earning a second income from his hard work and talent.

Kate admired him enormously for what he'd achieved. Yet there was a mystery about Freddie that she'd never quite fathomed. How did he know where Tessa was? It wasn't the first time he'd made uncannily accurate prophecies with the minimum amount of fuss. He was often silent for long intervals, staring into space, and Kate could easily have felt shunned and excluded from his very private world. But she chose just to love him and let him be, knowing he needed her bright spirit more than life itself.

He might find Tessa. But what if she was injured or sick? Would he know what to do? Kate was a trained nurse, an SRN, and now her thoughts ran along that scenario. What if Tessa was seriously hurt? She, Kate, should be there.

Kate got down from the wall and walked up and down on the road, clutching her cardigan tightly around her, worrying that wherever Tessa was she had only a cotton dress.

★   ★   ★

Freddie padded silently down the footpath, glad of the pale moonlight and the friendly shelter of the elm trees. Beeches and hazels grew along there too, and he knew each and every tree from his boyhood. He knew where he was by the scent of honeysuckle or the pong of the foxes' earth. He knew the sloping field where the turf was honeycombed with a vast rabbit warren, and saw them now, sitting totally still, listening to his footsteps, their erect ears rimmed silver in the moonlight. In a flash, they vanished underground as the shadow of a fox brushed through the grass.

Freddie paused at the crest of the hill, looking down at the haze over the water meadows. The gabled roof of the school was silhouetted against the night sky, its windows splashed with moonlight. Tonight the countryside wasn't peaceful. It bubbled with voices and the shadows of the search party moving through sweet-scented hay meadows, along the hedges, the torch beams probing into ditches and corners.

'Tessa. T E S S A . . .' The way they were calling his daughter's name was chilling to Freddie. Voices he knew, Lexi's ringing tones, Joan Jarvis, Gladys, and some of the men from the quarry. There was a hopelessness about the sound of the searching. Tessa would not respond. She'd stay in hiding, frightened, worrying about the trouble she was in. To her, those well-meaning voices would sound like the howling of wolves, the red-eyed dogs of storyland.

Only Freddie could rescue her from the place she had locked herself into. He knew her mindset. She was like him, frighteningly so.

It was obvious to Freddie that Tessa would have headed down to the mill stream, especially after hearing that poem. The words must have gone deep into her soul, the way he'd been affected all his life by a poem he'd learned in school – *The Lake Isle of Innisfree* by W. B. Yeats. With a new sense of urgency, Freddie lengthened his stride and was soon on the bank of the mill stream. He picked his way through the marshy ground, using his torch in the deepening darkness. The beam of yellow light attracted moths and maybugs, and bats twisted to and fro around Freddie, never touching him. And, like Tessa, he felt the wild creatures were leading him.

He almost lost his shoe in the deep mud and had to pull it out with a loud sucking noise. No wonder no one was searching there. The only way was to walk in the stream, and then he moved along quickly in the ice-cold burbling water. When he came to the hummocky place with the willows and poplars, Freddie began to feel Tessa was close. The sound of his huge footsteps splashing through the water would alarm her. So he paused to listen.

The leaves of the poplar tree chattered like shingle. He listened deeper, and heard the roar of the weir in the mill gardens, and the chug-chug of the water wheel. Then he sensed the fear, the aura of panic that twined its freezing tendrils over the water, hooking into his heart. He shone his torch down at the stream, and there, trapped in a tiny pool were the yellow heads of cowslips. Freddie's heart leapt. He'd found her. Tessa had been there. He reached down and tenderly picked one of the flower heads out of the water. It was fresh and unspoilt. Touching it, he could feel Tessa's unique energy on the fat pink stem. Her little hands had held that flower. So why was it in the stream? Had she fallen? Had she been swept into the dark mill pool?

Freddie's pulse roared in his ears and he began to shake with dread at what he might find. He tucked the wet cowslip into his top pocket, a small memento, he thought, if needed. Paddling cautiously, he approached the road where the stream poured through the tunnel into the mill. He'd have to go to the house and knock on the door. Freddie had never encountered Ivor Stape; he'd heard the rumours but reserved his opinion. Maybe the man wasn't so bad.

He stood by the tunnel, his hand on the stone wall which was still warm from the sun. The clink of glass came from the mill garden, and the faint whiff of alcohol, and the baying of the two basset hounds, muffled as if they were in the house. Shut in, he hoped.

Freddie vaulted up the wall onto the road. Opposite him was a wooden door set into an archway in the high boundary wall, the moonlight flaking on the cracked paint. Freddie turned the iron handle and pushed. It was locked. He'd have to go round to the main gate. He looked up at the high wall, and gasped. The round dark eyes of a tawny owl looked down at him. He saw the sheen of its brindled feathers and the sharp hook of its beak. The owl stared into his eyes in a meaningful way. It waited for Freddie to move and when he turned to walk on, it flew past him with a whoosh of ghostly wings. The tip of its wing brushed Freddie's cheek as the owl wheeled down towards the stream. It perched on a post close to the tunnel and hooted mournfully, its eyes watching him, calling him.

Annie hated owls. Birds of death, she called them. Old, ingrained folklore that haunted her soul. Freddie had managed not to be influenced by her attitude; he'd studied owls and had once picked up a baby one that had fallen from a tree. Owls were wise messengers to him. There was a reason for this owl's behaviour. He turned again, to walk away, and immediately the owl repeated its silent curving flight. Again the firm soft wing feathers brushed his face as it circled around him and returned to its post by the tunnel.

Freddie stood in the road, undecided, holding his breath, listening. And then he heard it. A small, weak, desperate voice coming out of the darkness. 'Daddy. Daddy.'

Chapter Eight

THE IRON GATES

Kate was still pacing up and down the road when she saw Freddie silhouetted against the moonlight. He was carrying Tessa, wrapped in his coat, her bare feet hanging limply, her head nestled against his shoulder.

Kate ran to meet them, her heart pounding with hope and fear. 'You've found her! Oh well done – thank you, Freddie. Is she all right?' She touched his shirt. 'You're soaking wet. Where was she? Oh dear God – she's cold as ice.'

Freddie was breathing hard, from shock and from the long walk home carrying Tessa.

'It's bad,' he said, his voice trembling. 'Very bad. Let's get her inside, Kate. She's fast asleep.'

'Well that's a good thing,' Kate said soothingly. 'Where did you find her?'

'She was curled up in a ball at the foot of that big ash tree, the one that hangs over the road where the stream goes under. And she was stark naked, not a stitch on her, Kate. I looked around for her clothes, and she said they were inside the mill house.'

'INSIDE the mill house?' Kate look horrified.

'That's all she could tell me,' Freddie said. 'She was shivering – and absolutely terrified. As soon as I wrapped her in my jacket, she went to sleep.'

'That Ivor Stape is up to no good,' Annie said, following them into the house. 'Living like a hermit in that gloomy old place. They say 'tis haunted.'

'Will you go and make some cocoa, Mother?' Freddie said bluntly. 'And a hot water bottle. Then will you phone the police station and say Tessa's been found.'

'I don't like that telephone. Wretched new-fangled contraption,' Annie chuntered, but she dragged herself into the kitchen and gingerly plugged in the new electric kettle.

Freddie carried Tessa upstairs and put her on the bed.

'She's so COLD,' Kate said, alarmed as thoughts of hypothermia raced through her mind. 'And she ought to have a bath – but not until she's warm and awake. There's only one way to warm her, Freddie. I must get in and lie beside her.' She took off her shoes and pulled the eiderdown open to get in next to Tessa's small naked body. Then she noticed something that made her heart turn over. 'She's got bruises at the tops of her legs,' she said. 'Freddie, she's only seven. Something awful has happened to her, I know it – and it's too terrible to tell anyone, Freddie – especially don't say anything to your mother.'

Freddie nodded. Priority was to get Tessa warm and safe. He pushed his rising anger deep down into the dungeons of his mind. 'What can I do to help?' he asked.

'Rub her feet,' said Kate, 'and we should call Doctor Jarvis.'

Freddie knelt down and found Tessa's cold little feet under the covers. He rubbed them vigorously with his big hands. Kate drew Tessa close, and held the sleeping child against the beat of her heart, and Tessa gave a sigh, her head snuggled on Kate's cushiony bust. 'Mummy's here. You're home now, home safe,' Kate murmured. 'Are you awake, Tessa?' There was no answer, and she felt the child slipping deeper into stillness. Instinctively, Kate searched her small wrist for a pulse. It felt steady, but without her nurse's watch she could only guess that it was slow, too slow. She knew that hypothermia could lead into coma, and coma into brain damage.

'Will you telephone Doctor Jarvis, Freddie, please,' she said, looking up at his worried face. 'And bring the hot water bottles upstairs for Annie. And – Freddie – no one must ever know. Whatever has happened to our daughter, Lucy mustn't know. And I don't want Tessa to remember it – the shame of it – it could ruin her life.' Tears glimmered in the corners of Kate's eyes.

Freddie went downstairs, the words cutting into his heart. That man. That evil man at the mill. Had he ruined Tessa's life? Freddie wanted to kill him. Strangle him with his bare hands. He told himself to calm down, told himself it was no good thinking like that. But this was justified rage. It smouldered while he made the phone call. He was awkward on the telephone at the best of times, embarrassed by the authoritative female voice saying, 'Number please.' He mumbled the

131

three digit number, and she snapped, 'Speak up please, will you. Hold the receiver closer to your mouth, sir.'

He was glad to hear Doctor Jarvis answer his telephone in a reassuring tone. 'Yes, I'll come down now, of course,' he said immediately. 'Just keep her warm.'

'Thanks.' Freddie put the mysterious black Bakelite telephone back on its pedestal.

Then something happened that reminded him of the owl who had helped him find Tessa, and how sometimes, in our blackest moments, we are given a gift.

He walked into the kitchen and looked at Annie who was putting cups of steaming cocoa on a tray. She held her finger to her lips. 'Listen!' she said. 'What's that?' Outside the kitchen door something was whimpering in the night. Freddie crossed the kitchen in two strides. He opened the door cautiously and a small white dog trotted in, wagging its stump of a tail, its pointed face clearly happy to be let in. Overjoyed, it ran ecstatic circles round the kitchen table.

'Where did you come from?' Annie said, captivated by the bright friendly little dog.

'Oh, 'tis you, is it?' Freddie said, and squatted down to pet the dog, pleased when it squirmed with joy and licked his face. 'He was following me,' he said to his mother, 'when I was carrying Tessa. He followed me home. Lovely little dog.'

'Perhaps he's lost?' Annie said. 'I've never seen him before; have you?'

'No.'

'Well, I'll give him a plate of scraps and let him go out in the morning,' Annie said kindly. 'Perhaps he'll find his way home. He's got no collar.'

But the dog had another surprise in store. When Freddie took the tray of cocoa and opened the hall door, the dog shot past him and up the stairs, straight into Tessa's bedroom. There was a cry of surprise from Kate. 'Well, you're a dear little dog. Where did you come from?'

'He followed me, when I was carrying Tessa,' Freddie said again. 'Better not have him in the bedroom, had we?'

The dog jumped straight onto the bed. He wormed his way on his belly until he was close to the sleeping child, making conversational whimpering sounds in his throat. He put his chin quietly on Tessa's arm, and looked up at Freddie appealingly. And Tessa stirred gently. She lifted her hand and put it over the dog's neck, and the corners of her mouth curved in a silent smile. But she didn't wake.

Freddie and Kate looked at one another, and the air around the bed seemed to shimmer.

'I think – maybe – our Tessa has found a friend,' Freddie said thoughtfully. 'A friend who won't let her down.'

'I'm not going to try and examine her down there while she's sleeping,' Doctor Jarvis said, folding up his stethoscope and putting it back in its box. 'If she woke, that could frighten her, especially if she has been . . . interfered with. I'll come in the morning and we'll talk to her together, Kate. See what she has to say about it. Let's not assume the worst.'

'Do you know Ivor Stape?' Kate asked.

'I do, yes.'

'Do you think he's . . .?'

Doctor Jarvis held up his hand. 'I'm sorry I can't comment,' he said. 'Professional ethics. I'm sure you understand that.'

Kate stared at him. 'I know – but if I find out he has hurt my daughter, I shall go down there myself, and confront him,' she said courageously. 'He won't get away with it.'

'Let's wait and see what Tessa tells us, Kate.' Doctor Jarvis looked at her kindly, his grey halo of hair backlit by the yellowy electric light bulb which hung from the ceiling on a twisted brown cable. 'You've done a good job, getting her warm. Stay with her in case she wakes in the night. Looks like the dog is going to stay too.'

'He's a stray,' Kate said. 'Do you know where he lives?'

'No – never seen him before.' Doctor Jarvis stood up, his knees cracking. 'I wish you – and young Tessa – a peaceful night.'

Kate tucked Tessa in tightly and spent the night in a chair close to the bed, her head on a pillow propped against the wall. The child slept deeply, hardly moving, and the dog snuggled close to her on the eiderdown, only once getting up, turning round and sitting down again. Kate was restless, and every time she moved, the dog wagged his stump of a tail and looked at her, his eyes reflecting the moonlight.

Through the open sash window, Kate could smell the roses in Annie's small garden, and the pink lilac which overhung the 'Anderson Hollow'. She listened for the nightingales, but there were none. It was too early in the year, Freddie said. She heard the church clock chimes, the shuffle of a hedgehog working its way through the garden, and the huff of the night express train steaming over the viaduct on its way from Paddington to Penzance. She didn't sleep at all. Her mind was full of anxiety about Tessa.

'Why?' she kept asking herself. 'Why is my child suffering so much? Why is Tessa like this? Why can't she be like Lucy? What will happen to her when she grows up?' For once in her life Kate began to feel she couldn't cope. What if Tessa couldn't go to school? Her mind replayed the conversation with Miss O'Grady. Monterose School was a two teacher school. Tessa had been fine in the first class with Mrs Robbins. She'd learned to read quickly, eagerly devouring books. She'd read the original *Peter Pan* by herself, and *The Secret Garden*. 'I haven't got enough books to satisfy her,' Mrs Robbins said. So Kate searched the jumble sales, always coming home with a few books. One day she found a scruffy little book with a brown cover, *Freckles* by Gene Stratton-Porter. 'It's not a children's book,' the stallholder told her, 'but it's lovely. It's about a lad who became the guardian of a beautiful forest in Indiana, called The Limberlost'. Kate left *Freckles* on the table, and Tessa picked it up, silently, and curled up in a chair, her eyes racing across the text. When she was reading, Tessa didn't like to be disturbed and would fly into a rage if Lucy pestered her to play, or if Kate wanted her to eat a meal.

So why should a teacher be actually refusing to have such a bright, interesting child in her school? It was shocking. And not fair. Kate spent the night drawing up a battle plan. She even planned what to wear. Her jacket with the big shoulder pads. Her scarlet blouse. Her black court shoes. She would march into school and demand an explanation. She'd insist that Tessa was given another chance. And if they refused, Kate would take it to the board of governors, in person.

But first she would head down to the mill and knock on Ivor Stape's door until he answered. She would be courteous but assertive. She'd ask for Tessa's clothes and demand to know what he had done to her daughter.

Kate was desperately tired, but the maternal savagery kept her awake for most of the night. Finally she fell asleep at three in the morning, and woke at seven to see Tessa's pale blue eyes wide open, watching her in silence.

'Tessa! My love,' Kate wanted to cry, especially when Tessa got out of bed and sat on her lap, leaning her head against her mother's ample breasts, listening to her heart beat. Kate had gently unravelled her plaits the night before, and her chestnut hair was wavy and still damp. 'Thank God you're safe,' Kate murmured. 'You're home now, darling, safe in your own bedroom. And you're nice and warm now.'

Tessa's face had a reserved expression, a slight pout, and the eyes of a soul in recovery, eyes ready to close and retreat into trance if disturbed. Even the sight of the dog on her bed didn't seem to register as a surprise. He was a wise dog. He kept looking at Kate as if telling her not to disturb Tessa. She needed stillness and quiet.

Silent contemplation didn't come naturally to Kate. She was bursting to ask questions, give advice, and move things on into brighter times. She wanted to talk with Tessa the way she talked with Lucy. But it wouldn't work. She wanted Freddie to wake up and come into Tessa's room, but a glimpse through the open doorway showed him still peacefully asleep, the white rays of the early morning sun spilling tablets of light onto the scarlet bedspread.

She could hear Annie down in the kitchen, up early as always, and humming hymn tunes to herself. She heard her go out and feed the chickens, hearing the corn being scattered like hard rain, the clucking and the heavy flapping of wings as they jostled for food.

'Granny's feeding the chickens,' she said, and Tessa's eyes changed for the merest fragment of a moment, a glimmer of light which quickly sank back into the reserved expression, into the nothingness of not sharing.

Kate winced when she heard Annie unplugging the new electric kettle, then the blast of water going into it, the struggle with the unfamiliar plug, and the predictable complaint. 'Damned silly contraption.' She wondered uneasily why Annie was doing so much clattering around in the kitchen. When she heard her coming upstairs, Kate braced herself for trouble in the form of recriminations aimed at Tessa.

'Can I come in?' Annie asked, pushing the door open. Kate looked at her in astonishment. Annie was smiling. She wore a snow-white apron and carried a tray with an even whiter cloth. It was laden with a wholesome breakfast. Boiled eggs under hand-knitted cosies, a pot of tea, and a toast rack crammed with toast, a pat of butter and a jar of marmalade. She'd brought Tessa's favourite glass, filled with creamy milk and one of the red and white drinking straws left over from the tea party.

'Annie! What a lovely, kind thing to do.' Kate's eyes filled with tears, and Annie looked pleased. She set the tray down on the bedside table. 'Breakfast in BED!'

'I thought it might help you,' Annie said, and she peered at Tessa. 'How is she?'

'Just quiet,' Kate said, praying that Annie wouldn't start a diatribe on Tessa's shortcomings. She was pleased when Tessa held out her hands for the glass of milk and drank it straight down, through the straw.

'So what happened?' Annie asked.

'We still don't know,' Kate said. 'I'm sure it will all come out in time.'

'You look tired out, Kate.' Annie sat down on Tessa's bed, and Kate felt glad to have her there, glad to see kindness in her eyes and remember who this woman actually was.

The dog was whining and looking expectantly at the food. 'He's hungry. Dear little dog,' said Annie, fondling the dog's silky head.

'He's my dog,' Tessa said, unexpectedly. 'His name is Jonti. AND – he taught me to swim.'

Kate and Annie stared at each other.

'SWIM!' Annie said in a sepulchral whisper. She opened her mouth to say something else and shut it again when she saw the warning glint in Kate's eyes.

'So – how did he do that, dear?' Kate asked, gently.

'He jumped in the pool and showed me how he kicked his legs and kept his nose out of the water,' Tessa said. 'And then I copied him. I swam across the pool.'

'What pool?' demanded Annie.

Tessa stopped eating. She dumped her piece of toast and glowered at Annie. 'I'm not telling you.'

The sparkle vanished from Annie's eyes and, in a moment of insight, Kate finally understood that Annie felt rejected by Tessa.

'Let's just enjoy our breakfast,' Kate said. 'We can talk about it later.'

But Annie was on the warpath.

'It's not your dog. How can it be your dog?'

'He IS my dog,' Tessa's eyes blazed. 'The man gave him to me.'

'What man?'

'I'm not telling you. I'll NEVER tell you.' Tessa got back into bed, curled up in a ball, and pulled the covers right over her head.

But later, when Annie wasn't there, Tessa did want to talk about Jonti. Kate had found him a tennis ball to play with, and Tessa seemed happy, throwing it across the lawn and squealing with delight when Jonti brought it back and dropped it at her feet. The little dog was exactly what Tessa needed, and Kate was reluctant to tell her Jonti might have to go back to whoever owned him. She made a card to put up in the Post Office, and Jonti sat looking at her, his head on one side. It stirred a memory of a dog Kate remembered seeing in a photograph. She went indoors and found the old brown photo album. Tessa always enjoyed looking at it, and she came straight away and sat next to Kate on the wooden garden seat. Jonti jumped up beside her, his head in her lap.

'Auntie Ethie!' she said, smoothing the photo of Ethie sitting on top of a hay cart. 'Did she drown, Mummy?'

'Yes, she did.' Kate turned the pages on, not wanting to dwell on the subject of Ethie. 'This is Granny Sally – my mum,' she continued, 'and this is me on my favourite horse.'

'Daisy!' said Tessa. 'She's enormous.'

'Here we are. Look!' Kate found what she'd been looking for, a sepia picture of her father, Bertie, as a young man, smartly dressed in breeches, long boots, a tweed jacket and cap. At his feet was a small white terrier, exactly like Jonti.

Kate watched Tessa's expression and saw a smile of delight come as she stared at the old photograph. She looked intently at Kate. 'That's the man who gave me Jonti,' she said firmly, 'and his eyes sparkled, Mummy, like yours.'

Kate felt goosebumps prickle her skin. 'So . . . where was Jonti when you first saw him?'

'In that man's arms,' she said, 'but then he was waiting for me on the lawn when I escaped.'

'You escaped?'

'I climbed out of the bathroom window,' Tessa said, and her eyes changed. 'I'm not telling you any more, Mummy. I want to play with Jonti.'

★   ★   ★

Kate wheeled her bike into the road. It was a new bike, a Raleigh, with a basket on the front and a Sturmey-Archer three speed. Freddie had given it to her for Christmas and she'd hardly used it. She felt conspicuous on it, sitting up so straight and high above the road, dressed in her black jacket with the wide shoulder pads, her red, ruffled blouse, black skirt and black court shoes.

'Don't you go down there on your own,' Freddie had said. 'That would be madness – asking for trouble.'

But Kate didn't care. She intended to confront Ivor Stape while the maternal savagery was on fire inside her mind. She was used to dealing with all sorts of characters from her nursing days. She'd thought about asking Joan or even Lexi to go with her, but Kate worried about gossip. If Tessa had been raped, Kate wanted it kept a secret. She didn't want it haunting Tessa's life, bringing shame on the family. So, with Lucy in school, and Freddie up at the quarry, she'd cajoled Annie into keeping an eye on Tessa, and Annie had promised not to question her.

'So where are you going, dressed up like that?' Annie asked suspiciously.

'It's private business. I won't be long,' Kate told her.

Kate was so angry that she pedalled energetically, and sailed down to the mill. With her dark hair flying and her cheeks rosy, she swept over the millstream bridge and around the corner to the entrance, skidding to a halt outside the high wrought-iron gates. They were closed, and apparently locked. She searched for a bell to ring but there wasn't one. She propped her bike against the wall, and looked through at the gloomy garden. Had Tessa really swum across that sinister pool? And why? It was still a mystery. Tessa had been silent all the morning, talking only in whispers to the dog. She'd refused to talk to Doctor Jarvis and allowed him only to feel her pulse and listen to her breathing. Wisely, he hadn't put pressure on her. 'She seems all right,' he'd said. 'We must give her a chance to rest and recover.'

Kate loved Tessa, but she also wanted to shake her. Instead, she shook the iron gates. 'Hello,' she called. 'Mr Stape. Are you there?'

Silence.

Kate unclipped the tyre pump from her bike and used it to bang the iron gates. It made an arresting kind of clang. From inside the house, the basset hounds set up a booming, howling bark. She saw them standing up against the window sill, their throats lifted like wolves. A movement deeper inside the room caught Kate's eye – a bobbing, evasive shadow of someone who wanted to hide.

Her heart pounded hard against the iron gates. She wasn't going to give up. 'Will you come out please, Mr Stape? I want to talk to you.'

No response. She heard Ivor Stape roar at the dogs. 'Quiet!' They stopped barking instantly, and disappeared from the window. Kate pictured them slinking under the furniture, their tails drooping.

'I'm not going to go away, Mr Stape,' she called, 'and if you don't come out and open these gates for me, I shall climb over the wall and come in.'

Silence. Kate looked up at the wall and noticed a place where a stone was missing. She could put her foot in there, hold on to the clump of valerian growing at the top, and swing herself over, like mounting a horse, and she'd done enough of that in her life.

'Mr Stape, I want to speak to you, and if you don't let me in, you'll be sorry,' she called, and rapped on the iron gates with the bicycle pump, harder and louder. 'I am going to count to ten, and if you're not out here, I'm coming over that wall. One – two – three – four—'

A door flew open at the side of the house, and a stocky little man emerged. He had broad, burly shoulders, wild grey hair, and the whites of his eyes glimmered under a bushy frown that made the top of his head look like a hat. His hands twitched at his sides and a ferocious pipe hung from his lips.

Kate drew herself up and stood very straight, glad of the shoulder pads and the high-heeled shoes. She wasn't tall, but she felt empowered by a sense of justice.

Ivor Stape came towards her. She saw the ferocious pipe in detail, and it was a model of a bull's head. An Aberdeen Angus, Kate thought. All part of the image. He stood inside the gate, puffing smoke, and trying not to look at the determined young woman who was searching the cobwebbed corners of his soul with magnetic, bright brown eyes.

'I'm Mrs Barcussy,' Kate said, 'and I will not have a conversation with you through this gate. Will you please open it and let me in?'

Ivor Stape fished in the pocket of his tweed jacket and produced a key. He unlocked the gate and held it open for her while she tried to get his evasive eyes to look at her. Once inside, she stood facing him, took a deep breath, and managed to be civil.

'Mr Stape, I'd like you to tell me how my little girl came to be here yesterday, and why she was found on the other side of the bridge, freezing cold, frightened, and with no clothes on. And I want her clothes back, please, right now.'

Ivor Stape looked at the floor, so that Kate only saw the top of his head. 'You'd better come in,' he mumbled, clenching the pipe between surly lips. 'Follow me, and don't mind the dogs. They won't hurt you.'

'I'm not afraid of dogs. I'm a farmer's daughter.'

Kate strutted beside him, her heart beating hard and fast. What would Freddie say if he saw her? But I'm doing it. *You'd be proud of me, Daddy.* Thinking of her dad helped Kate to imagine herself protected as Ivor Stape led her to the house and into a porch thickly covered in the glossy leaves of Virginia creeper. She heard a bird singing back in the garden as she followed him inside.

The room he led her into was a complete surprise. So unexpected that Kate momentarily lost her iron resolve and stood in the doorway, her mouth open, her eyes gazing in disbelief at what she saw.

Chapter Nine

INSIDE THE MILL HOUSE

'Where's Kate?' Freddie asked, sitting down at the table for his mid-morning cup of tea.

'She's gone off on her bike, dressed up like a dog's dinner.' Annie put the steaming mug of tea in Freddie's hand. 'She said it was private business, and she wouldn't be long. But she's been gone an hour already.'

Freddie immediately had a nasty feeling about where Kate had gone. He'd taken a detour and called at the mill himself early that morning on his way to the quarry, but the gates were locked. The house looked closed up, its curtains drawn, and everything quiet in the morning sun. Freddie walked around the perimeter, looking for another way in, but there wasn't one, only a narrow animal track going under the wall. Like Kate, he considered getting over the wall, but Herbie was waiting in the cab of the lorry, his elbow out of the window, his eyes puzzled and a bit impatient.

'I wouldn't bother going in there,' Herbie advised. 'He's a

curmudgeonly old crank. Got two bloodhounds, they say. Have yer arm off, they would.'

Freddie hadn't told Herbie why he wanted to go in there. He and Kate had agreed on secrecy. No one must know what might have happened to Tessa. Keeping a secret wasn't easy in Monterose, and he wanted to talk to Tessa himself, find out the truth before taking action.

Tessa was squatting on the lawn, painting a cardboard box with her Reeves paint box and a tiny brush. 'I'm making Jonti a bed,' she said, and Jonti wagged his tail obligingly.

'Can I do a bit?' Freddie asked.

'You can do that bit,' Tessa said, and she looked up at him. Her eyes were calm. 'Paint an elm tree, Daddy.'

Freddie took the brush and dipped it in the tablet marked *Viridian*. 'An elm tree is like a cottage loaf,' he said. 'It's got a big curly bit, then a small one on top, and a smaller one on top of that, and it's not just green. It's got light and shade in it.'

Tessa watched intently, her mouth open in awe as he painted the elm tree and added blue shadows and flecks of white. 'Ooh, Daddy – it looks real,' she said.

'Me tea's getting cold.' Freddie gave the paint brush back to her. 'You paint some grass underneath – otherwise it looks as if it's flying up in the air, don't it?'

Tessa giggled, and set about painting the blades of grass, while Freddie sat on the lawn drinking his tea and stroking Jonti thoughtfully. The way to get Tessa talking was to work with her, painting, or gardening, or polishing wood. He needed time to spend with her, especially today. When her hands were busy, she would talk. Watching her carefully painting Jonti's name in *Prussian Blue*, Freddie felt torn in two. Herbie was waiting for him up at the alabaster quarry, and Herbie was paying him. But right now, being a dad felt urgent and important. He was the one who best understood Tessa's mysterious mind.

'That man has got specimens all over his house,' Tessa said, pronouncing the word 'specimens' with relish, 'even in the bathroom.'

'Oh, ah,' said Freddie. He didn't like the sound of 'specimens'. His mind conjured up ghoulish body parts in jars. His brother, George, had had his appendix out, and the hospital had let him bring it home, pickled, in a jam jar. A horrible, grey, grub of a thing proudly displayed on George's mantelpiece, so horrible that Freddie made sure he sat with his back to it when he visited George.

'AND . . .' Tessa's eyes widened with the drama, 'one of them is millions and millions and MILLIONS of years old.'

Freddie kept quiet and listened in horror. An appendix that was millions of years old?

Kate was disinclined to give Ivor Stape credit for anything, but she detected a surprising note of respect in his manner when he invited her to sit down. 'Thank you, but I'd rather stand,' she said, thinking she would look more intimidating standing up. 'And first I'd like my daughter's clothes, please. Where are they?'

'I'll get them.'

She heard him go upstairs, slowly, as if his legs were painful. It gave her the chance to stare around the room which had quarry tiles and a beamed ceiling. Three windows on each side looked out into the garden, and there was an inglenook fireplace. There was one armchair, like an island in a labyrinth of tables. On one table was a black typewriter, piles of notebooks, and a bottle of Quink. On another was an electric flat iron, standing on a pad of linen, plugged in as if it had just been used. The basset hounds lay on a rug at one end, growling at each other as they gnawed loudly at two gigantic bones.

What amazed Kate were the stones arranged over the table tops and window sills, some twinkling with crystal, some smoother, others with spiral patterns set into them. Kate's education had included geography, but not geology, and she had no idea what crystals and fossils were. She gazed at the collection in awe, noting that each stone had a neatly written label. What did this man do with them?

Then she looked at the walls and gasped. Every available space was lined with bookshelves, maps and charts. He had more books than Kate had ever seen: old, expensive leather-bound volumes with gold lettering, sets of navy blue encyclopaedias, shelves of poetry books and Shakespeare; new books stacked in toppling towers, piles of yellow National Geographic magazines. Kate found herself imagining how Tessa would be completely entranced by a room such as this. *You'd never get her out*, Kate thought. She glanced at a dark green book with gold-rimmed pages which was balanced on the arm of the chair. It was Hans Andersen. Had Tessa been in here, reading it?

The room smelled of dust and damp dog, and a ripe winey aroma from a crowd of bottles stashed under one of the tables. But there was another smell, a faint whiff of something that alarmed Kate. She had noticed it on Tessa's hair. It wasn't tobacco. It was something Kate recognised from her nursing days. Gas. Chloroform gas, she was sure. What was this obviously educated man doing with chloroform gas? Kate couldn't see any evidence. Where was it coming from? She itched to walk around and peep into corners and cupboards, but the man was coming downstairs.

Again, she was dumfounded. He had put Tessa's blue and white dress on a hanger. It looked freshly ironed. Her vest, knickers and socks were neatly folded and clean, and he had stuffed her wet sandals with newspaper. Just seeing how small her clothes were caught Kate off guard and made her want to cry.

'My daughter is seven years old.' She glared at Ivor Stape. Then she lost control and snatched Tessa's clothes from the chair where he had carefully put them. She clutched the little dress to her heart, and felt the edges of an emotional tidal wave lapping at her strength as if suddenly she was made of sand.

'I tried . . .' Ivor Stape's eyes looked at her for the first time. Guilty, Kate thought.

'Don't SPEAK to me.' She held up her hand. 'You – you DISGUST me.'

A wave of giddiness overwhelmed Kate. Her skin went cold and sweaty with terror. What if she passed out on Ivor Stape's floor? No one knew where she was, and she had no control of the giddiness. Clutching Tessa's clothes, she sank into the chair, taking deep breaths, trying to hold onto consciousness.

She glimpsed Ivor Stape standing there looking alarmed, and oddly helpless. He started to talk fast. 'I didn't take your little girl, if that's what you think,' he said. 'She came into my garden, through the tunnel. She was dripping wet and clearly terrified. The dogs scared her. I carried her in here and gave her a blanket and a cup of cocoa, and hung her wet clothes by the stove.'

Kate looked at him sceptically through the waves of giddiness. Then her heart almost stopped. The basset hounds erupted into deafening barking, and the stones in his collection rattled and trembled with the weight of the dogs' powerful bodies charging through the table legs to reach the door.

'LIE DOWN!' Ivor Stape clambered after them and dragged both dogs, at an angle of forty-five degrees, across the floor and shut them in the kitchen.

In the shocked stillness, heavy footsteps crunched on the gravel, and three figures plodded past the window.

When Freddie walked into Ivor Stape's extraordinary room, he saw only the haze of golden light around the one chair. Kate turned her beautiful eyes to look at him, and so did her father, Bertie, who was standing beside the chair, earthy and twinkling with humour as he had always been. On the other side of the chair stood a silver-haired lady who looked like Sally. He recognised her as Kate's grandmother, from photographs he'd seen. Between them was a phosphorescent column of light stretching to the ceiling. Rays of light rippled from it, yet the light didn't illuminate the crystals, or the books, or Kate's glossy hair. It was sacred light which didn't come from the sun, and Freddie was certain that if he stared into it for long enough, he would see the radiant face and shimmering skirts of an angel. He was transfixed. To walk into a place he had considered to be evil, and find this shining capsule of truth was overwhelming. Not only was it totally unexpected but, he thought, stunned, it was exactly as Tessa had described.

Tessa had told him about the stones. She told him about the Hans Andersen book with the gold-rimmed pages. Clearly and fluently, she described Bertie and Kate's granny, down to the last detail, as if it was normal. Her pale blue eyes were translucent with honesty, and Freddie believed her. It confirmed what he suspected. Tessa was seeing spirit people. She had the gift.

He didn't know whether to be happy about it, or worried.

Kate was trying to stand up. 'It's all right, Freddie. Don't look so worried.'

'I told you not to come down here.' Freddie took her in his arms. She was quivering, and white-faced.

'I know you did – but I felt compelled,' she said. 'Nothing has happened. I only had a little giddy turn. Too much excitement.'

'You sit down.' Freddie led her back to the chair, not convinced that she was well. She sank into it, and he sat on the arm, holding her hand tightly and looking up at Bertie. Should he tell her? The words were out of his mouth before he could stop them. 'Your dad is with you, Kate,' he said, 'and your granny – in spirit. I can see 'em, clear as daylight.'

Kate stared at him in astonishment. 'Well, I can't see them.'

'I know you can't – but I can,' Freddie said, and added, 'just between ourselves, Kate.'

'But that's wonderful!' She beamed and the colour began to return to her cheeks. 'Someone was giving me strength.'

Ivor Stape was blustering, and they both turned to look at him standing between the two policemen. He pointed at Freddie. 'Your wife is an extremely courageous woman,' he said. 'You should take better care of her, and your little girl. What was she doing all alone, paddling up the stream? She ought to have been in school. She's a highly intelligent, interesting child. I'm a lonely old man, you see, and Tessa brought a bit of sunshine into my life.'

Freddie and Kate looked at each other. It was the first time in seven years that anyone had said something so positive about Tessa. As for taking better care of her – Freddie shook his head at Kate. 'Don't argue with him,' he whispered. 'They're writing it all down. He's gonna drop himself in it in a minute.'

'And I get the blame,' Ivor Stape continued, as one of the policemen scribbled down every word in his notebook. 'You don't think, do you? If I go to prison, what happens to my home, and my dogs – and my life's work – sitting in here going damp, gathering dust – years of dust? Ruined. All because you can't look after your child.'

Freddie heard tears in the man's voice and momentarily felt compassion for him. He'd seen his own father cry those kind of tears many times in his childhood. The bittersweet tears of someone who couldn't be the person he'd like to be. Tears of failure and frustration.

'I think you'd better calm down, sir. It's no good attacking Mr and Mrs Barcussy,' said the sergeant. 'And I think it's time for you to come to the station with us and make a statement.'

Ivor Stape snorted. 'Make a statement!' he mocked. 'What good is that?' He took the Aberdeen Angus pipe out of his pocket and lit it with a match, his hands shaking. He looked at Freddie and Kate, and loneliness echoed in his eyes, like a shout in a railway tunnel. 'You remember this when you blame an old man like me,' he said. 'Folks like you – you've got each other. I've got no one.'

'Come along now, sir.'

Ivor Stape looked intently at Kate as the two policemen bundled him out of the room. 'You remember what I said,' he told her, turning his head. 'That little girl – Tessa – she is a treasure.'

Kate had one last question she needed to ask. 'Did you give Tessa a dog – a white terrier?'

'No, I didn't and I've never seen a dog like that here.'

Freddie found himself looking again at the spirit of Kate's father and he could have sworn that Bertie winked at him and said something. It sounded like: 'Look in the bureau.' He would have liked some time to focus on talking to the spirit visitors, but he was concerned about Kate. She looked pale and had shadows under her eyes. He wanted to take her home, get her out of this extraordinary room. Yet another part of his mind wanted to linger and examine some of the fascinating collection of stones.

The two policemen escorted Ivor Stape outside.

'Will you follow us out please, Mr and Mrs Barcussy? – and close the door behind you.'

'What about the two dogs?' Kate said. 'Who's going to look after them?'

'We'll take care of that, rest assured,' said the sergeant. 'The important thing for you is to go home to your family and get some rest. You can come down to the police station tomorrow morning and make a statement.'

Freddie was eyeing the police car, a large black Wolseley. He couldn't resist touching it, and dreaming.

Once Ivor Stape was inside the police car, the sergeant got out again to speak to Freddie and Kate, in confidential tones. 'Between you and me, unless you can get Tessa to tell you what actually happened, we've got no reason to charge him. I know she's only seven, but you must sit her down and make her talk.'

Making Tessa talk was the beginning of the destruction of a hypersensitive soul. The more she was pushed, the more she recoiled into her mysterious shell.

'Just let her be,' Freddie advised, sensing Kate's determination to get the truth out of her. He refused to take part in any more interrogation sessions. Tessa needed him to be a safe, quiet, loving presence, a *rock of ages* where she could hide herself. 'I've got work to do,' he said to Kate. 'You sort it out. You're good at that kind of thing. You're the best person to do it.'

So Kate took Tessa down to the school, with the light of battle in her eyes. 'Don't you DARE run away,' she said. 'You stay in the playground with Lucy while I talk to Miss O'Grady.' It was the end of the school day, and Tessa's classroom was empty.

Kate sat down on a hard chair, facing the metallic grey figure of Miss O'Grady. She searched her cold eyes for a spark of love and found them chillingly barren.

'I believe in my daughter,' Kate said warmly. 'Tessa doesn't talk a lot, but she's bright, I'm sure she is – and artistic like her father. And she can be VERY kind. There's nothing wrong with her at all, and I would like you to give her another chance, please.'

'I see.' Miss O'Grady picked up a wooden ruler and smoothed it with her chalk-ingrained fingers. Her nails were cut sensibly straight, the cuticles dry and peeling.

'What is it that bothers you about Tessa?' Kate asked.

'She is stubborn. Obstinate, I would say. She won't do what the other children are doing. She won't play. She stands against a wall and does nothing. She won't do games or P.E. She won't eat her lunch. She won't answer if you ask her a question.'

'But that's no reason to exclude her, surely?' Kate said.

'No.' Miss O'Grady began to flip the wooden ruler over and over on the desk. 'It is something worse.'

'What?' Kate asked.

'It's – I'm afraid it's something evil, Mrs Barcussy.'

'Evil? What do you mean?'

'Tessa insists on talking about ghosts. She is adamant that she sees them, right here in the classroom.'

'Surely not – give me an example.'

'We had a child who came in crying because her granny had died, and I told the children to leave her alone – but Tessa shouted out, in the middle of a spelling lesson that she could see the child's granny. She even tried to describe what she was wearing. Then – very recently – she actually claimed she could see Alfred Lord Tennyson, if you please, in the classroom. I've told her and told her not to do it, but she does, and she does it in an extremely disruptive way. It frightens and upsets the other children – I've had parents complaining about it. I've punished Tessa, or tried to, but she just sits there, mutinous. Believe me, Mrs Barcussy, I've tried everything.' Miss O'Grady brandished the ruler at Kate. 'One day I smacked her hands really hard with this ruler – and do you know what she did?'

'What?'

'She picked up her own ruler and smacked me right back, and do you know what she said?'

'Go on,' Kate said, shocked.

'She screamed at me. "I hate you," she said – and her eyes looked EVIL. It's bad and disruptive for the other children, don't you think?'

'I can see what you mean,' Kate said, 'but I believe in my daughter. I know there's good in her, and I want to get to the bottom of this. Why does she hate you so? We must find a way to help her, not condemn her. Now, I suggest we invite the vicar to come and talk it over with us, and perhaps he can talk to Tessa. He is a school governor, isn't he?'

'Yes, he is – and of course it's a church school. I think that's a good idea.'

Tessa felt abandoned. She sat obediently on a chair in Miss O'Grady's office, her legs not quite reaching the floor, her eyes watching a honey bee climbing up and down the window pane. Trapped, like she was, desperately seeking a way back into the paradise of a garden in the sun. She heard its high-pitched whine of distress.

Her mother was there, next to her, leaning forward as if she was riding a horse, her bright brown eyes darting attentively from one to the other. Miss O'Grady was there, and so was the Reverend Reminsy. Tessa knew they were talking about whether to give her a chance to come back to school.

She didn't care, didn't want to go there anyway, and didn't listen to what was being said.

It seemed to Tessa that even her mother had abandoned her, and her father wasn't there to defend her. Freddie had taken Lucy for a walk in the woods, and Jonti had gone with them. That hurt as well. *Jonti is MY dog*, Tessa thought angrily.

Alone in the garden that morning Tessa had gone into the 'Anderson Hollow' under the lilac bushes. She'd sat underneath one, gazing at the exuberant blossom and the flakes of blue, blue sky between. For once the beauty didn't make her happy. It made her sad. She was no longer part of that beautiful world. She didn't belong to herself. She belonged to the adults in her life who wanted to own her and change her. She would be like the milkman's pony, forever in harness, blinkered, obedient and servile, not free.

How could she stop them trying to trap her and harness her? How could she protect herself? Tessa saw a caterpillar crawling up a weathered tree stump. It found a crack and went in there. Fascinated, she watched it spinning a thread around and around itself, twirling as it hung there, lit by a beam of sunlight. It was making a cocoon, a safe place to hide and change.

Suppose I did that, Tessa thought. *I'll be like a caterpillar and build myself a cocoon of white silk. I can hide in there safely, until I'm old enough to be a butterfly and fly away into the sky where no one can get me.*

So she sat, silent and detached, in the meeting, visualising the silver threads glistening in the sun as they wrapped her into a thicker and thicker cocoon.

'She's not listening! Look at her,' said Miss O'Grady's exasperated voice.

'TESSA!'

She jumped as the Reverend Reminsy brought his whiskery face uncomfortably close to hers. His eyes pierced the cocoon and looked into hers like two nails being hammered into a tree. 'If you won't talk and explain yourself, Tessa, then you are going to listen,' he announced. 'Look at me please, at my eyes. Do you know why I'm here?'

Tessa shook her head.

'I'm here because I'm a school governor – and I'm here to help you, Tessa. I have persuaded Miss O'Grady to give you another chance. She has kindly agreed to let you come back to school,' he said, 'BUT – you have got to change your ways, young lady. Do you understand that?'

Tessa nodded.

'You are not to run away. You are not to be rude and answer back. You are to do everything Miss O'Grady tells you to do, even if you don't like it. You are to eat your lunch and join in with games and try hard to make friends, Tessa. Do you understand me?'

She nodded.

'AND,' he continued, 'all this nonsense about seeing people who have died HAS GOT TO STOP.' He banged his hands together and Tessa jumped, frightened by the force of his tone and the way his eyes burned into her. 'Even if you do think you see them, you are not – I repeat ARE NOT – to tell ANYONE.'

The 'ANYONE' hung in the air between them. Tessa imagined all the people she knew disappearing down a hole and leaving her alone at the brink with no one to talk to, no one to share her dreams and ideas. She felt her eyes growing shiny with hot, thick tears.

'Do you understand why I am talking to you like this?' the Reverend Reminsy asked more kindly.

Tessa shook her head.

'I'm not just being unkind to you, and neither is Miss O'Grady, and neither is your mother. No – don't look away. Keep looking at my eyes, Tessa. This is to help you with your life, child. If you don't behave properly, like Lucy, then you won't have a happy, successful life. You won't have an education because no one will put up with you, and if you don't have an education you won't be able to get a job and you won't be able to grow up and get married and have a family of your own. Do you understand that?'

Tessa nodded. She felt the words being chiselled into her soul, like letters on a tombstone. She glanced at her mother.

'He's right, Tessa. You've got to try and be more like Lucy,' Kate said.

'Yes – I agree,' Miss O'Grady said. 'Lucy's such a good girl, and everyone likes her.'

'You've caused your mother a lot of worry and heartache,' said the Reverend Reminsy. 'Do you understand that, Tessa?'

Tessa nodded, her small hands gripping the seat of the chair. She felt her life was over. She was a failure at being a human being. It seemed impossible to her. There was no way forward. She looked at her mother and saw pain and anxiety in those bright brown eyes, eyes that usually shone with fun. 'I'm sorry, Mummy,' she whispered.

'I should think you are,' snapped Miss O'Grady.

Kate put her arm round Tessa's shoulders. 'Well, sorry is a good place to start,' she said warmly.

'You're lucky to have such a kind mother,' said Miss O'Grady, and her eyes glinted. 'I hope we can start again, Tessa. Otherwise you will be sent away to a home for bad children.'

Tessa's mouth fell open. A home for bad children? Far away from the places she loved. Away from her own home and family.

That one comment appalled and frightened her. Shock waves cracked through her aura like arteries of ink. It wasn't fair. Why should this bone-thin woman stir up such hatred in her? Tessa wanted to give Miss O'Grady a poisoned apple like the witch in *Snow White*.

She got down from her chair and walked towards her teacher's cruel eyes which seemed to be mocking her. She heard her mother's anxious voice. 'No, Tessa, sit down dear, please.'

Suddenly the cocoon she had constructed around herself began to spin crazily. The white silk threads turned black and unravelled in little spirals and coils. She felt exposed, as if her beating heart had been unwrapped and left on the floor in front of Miss O'Grady.

'Tessa!'

Kate moved forward quickly and got her arms firmly around Tessa as the child turned deathly pale and lost consciousness. 'I'm so sorry,' Kate said, 'it's all too much for her.'

PART TWO

1960

Chapter Ten

1960

The young man stood at the edge of the woods, under a beech tree; the afternoon sun touched the texture of his long hair and the wiry crinkles of his beard. He stood so still that he seemed part of the wood, a face staring from an ancient tree trunk, his bare feet disappearing into the leaf mould as if he had grown there.

He was listening to the voice of the beech tree, and watching the wind moving through cornfields far away, waiting for the same fan-shaped gusts to dive into the foliage above him. He was thinking that the wind came from the sea. It tasted faintly of salt. It painted the ocean in his mind, in jewel-like colours, lace over silk in the long stretches between waves. The wind raised a sable brush and painted him there, a crouched silhouette flying on a Malibu surfboard.

He wore a heavy denim jacket covered in bulging pockets he had stitched onto it in meaningful scraps of fabric: a square of his granny's old pinny, a patch from the curtains he'd once had, a piece of bottle green crushed velvet that had once been a cushion. He put his hand into it and pulled out a dog-eared notebook. Frowning, he added a few lines to the poem he'd been writing.

He stared across the open hillside to the girl who was still lying there, not moving, the wind ruffling her chestnut hair. The man glanced at the shadows of the wood on the bright grassland and figured it must have been an hour since she had moved. *Don't get involved, Art*, he thought. *Women, you don't need right now. Be free, man.*

But some magnetic force drew him towards the still figure of the girl. Something ancient in his soul. He padded over the springy turf, his bare feet enjoying the softness, his hair flowing in the breeze. Why was he walking towards this girl? He didn't know. He just let go, and let his feet walk.

There was an aura around the girl. It wasn't welcoming. It was a cry. A light and a colour that actually cried out to the sky, to the land, and to him. The closer he got, the more Art found himself captivated. He wanted to scoop the sleeping girl into his arms and take her to the wild shores of the Atlantic where the salt wind and the surf would heal her damaged soul.

He stood, on quiet feet, looking down at the satin folds of the sea-blue dress swirled over her slim body. An ant was crawling on one of her tanned legs. He watched it disappear into the diamond hole in the front of her sandals. He watched a tendril of her chestnut hair reach out into the wind as if trying to touch him. He felt the cry emanating from her aura, like a harmonic echoing from a bell, invisible, inaudible, but sensed in the sudden chill that crawled up his spine.

Art cleared his throat. It was a long time since he had spoken to anyone. 'Are you okay?' he asked.

There was no response. Art squatted down, thinking he might gently touch the girl's hand. He studied it for a moment, noting the smooth, tanned skin, the elegant fingers and shell-like nails which had been beautifully filed. The sun flashed on something metallic lying in a patch of thyme. A blue-black Gillette razorblade, a new one, with a stain of blood along its edge. 'Oh God!' he gasped. 'God – no.' He saw the blood in the grass around Tessa's left hand which was flung sideways, away from her face as if she couldn't bear to look.

Art acted swiftly then, his heart banging in fear, his mind hammering out prayers he'd learned long ago in another life-time. He ripped the scarf from his neck, turned Tessa over and tied it tightly around her arm just above the elbow, twist-ing, twisting it, and muttering, 'Stop. Stop. Come on. Stop bleeding.' He held her arm up straight and kept it there, watching it turn blue as the flow of blood slowed to a trickle. He looked down at Tessa's face, the chestnut lashes curled against her pale skin, her cheeks softly rounded, her brow smooth with a sublime peacefulness that told him she was already far away in some undiscovered land.

Desperately he scanned the hillside for another human being, but there was no one. He knew the hospital was miles away. There wasn't even a cottage nearby with a telephone.

The road! he thought, *it's her only chance.* Gathering Tessa's limp body into his strong arms, he ran towards the road, hearing the grinding gears of a car coming up the winding hill. With bare feet on hot tarmac, he straddled the road and flagged down the battered Morris 10.

He looked through the passenger window at a scowling farmer in a trilby hat. 'Can you help – please?'

The wings of the butterfly arched into Tessa's consciousness like stained glass in the gloom of a church. Its eyes watched her with unassuming wisdom. Twice it flew away, circled, and returned to pitch on her hand. Though her eyes were closed, Tessa sensed its cottony legs on her skin. She saw herself rise from the crumpled sea-blue satin and the chestnut curls of her hair lying on the hillside. Floating, she glanced down at it with a sense of relief. Her spirit was leaving! She followed the flickering colours of the butterfly into the woods where it guided her through towering tree trunks until its wings seemed to expand and dissolve into the spaces between the branches.

In a dream-like state, Tessa sat down on a moss-covered log, in a place she had visited before in her dreams. Fragrance drifted through the trees, from the haze of bluebells in the distance. A stream trickled nearby, like tiny bells, drawing threads of glittering light over the roots of trees and into pools where cresses grew. The banks were cushioned with moss so green that the whole wood seemed luminous with a light of its own.

Tessa stared into the light between the lime trees. It seemed to crackle like a sparkler she had held in her hand on firework night. It blazed with dazzling stars of silver and gold. From the centre of the light footsteps emerged, making no sound, across the woodland floor. She sensed them, welcomed them, allowing the presence to arrive and enfold her in healing light. She raised her left hand and turned it to look at her wrist with the blue veins like rivers in the sand. It shone, blue and white, and perfect. There was no cut. No blood. No pain. No reason. In spirit she was perfect.

She turned to gaze into the timeless loving eyes of the man in a saffron robe who sat beside her on the log. Tessa knew him well. He had talked to her in daydreams and trances, always serious, yet his eyes twinkled with mysterious humour. Like her mother's eyes, they radiated reassurance. 'All is well,' he said. 'You are welcome, Tessa. Stay here, and rest for as long as you need. Take all the healing you need. There is no limitation. But when you feel ready, you must go back. It is not time for you to pass into spirit. Go back and be Tessa, and be ready for change – a good change, and a kindred spirit – a friend to walk with you. You will know him by the intensity of his eyes.'

Tessa sighed. The longing to go home to the world of spirit ached in her heart. Wasn't it enough? Fourteen friend-less years? Fourteen years of being the one who 'made trouble'. She didn't want to make trouble. She longed to be 'normal', like the girls she envied. Confident, happy girls, like Lucy, like Fiona. Girls who never saw what she saw or wanted what she wanted or dreamed what she dreamed. Girls who had a place to go, a respectable niche in the world that would guarantee respectability. Not the wild, untrodden paths that Tessa wanted. She wasn't interested in anything her peer group talked about. Mostly it was clothes, boys, pop music, cookery. No one else wanted to talk about poetry, philosophy and art. Even those three labels had a nameless beyond, a forbidden realm of mysticism, and that was where Tessa wanted to be. Banned from using her true gifts, she felt useless and unwanted, sick, sick, sick of trying to conform. It seemed that as soon as she found something she loved and wanted to do, a barrier slammed down in front of her, fierce and iron hard, like a portcullis edged with merciless spikes.

'You must go back.' The man in the saffron robe spoke to her with love and kindness. 'You are needed.'

'I don't feel needed,' Tessa said. 'No one needs ME.'

'Gaia does.'

'Gaia? Who is that?'

'Gaia is your mother planet. Planet earth. She is sick, Tessa, and your strength and knowledge will lead the way to her healing. Many will follow you. I urge you, at this time, to study environmental issues. The Warriors of the Rainbow. The Findhorn Garden. The book called *Silent Spring*. Study them. Seek them out and do not let anyone stop you, Tessa. You are blessed with intuition. Your time will come.'

Tessa stared into his eyes. In her dreamlike state she felt change wash over her like an ocean wave. She felt suddenly strong, like a figurehead on the prow of a boat. A strong woman with her hair flying in the wind. A leader. *Is that me?* she thought, and the answer came from the man's voice.

'Yes, that is you. A strong woman. Not a girl. You were never a girl. You were born a woman. That is why you cried so much, Tessa.'

She nodded slowly. It made sense. More sense than anything she'd been told by the adults in her life. Yet part of her didn't want to be a woman. She was afraid, always afraid.

'You have nothing to fear but fear itself,' said the man in the saffron robe. 'You are on a journey. Look back with me and see how far you have come.' He held out his hands, and between them was an orb of pulsing light. Tessa watched it, mesmerised, and saw within it a succession of jewel-like images. Cowslips on the millstream. Raindrops on her skin. The wildflower meadows. The wood of the singing nightingales. And the alabaster angel Freddie had carved for her. Then she saw books. Books of magic and beauty, poetry and truth. She saw Alfred Lord Tennyson in the classroom, so bright, as if drawn by a pencil of golden light. Then she saw Jonti, and the horses, and the baby birds she had rescued, the creatures of the stream, the golden frogs and shimmering dragonflies.

'I do . . . actually like being on earth,' she said slowly, letting the words dawn in her like a sunrise.

Only then did she know, beyond doubt, that she had to go back.

She opened her eyes, bravely, to the whiteness of a hospital, a place that had always filled her with terror. The smell of

Dettol, the purposeful squeak of shoes, the rustle of starched aprons, the ringing voices, the steel in the eyes of nurses.

But this time she could smell something different – an earthy, woody smell that didn't belong there. A smell of turf and damp tweed. Her left arm felt cumbersome and strange. She touched it and felt the hot tight bandage, the tips of her fingers protruding from it like crayons. Who had brought her here? She turned her head in the direction of the woody smell, and was startled to see a pair of intense eyes watching her from a biblical kind of face.

'Who are you?' Tessa whispered.

The intense eyes crinkled and shone with a warm smile. 'I was about to ask you that question,' said Art.

Freddie was on the floor in his workshop, with Joan Jarvis's lawnmower in bits around him. He looked up, startled to see a young man with long hair and the scruffiest, weirdest clothes he had ever seen. *A blimin' hippie*, was Freddie's first thought, and furious rage burned through him. He'd heard about the hippies. A feckless bunch of timewasters. Herbie had seen them in Glastonbury, 'draped all over the market cross, picking their toes,' Herbie had said. 'We didn't fight the war for that lot, did we? And their hair! I could take me garden clippers to that. Chop the lot off, I would. Short back and sides. Dunno what this country's coming to.'

Freddie felt the rage reach his eyes, sparking with unaccustomed pain that spread into the roots of his hair. He stood up, ready to confront this brazen layabout who had dared to walk up his garden path. 'What do 'e want?' he asked brusquely.

Immediately he was disarmed by the gentleness in Art's eyes, and the quiet voice. 'Are you Mr Barcussy?'

'Yes.'

'Tessa's father?'

'That's right.'

'I did knock on the door,' Art said, 'but no one answered so I figured you must be in here.' His eyes roamed appraisingly over the stone carvings at the other end of the workshop. 'Are these yours? Awesome, man.'

Freddie looked at him silently. He waited. The sound of Kate feeding the chickens in the back garden bubbled through the workshop door, and the wind rustled in the elm trees.

'So – how come you know Tessa?' Freddie asked, sensing he wasn't going to like what he heard.

'I found her – up on the ridgeway – earlier today. I – look, I think you'd better sit down,' Art said, and he took Freddie's arm and guided him kindly to the wooden seat outside the workshop. Freddie didn't want this layabout sitting on his bench, but he went along with it, for the sake of peace.

'Tessa was lying there, all alone,' Art said, looking at Freddie with intense grey eyes. 'She tried to kill herself – cut her wrist with a razorblade.'

Freddie just stared at him, too shocked to speak. Art put his hand in one of the fabric pockets and produced the razorblade wrapped in a strip of newspaper. It had blood on it. Tessa's blood. And the razorblade was one of his, from the bathroom cupboard. He'd counted them that morning, and thought it odd that one had gone missing. Waves of nausea washed over Freddie. He held onto the bench tightly with his big hands, the wind chilling his sweating brow. 'Could you . . . fetch my wife please?' he asked. 'She's in the back garden feeding the chickens.'

Dazed, Freddie waited, breathing deeply, fighting the unmanly nausea. Pictures of Tessa swirled through his mind. He loosened his collar, feeling his chest caving in. Was she dead? Had his beautiful daughter bled to death, alone on the ridgeway? Whatever had happened, Freddie needed Kate there with him. The moments throbbed while he waited and, at last, through a white mist of shock, he saw her coming down the garden, sturdy and bright, her eyes finding him as she walked beside Art.

He hadn't told her!

Kate sat down next to him. 'Are you not well, dear?' she asked lovingly, and Freddie wanted her to hold him as if he was a little child. But he had to be strong.

'It's Tessa,' he said heavily, and looked at Art who had sat down cross-legged on the ground, facing them. 'Tell Kate . . . what you told me, will you?'

'What's she done now?' Kate asked.

'I found her up on the ridgeway,' said Art, 'and she'd cut her wrist – badly. She was unconscious, and so I took my scarf off and made a tourniquet above her elbow. There was no one around, and no chance of reaching a telephone – so I carried her to the road and flagged down the first car that came along. He was great – took her straight to Yeovil Hospital and I sat in the back with her and kept her arm up in the air – and talked to her. I didn't know if she could hear me, but I figured it might help her, poor kid.'

Kate looked horrified. 'Is she – did they bring her round?'

'She's all right now,' Art said, wiping a tear from his cheek with the back of his hand. 'No one knew who she was, so I stayed with her until she came round – then we had a talk. She's – really, really – a special girl. I was – gutted, man – to see her like that.'

There was a silence, like the silence that follows a broken window, the settling into stillness, the winking shards of glass reflecting the sky.

'Well – thank God she's all right,' Kate said, and then she did something Freddie would never have thought of doing. She reached out both her hands to Art and gazed into his face. 'Thank you. And I don't even know your name, dear . . .'

'Art. Short for Arthur.'

'And how did you get here from Yeovil?' Kate asked.

'I got the bus.'

'So – where do you live, Art?'

Art hesitated. 'I'm living free. Wandering. Searching, I guess. My folks have got a place in Truro – but we don't see eye to eye. They're stinking rich, and totally lost in materialism. Man . . . the whole of mankind lies sleeping in materialism, don't you think? I broke free of it.'

The shards of glass twinkled ever brighter.

Kate put a restraining hand on Freddie's knee, sensing the angry response that was pending. 'We must go to Yeovil as soon as we can,' she said, and looked caringly at Art. 'We're really grateful for what you've done. You saved Tessa's life.'

'Maybe.'

'Is there anything we can do for you in return?' Kate asked. 'Could we give you something?'

'Nah – thanks – I don't need stuff.' Art stood up. 'I was glad to help Tessa. She's a great girl.'

'She is,' agreed Kate, 'and we'll go straight over to Yeovil and see her, fetch her home if she's well enough.'

Art frowned. 'Tread softly,' he said. 'Don't tread on her dreams.'

At that moment, Tessa felt depressed and frightened. She kept her head turned away from her bandaged arm and the drip feeding a mysterious clear liquid into her. The curtains were drawn around her bed, but she could hear, and sense the loitering shadows of illness that hung over the ward. Coughs and moans, and subdued conversations. The busy footsteps passing to and fro alarmed her. The feet sounded huge, like doctor's feet, and she kept thinking someone was going to come through the curtains and enforce some medical procedure on her.

She'd come back, but already the world she was in seemed alien and too difficult. It was like being born all over again. Shocking. Only this time she couldn't cry. She had to pretend.

Tessa had told Art she didn't want to see her parents. She couldn't cope with them right now.

'I understand,' Art had said. 'I cut loose from my folks. I don't hate them. But I had to take charge of my life – take it back from being manipulated. It's my life, and now I'm living it and loving it. I'm free – totally. I live in the woods, parked up in a camper van, but I only sleep in it when it's raining. On clear nights I sleep under the moon and stars and listen to the nightingales, and the wind in the trees. I believe that's how we were meant to be – not wearing a collar and tie and sitting in a glass box all day.'

Tessa stared at him, her eyes wide open and round as she listened to his story. 'I've never met anyone like you before,' she said.

'People hate my long hair,' Art said, running suntanned fingers through his flowing mane, 'but I tell them Jesus had long hair.'

When he had gone, Tessa lay there thinking about him. Art hadn't asked her any questions or pushed her to explain why she'd tried to kill herself. He'd told her why he'd saved her life.

'Because you're beautiful,' he'd said, and he was looking at her eyes, not her body. 'You're a child of the forest. I'll bet you're into poetry and philosophy. I can see that, Tessa. You've been born for the Age of Aquarius. Hang in there, girl. I'll see you around.' Art stood up. He lifted Tessa's right hand from the starched sheet, kissed it tenderly, gave her an intense stare, and left.

The kiss made Tessa buzz all over. A new feeling fizzed across her creamy skin, warm and electric, like fresh toast. *I'm a woman*, she thought, *a strong woman*. The back of her hand tingled as if the kiss was embossed there, like a tattoo, there forever.

She slept deeply, and awoke to find her parents sitting beside the bed on two iron chairs, their eyes haunted with questions. She glanced at her father's anxious expression, then at her mother's hot eyes and cheeks.

'What happened, dear?' Kate asked.

Tessa looked at her silently.

'Why?' Kate asked. 'Why, Tessa?'

Tessa turned her head away and gazed at the tiny bead-bright bubbles around the glass jug of water on the bedside table.

'I brought you a rose.' Freddie handed her a peace rose in a twist of damp newspaper.

'Thanks.' Tessa buried her face in the cream, pink-rimmed petals, breathing the soothing peachiness of them, tasting the garden. She pressed her tongue hard against the roof of her mouth, a trick Lexi had taught her to stop herself crying.

'You must tell us why,' Kate said, and her voice broke. 'We're so HURT. I'm your mother, Tessa. I gave birth to you, gave you your life. Doesn't that mean anything?'

Tessa closed her eyes. She wanted to say, 'No comment', like people did on television.

'Tessa! No, don't shut us out, dear. I won't have it,' Kate said. She stroked Tessa's pale brow, moving a strand of hair tenderly away from her face. Tessa braced herself, and tolerated it, when what she wanted to do was shake her chestnut locks right over her face like a curtain.

'She's not ready to talk, Kate,' Freddie said.

'Well I am,' Kate said, and the spots of colour burned hotter on her cheeks. 'You're a lucky, lucky girl, Tessa. You have a lovely home and everything you could possibly want. Your daddy has worked day and night to keep us in such luxury. We've bent over backwards to help you, Tessa – we've done everything we possibly can, and more.'

Tessa felt her mouth closing tighter and tighter. Her head felt like a balloon about to burst.

'Why take your LIFE?' Kate ranted. 'It's so selfish, Tessa. Don't you see that? Oh – I'm so ASHAMED. Why must you hurt us so?'

'You don't like me.' Tessa met her mother's eyes.

'Of course we do. Don't talk so silly.'

'You don't. You've never liked me.'

'Well, you don't make yourself easy to like, Tessa. Why can't you be more like Lucy?'

Salt in the wound! Tessa couldn't bear to hear another word. She screamed at Kate. 'I knew you'd say that. It's all you ever say to me. You've made me hate Lucy and her smug face, Mummy. I'm not like Lucy. I'm like ME. And for once in your life, can't you understand that?'

The ward sister opened the curtains and intervened.

'Tessa,' she said kindly, 'you were doing so well. Please try to calm down.' She put a cool hand on Tessa's hot brow and stroked her hair back. She looked at Kate. 'I think you should go now. Your daughter needs to rest. And we can't have the other patients disturbed, can we?'

Freddie stood up and put his arm round Kate. 'You go and talk to the sister,' he said. 'I'll have a quiet word with Tessa.' Kate looked devastated. She wasn't used to failure. But life with Tessa had been one long, exhausting rollercoaster.

'I will not be calmed down,' Tessa screamed, her pale blue eyes brimming with angry tears. 'Why can't you try to understand me, Mummy? You just hate me, and blame me. You do. You DO.'

'If you don't calm down, I will give you a sedative – an injection,' said the sister, and Tessa sank back against the pillows in utter despair. She was glad when her mother walked away with the ward sister, and Freddie just sat close, his eyes holding her in one of his vast silences.

'Did Art tell you I was here?' Tessa asked.

'Ah – yes, he did,' Freddie said, and Tessa respected him for not criticising Art, even though he must have thought him 'a blimin' hippie'. ''Twere kind of him. We gave him a bunch of carrots and a few eggs.'

Tessa looked at the peace rose now falling apart in her hand. Art had said she was beautiful. Only one other person had ever said that in her whole life, and that was Ivor Stape.

Chapter Eleven

WHEN THE EARTH IS SICK

Tessa picked up the dead song thrush from the grass verge outside The Pines. She stood looking at its creamy, speckled breast, stroking its downy softness, and tears poured down her face. The morning sun seemed cruel in the way it lit the dead bird so brightly, gleaming on its beak, the blue-grey, closed eyelids, and the texture of its tightly curled feet.

She carried it tenderly, slowly, up the garden path. She wanted her father to be there, to do a silent, sharing lament with her. He would know why the bird had died, he would help her dig a little grave under the lilacs. But Freddie wasn't there. He was out in the lorry, working as usual. Tessa felt she couldn't bear to show the dead song thrush to anyone else, even her mother. She didn't want them to look at it, act as if it didn't matter, and say it was only a bird. Brisk dismissal of her deepest beliefs and feelings was pushing Tessa over the edge, and she didn't want to invite criticism. Best avoid it, she thought, best to just hide her true self, and try to conform.

Art had said new exciting things to her. He told her it wasn't long before she was fifteen and then she could leave school and be free, like him. She could run away and live in peace. He pointed out that she'd managed to survive fourteen years of her present life, and it was a journey. The last few miles were always the hardest. 'But hang in there,' he'd said. 'Freedom is worth waiting for. Come and find me,' he'd said, 'and I'll help you.'

Art would care about the song thrush, Tessa thought, as she buried it and picked a sprig of scented lilac to lay on the grave. She sat there for a while, on the grass, looking at her new circular skirt. Kate had bought them one each from Marks and Spencer in Yeovil. Lucy's had pink roses, and Tessa's had blue. Lucy couldn't wait to go dancing in hers, loving the way it twirled out and showed off her legs. But Tessa felt guilty as she smoothed her pretty new skirt. Why should she have a lovely, clean, ridiculous skirt when song thrushes were dying?

She went inside and found her mother making pastry in the kitchen.

'You look nice, dear,' Kate said.

Tessa sat down at the table and watched her dusting the pastry with flour, rolling it and turning it. She didn't say, 'I don't want to look nice,' and she didn't mention the dead song thrush. And nobody talked about her suicide attempt. It was forbidden territory. Hushed up. Hidden in a box marked FAMILY SHAME. The wound on her wrist was still covered with a plaster and nobody asked about it.

'Only two more days before we go on holiday,' Kate said cheerfully. 'Won't it be lovely?'

Tessa didn't answer.

'We'll come home as brown as berries,' Kate said. 'We're lucky to have this extra holiday, thanks to Joan lending us her caravan for a week. Won't it be fun? I've always wanted to stay in a caravan, and we all need a holiday.'

'After my messed-up suicide attempt,' said Tessa bluntly.

'It's hard for your dad to go on holiday,' Kate said, avoiding the provocation in Tessa's eyes. 'He never had a seaside holiday when he was young, and he never wants to go, but when he's there, he enjoys it.'

'I don't want to go,' Tessa said.

Kate stared at Tessa in disbelief. She put the rolling pin down very carefully. 'That's rude and ungrateful.'

'But it's true, Mum.'

'Never mind if it's true. I don't want to hear it. And neither does your Dad, or Lucy, poor girl. She's in the middle of her exams.'

Tessa felt the skin tightening over her cheeks. She met her mother's bright, expectant eyes in silence.

'I can't leave you here with Granny, Tessa. That's not what you want, surely? We've had lovely times at Weymouth, and you'll love it when we get there. You like swimming, don't you?'

Tessa shrugged.

'And you know how Jonti loves the beach.' Kate embarked on a tantalising list of the things they would do in Weymouth, but when Tessa just stared at her with gloomy eyes, she rounded it off with a threat. 'You are not going to cast a blight on our family holiday, my girl, so don't think you are. I won't have you spoiling it for Dad and Lucy.'

'That's exactly why I shouldn't go.'

Kate went on cutting the sheet of pastry into circles with a serrated tart cutter. 'If Lucy was here, she'd be helping me. She'd have had these tarts in the oven by now, and the washing-up done – and a smile on her face.'

'You just don't understand, Mummy,' Tessa said, holding on to her fury so tightly that it felt like a fever burning inside her. 'Why won't you LISTEN to me?'

'I will if you say something worth listening to.'

It stung, like a small hard pebble aimed at the heart. Tessa searched her mother's eyes. The love was in there some-where, but she felt Kate had shut it away behind a door marked NO ACCESS. 'I'm going out,' she said, and looked away from her mother's eyes to the window where green and silver foliage rippled in the wind.

'Where are you going?'

'For a walk with Jonti.'

'Don't be long then.'

Counting to ten didn't work for Tessa. She needed to count to a hundred. A hundred angry footsteps before she felt calmer, and then she could see the world clearly again. With Jonti trotting ahead, she walked up the road under the tower-ing elm trees, their young leaves rich and hopeful in the after-noon sun, the grass verge covered with mats of violets in every shade of pink and purple.

The church clock struck four, and she heard the whistle of a train in the hills. She watched the express train burst out of the cutting and tear over the viaduct with a ribbon of white steam flying over the roofs of the carriages. Freddie had often told her about that train. It was The Cornishman, and it never stopped at Monterose. She could see tiny faces looking out from carriage windows. Those people were going to Cornwall, she thought, and something tugged at her memory. Something Art had said about the magnificence of the Atlantic Ocean, the jewel green colours of it, the mighty rolling waves, waves so strong you could ride the foam on a surfboard and feel part of the wild sea.

When she thought about it, in that moment it felt as if the sea rushed through her heart, washing away the anger and sadness, filling her with light and sparkle.

Kate stood at the window and watched Tessa walking away under the elm trees, with the wind blowing her wavy hair and the blue and white skirt. The way she walked reminded Kate of Ethie. It wasn't a lady-like walk, it began as an angry stride, then became an aimless, dreamy wandering. She was glad to see Jonti escorting her at a business-like trot.

The look in her daughter's pale blue eyes stayed in Kate's mind. Such misery and hatred from a girl who had so much: why? Kate wanted to understand. Why had Tessa tried to kill herself? To Kate it had felt like a kick in the gut, an insult that shattered her maternal love. Love wasn't working. It wasn't enough.

Before Tessa, Kate's confidence had been a shining asset that others had envied. Her confidence had built a marriage, it had taught Freddie to laugh and smile; it had pacified Annie, and raised Lucy. They were so proud of Lucy, now doing her A levels at grammar school. Lucy was popular and successful. Kate passionately wanted Lucy and Tessa to have a career, and to marry Mr Right who would be tall, successful, and from a good family. She was sure that Lucy would do exactly that, and have a fairy-tale wedding in Monterose Church. But Tessa? What kind of future was there for a girl so gifted and yet so emotionally enigmatic? After the suicide attempt, Kate felt the gulf between them widening. Despite help from Doctor Jarvis, and a week off school, Tessa still hadn't told them why.

Kate felt one of her headaches coming on. She put the tarts into the oven and cleared the table, her head full of sharp pain. She took two of the soluble Disprin Doctor Jarvis had given her, and sat at the table with a sudden overwhelming feeling of wanting to give up. The pain in her head was excruciating, and it seemed to have something to do with wanting to cry. The uncried tears felt like a hot bar of pain, a bolt through her head from ear to ear.

The side door to The Pines was never locked. Kate liked to keep an open house. She didn't feel like seeing anyone right now, but the door opened and Susan came in, carrying an enormous willow basket. 'Hello Kate! I just popped in to give you these.'

'Lovely to see you!' Kate held out her arms and beamed at Susan. 'Cup of tea? Oh my goodness – look at those!' She stared at the glistening red strawberries that filled the basket. 'What a lot!'

'I thought you'd like them, Kate – we've got far too many – there must be about ten pounds in there. Can you use them?'

'Oh yes. I'll make jam.' Kate took down the huge preserving pan that hung on the wall. 'Pop them in here.' They tipped the basket and the strawberries thundered into the pan, leaving a red stained piece of newspaper at the bottom of the basket. 'That's so kind of you, Sue – thank you.'

Susan's quiet eyes stared at Kate, looking suddenly serious. 'You don't look well, Kate. Is something wrong?'

Tessa and Jonti crossed the brown and cream footbridge over the station platform. She wanted to ask Charlie, the station-master, about The Cornishman, but he was busy helping a farmer load his cows into the cattle train wagons that stood in the siding. There was much mooing and shouting and the rumble of hooves as terrified animals found themselves trapped in unfamiliar, swaying wagons. Tessa could see the whites of their eyes gleaming in the cracks, desperate for a last glimpse of green fields. 'Poor things,' she said to Jonti, and he whined in agreement.

She walked on up the street to the other side of Monterose, to where the cottages ended and a narrow tarmac lane led towards the wooded hills. There were two horses up there in one of the fields, and Tessa wanted to lean over the gate and see if she could get them to come close and let her stroke them.

They raised their heads and stared at her, then lowered them again to continue eating. So Tessa climbed over the gate in her flowery skirt, and tied Jonti to the bars with his lead. 'You stay there,' she said to his disappointed little face. 'I won't be long.' The lush grass brushed her ankles, and clumps of dandelions, moon daisies and clover grew thickly from the red clay soil.

Tessa had a special voice for talking to animals, a low-pitched, soothing tone. It was something she enjoyed doing, a time when she felt free to be loving and kind without risk of ridicule or judgement. She was thrilled when one of the horses came to her and lowered his graceful head to let her stroke him. She ran her hands along the crest of the mane, down the sleek shoulders and broad chest. She rubbed the hard, suede ears and rested her own cheek against the warm silk of his big bony cheek.

She spent a long time talking to him, then turned her attention to the other horse who was hanging back. 'Are you afraid of me?' Tessa asked. 'I'm not going to catch you, or ride you.' The mare raised her head and stared with dark, liquid eyes. As soon as Tessa moved towards her, she laid her ears back, curled her lips and tossed her head, looking distinctly unwelcoming. The breeze ruffled her long mane which was creamy white against the dappled grey of her coat. Her head was delicately shaped, with a fairy-tale kink in the nose, and small curved ears. Her legs were slim and deep grey. A seahorse, Tessa thought, longingly. 'You're so beautiful,' she said in her animal voice. 'I love you.'

She inched her way nearer, but the mare turned her rump towards her, the tail swishing angrily. 'You're like me,' Tessa said. 'You pretend to be angry and fierce when actually you're scared, aren't you?' The mare swung round again, pricked her ears and looked at Tessa in a new way. 'You've been hurt,' Tessa said, 'I can tell.' She sat down in the grass. 'There, you see, I'm sitting down, so I'm not going to hurt you, or use you.'

The mare walked towards her in hesitant steps, her head lowered, her nostrils flared. Tessa began to tingle with excitement. The mare was blowing softly at her, so she blew back, in horse language. She kept her hands still and let the beautiful creature come close and blow in her hair. She was aware of tension in the mare's muscles, and sensed that one wrong move would send her spinning away in alarm. To her intense joy, the mare lowered her elegant head, pressed it into Tessa's shoulder, and stayed there in a magic moment of understanding, a moment of building a bridge between two lost souls. Tessa kept still, but her body turned to velvet. *I've fallen in love*, she thought, *with a horse!*

She didn't see the person who stood in the lane, behind the hedge, watching her.

Kate was surprised to see Tessa come back with colour in her cheeks and light in her eyes. She had a mysterious smile that made Kate think she had been up to something. Best not to ask, she thought, as Tessa sat down at the table. It was set for high tea, with Freddie, Lucy and Annie already tucking in to slices of ham and cheese. Lucy was explaining her French homework to Freddie, laughing as he tried to pronounce some of the phrases she was teaching him.

'You're such a clever girl,' Annie said, and her face changed when she saw Tessa. 'Late again?' she said disapprovingly.

'Leave her be, Mother,' Freddie said, looking at Kate's pale, strained expression. 'Let's have tea in peace.'

'Did you have a nice walk, dear?' Kate asked Tessa.

'Yep.'

'Yes, thank you, not "yep",' Annie said, glaring at Freddie.

'Did you see any interesting birds?' Freddie asked.

Tessa hesitated. 'Not many – no – but this morning I found a dead song thrush. I've buried him under the lilacs.'

'I can't think where all the birds have gone,' said Freddie seriously. 'There used to be big flocks of yellowhammers, and linnets, goldfinches – where are they all?'

'It's the spraying,' Kate said. 'All the farmers are doing it now – it must be killing hundreds of birds. I know it's progress – but it's sad. Who knows what else those chemicals are killing.'

Tessa was listening with round eyes.

'The earth is sick,' she said, and everyone stared at her. Lucy rolled her eyes.

'Don't talk such rubbish,' Annie said.

'It's not rubbish, Granny,' Tessa glared at her. 'It's a prophecy coming true. *'When the earth is sick, and the animals begin to disappear, then the Warriors of the Rainbow will come and save her.'*

'Save who?' Annie asked.

'Gaia.'

'And who's Gaia when she's out?'

'The earth. It's her name.'

'Don't talk so silly. The earth isn't a person.'

'Would you like another cup of tea?' Kate asked, trying to divert Annie's attention. Her head was pounding and she didn't feel she could sit there through yet another confrontation between Tessa and Annie. 'It's *Dixon of Dock Green* tonight on television,' she added brightly.

'Don't change the subject, Mummy,' Tessa said angrily. 'This is important.'

'No, it's not,' said Lucy. 'It's gloom and doom, isn't it, Mummy? And we don't want to talk about it at tea-time.'

'You would say that, Lucy.' Tessa's eyes blazed at her sister. 'You undermine everything I choose to believe in.'

'No, I don't,' Lucy said. 'If you chose to believe in SENSIBLE things – things that matter – I wouldn't argue. It's for your own good. You can't go around talking about hippie stuff.'

'Quite right, Lucy,' Annie said triumphantly.

'It's not hippie stuff. Anyway, the hippies are trying to save the earth, which is more than you're doing.'

'Will you STOP!' Kate cried out suddenly. She put down the slice of bread and butter she'd been trying to eat, and clasped her hands to her temples. Her behaviour was so out of character that silence fell over the tea table.

Freddie reached out and patted Kate on the shoulder. 'Don't you upset yourself, Kate. What is it? A headache?'

'It's right on top of my head,' Kate said, almost crying with the pain.

Terribly concerned, Freddie turned to the two girls with a rare spark of anger in his blue yes. 'Stop your bickering, the pair of you – and you, Mother. Look what it's doing to my lovely Kate. What's the matter with you all?' Unexpected tears of passion poured over his red cheeks.

Tessa and Lucy froze into shocked silence. To see their invincible father cry was major.

'Come on, you lie on the sofa, Kate.' Freddie guided Kate to the sofa and put a cushion under her head. 'You lie quiet,' he said, and turned to the three shocked faces watching him. 'And you lot – finish your tea in silence and clear the table.'

Jonti got out of his box and crept across the floor to be with Kate. He jumped up and cuddled against her, whining and looking up at her. 'Dear little dog,' muttered Kate. She looked at Freddie and tried to smile. 'Goodness – I don't need to lie on the sofa like an invalid.'

'Yes, you do. You stay there.'

Tessa went to the airing cupboard and found a flannel. She soaked it in cold water, squeezed it and took it over to her mother. 'Poor Mummy, put this on your forehead.'

'Thank you, dear.' Kate glanced at Tessa's pale blue eyes and the anger had gone. In its place was real love and caring

– and fear and guilt. She let Tessa press the flannel over her eyes and felt her slim fingers cooling her throbbing temples. She could smell the heavy fabric plastic on Tessa's wrist and it reminded her that only a week ago her beautiful daughter had taken a razorblade and tried to end her life. Her beating heart was loud and frightened as she leaned over her mother. It had the desperate fragility of a bird fluttering against glass. *Tessa needs me*, Kate thought. *Even when she hates me, she needs me.*

'I don't know why I didn't see this coming,' Freddie said as he leaned on his car, watching reflections of the sunset in the well-polished roof, coppery clouds with the ragged shapes of crows and jackdaws passing through.

Doctor Jarvis looked over the top of his glasses. 'It's not your fault, Freddie. You're a working man with a lot on your plate.'

'Ah – but I shouldn't have let Kate suffer like that,' Freddie said and each word hurt like a hot stone in his throat. 'All these years. She's too good. Never complains.'

'Joan is the same,' Doctor Jarvis said. 'She'd kill herself for the family. Wartime women they are. Salt of the earth. Now she's killing herself for the grandchildren.'

Freddie felt too angry with himself to speak. The anger drove him into silence, and somewhere on the fringe of it, the doctor's perceptive eyes were observing him.

'I've given Kate a strong painkiller and a sedative,' Doctor Jarvis said. 'It'll knock her out and she'll sleep heavily. Let her sleep on in the morning, Freddie. It's years of exhaustion and worry over young Tessa – and your mother – she's not easy, is she? But, knowing Kate, she'll bounce back – let me know immediately if that headache gets worse or if she gets a fever.'

When he had gone, Freddie stood looking at the thundery sky. He went to the washing line and unpegged the eight white linen sheets and the sixteen pillowcases. They were heavy, still damp, and flecked with soot from the railway. Shocked at the weight of them, he hung them over both arms and took them inside. Kate had spent the day hand-washing them in the boiler, wringing them through the squeaking mangle, then hanging them out. Endless bending and lifting, he thought. When he'd held her hand, he'd noticed how sore and red the skin was and how her finger was swollen around her wedding ring.

He'd never meant it to be like this.

He dumped the sheets on the kitchen table and stood looking at them. Annie had gone home and he could hear the girls' voices from the living room, above the television.

'That's not true!' Tessa shouted at Lucy.

'Yes it is. It's time you grew up.'

'I don't want to grow up and end up boring like you.'

'I'm not boring. And at least I'm not an evil witch like you. And stop shouting. You'll wake Mummy and make her worse, and then we won't go on holiday.'

'I don't care. I don't want to go anyway.'

Freddie felt rage towering inside him like a wave about to break into a thousand stinging pellets of spray. He crossed the room in slow, deliberate strides, and turned off the black knob on the television. The monochrome image of *Dixon of Dock Green* vanished into a small hard white dot.

'Daddy! I was . . .' The protest died on Lucy's lips as she saw her father's face. It was dark and swollen, and his eyes looked frightened of the fury that glittered in them. And when he spoke, his voice was ominously quiet.

'Now I don't care what you're doing, you two girls are going to listen to me. I got something to say to you – so you sit there, and you remember this – for the rest of your life.' Freddie bit back the words that burned on his tongue. He'd say them to Herbie in the morning. He was aware that Tessa was particularly fragile right now. She was already crying, silently, wiping tears from her face with the back of her hand, and he knew she sensed the depth of his anger.

He went to the oak dresser, and took down a small ceramic owl. The memory it evoked was painful. 'When I were a boy,' he began, 'younger than you – seven, I was, I saw my old father lose his temper. Your granny had some lovely china – she was proud of it – loved it, she did. Some of it belonged to her family. And she kept it beautiful, all arranged along this dresser.' He paused, and let the memory wash over him like a cold merciless wave. 'Now my father was so angry about something I did at school that he flew into a blind rage, and he smashed every plate, cup and jug – even the teapot from the dresser. Cleared the shelves he did, chucked it onto the stone floor with such force. It was broken all to hell.

Terrible it was. Upset me, and your granny. That's what she had to put up with, all her life.'

'Poor Granny,' whispered Tessa, and her pale blue eyes watched him with compassion and alarm. Lucy was dry-eyed and her pretty mouth was pursed defensively.

'And when he'd done it,' Freddie continued, 'he was so sorry and ashamed, he sat there and cried. Sobbed his heart out. Wished he'd never done it – a grown man – a giant of a man he was, sat there crying like a child. And d'you know what your granny did?'

'What?' Lucy asked, her eyes wide.

'She just put her arms round him and calmed him down, and told me to get the dustpan and sweep up the broken china. Told me to put it in the rubbish bin. But I couldn't. I hid it, and then I dug clay from the stream, and I made this owl from the broken china.' He smoothed the owl's winking eyes with his roughened index finger. 'These were cup handles, and the feet were made from the curly handle of a jug. It's got some of my blood in it too, 'cause I cut me hands doing it. And d'you know what my father said to me?'

'What?'

'He turned round to me – I were only seven – and he said, "Don't you ever be like me, son". I vowed never to lose my temper like that. And I never have.' He paused, finding his eyes drawn again to Tessa. She was staring at something beyond him, something shimmering in the air. 'But,' he added with a new spark of anger in his eyes, 'when I come in and find you two girls bickering and hurting each other, and your mother lying in bed – ill and exhausted – and the sheets still on the line – I feel angry like that. Angry with you two. Disappointed. Disgusted.' His voice broke into fragments. 'I've loved your mother since I were nine years old. She was my dream girl, my sweetheart, all I ever wanted. She's precious to me, my Kate, more precious than gold.'

Freddie looked hard at his two daughters. Lucy seemed mature, preoccupied with her exams and her future. She didn't seem impressed by what he had said. He wondered if she'd even listened. But Tessa's eyes were silvery with light as she gazed at him, her creamy skin had a translucent quality, the last rays of the sunset in the fire of her hair. She had listened. She had cared. Freddie suddenly felt very small, like one person in a crowd, as if Tessa was seeing them all around him.

'Daddy,' she said, in a voice that sounded like a clear bell, 'I can see the stone angel. But she's not stone. She's real and she's enormous. Her wings are touching the walls, and she's made of light like the sun and moon.'

Chapter Twelve

BREAKING POINTS

'I'll have Tessa,' Lexi said, and there was an astonished silence. So she laughed and added, 'Must be mad.'

Freddie frowned. He thought Tessa didn't like Lexi. He wished Kate was downstairs, ready with the perfect answer, but she was still sleeping, and he had to make a decision. Tessa was adamant that she didn't want to go to Weymouth and 'endure a week cooped up in a caravan with Lucy', as she put it. He couldn't leave her with Annie.

Lexi was eyeing him expectantly, awaiting an answer.

'It's kind of you,' Freddie said, trying not to be rude, 'but . . .'

'Yes – I know,' Lexi said, rescuing him. 'You're wondering why, aren't you? Well, Tessa's been talking to me, and yesterday I watched her with the horses.'

'Horses?' Freddie stiffened with anxiety.

'She was in the field talking to them,' Lexi said. 'She didn't know I was watching, but something extraordinary happened. I've got an Arab mare, Selwyn, and she's a really bad-tempered horse – she hates everyone – and no one can catch her, including me. But Tessa sat down on the grass and talked to her, and Selwyn actually walked up to her and leaned her head against her. A horse doesn't do that unless they love you. I think Tessa has got a special way with animals.'

'Ah – she has,' agreed Freddie.

'I need someone to help me,' Lexi said, 'and I'd teach her to ride in return.'

Freddie was alarmed. He didn't want Tessa riding horses and getting involved with the Tillermans. But before he could find the words to answer, Tessa ran downstairs, a paintbrush in her hand. 'I'd LOVE that,' she said. 'Please Daddy – let me go – I promise to be good. I'm crazy about horses.'

'You'll have to help me look after them, Tessa,' Lexi said. 'Mucking out stables, tack cleaning and grooming.'

'I don't care. I'll do anything,' Tessa said firmly. 'And can Jonti come too?'

'I don't see why not,' said Lexi. She raised her eyebrows at Freddie. 'Well?'

'It's good of you, Lexi,' Freddie said, 'but you know how I feel about horses. I don't want her riding anything wild.'

'She won't be,' Lexi assured him. 'I am a qualified riding instructor, and we've got a quiet old thing she can learn on. I can lend her all the kit.'

Tessa looked at him pleadingly, and Jonti sat on his foot and gazed up at him, his head on one side. Freddie would have liked more time to think it over, but Lexi wasn't going to wait; he sensed her impatience already brewing. Lexi lived alone in a magnificent old house at the edge of the woods. Maybe, just maybe, it would be good for Tessa. A voice in his mind was urging him to let go.

'Well – it's only a week,' he said, 'if you can put up with her.'

Lexi grinned. 'I've had worse,' she joked.

Tessa was ecstatic. She wagged her finger at him like Kate would have done, and her eyes shone. 'You've made the right decision, Daddy. It's the best thing I've done in my whole life!'

'I'll bring her up in the car later,' Freddie said heavily.

'Come now if you like. I've got the Land Rover. Save you a trip,' said Lexi. 'You don't need much, maybe a mac if you've got one.'

So Tessa was bundled into Lexi's Land Rover with a box of books and a few clothes. Jonti jumped in beside her, squirming with enthusiasm. Freddie stood at the garden gate and watched them go. Ironically, a holiday without Tessa seemed exactly like the gift of peace that Kate needed for her recovery. He had a sense of foreboding too. His girls were growing up. The magic hours of childhood had gone. Freddie went to the car and opened the boot. In the corner, on a tartan rug, were the two Mickey Mouse tin buckets, and two small red spades, still with a glaze of Weymouth sand on them. He looked at them sadly, remembering the happy times with Kate in a deckchair, her bare legs soaking up the sun, while he made ever more elaborate sand sculptures with the two suntanned children. He remembered the light in their eyes, the screams of joy as they splashed in the sea. The donkey rides, the Punch and Judy. He'd loved it all. And he'd felt like Daddy. Loved, respected and wanted. He didn't want that to change.

He went inside and crept upstairs. Kate was sleeping peacefully, her skin smooth and rosy again over her cheeks. The pain had gone, leaving only the shadows under her eyes. Her glossy black hair was spread out over the white pillow, and he noticed a few threads of grey in it. He wanted her to wake up and rescue him from his gloomy thoughts, but he crept out again and shut the door quietly.

On an impulse, he went into Tessa's bedroom to see the picture she'd been painting. She'd left it on the table, her paint box still open beside it, the two sable brushes he'd given her for Christmas lying on a piece of newspaper.

Freddie gazed in awe as he saw the painting she'd done. It was stunning. Life-changing. In a moment of echoing brilliance, it re-awakened everything he'd tried so hard to forget.

Tessa had obviously worked with speed and passion to paint the angel she'd seen. She'd done the three of them, herself, Lucy and him sitting at the kitchen table, but very small and in remarkably life-like silhouettes, dark against the blazing light of a huge angel, painted in yellow and white, her wings like sun rays, filling the kitchen. She had painted bits of the dresser and the window in gloomy, mysterious colours, emphasising the incandescence of the angel, the awesome size of it, and the power.

Freddie wasn't sure if she had finished the painting or not. He felt it was the most startling image of an angel he had ever seen, yet it wasn't detailed. It made him want to cry with joy at the sense of recognition. He had seen an angel just like that, and nobody had believed him. In one instant, the experience had thrilled him spiritually, and devastated him emotionally, like being torn in two. He didn't want Tessa ever to feel like that.

It was all coming true, he thought, the words of Madame Eltura – but so much faster than she had predicted. Too fast, he feared, to be contained in a sensitive teenage girl. He wondered if that was why Tessa had tried to take her life – because of the extreme power of her visions, and the pain of constant ridicule and rejection.

She's my daughter, he thought as he studied the painting, *but who is she? Who is she as a soul?*

Kate slapped Lucy's face hard. 'How DARE you do this. I'm disgusted with you,' she cried. 'And who is that boy?'

Lucy stared at her, holding her face and swaying a little as they stood by the caravan in the dusk of evening. The sea was a chalky blue, the sky changing to violet over the winking lights of Weymouth. Further up the cliff-top campsite, Kate could see Freddie's silhouette holding the yellow box kite on its string. He'd still wanted to fly it, even without the two girls who had loved to hold the string, and feel the pull of the salt wind.

'Thank goodness your father's not here,' Kate said. She was trembling with fury, and with the shock of slapping her treasured daughter. 'I could SMELL you coming up the path,' she ranted. 'How dare you get drunk, Lucy! Where did you get it from? I hope you haven't spent the money Daddy gave you on . . . on booze.'

'I wasn't doing any harm, Mum. They were friends from school. They only gave me a bit of cider. Everyone was drinking it – and Jill's mum's potato wine.' Lucy's eyes blazed at Kate. 'We were only having fun. You didn't have to slap me like that. It's not fair.'

'You should have known better, Lucy. You don't just do something because someone else is doing it.'

'Why not? I was joining in and I enjoyed it,' said Lucy defiantly. Her eyes rolled and she swung round and was sick into the grass.

'Oh for goodness' sake, Lucy!' Kate pushed her into the green canvas toilet tent. 'Go in there.'

She got a bucket of water from the tank and sloshed it over the grass, feeling sick herself now. She glanced up at Freddie's silhouette and he was winding the kite in. Soon he would come padding down to the caravan, his face red from the sea air, his eyes peaceful.

'Don't tell Daddy. Please, Mum.' Lucy staggered out of the tent, her eyes desperate, her hair straggled over her face.

'You've ruined our holiday,' Kate said, 'and Daddy will be terribly upset. You'd better tell me who that boy was, Lucy. You won't be seeing HIM again, my girl.'

'That's not fair. He's a nice boy, Mum. You haven't even met him.' Lucy began to cry with rage. 'He's Jill's brother, and he gave me a lift back on his Vespa.'

'You've no business getting on the back of one of those scooters,' Kate ranted. 'You saw them all riding along the sea front, causing trouble everywhere. Fighting. They're no good – the scum of the earth – and your father hates them.'

'But you don't KNOW them, Mum. That's not fair. Why can't I have some fun? I'm seventeen, not ten.' Lucy pushed her hair back from her face, and her eyes seethed with resentment. 'And they invited me to go midnight swimming with them – and I'm going. You can't stop me.'

'Lucy!' Kate was hurt and appalled. She'd only just recovered from the upset with Tessa. Now her precious Lucy had turned on her. She couldn't understand it. Lucy had been a model daughter all her life. What had gone wrong? 'I would never have spoken to my mother like that,' she said, and her voice seemed disempowered, like something vanishing down a hole in the ground. 'You get undressed and get into bed,' she said through tightening lips. 'I've nothing more to say to you.'

She guided Lucy into the caravan and watched her lie down on the narrow bunk, fully dressed, and bury her head in the pillow. Kate covered her with a blanket, and shut the door on her. Dazed and upset, she sat on the caravan steps and waited for Freddie to come down from the cliff.

In her final three years at primary school, Tessa had been steel hard and silent. 'Communicates very little,' her reports said. Miss O'Grady had marked her work and tolerated her, but the hatred was mutual. Her threat had lodged in Tessa's mind. 'You'll be sent away to a home for bad children.' Tessa had spent time imagining such a place. It would be grey, inside and outside, like Miss O'Grady. Grey bars at the windows, grey porridge for breakfast, a garden of sticks and stones. It would be far away under a grey raincloud. The stress of trying to behave like Lucy made Tessa nervous and withdrawn. Her only happy times were when she was ill. Kate nursed her through measles, mumps and whooping cough, chickenpox and endless chesty colds. The last long summer term when she was well enough for full attendance was unbearable for Tessa. Yet she'd pushed herself through the eleven plus, passed it and gone to the grammar school where she was once again in the shadow of Lucy's perfection.

She'd remained a loner and a misfit, longing for a friend, forever feeling she wanted school to end and life to begin. When the Arab mare, Selwyn, had walked up to her and offered her silent love, Tessa had been overwhelmed. It was a key moment of change in her life. Minutes later, she had met Lexi.

Selwyn had walked away, cropping grass, and Lexi sat down on the turf beside Tessa. For the first time ever, they had eye contact, and Tessa discovered that Lexi didn't look so much like an ostrich when she was sitting close and being quiet. Lexi's eyes were honey bright and warm. Tessa looked right into them and saw something surprising. Loneliness. *Lexi thinks no one loves her*, she thought, and looked carefully at her aura, seeing emerald greens and orange around most of her lean body. But over the heart was a shadow. Tessa wanted to tell her that, but she kept quiet. Reading auras was a skill she was developing in secret. Increasingly, she felt like two people; the outside Tessa and the inside Tessa. And she believed Lexi's shrewd eyes were seeing the inside Tessa.

Lexi hadn't asked the usual questions like, 'How are you getting on at school?' and 'How's your mother?' She'd told Tessa about Selwyn. 'She's three-quarters Arab, if you can work that out – and she's eight years old. I've had her since she was a youngster, and she used to be a show-jumper. Jumped like a stag. I won lots of cups with her – she even beat some of the top horses, even though she's smaller than most of them. But then, one day, she just turned.' Lexi looked sad. She twiddled a piece of grass in her weathered hands.

'Turned? What do you mean?' Tessa asked.

'She wouldn't jump any more. Just refused. And she went so bad-tempered – she wouldn't even let anyone groom her. We tried to give her a rest and train her up again, but she wasn't having it. I'm fond of her, but I don't know why I keep her really – I suppose I'm protecting her. No one else would put up with her. She seems to hate everyone now.'

They both looked at Selwyn, who had turned her back on Lexi and wandered away, eating, her silver coat shining in the sun.

'She's beautiful,' said Tessa. 'I love her.'

She didn't tell Lexi that those words, 'She seems to hate everyone now,' had resonated deep in her heart. Yet she felt

Lexi understood. They stared at one another in silent empathy.

The upset at home had sent Tessa spinning into another emotional turmoil. She felt trapped by the family she loved. Her mother's headache had been frightening. *Is it my fault?* Tessa had thought. *Is she going to die?* Then it loomed again, the thought that sprang up like a billboard in front of her: *Everyone hates me.* She always added, except *Daddy*, and now she added, *except Art, and except Selwyn. And Lexi hasn't had time to hate me yet.*

So there is hope, she thought, as she clung to Jonti in the front of Lexi's Land Rover. *I'm getting a new life. For a week.*

Lexi carried Tessa's box of books towards the stairs, through a hall with a dusty parquet floor and walls covered in coloured rosettes and photographs of horses. 'You won't mind sleeping in the attic room, I hope.'

Tessa followed her up a second staircase which had bare boards and flaking cream paint on the walls. At the top was a bedroom with an iron bedstead, a basket chair, and a big table. Tessa was only interested in the view from the tall sash window. Fields and elm trees, and great silver skies.

'Can I open it?' she asked.

'Like this.' Lexi slid it upwards with her wiry arms. 'But at night, you'll get all sorts of moths coming in. And you can hear the nightingales.'

'And I can see Selwyn out in the field,' Tessa said. 'I shall watch her in the moonlight, and send her secret messages.'

★   ★   ★

'It's eleven o'clock. Lucy should be up by now,' Freddie said. 'If we're going to Abbotsbury, we should go soon.'

'I'll see if she's awake,' Kate said. She got up from the rug where they'd had breakfast overlooking the sparkling bay. Freddie lit a fag and tried to think calmly about what he was going to say to Lucy. Kate had told him, but he guessed she'd been playing it down, looking on the bright side as usual, protecting, always protecting her daughter.

The next minute, Kate was beside him, her eyes flickering with panic. 'Lucy's gone. Her bunk is empty. She's gone, Freddie! Where is she?'

'Check the toilet tent.' Freddie stood up. 'And look all round the caravan, and the bushes. She might have gone for a walk.'

'She was drunk!' Kate said. 'I thought she was out for the count.'

They searched the area around the caravan. It was the highest one in a line of five on the cliff overlooking Bowlys Cove, and no one else seemed to be around. There was no sign of Lucy at all. Freddie went to the edge of the cliff and looked down through clumps of sea pink and yellow kidney vetch. Nothing. But the thought of Lucy falling over that cliff filled him with a roaring, pulsing terror.

'I'll go down and take a look – she could have gone to the shop,' he said shortly, not wanting to alarm Kate. 'You stay here.'

He bounded down the cliff path towards the shop on the beach. He passed the seesaw where Tessa and Lucy had loved to play, and remembered them screaming with joy, one each end of the wooden seesaw. It had iron springs under each end which gave them a fierce bounce. He saw them licking pink ice-cream cones, sitting on the sea wall swinging their brown legs. His children were gone. It dawned like a dark sun in his heart, just as it had when he'd been flying the box kite on his own. Freddie hadn't had a carefree childhood. His childhood had arrived with Lucy and Tessa. He never wanted them to grow up.

The cliff towered over a stretch of black, slimy rocks festooned with seaweed. Further out towards the point were the barnacled hulks of two wrecked fishing boats. It was low tide and the blue-black clusters of mussel shells glistened on them in the sun. What if Lucy had fallen on to those treacherous rocks? No one would have seen her there. And the tide, in the night . . . Freddie felt sick with panic. Lucy. His little Lucy, with her blonde swirl of hair and dazzling smile. Right now, he'd forgive her anything – anything just to have her back.

White-faced, he went into the shop, past the colourful buckets and spades and kites hanging from the doorway.

'Have you seen my daughter – Lucy – she's got blonde hair – you know her, don't you?'

'Oh I know Lucy, 'course I do,' the man said. 'No, she hasn't been in here this morning. You don't look too good, sir. Do you want to sit down?'

'No thanks,' Freddie said. 'I've gotta find her.'

'She's a big girl now – a young lady, isn't she? Could she have gone off with her friends?'

'What friends d'you mean?'

'Those lads, on Vespa scooters, were here early this morning. Made such a noise – and left such a mess – crisp packets and broken bottles. I was glad when they'd gone.'

'Which way did they go?'

'They were going off to Burton Bradstock, they said. And they'd mostly got girls on the back, all dolled up with eye make-up – eyes like piss holes in the snow, some of 'em had. And skirts! I never saw skirts so short in my life.'

Freddie went back to the caravan and found Kate sitting on the steps, a piece of paper in her hand.

'Lucy left a note,' she said, and looked up at him with tormented eyes. 'And – oh, it's so cruel.'

Freddie took the pale blue sheet of Basildon Bond writing paper, his mouth twitching as he read the words Lucy had scribbled there in a leaking ballpoint pen.

Dear Mum and Dad,

I am fed up with being treated like a child. I am seventeen, and it's 1960, not 1940. Why can't you be like other parents and let me have some fun and have a boyfriend? All you want is for me to pass exams so that you can boast to your silly friends. You can't lock me up forever you know! So stop behaving like two old-fashioned fuddy duddies, and let me go out, and stop judging my friends. They're nice people, and I'm going to Burton Bradstock with them, on the back of a scooter. And if I want a drink I shall have one.

Lucy

Stunned and hurt, Freddie and Kate went into the caravan and sat together on the seat, sharing a bitter silence.

'Please, Freddie – let's get in the car and go and fetch her,' Kate said eventually.

'No,' Freddie insisted. 'I'm not going running after her. If she wants to throw her life away like that – let her – she'll learn a hard lesson.'

Kate look shocked. 'That's not like you, Freddie.'

'I can harden my heart,' Freddie said bitterly. 'That's what she's done. Hardened her heart against us.'

'She's young,' Kate pleaded. 'She's had years of studying, and she just wants to be like her friends. We must stand by her, Freddie.'

Freddie shook his head and retreated into the forests of his mind. He pictured the Somerset Levels on a windy day when you could stand on the ridgeway and see the shadows of clouds racing over sunlit pastures. Each bright meadow was a thought, chased by a shadow, and each hopeful green stalk was bent by the wind, its intentions shredded and scattered across the earth. The conflict in his mind tore itself apart like the wind ripping the grass. He could forgive Lucy anything if she had fallen from the cliff, but if she'd run away with some layabout on a scooter, he could never forgive her!

Tessa and Lexi sat on a tartan rug at the edge of the woods, an hour before sunset. A nightingale picnic, was what Lexi called it, but it was different from the picnics Tessa was used to. There were no cucumber sandwiches and boiled eggs dipped in salt, and no threats about eating nicely and eating crusts. Lexi had thrown the picnic together in a saggy canvas holdall. A sharp knife, a box of matches, a frying pan, tin mugs and plates, bread rolls, a lump of butter rolled in grease-proof paper, two onions, four chipolatas and two Penguin biscuits. 'You carry the whistling kettle,' she'd said, 'and keep it level – it's full of water.'

Lexi showed her how to cut a square of turf and light a fire. 'You can do it next time,' she said, building a ring of flat stones around the fire pit as Tessa chopped the onions, awkwardly, on one of the tin plates. 'We're having hot-dogs, like they have at the carnival, only nicer!'

Jonti wagged his tail when he heard the word 'dog', and gave a little bark. 'He thinks it's funny, don't you, Jonti?' Tessa said, her eyes streaming from the onions. She smiled at Lexi. 'Mum and Dad never let me do this. Light a fire and cook sausages. It's fun.'

'It's survival skills,' Lexi said. 'Who knows when we might need them?'

Nothing had ever smelled or tasted so delicious as the onions and sausages furiously fried in butter and stuffed generously into a bread roll, the burnt edges of onion glistening in the evening light. Tessa felt alive and contented as she sat on the rug with Lexi, munching, and watching the orange flames criss-crossing, the smoke blowing away from the woods. It felt right and good.

Lexi had surprised Tessa in a number of ways. Firstly, Tessa had seen her without the fierce make-up she sometimes wore, and was reassured to see that Lexi had freckles and a few blotches on her skin. She saw that her eyes had sadness and honesty. She found that Lexi didn't smile a lot, and didn't ask questions. It had seemed to Tessa that all the women in her life were hell-bent on interrogating and manipulating her. Only her father was a safe haven, and he was so often not around when she most needed him.

She felt grateful that Lexi hadn't mentioned her suicide attempt. Gratitude was a new feeling for her, and Tessa wasn't sure how to express it, so she kept quiet.

Lexi had brought some cocoa powder in an old paper bag, and they made two mugs of it from the whistling kettle, and sat sipping it, watching the sun go down over the distant Quantock Hills. Jonti was given a sausage to himself, and lay on the grass growling at it because it was hot. 'Best put him on his lead now, Tessa – do you think? – otherwise he'll be off after rabbits.' She showed Tessa how to damp down the fire and replace the square of turf. 'We can leave the stones here – use them another time,' she said. 'I'd love to do this again.'

'So would I,' Tessa said, and she thought of Lucy and her parents walking along the promenade in Weymouth.

Lexi sat in silence, her back against an ash tree, her eyes watching the darkening landscape. Tessa found her own tree, an oak, and sat against it. The purpose, and the magic, of this picnic was to listen to the nightingales who came every year to breed and sing in the woods that stretched along the south side of the Polden Hills. As twilight deepened, the blackbirds stopped singing and sounded their alarm call, warning each other about the owls now flying silently through the shadows. The stars came out and the wind sighed in the leaves of the woodland canopy.

The whole world seemed hushed, like a symphony of whispers. Tessa felt the power of the dark trees behind her, the ancient wisdom of them, the sense of benediction they breathed upon the earth. The first notes of a sole nightingale, unbelievably loud and pure, burst into the purple twilight, floating on the wind like a diamond point of light upon the sea. Lexi's eyes shone and she smiled at Tessa.

They listened as a second nightingale, then another and another joined the warbling, flute-like chorus until it became a golden sheet of music rippling above the voice of the wind. Tessa felt magic pouring through her, as if she sat in an open doorway and became translucent, letting the stream of sound infuse her with sparkles. She gazed at the dome of the night sky and saw that it was a dark, concentric rainbow beginning on the far edges of the world, with a flush of pink and orange, then palest yellows and aquamarine leading higher into indigo and violet. *No book will ever tell you that*, she thought, remembering something Freddie had said to her: 'You can read every book in every library on earth, and still not know the wonders you can see for yourself.'

She touched the slim scar on her left wrist, and Jonti whined and climbed onto her lap. *I'm glad I came back*, Tessa thought, *I would have missed this beautiful, magical night. I will wear it around my shoulders for the rest of my life, like a cloak of stars.*

As she imagined the cloak of stars, she could feel its velvet swirling around her, and a startling thought flew into her mind. *Perhaps I'm a witch.*

Chapter Thirteen

HILBEGUT

Kate put on her black jacket with the shoulder pads, and swept her hair back into a sleek bun. She went into Tessa's bedroom, picked up her portfolio, checked that the paintings were inside, and carefully closed it, tying the tapes into neat bows.

Annie looked at her suspiciously as she wheeled her bike out of the shed. 'Where are you off to now?'

'A little bit of private business,' Kate said. 'You hang on to Jonti. I don't want him running along the roads with me. Shut him in the kitchen, will you please?'

'I hope this isn't another of your crazy ideas,' Annie said, clipping Jonti onto his lead.

'No – it's one of my GOOD ideas.' Kate had a twinkle in her eyes. 'I'll be an hour or so.'

'Does Freddie know what you're up to?'

'Not yet.'

'And what am I supposed to do with this . . . contraption?' Annie pointed at the green and cream washing machine which was shuddering in the scullery, its lid rattling as it swooshed the sheets to and fro.

'Switch it off in twenty minutes – that switch on the wall. I'll drain it when I get back. Don't put any more Omo in it. You don't need to touch it.'

'I never had a MACHINE to do my washing,' Annie said. 'Look at all this foam bursting out of the lid!'

'It will be all right,' Kate said, and she pushed her bike down the path and rode off on it, leaving Annie scowling at the new washing machine.

Kate sailed down the hill, and out towards Hilbegut in the September sunlight. She followed the road through the river valley, then under the railway and up over the hills, pedalling vigorously, with Tessa's portfolio propped precariously in the front basket.

Hilbegut Court had been part of Kate's childhood. She'd lived next door at Hilbegut Farm, and had often been sent to carry a billy can of fresh milk to the squire. When he'd died, Hilbegut Court had been left derelict for years, until an eccentric academic had bought it and founded an expensive private school. His enterprise had fascinated Kate and she'd followed the frequent reports in the local papers, and listened to the gossip.

'You can't get Tessa in there,' Freddie had said. 'That's for toffs – and it's the most expensive school in Britain, they say. You should see the Daimlers and Jags going in there – and Rolls Royces.'

Undeterred, Kate swept through the grand gates on her bike, and down the sun-dappled drive of copper beeches, thrilled to see the magnificent trees she had loved as a child. It was early September and the trees were shedding their heavy crop of beechnuts, carpeting the ground with their bristly cases. The wheels of her bike crackled over them, and she remembered Freddie's story about how he was always hungry in his childhood and used to fill his pockets with beechnuts to sustain him on his long walk to school. Kate was proud of what Freddie had achieved. A new lorry now stood in the road outside The Pines, next to the black Wolseley, and his haulage business was thriving.

A few heads turned to watch Kate pedalling down the drive, her eyes alight with anticipation. She was excited by the sight of scholarly-looking boys in the grey tweed uniform, shoes polished, faces clean and earnest. Exactly the sort of boy she hoped Tessa would meet. She imagined the white wedding, the grey top hats. At least one of her daughters was going to do it right, Kate thought, satisfied.

She propped her bike against the wall, tucked Tessa's portfolio under her arm, and bustled up the steps. The entrance doors were open, so she straightened her spine and walked into what had been the great hall. It was now divided into offices and classrooms, tastefully built with timber panelling. She eyed the door marked *Headmaster*, but before she could knock, a secretary sprang out from the next-door room, a petite woman with fierce eyes, a beehive of silver hair, and well-powdered high cheekbones.

'Can I help you?' she asked stonily.

Kate thought, *Ah – the guard dog*. She'd heard about this iconic secretary who protected the exhausted headmaster from predatory parents.

'Good morning,' Kate said pleasantly. 'I'm Mrs Barcussy from The Pines at Monterose. I'd like to speak to the headmaster, please.'

'Have you made an appointment?'

'No. But I'm sure he will want to hear what I have to say.' Kate took a step towards the hallowed door.

'Nobody sees the headmaster without an appointment. And the waiting list for appointments is long.'

'I'm sure he will want to see me,' Kate said confidently. 'I have a VERY talented daughter, and I know how much he cares about helping talented young people.'

'This is a boys' public school, Mrs Barcussy.'

'But I read in the *Gazette* that the school is now taking girls, especially those with a rare talent, like my daughter, Tessa. Believe me, when he sees her work, he will want her in this school.'

'I'm sorry, Mrs Barcussy, but the headmaster is extremely busy. He cannot see you now.'

'Then I'll wait.' Kate sat down on a chair that looked like a throne. She beamed at the secretary's appalled face, and said in a conspiratorial whisper, 'He's bound to come out of that door sometime, isn't he?'

The two women eyeballed one another.

'I don't mind waiting,' Kate said. 'Isn't this a lovely chair? It's nice to sit down. I've just ridden six miles on my bicycle, and the countryside is so beautiful in September, don't you think?'

Eclipsed by Kate's radiant confidence, the secretary looked annoyed. 'I will see if he's got five minutes,' she hissed, and opened the hallowed door just wide enough to allow the silver beehive hairdo to pop though. 'Excuse me, Mr Perrow, but I have a very persistent lady here.'

Freddie arrived home at lunchtime to find Annie shovelling foam out of the scullery. She was piling it into a bowl and tipping it onto the lawn where it made a three-foot high meringue, hissing with popping bubbles. Jonti was crouching in the grass growling at it.

'Look at this!' Annie said, her face pink from exertion. 'Kate went off on her bike again, and left me with that out-of-control contraption.'

Freddie raised an eyebrow. He wished Kate was there to laugh about it.

'She said to switch it off, but I couldn't reach the switch for the foam. It was coming at me,' Annie said.

Freddie strode into the scullery, turned off the switch and there was peace. 'It'll burn the motor out if you let it run too long,' he said. 'Did Kate say where she was going?'

'No – but she had a look in her eye.'

'Hmm.' Freddie sat down at the table. 'You go and have a rest, Mother, I've got some paperwork to do.'

When Annie had gone, he turfed the money out of his pockets and sorted it into piles on the table. Pound notes, ten shilling notes, and some silver, mixed up with crumpled receipts, Fox's Glacier Mints and bits of string. He counted it, clipped it together and put it in the wooden box they kept on top of the dresser. He was replacing it when Kate came up the path, wheeling her bike. She looked jubilant, and when she saw him in the window, she quickly unpinned her hair and shook it back from her face.

'Now, what do you think I've done?' She gave him a hug, then took off her jacket and hung it over a chair.

'You're hot,' he said.

'I'm boiling,' Kate said. 'I rode all the way to Hilbegut and back.'

'What for? A ride?'

'No.' Kate's eyes were sparkling. 'Guess what I've done, Freddie?'

'What?'

'I . . . have got Tessa the chance of a scholarship at Hilbegut School!'

Freddie was shocked. His first thought was to say, 'Oh no,' but he managed to keep quiet. Seeing Kate happy was a rare treat after the summer of conflict they'd had with Lucy. They'd stayed awake at night talking about it, and worrying. 'We can only stand by and pick up the pieces,' Kate said repeatedly, as Lucy's social life got wilder and wilder. Freddie hated her boyfriend, Tim, and his lifestyle, his hair, his insolent grin, his arrogance and his noisy scooter.

Freddie found it hard to maintain stability. It felt as if he and Kate were being torn apart by their differing views. Kate had been to a private boarding school and she wanted Lucy and Tessa to 'marry money'. It cut deep into Freddie's confidence. He began to feel that love was not enough now – he needed attitude as well. The idea of Tessa, of all people, going to Hilbegut School appalled and frightened him. He felt unable to bridge the widening gap. His children, and his self-esteem, were being splintered away from him.

'Don't look so worried, dear,' Kate said, flopping into a chair. 'I'd love a glass of water. I couldn't spit sixpence!'

'I hope you didn't say that at Hilbegut School.'

Freddie got her one. He looked into her eyes in silence, seeing the dancing light in them, something he had loved, yet now it looked dangerous. It looked like a glittering curtain screening something low and undesirable. He wanted to rip it aside.

'I met Mr Perrow,' Kate gushed, 'and he's such a powerful man – but so understanding. They call him Robin Hood in Hilbegut. He makes the rich pay for the poor. He takes a rich man's son and uses the fees to give scholarships to talented children like Tessa. As soon as he saw her artwork, he was interested.'

'You showed him Tessa's paintings?' Freddie was even more shocked. 'I don't think she's going to be happy about that. Those pictures are private to her.'

'Oh, it doesn't matter,' Kate said, 'it got her IN!'

'Even the one . . . with the angel – did you show him that?'

'He picked it out,' said Kate. 'You should have seen his face, Freddie. He stared at it with such an intent, intelligent look in his eyes. Then he stared at me with a piercing gaze, and he said, 'This girl is a visionary – she needs to be here – we have an extraordinarily good art teacher who will know exactly how to nurture Tessa's talent.' He said they could get her into the best art college in the country!'

Kate paused to take a breath. Her bright brown eyes looked at him expectantly. 'Well, say something, Freddie.'

'A visionary? Is that what he called her?' Freddie shook his head. The word swam through the dark waters of his mind, like Tessa, so long ago, swimming naked and afraid across the Mill Pool. A visionary! His thoughts rolled back, fourteen years, to Madame Eltura. She had used that same word. He thought of the sealed envelope now lying in the secret drawer of Granny Barcussy's bureau. Should he open it? Was now the time? Or should he destroy it? If those words got into the wrong hands . . . 'But he hasn't even met Tessa,' he objected. 'Surely he's not daft enough to award a scholarship to a girl he hasn't met! Even I wouldn't do that.'

'That's arranged,' Kate said, beaming at him joyfully. 'He wants us to take her there for an interview – a chat, he said – after school today. I said we'd go.'

'So . . . you want me to take you in the car?'

'Yes please, dear. I'd be so proud to arrive there with you in our lovely car.'

'And . . . you want me to agree to this?'

Kate gazed at him trustingly. 'Of course, dear. It goes without saying. We must support Tessa. It's a golden opportunity for her. Let's not stand in her way.'

'She's more likely to stand in her own way.'

'Then we must talk her round. You know how unhappy she is at the grammar school. She can't wait to be fifteen and leave – then what will she do? Work in the shoe factory? What else is there round here, Freddie? Can you really see Tessa on a factory assembly line sticking soles on shoes for the rest of her life? When she could go to Hilbegut and spend two wonderful years doing Art and English which is what she loves. She can take her A levels there and get into Art College. Wouldn't you have loved a chance like that?'

'Ah – I would have,' Freddie said, feeling Kate's enthusiasm again sucking him towards a place he didn't want to explore. 'Well, I suppose it won't hurt to let her go and have a look at this man and his fancy scholarship.'

'I'm not going,' Tessa said wearily. She wanted to put steel in her voice, and in her eyes. Ice blue, blade sharp steel. She had used it frequently, but today the energy she needed to manifest it just wasn't there. At the end of the school day, she wanted to crawl into a cave and be left alone. Her mother knew that, and mostly respected it. So why were BOTH her parents dragging her out to see this intimidating school with its hordes of horrible boys? And why today? 'You know I hate Thursdays,' she added.

'Well, this could be your lucky Thursday.' Kate turned in the front seat of the Wolseley to look at her daughter's mask of a face.

Like Freddie, Tessa saw the glitter in Kate's eyes. *Delusion,* she thought. *Mum just can't stop believing she can make me into someone else.*

She glanced miserably at the river valley, and a train burst out of the hills and sped over the viaduct, like a symbol of her escaping freedom. Tessa waited for Freddie to say what she knew he would say.

'Ah – that's The Cornishman.'

Tessa watched his eyes in the driving mirror and thought they looked wistful. Did he share her secret dream? *Maybe he does want to escape,* she thought, *and he's trying to conform to what Mum expects.*

Since her meeting with Art, Tessa had built the dream of running away to Cornwall. She would go on The Cornishman. She'd even taken to timing her walks with Jonti so that she could watch that train go through, and feel the fierce energy of it reinforcing her dream. Once she had leaned over the bridge and thrown a moon daisy onto its roof as it thundered through the town. 'Take my love to Art,' she'd said, aloud. But when the train had gone, the moon daisy lay forlornly on the track, dying and discarded.

Her dream was so secret that she hadn't written it in her diary. Kate or Lucy would read it and make a fuss. Sometimes Tessa felt her mind was like a vast museum of dreams, with more and more archives and exhibits in glass cases to which she alone held the keys.

'Can't you tell her, Dad? I'm not going.' Tessa looked at Freddie's eyes in the driving mirror. Cornflower blue, and glistening with secret thoughts which he kept firmly under the tweed cap he always wore. Today it was his best one, clean and grey like lichen on tree bark.

'You let me do the driving, Tessa,' he said. 'If I go arguing with you we'll end up in the ditch.'

The narrow road across the Levels made this a serious possibility. One wheel on the spongy grass verge and a car would roll into the peat-black rhyne below. Tessa knew the rhynes were fifteen foot deep, and some of them yielded up blackened stumps of prehistoric trees which the dredger had dumped along the banks. She stared into the tea-brown water, wishing she was a carefree child again, searching the banks for the green shells of freshwater mussels.

She thought about the look in her mother's eyes. It was screening sadness. In her diary, Tessa had written of their 'summer of discontent'. Until that summer, she thought her mother's optimism was invincible. Lucy had been there like a bright star, until the Weymouth week, and suddenly the family's golden child had turned hostile and hormonal.

To Tessa, it had felt like a thunderstorm, brooding with anger, firing barbs of stinging rain. The storm was inside their home, under beds and under tables, billowing around heads and hearts. It was inside Lucy. Even Tessa missed the old Lucy. The new, resentful, bolshie Lucy rarely wanted to talk to her now or do any of the things they had done together. Increasingly, her parents were turning to Tessa to salvage their dreams. She began to feel responsible for their happiness.

The tyres crackled over the beechnut carpet and the car swept up the drive to Hilbegut School. Tessa made up her mind to be polite but uncooperative.

'You look smart, Daddy,' she said as Freddie got out of the car.

''Tis me wedding suit,' he said. 'Weddings and funerals.'

'And special occasions. Like this golden opportunity for our daughter,' Kate said, her face radiant as she led the way in.

Freddie took Tessa's arm. He looked into her eyes. 'You be proud,' he said. 'Proud of yourself and what you can do. I'd have given anything for a chance like this, Tessa.'

The headmaster came out to meet them, and all Tessa saw were his ancient eyes finding hers, like a man high above her on a tall ship, throwing a lifeline down as she struggled in the cold deep ocean. She had no choice but to grasp it.

'Tessa!' he said, as if he'd found a diamond in the sand. 'I'm honoured to meet you.'

Tessa took the hand he held out to her, and felt its bones squeezing her bones. She looked at his aura and saw a flare of aquamarine and white with a tired shell of a man lurking inside. *He doesn't want to die*, she thought, *he really wants to be here, and he wants to meet ME*. She didn't dare to speak, but gave him a smile, from her eyes.

Mr Perrow shook hands with Freddie, holding onto his hand for a long time as the two men studied each other's eyes.

'I thought we'd go over to the Art Department.' Mr Perrow took them along the side of Hilbegut Court and across the yard to what had once been the stables and coach house. Tessa followed, staying close to her father. They passed a group of boys who were standing under a big horse chestnut tree, with books and folders under their arms. They glanced curiously at the girl with the chestnut hair and pale blue eyes, appraising her; one of them, with a quiff of hair falling across his face, eyed her up and down. Tessa set her face to mutinous and stony. She turned her head away from them.

Mr Perrow showed them in to a spacious studio with a high glass roof. Immediately, Tessa felt a change. The energy in there was calm and beautiful, like a glade in the woods. The walls were covered in colourful artwork. Tessa glanced at her father, seeing his eyes light up with interest.

'Ooh, isn't it lovely?' Kate said. 'And I remember this as a stable block.'

They were introduced to Mrs Appleby, the art teacher, a pale-skinned, pale blonde creature with luminous eyes and a soft voice. She wore a denim smock covered in paint, a tie-dyed orange and purple skirt, and open-toed sandals. 'Tessa! How wonderful to meet you, dear,' she said. 'I hope we can work in harmony.'

Tessa looked at her, intrigued. Was this enchantress actually a teacher? She drifted around the studio and Tessa followed her silently, surprised at the variety of media. There were fat tubes of paint, and more brushes than she'd ever seen, boxes of charcoal, and trays of pastels in wonderful colours. There were stacks of sugar paper in different shades, there was cartridge paper, and luxuriously textured 'Bockinford'. 'And these are something new,' said the enchantress, showing her some brand new boxes of rich, brightly coloured sticks. 'These are oil pastels – they're gorgeous – I can't resist them.'

'I've never used pastels,' Tessa said, and she itched to pick them up and stroke them across the paper. 'I've never used anything except pencils and my paint box.'

'Well, you can do all that here – and we have a pottery next door, and a textiles department where you can do tie-dyeing and Batik. You can make yourself some clothes.' Mrs Appleby smiled beguilingly at her. 'I made this skirt.'

'It's lovely,' Tessa said. She could feel herself thawing, especially when Mr Perrow steered her parents away to look at the pottery and woodwork rooms.

'Do you paint at school?' asked Mrs Appleby.

'Only because I have to,' Tessa said. 'We just do still life – bottles and fruit – I find it boring. I don't see the point in copying something that you can see anyway. I think art should show you something you've never seen before.'

Mrs Appleby touched Tessa's sleeve like a butterfly pitching there. 'I think we're kindred spirits, Tessa. I'd really like to work with you.'

'Shall I show you my paintings?' Tessa asked.

'Oh, please – do.'

Tessa untied the ribbons of the portfolio, and took out her detailed pencil drawings of Selwyn. She laid them along the workbench in order. 'They tell a story,' she said, 'and it's a true story about a horse I'm in love with. She's called Selwyn, and I worked all the summer with her at my friend Lexi's place.'

'She's beautiful.'

'I'll tell you her story if you like,' Tessa said, moving to the first picture. 'This is Selwyn with tears in her eyes because no one understood what was wrong with her. Then, this is Selwyn making a face and being a bad tempered horse – see, she's got sparks coming out of her aura.'

'Her aura?' Mrs Appleby raised her eyebrows. 'Can you see auras?' she whispered.

Tessa checked to see if her parents were out of earshot. 'Yes,' she said. 'Yes – I do.' And when she spoke those words to another human being, she felt an archway of light open in her mind. 'I'm not supposed to talk about it. In case people think I'm mad.'

'I don't think you're mad, Tessa. You're a sensitive, gifted girl, and here, in this space, with me, you will be free to express yourself.'

Before Tessa could stop them, the tears brimmed over and ran down her cheeks. *The brimming river*, she thought, *it's been dammed since I was seven years old*. She brushed her tears away with the back of her hand. She wanted to tell Mrs Appleby that she'd tried to kill herself, and why. Instead she said, 'I'll go on telling you about Selwyn. Now – this next picture is Selwyn sharing her secret with me. Everyone assumed she was being bad-tempered and awkward, but she wasn't. I listened to her feelings in a special way I have with animals, and she told me she had hurt her back trying to jump too high – and now she can't bear anyone to ride her or even put a saddle on her – and she was devastated because she couldn't jump anymore. So I told Lexi, and Lexi is trying to find a vet who can treat her.'

'Poor Selwyn.'

'I can ride now,' Tessa said, 'but I'll never ride Selwyn, and she knows that, so she lets me lead her around and groom her and talk to her, and I try to send her healing for her painful back. She lets me touch it now.'

'That's wonderful, Tessa!'

Tessa smiled, and the smile felt warm and brand new. 'So,' she continued, 'I took the pictures onwards to help Selwyn recreate herself. This one is Selwyn as a unicorn in the pastures of heaven. And this last one is Selwyn as Pegasus, with wings, coming out of the sunlit clouds.'

'These are extraordinary!' Mrs Appleby raised her soft voice to a squeak of excitement. She touched the rippling mane with a manicured finger, as if she was touching the real Selwyn. 'It must have taken you hours to do this, Tessa – what pencils did you use?'

'I've only got two,' Tessa said, 'an HB and a 2B.'

'So who taught you to draw like this?'

Tessa shrugged. 'I just can.'

Mrs Appleby's luminous eyes shone into hers. 'It's not only the drawing skill,' she said, 'it's the emotion in them. These pictures mean something. They – they speak to my soul.'

'My Dad has helped me. He does stone carving, and he

used to paint. He helped me a lot when I was little, but now – well, he's usually working. Shall I show you some more?'

'Yes please – oh my goodness, what's THAT?' Mrs Appleby exclaimed as Tessa shyly pulled out the angel painting which had so impressed Freddie.

'I'm not allowed to talk about angels, so I painted this one,' Tessa said, and her heart began to beat faster with anxiety. Had she gone too far? She could hear the footsteps and voices from the studios beyond, and the squeak of Freddie's best shoes. Her mother was doing most of the talking as usual.

'This is a startling, surprising picture. It's refreshing. I've never seen a painting like this before,' Mrs Appleby enthused. 'Has it got a story too?'

'Yes, it has.' Tessa was silent for a few seconds, feeling yet another dam bursting in her consciousness. She'd made up her mind to be mutinous and monosyllabic, and not talk. She'd thought such a strategy would put them off trying to entice her into the school with its horrible boys. But Mrs Appleby's soft voice had somehow opened her up. After years of silence, Tessa found herself talking – freely – the way she talked to Selwyn. It felt as if the horse was in the studio with her, like a guardian who held the key to her soul. 'Well, Dad was really upset with us one day,' she began. 'He's rarely angry, but he was then, and the anger was hurting him so much, I couldn't bear it. I looked at him to try and convey how deeply I understood, when I saw the angel in the room with him, like a sunrise. Her wings were reaching the walls and her face was so dazzlingly bright. I tried to tell Dad but he clammed up on me, so I tried to paint her. I did it really quickly.'

She turned and saw her parents standing behind her, with Mr Perrow. Their eyes were shining with excitement, and pride. *I can't let them down*, Tessa thought. She felt energised by the talk with Mrs Appleby. She felt a bond with her. *I could do this – I could do art and English. If I can survive in this place. For now.*

They stood outside under the horse chestnut tree, talking about A levels and Art Colleges. Tessa glanced at her father. His eyes were sparkling, and he was fully engaged with the conversation. For once, he hadn't noticed the sparrowhawk, but Tessa watched it hovering, high in the blue air above Hilbegut. She gasped as it swooped above them. The underside of its blade-like wings were a rich cream, its hooked beak glinted and its eyes gleamed like tiny mirrors. And now, the high-pitched scream of a young swallow, snatched from the sky, and carried west. *I am that swallow*, Tessa thought.

Chapter Fourteen

TURNING POINTS

'I'd like a chat with Tessa on her own,' Mr Perrow said, 'before we finalise our agreement and give you the formal offer of a two years' scholarship. Is that all right with you, Tessa? You can have someone with you if you wish.'

'I'll come on my own,' Tessa said, looking firmly at her parents and trying to ignore the flicker of fear that passed through Kate's eyes. She read its warning message. It said something like, 'Don't tell him the whole truth.'

She followed Mr Perrow into his study. Instead of sitting behind his desk, he led her to two bucket chairs, and sat down beside her. 'Have you got any questions you'd like to ask me?' he said.

'Yes – do I have to wear my hair in plaits if I come to this school?' Tessa asked.

'No – it's your hair,' he said, 'and you're a young lady now, not a child.'

'And do I HAVE to do games?'

'No. It's there if you want to do it.'

'And do I HAVE to pretend to be like everyone else?'

'Definitely not. We want YOU here, Tessa, not a sheep.'

That made her smile. She fiddled with the soft ends of her chestnut plaits and wondered whether she dared unplait it right now in the headmaster's office. Her mother would say, 'That's VERY bad manners'. She decided to wait until she was in the car, and then undo the hated braids.

Mr Perrow's eyes were searching hers. 'Is there anything else I need to know about you, Tessa? Perhaps something your parents wouldn't have told me?'

Tessa hesitated. 'There are lots of things like that.'

'It doesn't have to be a good thing. It can be a bad thing you want to be honest about,' said Mr Perrow. 'Trying to be perfect can destroy us! It's better if we can be open about who we really are. If there is anything, Tessa, anything at all you think I should know, then please tell me now.'

'I need to think about it,' Tessa said.

'Take your time.'

Her thoughts jostled for attention. She would be fifteen in November, so there was still the option of leaving school and 'being free'. Art had sent her a postcard that she treasured. It was a picture of a suntanned man crouching on a surfboard, his hair flying as he rode on the avalanche of foam from an enormous wave. Behind him the ocean sparkled and more indigo blue waves were towering and breaking. It had been sent from St Ives in Cornwall, and Tessa knew it had a railway station. She could go, on The Cornishman. But first she'd have to earn some money, and deceive her parents, or break their hearts like Lucy had done. Or both!

So what was there to lose by telling the truth to this wise old man who had followed his dreams and created a school? A school which had teachers like Mrs Appleby. She took a deep breath and tried to make her voice adult and mechanical. 'I tried to kill myself . . . a few months ago.'

She waited for his reaction with a thumping heart, thinking her mother would never forgive her for wrecking this chance of a scholarship. Her father would retreat into his silent land where pain and disappointment made stony places where no plant could flourish. She wished she hadn't said it.

But Mr Perrow only raised his eyebrows. He leaned forward, his calm eyes inviting her to talk.

'Mum tried to hush it up,' Tessa said. 'I'm not allowed to talk about it to anyone. Even my sister doesn't know. Nobody knows why I did it.'

'Do you want me to know?'

'I did want people to know, but it doesn't matter now. My life is better, since I met Selwyn and Lexi.' Tessa looked at Mr Perrow steadily. 'I'm a loner. I never had any friends, and my family think I'm a troublemaker. But I don't actually want to make trouble. I'm hypersensitive. I can hear and see things which other people don't.'

'What kind of things?'

'Unacceptable things. Spirit people, for example.'

Mr Perrow narrowed his eyes. He fidgeted and raked his bone-thin fingers over his remaining strands of grey hair, plastered to his weather-beaten scalp with Brylcreem. 'Do you see any spirit people in this room?' he enquired.

Tessa felt her face relax into a smile of relief. 'Can I tell you?' she asked. 'No one ever lets me do that!'

'Yes – please tell me.' He sat forward, clutching the arms of the chair.

'There's a lady in a green dress,' Tessa said at once. 'She's lovely. The dress is bright green, and she has an emerald ring on her finger, and a necklace of tiny white seashells. And – she's got a white fluffy cat in her arms. It's a male cat and he's purring, a lot, and he's purring for you, not for her, because he's your cat.'

Mr Perrow looked suddenly vulnerable. His hands trembled and he pressed them together hard. He stared at Tessa with startled eyes. 'My wife!' he whispered. 'You saw my wife – green was her favourite colour – you couldn't possibly have known that! And the cat! He was indeed my cat. I adored him. Largo, he was called, after a piece of music. I'm astonished, Tessa – astonished – and grateful. What a gift – what a marvellous gift you have. It's going to help countless people – one day.'

Tessa beamed. She watched Mr Perrow reconstructing his headmaster image, the wonder on his face dissected by a frown. She knew what was coming. *Goodbye smile*, she thought.

'BUT,' he began, 'you're too young to own such a gift – and, listen to me, young lady, it is a GIFT and not a curse as you've been led to believe. That's why, Tessa, you MUST accept this scholarship. We will help you to build a strong career – a safe platform to support you until you can do your true work. No – don't switch off – keep that light in your eyes, always. The world needs it.'

Tessa heard the passion in his voice. She tried to respond. She tried to snatch back the smile, like the sparrowhawk catching the swallow. But the life of the smile was gone, diving into the dark.

'I'm like a bird in a tunnel,' she said. 'A bird that must walk forever, believing that when it reaches the exit, it will be too old to fly.'

Back at The Pines, Annie dragged herself up the stairs, a tray of cocoa and lardy cake balanced awkwardly on the arm that wasn't clinging to the banister. She put the tray down on the lid of the blanket box and listened to the crying coming from Lucy's bedroom. It didn't sound normal to Annie. She'd watched Lucy come stumbling home, bent double with pain, her face red and smudgy, her short blonde hair backcombed and sprayed into what Annie thought was a ridiculous beehive.

She tapped on Lucy's door, and the crying stopped. 'Go away. I hate you all,' Lucy yelled, and her voice was cracked and growly.

'It's Granny, Lucy, and I'm not going away. I brought you lardy cake and cocoa.'

'I don't want FOOD. I'm slimming. Go away.'

'I'm coming in.' Annie pushed Lucy's door open, and went in. She stood there, solidly, in her slippers, the tray in her hand.

Lucy was lying on the bed with her face to the wall. A tangle of clothes and shoes protruded from under the bed, and there were posters on the wall of Elvis and The Beatles. Lucy's red Dansette record player was on the floor with a stack of 78s on the spindle, ready to play. A black leather jacket with studs hung over the pink chair in front of Lucy's kidney-shaped, glass-topped dressing table with its pink net skirt.

Annie looked at the jacket disapprovingly. 'Whose is that?'

'No one's. It's none of your business.'

Annie eased the tray onto Lucy's bedside table, among the bottles of nail varnish. She put the lid on a jar of Pond's Cold Cream which was lying open. She sat down on the bed, and stirred the cocoa with a teaspoon, loudly. 'This cocoa's lovely and hot. Why don't you have a sip? Wrap your hands round it. 'Tis comforting.'

Lucy gave an extravagant sigh and turned over. 'Don't you ever give up?' she quipped.

'No,' Annie said. 'Never. Not on you, Lucy. I've given up on that sister of yours. But not on you. Here you are. Drink up.'

Lucy wrapped her fingers around the mug of cocoa. It was her favourite mug, with The Beatles on it, and it was deep – deep enough for her to breathe the chocolatey steam and feel the warmth in the palms of her hands. She sipped it in silence, her eyes staring blankly out of the window.

'I was a girl, once,' said Annie, 'and I brought up two daughters. I know more than you think I do, about girls growing up.'

Lucy looked at her then. 'Oh Gran,' she muttered, and put down the cocoa mug. 'You're so kind. Coming upstairs with your bad leg. Where is everyone?'

'Kate and Freddie went out in the car, all dressed up. They were fetching Tessa from school and taking her out some-where. That's all I know.'

'They didn't bother inviting ME, did they?'

'Well – you don't usually want to go these days, do you?' Annie said, and the words died on her lips as she studied Lucy's blotchy complexion and desperate eyes.

'Oh no – it's happening again,' cried Lucy, suddenly doubling up with pain. She rolled onto her side and curled up, clutching her stomach. 'It's cramp. Terrible cramp. It keeps happening, Gran. What's wrong with me? I'm so frightened.'

Annie gave her a hug. Lucy was hot and tense, her shoul-ders hard, her breathing panicky and fast. She clung to Annie like a terrified cat.

'What kind of pain is it? Whereabouts in your tummy?'

'It's like – waves of cramp – low down and round my back as well. It comes and goes – and it's worse every time.'

'Is it your period?'

'No . . .' Lucy wept. 'I can't tell you, Gran. I can't.'

'Shall I call Doctor Jarvis?'

'No. And don't tell Mum either. Please, Gran. Please.'

Annie looked at her shrewdly. 'Has it gone now? The pain?'

'It's easing.' Lucy looked shaken. She lay back against the pillows, her hands over her tummy. 'Please, God, don't let it come again.'

'Will you let me feel your tummy?' Annie asked, and Lucy nodded. Annie heaved herself to her feet. She put both hands gently on the baggy black top Lucy was wearing, and felt her tense body, running her hands over it, over the womb. She left them there for a few long minutes, trying to sense what was wrong. She remembered that years ago she had used her hands to give secret healing. She'd never talked about it, but Freddie knew. It was a gift from long ago, her most precious secret. She kept it hidden like a jewel. Strictly private. But she trusted it. *I'm never wrong*, she thought as she felt a spark of life, another life, in Lucy's womb. A dying spark, like one from a bonfire, floating into the sky like an orange star, then vanishing into nothingness.

'You're pregnant, aren't you?' she said.

Lucy nodded, smearing tears from her cheeks with the corner of the sheet. 'Please, please, Gran – don't tell Mum and Dad. Please.'

'I won't,' Annie promised. 'But you should, Lucy. Are you bleeding?'

Lucy put her hand down, and found the blood, unexpectedly reddening her clothes. She looked at Annie in horror. 'What's happening? I can't be pregnant and have a period, can I?'

'You're losing it, dear. It happened to me a few times. Terrible it was. This baby isn't meant to be born,' Annie said. She tried to speak gently. She loved Lucy, but she was shocked at her behaviour. 'You must let me ring the doctor, Lucy.'

241

'No, Gran. No. He'll tell Mum and Dad.'

'You've gotta forget about that, Lucy. Whether you like it or not, I'm going to ring Doctor Jarvis. And you'd better tell him everything – if you did something to bring this on. Did you?' Annie looked suspiciously at a glass bottle sticking out of the pocket of the black leather jacket. She pulled it out. 'Gin! You've been on the gin. Is that what he gave you?'

'A girl I know told me gin would get rid of it,' Lucy said.

Annie tutted. She hobbled out of the room and down the stairs, leaving Lucy screaming and crying. 'No, Gran – please don't. Please! It'll ruin my bloody life.'

'Swearing at me now. My own grandchild!' Annie muttered. She scowled at the telephone on its high pedestal, took a deep breath and picked it up. The receiver shook in her hand as she waited for the operator.

'Number please.'

Annie shouted into the mysterious black hole. 'I gotta talk to Doctor Jarvis. I don't know his number.'

Tessa sat on a canvas chair in the hospital waiting room, looking at the flowers in her hand. She'd picked them for Lucy, thoughtfully choosing the ones she hoped her sister would like. A pink rose, some white chrysanthemums, marigolds and blue Michaelmas daisies. She'd made a posy with a ring of scented herbs around the flowers. Mint, lemon balm and lavender. Then she'd decorated a strip of drawing paper, cut a scalloped edge, and wrapped it around them. She'd put a wish into every flower. A wish for Lucy. While Tessa was making the posy in the garden, a tiny, birdlike woman had been there, advising her which flower to pick. 'The lemon balm and lavender will calm the mind,' she'd said. 'The mint will bring clarity. The marigolds have healing power and their petals can be used to make ointment. The rose is for healing the heart.'

Tessa had glanced at the woman's lively face and thought she recognised her from an old photograph Freddie had in a silver frame. 'Are you Granny Barcussy?' she asked.

The reply came to her from a great distance, like a voice ringing across a valley in the mountains. 'I am, dear. I am Granny Barcussy, and I'm with you all the way, Tessa. I'm your spirit Granny, your forever Granny.'

Then she had vanished into the light like a thistle seed on the wind, leaving Tessa standing perfectly still in the morning sun, the posy in her hand.

'You can go in now, and see Lucy,' Kate said, coming into the waiting room with Lucy's clothes rolled up in a bundle under her arm. 'Daddy is sitting in the car with a face like thunder.'

'Why is he so angry?' Tessa asked.

'Oh, he'll get over it. Don't you worry about it,' Kate said. 'You go and see Lucy – she's in a room by herself. Second door on the left.'

'You've been crying, Mum.'

'Yes, I did have a little cry,' Kate admitted. 'But it will all blow over. You just think about that scholarship. We're so proud of you.'

'That's a change!' Tessa said, and immediately regretted it when she saw the hurt in Kate's eyes.

Tessa hadn't been told what was wrong with Lucy. She shook her hair back, took the posy, and walked in to see her, a bit apprehensively.

Lucy was lying propped against a stack of pillows, wearing the frilly nylon nightie Kate had taken in for her. The blonde beehive had collapsed into a wiry mess, and for once Lucy wore no make-up. Her skin looked mottled and unhealthy. She looked at Tessa with hard eyes. 'Hiya.'

'Hiya. I brought you these from the garden.' Tessa put the posy into Lucy's hands, but she hardly glanced at it.

'Thanks,' she said and let the posy fall onto the sheet, the flowers pointing away from her.

'So how are you?' Tessa asked.

Lucy turned her head away and stared at the wall. 'Who cares?'

'I do.'

'That's news to me,' said Lucy bitterly.

'What's actually wrong with you? Nobody's told me why you're in here, Lucy.'

'Oh, they wouldn't have, would they?' Lucy turned and looked at her with haunted eyes. 'Well, I'll tell you, and it's not pleasant, little sister. Maybe it'll help you grow up. I had sex with Tim – yes, sex – S-E-X, little sister. And I got pregnant. I'm in here because I had a miscarriage.'

'What's that?' asked Tessa, shocked.

'My baby came too early, and the pain was awful – the worst pain I've ever had. Gran found me screaming on the bed – while you lot were swanning round that posh school – I begged her not to ring the doctor, but she did, and he went and told Mum and Dad, and now my life is RUINED. Dad won't even speak to me.'

Tessa sat down on the bed. She felt Lucy's desperation. But she couldn't think of the right words.

'The baby's dead,' Lucy said in a rasping voice, and she lifted her hands in a gesture of hopelessness, and let them fall, limp, on the sheet. 'Everyone thinks I wanted to get rid of it. Mum cried and cried. She said it was her grandchild and she said I'd broken Dad's heart. No one cares how I feel. It's always been good old Lucy. Well, good old Lucy has HAD ENOUGH.'

'I care how you feel,' Tessa said.

'Don't make me LAUGH.' Lucy's eyes blazed with bitterness. 'You've done nothing but make trouble since the day you were born. And what do you get for it? A scholarship at a posh school! I've done everything right, all my life, being little miss perfect. And just because I wanted to grow up and have some fun for once, what do I get? A load of blame – and a . . . a dead baby.'

The ripples of anger shook Tessa's heart and soul. She felt powerless. She saw the cracks radiating out through the bedrock of her family. Her father's 'Rock of Ages' splintered.

'But I do love you, Lucy,' she said.

'Love? YOU? You don't know what love is,' Lucy shouted. 'Wait 'til you get a boyfriend – if you ever do . . .'

'But love isn't just to do with boyfriends.' Tessa picked up the posy and tried to give it to Lucy again. 'I put lots of love into picking these flowers for you.'

'It's too late for flowers.' Lucy sat forward and fired words at her like missiles. 'Bloody well go away, go and turn into a bloody snob at your posh school. I wish I didn't have a sister like you. Go on. Go, and take your stupid flowers with you.' She flung the posy at Tessa's face, and the petals of the pink rose scattered over the bed.

Devastated, Tessa jumped to her feet, and stormed out of the room. She glanced at a clock on the wall of the corridor. Was there time? She checked the car park and saw the black Wolseley still there, waiting for her. She turned and ran through the hospital to the back entrance. She ran across the gravel, over the lawn and down the bank, then on, down the hill towards the station.

'What have we done wrong?' Kate kept saying, over and over again. Freddie held her against his heart, silently. They sat on the stairs, close to the phone, with Jonti on Kate's lap. 'One in hospital with a miscarriage, and the other one gone missing. What have we done wrong, Freddie? We've bent over backwards for those girls.'

Freddie just cuddled her, and let her talk. Outside the hall window he could see swallows gathering on the wires, and the gleam of red that was the roof of his new lorry. The warm smell of cows and apples drifted in from the farms.

'We should be happy,' Kate said. 'We've got so much

– and now this scholarship. Such a wonderful chance for Tessa. I hope she hasn't just thrown it away.'

'Ah . . . well . . . there's times when I wish they'd never been born,' Freddie said.

'No, Freddie, you don't mean that.'

'I do. You are my world, Kate. You're all I ever wanted. I married you, not Lucy and Tessa. They'll leave home anyway, one day, and it'll just be the two of us – again.'

'But not like this!' Kate said. 'We've invested our lives in those two girls. When you have your children and they're so little and sweet, you never imagine them hating each other – and causing so much worry. I don't want them to leave home under a cloud.'

'Well – they haven't left home yet. Tessa will come back. I know it, Kate, and we can make it happen.'

Kate stared into Freddie's eyes, noticing the flecks of deep violet and turquoise that now gave colour to his sadness. Beyond the sadness was knowledge, mysterious knowledge that hadn't come from books. She waited for it to emerge, and it did.

''Tis no good sitting here moaning,' he said. 'We know where Lucy is, so we ought to concentrate on Tessa. And I believe that if you go into a person's mind – or soul, whatever you want to call it – if you go in there as if it were a garden, you can speak to them, but not with words, with silence.'

Kate frowned. 'That sounds like prayer to me.'

'Call it what you like. Call it magic, call it telepathy if

you like, but it works, Kate. I've done it many times in my life, secret times. But you have to promise not to talk, and that's hard for you, isn't it?' His eyes twinkled with sudden life.

'Right. I'll be quiet. You're in charge,' Kate said and pursed her lips.

Freddie held her head against his heart, and closed his eyes. His bond with Tessa was strong. Unbreakable. He visualised it as a garden of light. He asked for help from the spirits, and first to appear was Granny Barcussy. She showed him a pink rose, with its petals scattered. 'Each petal is a teardrop,' she said, 'and a lesson in letting go.'

Even when she disappeared, Freddie stayed in the garden of light, listening and watching. He was aware of gold around him, gold that flowed like fabric. It drifted, then became still, and he saw a man in a saffron robe, a man he'd seen in Tessa's paintings. The man had humour and wisdom in his dark eyes. Freddie listened attentively. 'You have only to remember the way you communicated with Tessa, long before she could talk,' the man spoke softly, almost in a whisper. 'Send the love. Send the welcome. And she will come home.'

Jonti startled them both out of the trance. He barked, leapt off Kate's lap and ran to the door, his tail wagging the whole of his small body. Freddie and Kate looked at each other with hope in their eyes. 'Let him out.' Kate got up from the stairs and opened the front door. Jonti shot out, his paws hardly touching the ground. He flew down the road under the elm trees, his ears flying back, his mouth smiling as he ran to welcome the girl he loved.

Tessa came in looking tired, with Jonti in her arms. 'He's soaking wet,' she said. 'He was coming through the puddles like a speedboat.' She took Jonti's towel from its hook, stood the happy little dog on the kitchen table, dried him thoroughly, and gave him a Bonio biscuit.

'You're soaking wet as well,' Kate said, touching Tessa's hair which hung in curls over her shoulders.

Freddie looked at Tessa's eyes. 'We're – glad you came home,' he said, his voice shaking with emotion.

Tessa seemed overwhelmed. Her face sparkled with raindrops, and Freddie sensed her defensiveness softening in response to his welcome. He sensed a momentous change in Tessa's mindset. 'Where were you?' he asked nervously.

'Did something happen with Lucy?' Kate asked.

Tessa shrugged. 'Lucy – oh, it doesn't matter,' she said. 'I'm sorry – I kind of panicked. I went to the station and bought a ticket to Taunton.'

'Taunton! Whatever did you want to go there for?'

'It doesn't matter,' Tessa said, 'because the train was late, twenty minutes, Charlie said. I stood on the platform looking up at Lexi's fields, and I saw Selwyn. She raised her head and looked at me, and I'm sure she knew it was me, even from a distance. She stood there tossing her mane and whinnying. She sort of . . . rescued me, like I rescued her. So I abandoned the train idea and went up to Lexi's place. We brought

Selwyn in because she hates the rain, and I rubbed her down and gave her a bran mash.'

Kate beamed. 'That's my girl!' she said. 'Horses are great teachers.'

'So is Mrs Appleby,' Tessa said. 'I've been thinking, and I really do want to go there – so – thanks – thanks, Mum and Dad for – for believing in me. I won't let you down.'

Freddie gave Kate a secret smile. They both knew it was the first time in Tessa's life that she had spontaneously said thank you.

'It won't be easy,' Freddie warned.

'I know that, Dad. But I'm a warrior!'

'I'm in love with her, Mum,' Tessa said as the two of them stood close to Selwyn in Lexi's yard. She was brushing Selwyn's dappled grey coat in long firm strokes, and the horse was clearly enjoying it. But if Kate tried to touch her, Selwyn made a face, laying her ears back, and tossing her silver mane.

'I've never not been able to make friends with a horse,' Kate said, disappointed. 'I'm sure if I spent time with her she'd learn to trust me.'

'She might, Mum – or she might not,' Tessa said. 'Lexi's tried everything with her; she's been really kind, but Selwyn is afraid to give her trust in case it means she has to be ridden again. I talk to Selwyn a lot, and I've promised never to ride her, even if I want to – which I do.'

'You've done a wonderful thing for her,' Kate said. 'Lexi is so pleased. But – don't break your heart over her, dear. What if Lexi has to sell her?'

'She won't,' Tessa said fiercely.

'But . . .' The words died on Kate's lips when she saw the passion in her daughter's eyes.

'She definitely won't,' repeated Tessa, and she went on brushing Selwyn, lifting the fronds of her cream mane to groom underneath. She could feel the mare's anxiety about Kate being there.

Tessa was to start at Hilbegut School the following day, and Kate had insisted on walking up to Lexi's place with her. Tessa wanted to be alone, but she knew her mother was upset about Lucy so she tried to compensate by being a normal kind of daughter.

'I was in love with a horse once,' Kate said.

'Daisy?'

'Yes, Daisy – but she wasn't difficult like Selwyn. She was easy to love.'

'Selwyn isn't difficult, and you shouldn't say that when she's listening,' Tessa said. 'She picks it up, Mum. She's hypersensitive, like me. She didn't start out being difficult. She was a willing and brilliant showjumper. Then she hurt her back.'

'I know,' Kate said, 'but it's you I'm concerned about, dear. I want you to REALLY fall in love one day.' Her eyes brightened with the thought. 'You're still young, but I hope with all my heart that you'll fall in love with one of those handsome boys at Hilbegut. A nice boy, from a good family.'

'Mum!'

'But it's important,' Kate said sadly. 'Look at Lucy.'

'I've been looking at Lucy all my life, Mum. And she told me what happened – about the baby.'

'Our grandchild,' Kate said bitterly, and to Tessa's alarm she began to sob uncontrollably.

'Mum! I've never seen you cry like this.' Tessa put Selwyn's brush down. She steered Kate towards the hay barn and sat her down on some bales of hay. Jonti sat between them, whining and looking up at Kate. Tessa put her arms around Kate, feeling the hard knots of tension across her shoulders. Suddenly she felt like the adult, comforting a child, and she felt the helplessness of not knowing what to say. She looked up at the shining figure of her grandfather, Bertie, standing close. He put a finger to his lips and shook his head. Silence, he was telling her. Loving silence is best.

So Tessa kept quiet, her cheek against Kate's hair. She noticed the threads of grey glinting in the sun, and the gleam of a few teardrops that had fallen onto Kate's neat brown shoes. She felt the sobs, like earthquakes, shaking her mother's solid body. She let her cry all of her tears.

Kate sat up, drying her face with a small embroidered hanky. 'Don't tell your Daddy,' she said, looking into Tessa's eyes. 'He's upset enough, without me adding to it.'

'I won't,' Tessa said, and she looked up again at Bertie, surprised to see a tiny baby in his arms. The baby was sleeping peacefully, wrapped in a white crocheted shawl that Tessa had seen before, somewhere. Lucy's baby. Lucy's child. She longed to tell Kate. But Bertie shook his head. They both knew what the reaction would be.

'I did so want to be a Granny,' Kate said, 'even – if it was illegitimate, I'd still love it.'

The spirits of Bertie and the precious baby melted into the shimmering air as if curtains of gauze and silk had swung over them.

Kate looked at Tessa with passion in her eyes. 'Don't go off with that hippie,' she pleaded. 'Try and made a decent life for yourself – please try and get through school, Tessa. I want to see you happily married to a nice man one day. Promise me you'll try.'

Tessa sighed. 'I'll try,' she said, and added another load to the emotional baggage she was already carrying. And the dream of finding Art grew ever brighter.

Chapter Fifteen

1963

GIRLS IN BLACK

Tessa leaned out of her window to watch Freddie drive away in his new mink-brown Rover 90. She caught a glimpse of his blue eyes, full of emotion, seeking the last contact with her from under his cap. He didn't smile. She stood in the window with mixed feelings, watching the back of his car getting smaller and smaller. At the end of the long drive it turned left, accelerated, and was finally gone. *I'm alone*, she thought, *alone in the world*.

'This is like a blimin' rabbit hutch!' Freddie had said when they'd arrived and found the low, black-timbered huts of an old army barracks, now converted into students' bedrooms. Tessa had found his comment funny, and endearing. She imagined her mother laughing when Freddie got home and said that.

A sense of euphoria swept over her when she turned to look at her room. It was small. The narrow bed against the wall was covered by a blanket with arty splodges of subtle colour. The floor had yellow lino which gave it a sunny feel. There was a slim white wardrobe, chest of drawers, and an oval mirror set in a recess with a square of Formica top and a tubular, canvas chair. Along the wall over the bed was a high shelf which seemed like a gift. *This is my place*, Tessa thought joyfully. *I can do what I like!*

She threw herself on the bed, propped her feet against the wall, and lay looking at the ceiling of Room 11 in Hut 5, planning how she would cover it with her postcard collection and her pictures of Selwyn. She listened to the sounds of other girls arriving, and decided to fix her hair first. She undid her suitcase and pulled out some narrow ribbons, choosing purple, turquoise, and lime green. Her hairbrush was right at the bottom so she tipped everything onto the bed in a chaotic heap, then sat on the canvas chair in front of the mirror. Separating one strand of her chestnut hair, she divided it into three, and plaited the ribbons into it, making a long, multi-coloured braid on one side of her head. It made her look interesting, and different, she hoped, and the turquoise complemented her pale blue eyes. She found the little tie-dyed make-up bag she'd made at Hilbegut, and applied silver eyeshadow and midnight blue mascara.

Kate had insisted that she arrived 'looking respectable'. *Freedom!* she thought, and tore off the Donegal tweed skirt and hand-knitted sweater that Annie had made in maroon red, a colour Tessa loathed. She flung them up to hit the ceiling, like wild escaping mallards, and stuffed them under the bed, right into the far corner. She put on her new black jeans, and one of Freddie's old shirts which she had tie-dyed in purple.

Leaving everything in a heap, she strolled outside, feeling like an art student and hoping she looked cool and experienced. Discreetly observing more students arriving with fussing parents, Tessa headed for a group of lofty elm trees that shaded the lawn. She touched them and gazed up into the bushy branches. The leaves were old and bottle green at this end of summer, and deeper into the garden was a sumach tree already turning fiery pink and orange, its blade-like leaves flickering like flames. Tessa had never seen a sumach tree and she sat down under it, then lay on her back, hypnotised by the fire of its colour against the blue sky. *What a feast for an artist*, she thought.

'Excuse me, are you in Room 11?' said a voice.

Tessa sat up, and saw a girl with a wide smile that reached the tips of the two curls in her perfect shining bell of dark hair. She had eyes greener than Somerset. 'Hiya mate. I'm Jen, from London – and I'm next door to you in Room 10. I dig the shirt! And the braid. You look like an interesting character.'

Tessa beamed. 'Hiya!'

'What's yer name?'

'Tessa.'

'Want a coffee? We're making a brew up. Come and join us. Got yer mug unpacked? I can lend you one if you haven't.' Jen talked fast, moving her mouth extravagantly, and she hardly gave Tessa space to reply before gabbling on to her next thought. 'What d'ya think of this place? Right dump, in't it? Out in the bloody back of beyond. Gives me the creeps. All them flipping trees and green fields. Boring, aren't they? Come on then – Tessa – you coming or not?'

'If you want me to.'

'Course I want you to, ya 'nana. Come on.' Jen stretched out a wiry white arm and pulled Tessa to her feet. 'Cor, you're tall. You could be a model. Where are you from?'

'Monterose – in Somerset.'

Fascinated, Tessa walked with Jen into Hut 5. At the end of the hut was a room with a row of boiling rings, a fridge, kettle and two irons. Jen put five mugs on a tray. 'You shovel coffee, and I'll do the milk,' she said, handing Tessa a teaspoon.

'All five?' asked Tessa.

'Yeah, I said – we're having a brew up.'

Tessa carried the laden tray down to Jen's room, slightly nervous about meeting the other three girls. Years of being a loner and getting pushed out of peer groups at school had made her socially anxious. She still hadn't found a real friend, even at Hilbegut. The girls there had been mostly from rich families and talked about exotic holidays abroad, shopping in London, and boyfriends. Tessa had kept the boys at arm's length, much to her mother's dismay.

'Coffee up! This is Tessa. She's my mate next door in Room 11,' Jen said. 'Come on, move up, you two.'

Two girls sat on the bed, their backs against the wall. 'Mel and Noni,' said Jen, 'and this is Faye.'

Mel and Noni smiled at Tessa, and she sat down on the bed. They couldn't have been more different. Mel was plump, bright-eyed and reassuring. She didn't look at all like an art student. Noni was tiny, with chicken-bone wrists covered in silver bangles. Her face was old, her eyes calm and mysterious.

Faye was sitting on an orange cushion on the floor. She didn't smile, but glanced shrewdly at Tessa, the whites of her eyes huge and dramatic, looking out from caves of heavy black eyeliner and mascara. Her mouth was surly and her cheeks hollow.

'Faye's on the other side of you, in Room 12,' Jen said, 'and she's got a flipping great cello in there. I hope you like music, Tessa!'

Tessa wasn't sure what a cello was, so she kept quiet, exchanging hostile stares with Faye. *She looks like an insect*, Tessa thought, *ready to sting*! She felt Faye's eyes raking her over, criticising every detail of her clothes, her hair, her face. She remembered that Faye had been sitting alone under the elm trees, smoking, and watching her arrive in Freddie's Rover 90, smirking at everything they unloaded, especially her brand new BSA bike, and her mother's personalised leather suitcase with *Oriole Kate Loxley* embossed on the lid.

'Have you got your letter, Tessa?' Jen said as they tucked in to Mel's chocolate-coated digestives and fig rolls.

'What letter?'

'It's got your grant cheque in it – and your timetable, and what group you're in. It should be in your room.'

Tessa fetched the smooth white envelope from her room and sat down again on Jen's bed. She tore it open. Inside was a cheque from Somerset County Council for £1,300. She stared at it with round eyes.

'Your face!' Jen laughed. 'It's a lot, isn't it? But it's got to last you a whole year, and you have to buy all your art materials with it – and clothes – and travel –'

'We're going to Bath tomorrow to get black duffle coats,' Mel said. 'Want to come? We're hitching.'

'Hitching? What's that?' Tessa asked.

Faye looked at her scathingly.

'Where've you been all your life?' Jen asked, but her green eyes were kind and humorous. 'Hitchhiking. You stand at the side of the road, stick your thumb out, and someone stops and gives you a lift, especially if you look like a student. That's why we need black duffle coats and college scarves. I can see we're gonna have to educate you, Tessa! – But don't look so worried, we'll look after you, won't we girls?'

Everyone smiled, except Faye, who now looked bored and was picking threads out of the knee of her black tights, and winding them tightly round her finger.

'So what group are you in, Tessa?' Mel asked.

Tessa unfolded her letter which was on *Bath Academy of Art* headed paper. She glared at it. 'There must be a mistake,' she said. 'They've put me in the Photography Group. I don't want to do THAT!'

'Yeah, we've all got the same issues,' said Jen. 'I'm in the Textiles group and I can't stand sewing. If God wants to punish me when he gets me up there, he'll sit me down with a needle and thread.'

'We're in Ceramics,' said Mel, 'and I've never made a pot in my life.'

'Give it here.' Jen took Tessa's letter out of her hand and scanned it with her green eyes. 'It's not just Photography – you're in Painting as well – same as me – and look, you've got three subsidiaries – Calligraphy – what the heck's that?'

'Lettering,' Tessa said. 'I HATE lettering.'

'. . . and Sculpture,' continued Jen, 'and Visual Communication – we've all got that.'

Tessa could feel her face going hot. *I've been here an hour*, she thought, *and they're telling me what to do*. She stuffed the anger into the far corner of her mind, aware that Faye's big eyes were watching her in a calculating way. Waiting to see her fall apart.

'You've got to go along with it,' Jen said. 'We're first years – the lowest of the low – and it's only work, Tessa. The rest of it's going to be fun.'

'Fun?' Tessa felt herself disappearing into a familiar black hole. 'Fun' was another word that clicked her defences into place. Fun meant failure. Fun meant rejection.

'Don't worry, Tessa.' Mel looked at her with kind, bright eyes. 'We'll look after you. We're all in the same boat.'

'Yeah – you stick with us and you'll be okay,' said Jen. 'Here y'are – have another biscuit.'

★   ★   ★

'I'll never get my fat legs into those,' Kate said, eyeing the slim pair of jodhpurs Susan had pulled out of a drawer. 'Haven't you got a bigger pair?'

'No.' Susan frowned. She caught the twinkle of mischief in Kate's eyes. 'You could borrow a pair of Ian's trousers.'

'Will he mind?'

'He won't know. He's gone to an auction.'

Giggling, the two women raided Ian's wardrobe which smelled of cedar wood and red wine. 'How about these?' Susan dragged out a pair of cavalry twill trousers and held them against Kate who stood there in her blouse and petticoat.

'They're miles too long,' Kate said, laughing. 'They'll be in concertinas round my ankles.'

'You can roll them up. Go on, put them on.' Susan threw the trousers at Kate, her eyes sparkling with fun. 'Ian won't know. Men never know what clothes they've got, do they? Come on – take your Charlie off. You can't ride a horse with yards of lace petticoat flying.'

Kate grinned wickedly at Susan, and stepped into the heavy pair of trousers. She stuffed her petticoat down inside, and fastened the leather belt. The two women stood in front of the mirror laughing at Kate's reflection. 'Well!' she said, 'I look ready for the sack race. Let's hope nobody sees me.'

In high spirits they skipped downstairs and headed for the stables. It was the first time Kate had had any fun for years. She'd met Susan in the post office and Susan had noticed how pale and tired her friend looked. 'Come home with me, and have a ride, Kate,' she'd said. 'You must be feeling lonely with Tessa gone to Art College. It'll do you good to have a ride.'

It was doing her good, Kate thought. The laughing and larking about with Susan was something she had missed. The endless washing and ironing, cooking and cleaning, keeping Annie happy, and coping with her two girls had taken its toll. Kate was exhausted, and Freddie hadn't noticed. He was preoccupied with his engines, his stone carving, and the vegetable garden. They both fell into bed at the end of the day, mentally and physically tired, and lovemaking was last on the list.

There was an uneasy truce with Lucy. After the miscarriage Kate had persuaded her to enrol for a secretarial course at Taunton Tech. Lucy caught the train every day to Taunton and often came home late, but she'd stuck to her course and found a job with a firm of solicitors in Taunton. Kate knew she wasn't happy, and her relationship with Freddie had been damaged, it seemed, forever. Freddie was silent and grim-faced in Lucy's company, and there was an occasional flare-up, usually about the length of Lucy's skirt or the smell of alcohol on her breath. Kate found her own role as peace-maker very stressful, and getting Tessa off to college had been yet another emotional rollercoaster.

Kate knew Freddie didn't want her to go horse-riding, especially with Ian Tillerman around, and she tried to respect his wishes. But this morning she felt rebellious. With the October countryside basking in an Indian summer, she wanted to be cantering through the sunlit woods with Susan.

'I haven't been on a horse for years,' Kate said as they saddled up in stables next door to each other, and led the horses into the yard.

'You'll be all right on Toby,' Susan said. 'He's very steady. Lexi uses him sometimes, for teaching.'

'He's gorgeous.' Kate gave the kindly black horse a hug round his solid neck. His dark eyes were peaceful and he stood rocklike while she turned the stirrup to her foot and swung herself up, her heart beating hard with excitement. She adjusted the stirrup leathers and gathered the reins. 'Let's hope these trousers don't fall down!'

Kate loved being out in the soft October light, trotting past orchards where trees were laden to the floor with heavy scarlet apples, and standing up in her stirrups to pick clusters of pale green hazelnuts from the lush foliage of coppiced hazels. Entering the woods, the horses walked peacefully, side by side, the path ahead lit by a shaft of sun slanting through the beeches. The woods created silence, the horses' hooves making no sound on the carpet of leaf mould, the contented, magic quiet that didn't need conversation. Kate didn't want the ride to end. She felt healed by a joy she had forgotten, a sense of being fully alive and awake, and part of the planet in its ripest, most rich, abundant harvest time.

'I'd love to do this again,' Kate said as they returned down the road towards the stables. 'It's done me the world of good.'

'You look better,' Susan said. 'You've got colour in your cheeks, Kate. We could do this once a week if you like – I'd enjoy it too.'

'Freddie won't like it,' Kate said sadly. 'He doesn't want me to ride. He worries.'

'But he doesn't own you, Kate. You've got to have some free time – one afternoon a week isn't much. You've had such a hard time, haven't you? – with his mother there – and Tessa. You're worn out, Kate – worse than you were in the wartime when we were nursing. At least we had fun sometimes, didn't we?'

'Yes, we did – and I miss it.'

'Does Freddie have to know?' Susan asked. 'Can't you just say you're spending time with me? It won't do any harm, surely? What the eye doesn't see!'

Kate was tempted. Why not?

'What about Ian's trousers?' she laughed. 'Can we smuggle them out once a week?'

So it was arranged for Kate to ride every Tuesday with Susan. She went off on her bike, with Ian's trousers in a brown paper bag in the basket, and Freddie never questioned her about it. Spending time with Susan was obviously good for Kate. It was Annie who made a fuss. 'Gallivanting off again on that bike,' she complained. 'I never had a life like you.'

All through autumn the rides continued, even when storms howled in the tree tops and golden leaves sped through the woodland twilight like shooting stars. As the winter light sharpened, the bare branches turned to stone like the vaults of a Gothic cathedral. Frost glistened in the blue shadows of the hedges and there was a sense of shifting time.

On their rides, Kate watched for the winter birds, the vast flocks of fieldfare and redwing, snow buntings and bramblings. They didn't come. The hawthorn berries hung heavy on the trees, uneaten, and carpets of apples remained under the orchard trees like cobblestones, far into the winter. She couldn't help feeling that something was wrong. Could it be true what Tessa had said? That the earth was sick?

'But I don't WANT to use yellow ochre,' Tessa said furiously. 'I hate yellow ochre.'

'Tough. I'm your painting tutor and you'll paint the way I think you should paint.' Tony Bulletti's penetrating stare challenged Tessa. He was much shorter than her, a stocky dwarf of a man with an angry quiff of hair that flew over his face. Tessa had hated him on sight. It was deep. *Ivor Stape*, she thought, *that's who he reminds me of – and he's got eyes like acid drops*.

'I don't want to paint like this,' she said stubbornly. 'I like pure spectrum colours.'

'Pure spectrum colours are what they use in Primary School. This is Bath Academy of Art, girl.'

'My name is Tessa, not girl. I don't care who you are, and I don't care if you have got your sludgy brown paintings in the Tate Gallery. That doesn't give you the right to bully me.'

Jen was looking at Tessa in concern. 'Don't push your luck, Tess. Back off,' she mouthed.

'Where's your turps?' Tony Bulletti demanded.

'Here.'

'Right. Take a rag and scrub it all off, and start again.' He sloshed turps onto a cloth and smeared it over Tessa's painting. 'And don't give me the drama queen stuff.'

He walked away, leaving Tessa holding the two ends of a paintbrush she had snapped in half, her face locked into fury.

Moments later Faye was beside her, offering her a new paintbrush. 'Borrow this one. I'm not using it.'

'Thanks.'

Later that day, back in the haven of her bedroom, Tessa heard a tap at the door. She opened it, surprised to see Faye standing there.

'I'm looking for someone to hitch up to London with me,' Faye said, 'for a concert at the Royal Festival Hall.'

'What kind of concert?' Tessa asked. It was December, two weeks before the end of her first term at Bath Academy of Arts. Faye had hardly spoken to her, apart from the odd, begrudging 'Hello,' but Tessa felt she knew Faye by the music that came through the wall. Faye practised her cello most evenings, working on the Bach sonata for solo cello. Tessa's experience of music had been confined to Freddie's radio blaring out *Music While You Work* in his workshop, the town band playing marches, the Gilbert and Sullivan operettas they had done at the grammar school, and Lucy's record player blaring out The Beatles and Cliff Richard. None of it appealed to Tessa. Yet once she had been deeply moved by hearing the church organ, feeling the stone-trembling power of it. And once, at Hilbegut, hearing Wagner's *Tannhäuser Overture* in assembly. It had moved her so much that she'd felt profoundly disturbed for days.

'It's the Brahms' *Symphony No 1*,' said Faye, her eyes coming alive with passion. 'It's SO powerful – and SO magical. It's got this theme tune that keeps coming back, like the light in the forest.'

Tessa stared at her. She didn't know what a symphony was. She'd never been to London. Hitchhiking with Faye sounded scary. But the light in the forest? Words that spoke to her soul. Words like that, from a girl who had shown her nothing but scorn and hostility!

'And in the second half of the concert,' Faye continued, now with stars in her eyes, 'it's the Respighi – *The Pines of Rome*, and it's STUNNING. It blows my mind. It's got a nightingale's song in it, a recording of a real bird.'

Tessa couldn't speak. Suddenly she was back in Monterose, on the edge of the woods with Lexi and Jonti on that magical night of the nightingale picnic. The night of the cloak of stars. She was completely overwhelmed. The sobs welled up in her, old sobs that had been there all of her life, sobs that lurked in the catacombs of her soul like gremlins, never, ever satisfied with her efforts to appease them. She slumped onto her bed, crying bitterly, her hands over her face.

She expected Faye to slam the door and stalk off, but she didn't. Faye came right into her room, closed the door quietly, and sat down beside Tessa in silence, and let her sob.

'I'm sorry,' Tessa said, when she managed to regain control.

'You don't need to apologise.' Faye looked at her with concern in her eyes and Tessa felt it was the first time she'd seen a spark of humanity in Faye's eyes. Or maybe she'd never looked, she thought.

'I'll go with you,' Tessa heard herself saying.

'Great!' Faye looked pleased. 'Wear a mac. It usually pours with rain when I'm hitchhiking.'

Faye didn't ask why she'd been crying. Instead, she fetched her cello from her room, and sat on Tessa's bed with it, her skinny legs planted firmly on each side of the glowing instrument. 'I'll play you the theme tune, the one like the light in the forest,' she said, 'then you can listen out for it.'

'Okay.' Tessa looked at the cello in awe. She felt the vibration from its belly as Faye tuned it and drew the bow across the taut strings, and played eight evocative notes.

'That's it,' she said, and played it again. 'Then – at the end of the symphony – it leads into this really emotional tune as if you've come out of the forest and ended up on the wild Atlantic coast of Cornwall, with the sun making a sheet of light on the water.'

Again, her words touched something deep and sacred in Tessa's soul. She listened, spellbound, as Faye played the eight-note theme again and then flowed on into the 'really emotional tune', her arm moving in waves, her eyes closed under their fringe of black mascara. A girl in black, with the brightest aura Tessa had ever seen, light blue, lemon, and pure white. An angel in disguise, she thought, a streetwise angel. She wanted to tell her so, but Faye's defences were intimidating and strong.

'Meet me straight after class Friday afternoon – at the main gate,' Faye said, gathering up her cello and bow. 'See you then, Tessa!'

Freddie walked up through the woods, his boots crunching over frosted leaf mould. Overhead the twigs made a lattice of ice against a dove grey sky. He turned his collar up and drove his hands deeper into the warm pockets of his heavy overcoat.

He wanted to see for himself what was happening in the woods, why it was no longer silent, why the wild creatures were moving out. A family of badgers had set up home in the hedge opposite The Pines. The rooks whirled in the sky in huge, distressed gatherings, searching the tree tops for a new safe haven. Rabbits sat along the grass verges, ill and dying from myxomatosis. And a new smell drifted through the wood, the smell of petrol and sawdust.

Freddie had loved those woods since his childhood. Since his early courtship with Kate. Even now, walking up there in the frost, he thought nostalgically of their first picnic together, the pony and cart plodding through the lime trees and hearing the hum of thousands of bees in the linden blossom in early summer. The times when he had walked through those lime trees on his way to Granny Barcussy's cottage, and seen the spirit of his grandfather there, shining in the dappled twilight.

It was lunchtime, and today he'd chosen not to go home. Kate was out with Susan, and Freddie hadn't felt like coping with his mother's negativity. He'd been depressed just lately, especially after reading Tessa's latest letter. She hated her painting tutor at college. She hated the painting classes and the sludgy colours they insisted she used. She hated being in the photography group, didn't see the point of it. She hated life-drawing. She missed Jonti and Selwyn. But, she'd written, at last she had friends, and this weekend she was hitching to London with Faye. Freddie found that very alarming, the thought of his little Tessa standing at the roadside, thumbing a lift, like a hippy. Everyone does it, she'd said, but that didn't reassure Freddie.

He missed both his daughters. Tessa because she wasn't there, and Lucy because he felt estranged from her. She no longer ran to meet him with shining eyes. She no longer adored him. She was sour-faced and rude. It made him feel cast aside and powerless.

Jonti trotted staunchly beside him through the wood, his paws rustling on the crisp ground. They walked along the edge of the nightingale wood, between coppiced hazel and ash, and Freddie could see Lexi's place across the fields which were silvery with frost and the blue shadows of hedgerow elms. It would soon be the shortest day, Freddie thought, and he smiled as he heard a song thrush shouting across the valley.

Then, suddenly, came the sound he dreaded. Chainsaws. Men shouting. Birds rising in panic from the wood. He stooped and picked up Jonti. 'You stay with me,' he said, and the little dog looked up at him and licked his face.

Freddie stood still and Jonti listened with him, ears pricked, nose twitching, hackles at the ready. The whole wood seemed to be listening. A few snowflakes scattered down, as if shaken loose by the tension. Jonti began to whine and tremble in Freddie's arms as if he sensed impending doom.

The chainsaws stopped, a man shouted, and there was a mighty echoing crack. The trees stiffened and the woods shuddered with a great gasp of shock, followed by a sickening and thunderous crash. A sense of finality ricocheted through every twig and every crystal of frost.

A giant had fallen.

Freddie felt it in his heart. And he knew. It was a lime tree. He walked quickly now, in the ice-cold air, towards the Lime Wood, holding the memory in his heart of that summer day with Kate, the day of the bees in the lime flowers. He felt as if his entire life had gone suddenly cold. Yet he felt compelled to go on. He had to see it.

Minutes later he stood by the fallen lime tree looking down at the mess of broken twigs. He sensed the tree still quivering with shock, its nerves twitching like those of a dying animal. All around were the stumps of other lime trees, newly sawn, their majestic trunks cut into lengths and stacked, waiting for the two long timber lorries to come roaring up the new track and take them away.

Freddie put Jonti down, and walked over to the man who stood beside the fallen tree, a chainsaw in his hand. Freddie wanted to wipe the satisfied grin off his face. He wanted to challenge his right to destroy hundreds of years of ancient woodland. He stood in silence, like a man at a funeral, his head bowed, his grief sealing the door to powerless anger.

There was nothing he could do.

Or was there?

Snow floated down from the leaden clouds, tiny flakes like petals from plum blossom in springtime, then large flakes like gypsy lace, hurrying, as if to cover the fallen lime tree in crystal. As he watched it pitching on the wreckage, Freddie noticed the seeds still hanging in delicate clusters from the twigs. With frozen red fingers, he gathered a handful of the round seeds and tied them into his hanky, like money.

'What d'you want them for?' asked the man with the saw.

'The future,' said Freddie, looking through the snow at the man's eyes, 'and for my daughter, Tessa. She wants to save the world.'

'Don't 'em all?' the man said. 'Bloody hippies.'

'She's an art student. Bath Academy of Art,' Freddie said, and walked away into the whirling snow.

The grin on the man's face haunted him like a joker in a pack of cards, forever impudent. He felt sadness gathering itself into a spike of pain in the middle of his chest. A hacking cough had plagued him for weeks, and it came now, convulsively, causing Jonti to pause and look up at him, one paw in the air. The pain seemed to ignite like a blowtorch, scorching his throat. He loosened his scarf, and touched his brow with frozen fingers. His skin was hot and sweaty, and the pulse roared in his ears. The cough got tighter and suddenly he was struggling to breathe. *I've gotta get home*, he thought. The weather was closing in, blowing curtains of ice around him, the snowflakes hard and fast, obscuring the glimpse of landscape between the trees. He couldn't see Lexi's place, or the rooftops of Monterose, or the station with its signal box and footbridge.

The faces he loved swam before him. Kate's bright brown eyes. Lucy. Tessa. His mother. *No one knows where I am*, he thought, and tried to walk faster. But with every step his breathing tightened until he was gasping. He stumbled the few steps and reached the rustling shelter of the Evergreen Oak tree, leaned against it, and slid to the floor, fighting for breath. As he closed his eyes he heard Jonti running off into the snow, his paws pattering over the frozen ground.

Chapter Sixteen

LONDON

'Have I got to drag you away from that river?' Faye said, tugging the sleeve of Tessa's black duffle coat.

'Sorry.' Tessa feasted her eyes one last time on the night river. Its silver and black swirling tide, its rippling reflections of coloured light fascinated her. She tried to take some snaps of it with her Brownie Box Camera, for her project on water. Reluctantly she tore herself away and followed Faye's thin legs into the Royal Festival Hall. Seeing the River Thames had been the best surprise so far, even breathing the cooler, fresher air that seemed to hang over the water. She felt shell-shocked from their ride to London in the cab of a lorry with a loud, impatient driver. He'd talked non-stop, smoked non-stop and kept turning his head to look lecherously at the two girls he'd picked up. He'd dropped them at Baker Street tube station, and Faye had bundled Tessa down an escalator (her first) and onto a tube train. It had felt like a hectic journey into the screaming tunnels of hell.

Walking into the humming auditorium of the Royal Festival Hall was a different experience, a magical, expectant space, full of quiet, serious people. Faye quickly made herself at home in her seat, taking off her duffle coat and college scarf and making a nest with them. She gave Tessa one of her rare smiles. 'We made it!' she whispered, and offered her a Murray Mint. 'Unwrap it now. No one dares rustle paper when the performance starts.'

Tessa was awed when the members of the orchestra came in so solemnly, clutching their gleaming instruments, more than she had ever seen in her life. She tried to pretend she was used to it, like Faye, so she watched calmly, but inside she was fizzing with excitement. She wasn't sure she could sit still for long, with questions bobbing through her mind, and so many serious people to study. She wasn't sure whether she would like this kind of music or not. 'Even if you don't like it, you've got to sit there in total silence,' Faye had warned. 'If you cry, sneeze, cough or unwrap a sweet, you can get chucked out by some usher in a penguin suit.'

What have I let myself in for? Tessa thought, as the conductor lifted his baton to begin. But, from the first haunting note, she was captivated. The music swept through her and around her like the tide in the river, bearing her away like a water baby to distant, enchanted lands. She felt totally absorbed by it, as if there was nothing else, no world beyond the music, no more fear, no more anxiety, no more anger. She was the music, and the music was her.

275

When the eight-note theme came in, a smile passed between the girls. *The light in the forest*, Tessa thought, and each time it came, it was more intense than the last, until she could hardly bear it, and yet wanted it. Finally it led into the 'big emotional tune' Faye had described; it was greater than the river, the brimming river she had tried so long ago to find. It swallowed her, body and soul, and she went with it. She emerged, from the dark forest, into a sunlit ocean. She rode the waves, on and on, into the light. She never wanted it to stop.

The applause at the end was a different kind of surge. An overpowering feeling of oneness such as she'd never experienced in her life. *I belong*, she thought. *I belong in this music, with people like this.*

In the interval, Faye asked her how she felt.

'There aren't any words,' Tessa said. 'I've – never experienced this kind of music before – but I'm LOVING it. I feel like an explorer discovering a new land.'

'Great!' Faye said. 'I know what you mean. I can't believe you've never heard classical before. I grew up with it.'

'Lucky you, but have you ever heard a real nightingale singing?'

'No. I'm a total townie.'

'I have,' Tessa said. 'At home we had nightingale picnics under the stars.'

A wave of homesickness gushed over her. Jonti, and Selwyn, and Lexi. She let it pass. Two weeks and she could go home for Christmas, back to being Tessa the troublemaker. *Maybe I'll just stay in London*, she thought in excitement. *I'm old enough to work.*

In the second part of the concert, when she heard the nightingale's song in Respighi's *The Pines of Rome*, it sounded lost and distant. Impressive, but nothing like the golden sheet of birdsong she'd heard on the night picnic with Lexi. The deep feeling of belonging came again with the applause at the end, resonating in her like a gong. *I'm not homesick for home*, she thought, *I'm homesick for who I am.*

They walked out into the humming night of London. It was snowing, and the snowflakes were pale orange in the street lights.

'How are we going to get back,' Tessa asked, 'on a night like this?'

Jonti usually barked when he wanted to come in, but tonight he did something that spooked Kate. He sat by the gate in the snow, lifted his nose to the sky, and howled like a wolf.

Kate took her red umbrella from the cupboard and picked her way down the slippery path, to fetch the little dog in. 'What's the matter, Jonti?' She looked up and down the road. It was a whiteout, and the snow was drifting in a biting wind. Freddie's lorry had a white roof, and so had the car. Kate frowned. Where was Freddie? She tried to catch Jonti but he wasn't having it. He ran further down the snowy road and sat there howling. There didn't seem to be a living soul on the road, and the thick snow blotted out the town. Kate suddenly felt isolated. It was getting dark. She listened for the sound of

Lucy's train arriving from Taunton, but it didn't come. The town was silent.

Kate searched Freddie's workshop, but he wasn't there. She went to Annie's door and pushed it open, to find Annie asleep in her chair by the fire, her knitting trailing over her lap and the old kettle boiling itself dry on the stove top.

'Annie,' Kate shook her arm gently. 'Can you wake up please?'

'Wake up? I wasn't asleep,' Annie said grumpily. 'Just closed my eyes for a minute.'

'It's snowing,' Kate said.

'Oh dear – I hate snow,' Annie said. 'I know it's pretty but I can't go out on those slippery paths.'

'Do you know where Freddie is?'

'Freddie? Isn't he back?' Annie stared at her. ''Tis nearly dark!' She got up and went to the window. 'He took Jonti for a walk – that was lunchtime. Said he didn't want no lunch.'

'Jonti's out in the road, howling – listen to him!' Kate said.

'That's bad,' Annie predicted. 'Dogs don't howl for nothing. Something's happened to my Freddie, and that dog knows.'

'Oh, I expect he's just yarning to Herbie,' Kate said, trying to look on the bright side.

'No. I feel it in me bones. Something's happened,' Annie insisted. 'Freddie's not well. He's had that terrible cough for weeks now. And . . .' she looked accusingly at Kate, 'he was upset about something – I could tell. Someone's got to go and look for him.'

'What was he upset about?' Kate asked.

Annie hesitated. 'About – you.'

'About me?'

'That Ian Tillerman came up here, wanting Freddie to haul a load of hay bales, and Freddie wouldn't do it. So that didn't go down very well. But Tillerman kept on arguing and calling Freddie "my man", like he does. Then he said something about you – something about you riding horses with Susan. And Freddie just walked away.'

'Oh dear!' Kate immediately felt guilty. She'd intended to tell Freddie, but hadn't done so. The moment never seemed to be right. And she didn't want to give up her riding. She brushed it aside. 'We can talk it over later.'

'Someone's got to go and look for him,' said Annie again. 'He could die out there in the snow if he gets one of those asthma attacks.'

'I'll go,' Kate said. 'You make a flask with that boiling kettle – hot strong tea with sugar.'

Kate pulled on a thick sweater, and tied a square woollen scarf tightly over her head. She put on her wellies, and a yellow plastic mac she had bought in Weymouth. It was too long and flapped around her ankles.

Annie's eyes were worried as she handed over a small Thermos flask with the cup screwed firmly on top. 'Don't go slipping over, Kate,' she said. 'And take the rubber torch.'

'I'll be fine, don't you worry,' Kate said cheerfully. 'I'm a farmer's daughter.'

Snow pelted her face and the east wind moaned through the bare elm trees. Jonti was shivering when she reached him and clipped him onto his lead. 'Find Freddie,' she said, and the little dog stopped howling and barked. He led her along the slippery white road, pulling at his lead.

'We could doss down with that lot,' Faye said, as the two girls walked under Waterloo Bridge.

'Who are they?' Tessa asked innocently, glancing at the bundled shapes of homeless people, surrounded by sheets of cardboard and piles of coats.

'Homeless people. They sleep here all the time,' Faye said.

Tessa was shocked. She stared at the soles of a man's boots as he slept across the pavement, and wondered how he had ended up homeless. She wanted to stop, and ask him why, but Faye dragged her away. 'Come on. Don't get involved.'

'But where are we going?' Tessa asked.

'We can go to my mum's place,' Faye said, joylessly. 'She's a bit weird, but she won't mind. Then we can hitch back in the morning. I haven't got enough money left for the tube, have you?'

'I've got a ten-bob note,' said Tessa.

'That'll do.'

Faye led her into the underground and down another escalator. Tessa followed, her head still full of the music. She felt excited to be staying in London. She wanted to be there in daylight. Faye didn't seem interested in London, but to Tessa it was an undiscovered, glittering new place, full of history and romance, and interesting people. 'We could go to the Tate Gallery in the morning.'

'No. It'll take too long,' Faye said. 'I haven't done my project homework yet. Have you?'

'No,' Tessa sighed. 'I feel like chucking it in actually.'

'Yeah – join the club.'

'Don't you get on with your mum?' Tessa asked.

Faye shrugged. 'Be warned, Tessa, my mum is on another planet! I can't have a conversation with her. Never could. I've spent most of my life with Dad. They're divorced now.'

'Divorced. Aw, that's a shame.'

'It's no big deal. Dad's met someone else, but she hasn't. She likes being on her own – she doesn't even want me around. I'm an embarrassment,' Faye said bitterly. 'Come on – I'm not wasting time talking about her.'

Tessa sensed the pain in Faye's mind. She'd never met anyone with divorced parents. No one had ever spoken the word 'divorce' in her family. Meeting Faye's mum wasn't going to be easy.

Faye's mum lived in a penthouse flat in Belgravia. Plodding through the streets with Faye, Tessa began to feel strange and unsettled. Something tugged at her consciousness. A voice. Phone home, it insisted. They passed countless phone boxes, but Faye wouldn't stop, and she had very little money left. The snow was closing in around London, and both girls were soaking wet, their sodden duffle coats heavy, their jeans and shoes cold and dripping. Tessa suddenly thought of Jonti. *He's an old dog now*, she thought, *and he shouldn't be out in the snow*. She felt that Jonti was shivering. She heard him howling in her mind. Was he lost? Something's wrong, said her footsteps, something's wrong.

Dazed, she found herself arriving at Faye's mum's place. The door opened, and a woman who looked like a goddess beckoned them inside. Tessa couldn't believe she was Faye's mother. Her name was Starlinda. She had extraordinary eyes, wide open, wide apart and curving upwards at the outer corners, and a wide pearl pink smile. Everything about her was pearly, her lips, her nails, her shimmering hair, her white kaftan with silk embroidery, her slippers of exotic oriental satin.

'This is Tessa,' Faye said. 'We're stuck in London – been to a concert – can we stay the night?'

Starlinda fixed her extraordinary eyes on Tessa. 'Welcome,' she said in an oceanic whisper, 'we've been waiting for YOU.'

'Mum!' Faye rolled her eyes. 'Can we come in? We're soaking wet and starving.'

Starlinda looked them over, her nose wrinkling. 'You look like two steamed puddings,' she said, and laughed heartily. Two dimples appeared on her cheeks. 'Take everything off – well, almost everything – then you can come in!' She fetched a gigantic white plastic laundry basket. 'Dump it all in here.' Then she fetched two white towelling bath robes. 'Put these on.'

Tessa didn't want to take her clothes off, but the towelling robe looked enticingly cosy, so she followed Faye's example and stripped down to her bra and panties.

'What pretty hair, Tessa.' Starlinda touched the coloured braid in Tessa's chestnut hair. 'There, you look so much better in white,' she said, and the eyes looked into hers very deeply again. 'And you really shouldn't wear black, dear. You're a starchild.'

'Mum!' growled Faye. 'Can't you try to be a normal parent for one hour? We just need a bowl of soup and a bed.'

'You know where the kitchen is,' said Starlinda, and her face changed when she looked at Faye. 'Help yourself. It's all vegetarian.'

Tessa looked alarmed. She imagined plates of putrid cabbage.

'I'll fix us something – student-style – beans on toast,' Faye said. 'Don't look so worried, Tessa.'

'Come and sit by the fire, Tessa, you're shivering.' Starlinda led her to a purple velvet chair next to the electric bar, flame-effect fire. She sat down opposite, and looked at her with unwavering interest. Normally Tessa didn't like people staring at her, but this was different. She gazed back, finding a strange restorative power in the minutes of silent eye contact. She felt she knew Starlinda from some distant time. What happened next was the ultimate surprise.

'It's not the dog who is shivering and lost,' Starlinda said. 'A little white dog. Am I right?'

'Jonti!' Tessa whispered. 'How – how did you know? He's my dog, and I was worrying about him.'

'He's quite all right, dear – but I think you need to phone home, don't you? There's a phone right there beside you. Please do use it.'

Tessa looked at the cream telephone. 'Thank you – I do.'

'Do you want me to leave the room?' Starlinda asked.

'No,' Tessa shook her head. She lifted the receiver and dialled her home number with her finger in the round chrome dial. She heard it ring once, and Annie answered immediately and breathlessly.

'Hello, Granny, it's me, Tessa. You don't need to shout – I can hear you.'

'Oh, it's Tessa!' Annie shouted as if she was yelling across a farmyard. 'What are you ringing up for?'

'Can I speak to Dad, please?'

'No, you can't. He's not here. And nor is your mother.'

'Where are they?' Tessa asked in surprise.

Annie started to wail and sob. She couldn't speak.

'Calm down, Granny, it's okay,' Tessa said, concerned.

'It isn't,' Annie wept. 'Your father's ill, Tessa, and he's gone missing in this terrible, terrible blizzard. No one knows where he's gone. Your mother's gone out too, looking for him, hours she's been gone – and Lucy can't get home because of the snow – she's stuck in Taunton. I'm worried SICK, Tessa. I wish you weren't up at that art college.'

'I'm actually in London,' Tessa said.

'LONDON! That's a dreadful place. There are thieves and gangs of hooligans.'

'I'm quite all right, Granny. I'm staying in a beautiful flat with my friend's mother.'

Annie didn't reply and Tessa could hear her breathing in panicky gasps. 'Don't hang up, Granny. Stay on the phone.

Let me think a minute,' she said calmly, and closed her eyes. She was aware of Starlinda somehow helping her without doing anything. She imagined her father's steady blue eyes. 'Where are you?' she asked, and it came to her in a flash. 'I know where Dad is, Granny,' she said. 'I can see him clearly, and he's under the Evergreen Oak tree, the one on the way to the Lime Wood – and he can't breathe. He needs an ambulance, Granny.'

She heard Annie give a little cry.

'Put the phone down now, Granny. I'll organise it all from here,' Tessa said calmly. 'I'll ring for an ambulance and tell them exactly where he is.'

'But how . . .'

'Do as I say. Put the phone down.'

She heard another wail, and a click.

She looked at Starlinda. 'There's a crisis at home. Can I make another call, please?'

'Yes – of course – whatever you need to do, Tessa.' Starlinda was looking at her with admiration and sympathy. 'I knew it,' she said, 'you're one of us.'

Kate made her way through the woods with Jonti tugging her along, the snowflakes buttercup yellow in the beam from the torch. The snow gusted between the trees, glazing the moss, covering the dead rabbits with shrouds of crystal. Overhead the bare branches roared and creaked, bending to snapping point in the wind. Being in the woods was alarming, with twigs and small branches falling around her, and

Kate began to feel afraid, not only for herself but for Freddie. Without Jonti's gallant little figure bobbing ahead of her, she would have turned back. The voice of reason kept telling her it was madness to walk through a lonely wood in the dark and the snow.

She pressed on, thinking about Freddie. He'd been so gloomy recently. He'd lost that spark of life, that twinkle in his eyes. Kate couldn't remember when she'd last seen it there, or when it had gone. Two years ago, she thought. In Weymouth. It had gone with Lucy's letter. Freddie had adored Lucy. She'd been a shining presence in his life, and he'd taken her words to heart. No matter how often Kate told him Lucy was just young and needed to find her own way in the world, Freddie had remained stone-faced and unforgiving. She felt he was grieving for Lucy, as if she'd died.

He was proud of Tessa, and close to her in a different way. He saw himself as Tessa's spiritual guardian, believing he alone understood her, feeling he had to protect her hypersensitive soul from the world. It had been hard for him to let Tessa go to Art College. He read her letters eagerly, hoping for the kind of success and confidence Tessa had experienced at Hilbegut. But it soon became obvious that Art College wasn't easy for her. While Kate felt happy that Tessa at last had a group of friends, Freddie seemed to think the art she was doing was 'soul-destroying,' as he put it.

Kate hoped Freddie would take up his stone carving again when Tessa had gone to college, but he hadn't touched it.

His chisels lay forgotten in a box, and a carving of a lion he'd started was pushed into a corner, half buried under bits and pieces of engines. It even had drips of black oil staining the cream Bath stone he liked to use. Kate also understood Freddie's deep attunement to the natural world. She saw how he cared about the birds disappearing and the rabbits dying. The book by Rachel Carson, *Silent Spring*, had touched their hearts. It was on everyone's lips. In the papers. In the pub. On the television. Everyone in rural Somerset knew about it, and saw its grim predictions coming true. To Freddie it was the wilful destruction of everything he loved and treasured. After the war they'd had high hopes of raising their girls in a beautiful, abundant, healthy world. *Silent Spring* felt like a betrayal. A different kind of war. A war against nature.

As Kate walked through the dark woods, those thoughts stacked up in her mind like a card house. Freddie was actually fragile. One wrong move could bring everything collapsing. As a nurse Kate had seen grown men completely destroyed by emotions they had tried to deny. Was that happening to her Freddie?

'How far have I walked?' she wondered, and stopped. She shone the torch around and saw only snow and tree trunks, dead ferns and arching brambles. Nothing she recognised. She walked on, and noticed the coppiced hazels with tiny new catkins hanging bizarrely in the bitter winter. *I'm in the nightingale wood*, she thought, *above Lexi's place. I could walk down across her fields and get help.*

She knew she wasn't far from the great scar which had appeared in the hillside woods. She'd heard they were felling the trees for timber, then planting Christmas trees on a commercial scale. Another thing that had devastated Freddie.

I'm coming to the Lime Wood, Kate thought, and remembered the long ago picnics in high summer, the sound of bees and the scent of bluebells.

Jonti was pulling harder at the lead now, his stump of a tail wagging. Kate shone the fading torch beam and found a small oasis of dry ground under the shelter of a massive tree. It was there, at last, that she saw the soles of Freddie's boots and the snow-covered folds of his overcoat as he lay against the trunk of the Evergreen Oak.

'Before you go, Tessa, there's something I want to give you.' Starlinda handed her a small gold-rimmed card. It said '*STARLINDA – Clairvoyant Medium and Healer. Readings by appointment*'. It gave her telephone number and she had handwritten her address on the back. Taped onto it was a tiny piece of crystal which was white at one end and gold at the other. 'This is citrine,' Starlinda explained. 'It's the golden crystal. It carries the healing energy that this planet needs, and it's your link with me. If you need me – hold the crystal – pick up the phone and I'll be there for you, Tessa. You're one of us.'

'Thanks – but what do you mean exactly?' Tessa asked, looking curiously at the golden crystal.

'You're very young, and you've got a lot of living to do,' Starlinda said, 'but when you're ready, come back to me and

I'll help you to train for your true work. It's not by chance that you ended up here today.'

'Train for what?'

'To be a medium and a healer.'

'A medium? I don't know what that is.'

'A medium talks with spirit people.'

Tessa gasped. She stared into Starlinda's eyes. 'I've done that all my life. But I have to do it in secret.'

'Poor girl – you're in chains, aren't you?'

Tessa nodded silently.

'The New Age is dawning. The Age of Aquarius,' said Starlinda, and her voice was gentle and reassuring. 'And you will be needed, Tessa. Don't hold back. I think you know already that you are a healer. There is training – wonderful training you can do with kindred spirits. Keep that card and crystal, even if it takes years, and come back to me when you're ready.'

'Thanks,' Tessa whispered, aware that Faye was rolling her eyes and fidgeting.

'Come back tonight if you need to,' Starlinda said.

'I might.'

'I'm not staying,' Faye said. 'I've got a project to finish.'

Starlinda gave them both a hug. 'Try to remember I AM your mum,' she said to Faye.

'Why don't you like your mum?' Tessa asked as the two of them ran downstairs to the street. 'She's lovely.'

Faye glowered. 'She's a pain.'

'Why?'

'Don't ask!' Faye set off along the street. 'If you want to see London – get on the Bakerloo line to Trafalgar Square,' she advised. 'You'll like that – and you've got the National Gallery there too. I'm going the other way. See you tomorrow?'

They parted, and Tessa made her way nervously to Trafalgar Square, emerging from the unfamiliar tube journey with a new sense of independence and adventure. London was hers to explore. She didn't care about her college work. Her mind was in a different dimension, still hearing the haunting music as if it was part of her, a part that would never leave. Her father was in there with her, talking to her from a great distance. She imagined him standing beside her in the bright city sunlight, his eyes full of astonishment when he saw Nelson's Column and the four enormous lions. *How strange*, she thought, *he is here with me – he's really here – I can see him*!

Chapter Seventeen

A LIGHT IN THE FOREST

Kate had never felt so alone and shocked. The stillness of Freddie's body lying against the tree was like coming to the cliff and looking over the edge of her life, the place where it ended.

She dropped Jonti's lead and let him go. His eyes shone green in the torch light as he snuggled into the heavy folds of Freddie's coat, his breath making steam in the cold air. Panic roared in Kate's ears, before her nursing training kicked in. Keeping calm was number one. Searching for a sign of life. Listening. Speaking words of comfort and hope.

She made herself walk forward, terrified that Freddie might have been shot by a careless poacher. Shot and left to die.

'Freddie? Darling – it's me, Kate,' she said, and listened.

A rasping breath, a twitch of his gloved hand on Jonti's back sent her rushing to his side. She dropped to her knees, and shone the torch on Freddie's face. His eyes were closed, his lips looked blue, but he was still breathing, rapid and

291

shallow, each gasp tight and difficult. Kate found his wrist and felt the pulse. It was fast.

Kate acted quickly and calmly. She knew that Freddie was very close to death. 'Don't try to talk, dear,' she said. 'I've brought your medicine. Try to take a sip.' She held the bottle to his frozen lips, and after a few more gasps, he managed to swallow some of it. Kate kept talking to him. 'I'm here now, Freddie. I won't leave you.' As she said those words, she realised she would have to leave him, to get help. She planned to run down across the snow fields to Lexi's place. Without swift medical attention, her beloved Freddie would die there in the stone cold shadows where the distant hours of summer were long forgotten.

Annie's flask was in the deep pocket of her plastic mac. Kate unscrewed the cup. 'Listen to me, Freddie. I want you to try and take sips of this hot tea. It will help you – even breathing the steam will help. That's it! Turn your head a little.' She held the cup to his lips. Freddie's eyelids flickered and he looked at her with black, terrified eyes. 'Don't worry, dear. It will pass. I won't let you die. No – don't try to talk,' Kate said, and gave him one of her smiles. 'We'll soon get you out of here and into a nice warm bed.'

Her encouragement seemed to give him strength to drink in tiny sips. But what would happen when she left him to get help? She must go quickly. It would take at least an hour, she reckoned, for her to phone an ambulance from Lexi's place, then for it to come out in the snow. Lexi might drive him to hospital – but how would they get him down there? He needed a stretcher.

Her desperation rocketed as she talked calmly to Freddie. His eyes stayed terrified, locked into hers in the eerie incandescence of the snow. The storm was easing and welcome glimpses of the moon filtered through the trees.

'I will HAVE to leave you for a few minutes, dear,' Kate said gently. 'I'll go down to Lexi's place and get some help for you. It's not far.'

Freddie struggled to speak. He clung to her like a drowning man. He gave her the lime tree seeds, tied in his hanky. Kate looked at them, puzzled at the urgency in Freddie's eyes. He gasped out a few words. 'They cut – my lime tree – down.'

'Don't upset yourself, darling. Now I MUST go for help.'

'Plant – the – seeds,' Freddie begged, and closed his eyes again, the effort of speaking draining the last dregs of his strength.

'We'll plant them together, dear, when you're better,' Kate said confidently. But she didn't feel confident. She felt terrified and powerless. She looped the end of Jonti's lead over Freddie's hand. 'Jonti will stay with you. I won't be long.' She kissed him tenderly on his cheek. 'May God take care of you.'

Quickly she walked away, shining the torch on the snowy ground and fought her way along a narrow winding path towards the edge of Lexi's fields. She squeezed through the barbed wire, tearing her plastic mac. Moonlight shone over the snow fields, and the tall elm trees along the hedges cast bars of indigo shadow. Kate was scared that Freddie would die, alone in the wood in the cold. She could hardly bear it. Keep hope alive, she told herself. And hurry.

She ran through the glistening new snow, awkwardly, twisting her ankles on the uneven ground. She could see the rooftops of Lexi's place, two fields away, and was surprised to see a lot of lights in the yard. What if Lexi was about to go out somewhere and lock the house? Where would the nearest telephone be?

Breathing hard, Kate tried to run faster, slipping and sliding across the moonlit snow. She couldn't let Freddie die. What about her girls? They'd be devastated. A family ruined. A family without a rock. 'Why Freddie?' she agonised. 'Why should it be him? Please God – please don't let this happen to us.' Her own breathing and the pounding of her heart became painful. Exhausted, Kate fell heavily into the snow, hurting both wrists. She picked herself up, and paused for a moment to get her breath.

A blinding light shone into her face as the beam of a powerful torch swept the field. Voices called out. Kate stood in the snow, trembling, trying not to cry as she saw a miracle happening. 'Am I dreaming this?' she said, aloud. The steady crunch of boots in the snow, the torches, the two men carrying a stretcher! And that white van in Lexi's yard was an ambulance.

'Kate!' Lexi came striding towards her, dressed in a sheepskin coat and woolly hat, a torch in her hand.

'Oh thank God! Thank God!' Kate was overwhelmed. 'Are they here for Freddie?'

'Yes – we know where he is, Kate – goodness, you're in a state!' Lexi said. 'Were you trying to get help? Is Freddie okay?'

'No – he's bad,' Kate said. 'Please hurry.'

She heard Jonti barking in the wood. They all hurried up to the place in the fence where Kate had got through.

'I can't believe this,' Kate said. 'Someone must have found Freddie. Who was it?'

'Tessa,' said Lexi. 'She rang me from London.'

Kate's eyes rounded. 'Tessa! But how could she have known that? She's in London!'

'Well, she did,' Lexi said. 'Apparently she rang home and her granny told her Freddie was missing, and that he was ill. Tessa knew exactly where he was. She said he couldn't breathe and she rang 999 – from London! – and organised an ambulance. Then she rang me and told me to expect them and asked if I would guide them up here – she said he was under the Evergreen Oak. Is he?'

'Yes – that's where he is – well, what a blessing. But Lexi – how did Tessa know?'

'She's psychic,' said Lexi bluntly, 'and you should be proud of her.'

'Psychic!' Kate fell silent as she followed Lexi into the wood, tasting the new word in her mind. Psychic. It echoed in the undiscovered realms of her consciousness.

★　　★　　★

Tessa stood by the fountain in Trafalgar Square. She'd never seen anything like it in her life. The massive jet of water, peppermint white in the morning sun, fascinated and excited her. She gazed and gazed, and took the last two shots on her precious roll of film in the Brownie Box Camera. Then there were the lions. Awed at the size of them, Tessa had spent a few of her last pennies on a postcard and a stamp. Her dad had never been to London, and he'd love the postcard. It would inspire him, especially if she wrote him a message on it. Bundled in her stiffly dried duffle coat, Tessa sat down on a bench and filled the back of the card with her neat writing. She was annoyed when a man came and sat beside her. He smelled of garlic and aftershave.

'You're a pretty girl,' he said, staring at her. 'Where are you from?'

Tessa glared at him. 'Planet earth,' she said rudely, 'and I want to be alone.'

'A lovely girl like you shouldn't be alone. I will show you London. I can pay for a taxi, and a meal.'

'No thanks. I said – I want to be alone.'

'I'll take good care of you.'

'Will you GO AWAY and stop pestering me.'

'Mmm, you are fiery. I like fiery women.'

Tessa snatched up her canvas haversack, stuffed her camera, pen and postcard into it, and marched off, stomping in and out of the pigeons. She sat on a different seat on the other side of the square and continued writing Freddie's postcard, but the feeling of sharing wonder had gone. *I hate men*, she thought furiously. Aware that he was still prowling, watching her, Tessa scanned the buildings around the square, and her eyes found the National Gallery. She popped the postcard in a letterbox, crossed the road and went up the steps.

It was warm and quiet in there, with huge leather seats. Entranced by the enormous paintings, she wandered through the galleries and sat down in front of Giovanni Bellini's *Agony in the Garden*. It spoke to her soul. The sunset sky, the rocky land-scape, the pain of the lonely figure of Jesus kneeling on a rock. *It's my life*, Tessa thought, *and that angel in the clouds – so far away, so small – it's like the real me – small and far away, but waiting!*

Tessa had chosen to stay in London on that Saturday morning. She even thought of staying there forever. Dropping out of college.

'Don't be an idiot,' Faye had said. 'We haven't done a term yet. Give it a chance.'

Starlinda had given Faye her train fare back to Bath, and Faye had accepted it grudgingly, and then hitchhiked. 'I'll be fine,' she assured Tessa. 'You do your own thing.' Starlinda had told Tessa she could come back and stay another night. The idea of a whole day to herself in great big beautiful London was intoxicating. So many places she wanted to see. Big Ben. Westminster Abbey. And the river – always the river. Time alone was precious thinking time. She planned to find a bank and draw out another ten shillings, maybe even a pound, to tide her over.

But first, she must go in a phone box, armed with a pile of pennies, and find out how her father was. She rang Yeovil

Hospital, and was shocked when her mother came to the phone and told her, in a hushed, flat voice, that Freddie was fighting for his life. 'Everyone is here, round his bed. Lucy's here, and Uncle George, and the vicar is on his way,' Kate said. Then the pips went, ending the phone call, using the last of Tessa's coins.

Tessa stayed in the phone box, her hand on the receiver, like a stone statue of a woman weeping in a garden. A bitter flame burned through her heart. 'Everyone is here –' Kate had said. *Except me*, Tessa thought, *me, the troublemaker. No one cares that I'm not there. But Dad would care. Dad would care.*

A shadow darkened the space inside the phone box, and the man who had pestered her was leering at her, his greasy face pressed to the glass.

Tessa shoved the door open and confronted him. 'Will you PISS OFF and leave me alone,' she screamed, 'or I'll call the police.'

His smell and his laugh followed her as she ran wildly across Trafalgar Square, dodging people, scattering the pigeons, her haversack flying from her shoulder. At the corner, she dashed across the road with the surge of people crossing when the lights were red. She paused by a man selling newspapers. 'Which way is the river?' she asked.

'Down that street.'

She ran blindly down the street and came to the embankment. The gleam of the water between the trees. The incoming tide. The healing power of this great river which seemed to bring the lost energy of Earth's wild places sweeping boldly into London. Even the sky seemed brighter, more silver, over the river. The wind easterly and far away down river was the embryo of a storm, like a pearl in the womb of the wind.

My dad is dying, Tessa thought. *Where are you, Dad? Don't die. Don't leave me. You're all I have.*

Annie watched from the window as the Reverend Reminsy got out of his car and walked up the path. She hobbled to the front door and opened it.

'Mrs Barcussy – I'm going to Yeovil Hospital now to see Freddie. Would you like a lift? I can take you, and bring you back.'

'But what about the snow?'

'It's not too bad, melting a little on the roads now.'

Annie battled with herself. She still had a terror of going out, especially in the snow. She imagined slipping over and breaking her hip the way Gladys had done. 'Thank you, but 'tis best if I stay here,' she said. 'I can keep the fire burning and look after the house.'

'Did you know how seriously ill Freddie is?'

'Kate rang me. She said not to worry.'

'Well – she's asked me to come and – and give him a blessing.'

'A blessing? I hope you don't mean the last rites, Vicar.'

The Reverend Reminsy hesitated. 'Where there's life, there's hope,' he said. 'Are you sure you don't want to come?'

'I won't come, thank you.'

Annie watched him drive away. Surely Freddie wasn't that bad? Kate hadn't been honest with her. Pulling the wool over her eyes as usual! She thought back to Freddie's childhood. He'd been ill with bronchitis every winter. The cold weather made him worse, and Annie had spent countless nights sitting with him as he struggled to breathe. With no money to pay the doctor, she'd used her own remedies. Hot mullein tea. Friars Balsam. Ipecac. Hot flannels and eucalyptus. But, beyond the remedies, Annie had a gift she had almost forgotten.

She went to her special drawer in the rosewood sideboard and opened it. She reached into the back and took out a brown paper bag. Inside was her favourite photograph of Freddie at seven years old, white-blonde hair, intense, knowing eyes. He wasn't smiling. Freddie hadn't smiled a lot, until he met Kate. Annie took out a tiny matinee coat, hand-knitted in pale blue wool. Freddie had lived in it as a baby for the first year of his life, and Annie could still feel him when she held it.

She sat down by the fire, in Levi's old chair, and put the photo of Freddie on her lap. She held the little matinee coat close to her heart, and remembered her way of healing. With her eyes closed, she asked for healing love to flow through the palms of her hands. It came, instantly, glowing with warmth. Her hands felt hot. She imagined how the healing love would look, and it was a beam of coral-coloured light, coming across the universe from the source of all joy. It was limitless and powerful. She let it flow, the way she used to, and visualised it reaching Freddie as he lay in hospital. 'My son is not going to die,' she affirmed. 'He's going to get well.'

Flames flickered white gold and orange, and then a deep crimson as the fire died down. Annie sat for a long time, focused on her prayer. She opened her eyes and gazed at the eastern sky where the tight pearl of a storm was melting away into patches of blue. She thought suddenly of Tessa, alone in London.

Melting snow gushed down the streets of Yeovil, carving winding torrents through piles of slush. The late afternoon sun was a corn-gold reflection blazing from windows and dusting the bare elm trees with light. Tessa hurried up the hill towards the hospital, her wet socks squelching in her shoes, the ends of her jeans heavy with water. Her duffle coat was again sodden wet and so was the coloured braid in her hair.

Not knowing what to expect, she braced herself and walked into the hospital foyer. A tall Christmas tree stood there, with pink and green fairy lights, baubles and toys hanging on it, and a pile of wrapped presents underneath.

The receptionist didn't look friendly.

'You shouldn't come in here in such wet clothes,' she said.

'I just hitchhiked from London.'

'Hitchhiked?' The receptionist tutted and looked her up and down. 'What is it you want?'

'I want to see my father — Mr Barcussy — where is he?'

'I'm afraid visiting hour is over. Come back at seven o'clock.'

'I can't do that,' Tessa said desperately. 'I'll have nowhere to sleep.'

'Nowhere to sleep! Oh, you're homeless are you?'

'No. I'm an art student. The banks are closed and I haven't got enough money to phone my family or catch a bus back to Monterose. I hitched from London, I've had no lunch, and I want to see my father – please.'

The receptionist tutted again and rolled her eyes.

'You must let me,' Tessa was close to tears and angry. 'If you don't, I shall walk through every ward until I find him and you can't stop me. You've no right to treat me like this when my dad is dying.'

The receptionist sighed and lifted the wooden counter lid to let herself out. 'Follow me, and I'll see what I can do.'

She set off huffily in her dry, clean uniform, and Tessa squelched after her with grief and anxiety knotted together in her stomach. Along the corridor were little signs of Christmas, holly and tinsel and snowmen made of cotton wool. A cardboard Santa pointed the way to the Children's Ward. They walked on, through smells and sounds, until they reached the Men's Ward.

'Wait there.' The receptionist went into the office marked *Ward Sister* and Tessa could hear her indignant voice. She heard the word 'hippie'.

'Leave it with me.' The ward sister came out in her navy blue uniform. She didn't look at Tessa's clothes. She looked at her eyes, kindly, with searching love, and Tessa felt the anger draining away like the drips on the end of her jeans.

'I need to see my father. I've hitchhiked from London.'

'You poor girl! Tessa is it?'

'Yes – how did you know?'

'He's been waiting for you, dear. He's so proud of you! Come with me. We'll draw the curtains round his bed and you can spend a bit of time with him. He's very weak and can't talk much – so you must do the talking.'

'Mum said he was fighting for his life,' Tessa said.

'He was indeed. But round about midmorning, he started to respond to the treatment. He's sitting up now and he's had a bowl of soup. Now take off that wet coat – then you can hug him – I'll hang it over the radiator for you.'

'Thanks.'

Under her coat, Tessa had a turquoise sweater from C&A, and a string of ethnic beads she'd found in a junk shop in Bath.

'Dad!' She ran to the bed, and Freddie held out his arms to welcome her, as he'd always done. 'Oh Dad – I've missed you so much.'

Freddie just held her, patting her hair, and whispering, 'That's my girl,' and when they finally pulled away from each other, he said, 'You look beautiful – like a beautiful angel.'

'Dad!' Tessa was moved, and surprised to see tears on Freddie's rough red cheeks, running into the stubble around his chin. His eyes looked at her with a raw spiritual hunger. 'What happened, Dad?' she asked.

'They – cut – my lime trees down.' Freddie hunched forward, gripping her hand, the effort of talking, and the need to cry seemed to be paralysing him. Tessa was alarmed. She put her arms around his tense shoulders, and held him. It felt weird to be doing what he had done for her so many times. She sensed the hot pain inside him, and remembered how she had healed Selwyn, how the horse had trusted her and come to her with the burning need to be understood, to be heard, to be given love. So she talked to Freddie in the same way, in the same special voice. The words didn't matter. It was the resonance and the love that reached the spirit, like the light in the forest. Those eight haunting notes, still in her mind. She let them sing, and visualised the light. She saw that years and years of 'men don't cry' had become the dark forest in Freddie's mind.

'NO!' said Kate and Annie together.

The consultant looked at them over his glasses, tapping his Parker pen on the arm of his chair. 'Why such a wall of resistance?' he asked.

'Absolutely no,' Kate said passionately. 'I will never, never let Freddie go to one of those places – and I was a State Registered Nurse. I know a bit about Hospitals for the Mentally Ill. My husband is not, and never has been mentally ill.'

'I agree,' Annie said. 'Freddie had a tough childhood – tougher than you would understand – Doctor. And he's always been strong.'

'That's precisely the problem,' said the consultant, pouncing on the opportunity to elucidate his case. 'Strength is denial, especially in men. It can lead to depression later in life, and that is what Mr Barcussy is suffering from now.'

'What rubbish.' Annie drew herself up very straight in the hospital chair. 'My son has always been taught to pull himself together. He's ill from bronchial asthma, not this fancy, new-fangled depression. I don't believe in it. No. We'll have him home and he'll soon get better, won't he, Kate?'

'I don't think it's rubbish,' Kate said carefully, 'but we've got a lovely home and a nice garden, and Freddie will soon get over this. He needs to get back to doing his stone carving and gardening, then he'll be happy.'

The consultant frowned over his notes. 'Yes – but – that's another issue. The stone dust is lethal. With his chest condition, your husband must never do stone carving again. He must find another hobby.'

Annie and Kate looked at each other. 'It's not just a hobby,' Annie said. 'It was his passion – and he earned a lot of money from it.'

'Nevertheless, it will kill him. The stone dust, and the cigarettes, and the fumes he's getting from working with engines. All that has to stop.'

Annie's face went crimson. She struggled to get up. 'I'm not gonna sit here and listen to this!' She brandished her ebony walking stick at the consultant. 'I've never heard such a load of codswallop – especially from an educated man like you. Good day.'

★   ★   ★

After Christmas, Tessa borrowed Kate's bike and rode into town. She called at the bank and drew a precious ten pounds out of her student grant money. Then she rode up through the woods to Tarbuts Timber.

It was a crisp blue day in January, the air still and expectant, and there were song thrushes singing in what was left of the woods. Tessa was due back at Art College the next day. Despite her resolve to drop out, she'd decided to stay there. She'd made the decision with a heavy heart, and she'd done it to please her parents. Freddie was home now, in the chair by the fire, mostly staring out at the sky, miserable because he couldn't smoke, and anxious about how he was going to earn money and keep the family. He wanted Tessa to go back to college. And so did Faye. She'd spoken to her on the phone, and Faye had said, 'Don't be daft, Tessa. It's only six months and we'll have done our first year – and we've got the long summer break. Then you can do your own thing.'

Tessa had found some flower pots and planted the lime tree seeds with Freddie. They'd stood them outside, along the garden wall. 'Water them, Dad, when I'm not here,' she'd said. Those little pots were a symbol of hope, and so was her plan for today. It meant parting with some of her money. She'd needed to buy a better camera for her coursework, but that would have to wait.

She pushed the bike up the steep muddy track to the timber yard with the ten pounds safely in the back pocket of her jeans. She swept into the yard, her hair and college scarf bright in the winter sun. A few annoying wolf-whistles came from the workmen who were loading piles of bare-rooted young Christmas trees into wheelbarrows. A man who looked like the foreman came to greet her.

'What are you doing here, young lady?'

'I've come to buy some lime logs.'

'Lime logs?'

'For my Dad. He's a sculptor, and he's been told he can't do stone work any more because of his health. So I want to get him into woodcarving, and I've been told that lime is the best wood to start with. So I've drawn ten pounds out of my student grant, to buy him some.'

'Oh, you have, have you? And how are you going to get them home? Not on your bike, surely?'

'No. I'd like them delivered, please. Today,' Tessa said, looking him in the eye. 'Please?'

She saw an answering twinkle in his eyes. 'Who is your father? Do I know him?'

'Freddie Barcussy.'

'Ah – Freddie. I know Freddie. Been very ill, I heard.'

'Yes – and doing some woodcarving will help him get well,' Tessa said. 'It's therapeutic, don't you think? Poor Dad, he's got to give up smoking too. I'm sure you can spare a few of those lovely logs.'

The man grinned. 'You're just like your mother,' he said, 'and you keep your money. I'll sort out a few nice logs for Freddie and bring 'em down.'

When the logs arrived later, Freddie's reaction was not what Tessa had hoped it would be.

'Whatever did you do that for?' he grumbled.

But Kate was enthusiastic. She dragged Freddie out of his chair. 'Now you come and look at these beautiful logs,' she said, 'and get those chisels out. I'd LOVE a woodcarving of an owl. Or a squirrel.'

''Tis different from stone,' Freddie said. He smoothed his hands over the pale new wood. 'I suppose I could have a go. Gotta start somewhere.'

Kate and Tessa retreated and left him looking at the lime logs. 'That was a good idea,' Kate said, smiling at Tessa. 'We're so proud of you. You've changed so much, haven't you?'

'Maybe I have,' Tessa said. She longed to tell her mother about London, and Starlinda, but she didn't want to stir the waters.

'Is it Art College that's changed you? Kate asked.

'Selwyn changed me,' Tessa said, 'and Hilbegut. But I've got friends now, Mum. Real friends. We're all in the same boat at college.'

'And have you met any men?' Kate asked.

'Men?' Tessa bristled. 'Sure – there are men students – and I like most of them, as friends, Mum, not as potential husbands!'

Kate looked disappointed. 'Well, I did so hope you'd meet someone nice,' she said. 'A nice boy from a nice family who would look after you.'

'I don't need looking after, Mum. Especially by a MAN!'

'But surely you want to get married and have a family?'

'No,' Tessa said. 'That's the last thing I want.'

'Oh, you'll change,' Kate said confidently, 'when Mr Right comes along. I dream of a beautiful white wedding for you, and a nice home of your own – and children. Won't it be lovely?'

Tessa opened her mouth and shut it again. *If only you knew what I really want!* she thought.

'Signal left,' Freddie said, his hands braced against the dashboard as Kate hit the brakes. The Rover 90 stalled and lurched to a halt. Tessa was thrown forward, banging her chin on the back of the seat.

'Oops – sorry!' Kate said, laughing it off. 'Should have changed down, shouldn't I?'

'Start her up again,' Freddie said calmly. 'Wind the window down and give the hand signal for turning left.'

'There's so much to do at once,' Kate protested, but she managed to stick her arm out and rotate it to signal left. Shakily she turned the heavy car into the gates of Bath Academy of Art and drove it briskly down the drive, the L plates fluttering from the back bumper. She wanted to look confident and in control. It had been hard to persuade Freddie, and Tessa, that she was capable of driving after only a few lessons. 'I'm not going to let you do that long journey when you've been so ill, Freddie,' she'd said. 'I'll drive up there – then I can sit back and let you drive me home. It'll be lovely. And Lucy will have something hot in the oven for us when we get back.'

Kate knew that Freddie was still more debilitated than he liked to admit. Christmas and New Year had been difficult. Despite her determined efforts to create seasonal joy, there had been disruptive cross-currents in the family. She'd hoped that Lucy would be reconciled with her father after the harrowing time when he'd almost died. Lucy had held his hand in hospital, and cried with the rest of them. But once Freddie was home again, she'd reverted to being hard-faced and full of resentment. Kate put all her energy into trying to make everyone happy.

'Thank goodness Tessa is settling down,' she said, as Freddie set off on the long drive home through the winter sunlight. 'I enjoyed seeing her little room, and meeting her friends. Such interesting girls! Faye is a bit – well – sullen – but Tessa seems to like her.'

'Ah – she does,' Freddie said, happy to be driving again with Kate in the passenger seat beside him. 'It's Lucy we've gotta worry about now.'

'I asked her to cook tea for us today,' Kate said brightly. 'She'll soon get tired of that silly Tim.'

Freddie was silent. She looked at his profile, and saw the tension in his jaw. She wondered why a man with such wisdom found it so impossible to forgive.

It was getting dark as they drove into Monterose and up the lane to The Pines. The house looked oddly unwelcoming, with only a light on in Lucy's bedroom, and no smoke coming out of the chimney. A blue van was parked in the road, and two men were carrying Lucy's dressing table down the path.

'What's going on?' Kate got out of the car and picked up Jonti who squirmed and licked her face in excitement.

'That's Lucy's dressing table! Where are you taking that?' she asked, frowning at the two men. 'Oh – it's you . . .' Kate was shocked at the precarious arrogance on Tim's face as he shuffled past her and loaded the dressing table into the back of the van. She tried to confront him, but he wouldn't meet her eyes. 'Ask 'er!' he mumbled, and jerked his head at Lucy who was coming through the front door with a pile of clothes draped over her arm.

'Mum!' Lucy looked guilty. 'I thought you'd be gone all day.'

'Hello, dear.' Kate went to her daughter, her eyes puzzled. 'We're tired out, and cold. But I drove all the way to Bath, and we took Tessa in and saw her bedroom. It's a lovely place, and Tessa introduced some of her friends to us.'

'Good for her,' said Lucy. Her tone was sarcastic, her eyes rebellious. She looked cold, bundled in a baggy brown sweater, a chunky knit that was obviously Tim's, a red scarf wound around her neck. Her legs were covered in thick black tights, her hands in woolly black gloves.

'Did you manage to make the casserole?' Kate asked. 'We're hungry – haven't eaten all day. And Freddie's really tired. He's still not well, you know, and he's going to miss Tessa.'

'Yeah. Pity he won't miss me.'

'What d'you mean, Lucy?' Kate look bewildered. 'What's going on?'

'Isn't it obvious? I'm moving out, Mum.'

Kate felt the shock hit her, right in the middle of her sturdy little body. She saw Lucy's eyes harden as Freddie came and stood beside her in silence.

'And no, I didn't make a casserole,' added Lucy. 'And I haven't lit the fire either. No time for that. Good old Lucy has had enough. I'm moving out. Excuse me, I've got stuff to pack.' She twisted past her parents, carried the clothes to the van and flung them in.

'But – Lucy – Lucy – NO!' cried Kate, doubling up with grief. 'Don't do this – please . . .'

She marched after Lucy and grabbed her arm. 'Please listen to me, Lucy. I'm your MOTHER. Lucy – you have a responsibility to your family – all we've done for you.'

Lucy shook her off. 'Don't manhandle me.'

Kate followed her through the kitchen and up the stairs. 'I'm not having it, Lucy. Why do it like this? Why try and sneak out when we were taking Tessa to college? Why couldn't we have talked it over? We still can. It's not too late, dear. Won't you change your mind?'

'No,' Lucy sighed, and Kate thought she saw a glimmer of compassion pass through her eyes. She looked down at Lucy's bed, now stripped to the green and white striped mattress, the pink paisley eiderdown and the frilly nylon pillowcases gone. The bedside lamp, the grey and cream radio, the two ageing teddies – gone. A box of shoes stood by the door, each pair with a special memory of a party or a birthday. On top were the strappy silver dancing shoes they had given her for Christmas.

It was the poignancy of seeing those elegant little shoes that broke Kate. She sat on the edge of the bare mattress, with the silent sting of powerless tears on her cheeks. Lucy rolled her eyes. Heartlessly, she picked up the box of shoes and marched out with it.

Kate could hardly breathe. She had chosen the shoes with such care and love. They were expensive, more than they'd planned to spend, so Kate had secretly added some money she'd made from selling her homemade butter. She knew how much Lucy wanted them. On Christmas morning, when she'd opened the parcel, there had been stars in her eyes. Stars they hadn't seen for so long. Freddie's eyes had twinkled in response. But it seemed the stars were now only temporary visitors, just passing through. Stars that popped in the sky and vanished like bubbles.

When she says goodbye, I should hug her, and wish her luck, Kate reasoned with herself, but even as the thought came, she heard the rattle of the van's engine. She went to the window and saw Freddie standing by the passenger door. He was saying something to Lucy, and Lucy wasn't listening. Her face was pale and hard as china.

Kate flung the window open and leaned out. 'LUCY! Don't go without saying goodbye.'

Tim was at the wheel. He glanced up at her, smirked, revved the engine, and took off into the twilight with black smoke spiralling from the exhaust. Hatred came and squatted in Kate's heart, alongside the burning grief. She stood in the window, feeling the blue shadows of frost creeping across her skin like a paralysing tide. *I must be a terrible mother*, she thought, and the memory of three-year-old Lucy danced, vivid and radiant, in her mind. *I'm no use to anyone now*, she thought, and the house felt suddenly empty and deathly cold.

She sat in Lucy's abandoned bedroom, staring at the bare walls, the yellowing curls of sellotape where posters had been. She listened to the sounds of Freddie lighting the fire, snapping sticks and crumpling paper. Kate crept downstairs. She didn't want the intensity of her grief to disturb Freddie. She must be strong.

His face was flushed in the firelight. His eyes looked at her, instantly reading her distress, and Kate couldn't stop herself sharing it.

'She didn't say goodbye.'

'Ah – she wanted to,' Freddie said, 'but Tim wouldn't wait. In such a blimin' hurry he was! He's got a hold over our Lucy. He's only got to say jump and she jumps. I told her: "You're gonna regret this," I said, "you're gonna wish you'd listened to me." But no, she knew better! Gone off to live in Taunton in some flat he's got.' Freddie shoved the bellows into the base of the fire and made it crackle and flare with light. 'Don't you upset yourself, Kate. She'll come crawling back one of these days, you'll see.'

Kate sat down with him on the hearth rug and warmed her hands. Together they stared into the comforting flames.

'We can only stand by, and pick up the pieces,' said Kate.

Chapter Eighteen

THE DAWNING

'Tessa will be terribly upset,' Kate said, crying as she tenderly wrapped Jonti's stiff body in a cloth and placed him inside the plywood coffin Freddie had made. Together they laid the little dog to rest under the lilac tree in the 'Anderson Hollow'. 'He's been such a wonderful dog,' she wept, 'and we never knew where he came from.'

Jonti had died in Kate's arms, a few hours after the vet said his heart was failing. Minutes before he died, the little dog had stared at Kate, licked her hand, and was gone, peacefully. She'd felt he wanted her to fetch Tessa. But Tessa was at college in the middle of her end of year exams.

'We shouldn't tell her,' Kate said, 'until she's finished the exams.'

Freddie disagreed. 'We should,' he said, 'and it's no good writing a letter. She'll be home at the end of the week. You should telephone. Tell her what happened.'

He stood beside her as she made the phone call to the students' hostel that evening. Tessa came to the phone. 'Hello Mum!'

'I've got a bit of sad news, dear,' Kate said. 'It's Jonti. I'm afraid he's died, he—'

'No he hasn't,' Tessa said at once. 'He's with Grandad.'

Kate was speechless. *My daughter is mad*, she thought, not for the first time. She handed the phone to Freddie. 'You talk to her.'

Predictably, Freddie didn't talk. He listened for a long time and Kate sat at the table by the window, with Jonti's collar in her hand. She watched Freddie's face and saw sparkles of excitement coming in. Then, suddenly, they vanished, and disappointment rumbled in his voice as he said, 'I'm sorry to hear that. Very sorry. Well – you come when you can.'

He put the phone down and looked at Kate, helplessly. 'She's not coming home.'

'What?'

'She . . .' Freddie opened his big hands as if trying to find words in the air, 'she's going to Cornwall.'

'Cornwall! What – with friends?'

'No. On her own.'

'On her OWN! She can't do that,' cried Kate. 'We must stop her, Freddie. Ring her back and stop her.'

'We can't stop her.' Freddie pulled out a chair and sat down close to Kate, his hand on her shoulder. 'Don't you upset yourself, love.'

'But we MUST stop her. Where's she going to sleep? How can she afford to eat? She'll be in a strange town, hundreds of miles from home, with no money and no friends.' Kate seemed to be winding herself into a frenzy, her eyes dark with panic. 'We can't stand by and let her do that. And for another thing, she's got a responsibility to her family. She can't just go off when she thinks she will, Freddie. Doesn't she care about us? Doesn't she care about Jonti? It's so ungrateful – and after we've decorated her bedroom – it looks so lovely – it was going to be a surprise.' Kate put her head in her hands.

'Now you listen to me.' Freddie held her close and waited until she'd taken some deep breaths and was looking at him again. 'Tessa is a young woman now, and whether we like it or not, we've gotta let her go, Kate. Let her make mistakes. How else is she going to learn?'

'It's so ungrateful,' repeated Kate.

'No – you've gotta forget that,' Freddie said firmly. 'Tessa's all right. She does love us, and she'll come home when she's ready. But if we make a fuss she'll turn against us, like – well, like Lucy. And as for Jonti – she said you were upset, Kate, at what she said.'

'I was. I thought we'd left all that nonsense behind, years ago – she's been so much better lately. Now she's talking about her grandad, who died before she was born. Didn't we drum it into her that she was never to say things like that?'

'Kate! Kate, listen to me.' Freddie suddenly had strength in his voice, and in his eyes. She looked at him, astonished, as the passion of what he believed shone through his whole being. 'You can't change who Tessa was born to be, any more than you can change the wind and the tide, the sun and the moon. Tessa has got a rare gift, Kate, and we have to let her use it. To forbid and deny it is a sin – a sin against every-thing we live for – a sin against Tessa's soul. No – you hear me out,' he looked into her troubled eyes and his intense, crystal-blue gaze quietened her panic. 'Believe me, I know. I had the same gift, Kate, and it was beaten out of me, that ability to see spirit people and angels. It's haunted me all my life. I'd give anything to have my life over again, and do you know what? I'd use it. I'd be honest about it, and not let people knock it out of me. As Mr Perrow said – it's a GIFT and not a curse. Nothing would make me prouder than to see Tessa have the courage to use her gift – and I believe that's what she needs to do. She can't use her gift here, with us and my mother, and Lucy, constantly condemning her for it. No wonder she wants to go off on her own.'

Kate looked devastated. 'We've failed her,' she said sadly. 'Well – I have anyway.'

Freddie looked at her wisely. 'You can parent the body, but you can't parent the soul.'

Tessa had never seen her home town from the railway. Her face was pressed to the window as The Cornishman belted through the hills. She glimpsed the pink cliffs of the alabaster quarry, the fields of ripe corn and the nightingale wood which now had an ugly scar of cleared hillside where acres of young Christmas trees grew in regimented lines. The train flew over the viaduct and the river valley with its sheep pastures, through the wild flower meadows which Tessa had renamed 'the killing fields', now barren squares of rye grass.

The train was flying through sadness, through the song that had so touched her heart – *Where Have All the Flowers Gone?* Tessa didn't feel she could bear to go home. Not this summer.

For three years, she'd spent her holidays working at Lexi's place, and Lexi had paid her £3 a week. She'd saved it all for this one trip. It was her 'ticket to freedom' fund.

Monterose was gone in a flash, a muddle of rooftops, a church tower, a few farms, a green bus waiting at the station. It seemed unreal, like a fast rewind of her life. It added one more load to the huge emotional baggage. The exhaustion of exams, the working all night to set up her end of year exhibition, the worrying, then the bittersweet parting, the saying goodbye to the best friends she'd ever had. She felt like an arrow being fired from a bow, flying out there, alone, to an unknown target.

The train dived through the tunnel and headed out across the Levels towards Taunton. Tessa didn't want to talk to anyone. She made a cushion from her rolled-up duffle coat, closed her eyes and slept, her hand curled around her rucksack. She didn't know, and didn't much care where she was going to sleep that night.

When she awoke, the train was pulling out of Redruth, through a strange new landscape of small fields with high stone walls, and heather-covered hillsides with massive granite boulders and the tall chimneys of tin mines. She disembarked at St Erth, and caught the local train to St Ives, staring excitedly out of the window as it rattled across the saltmarshes and past the vast empty beaches of Hayle. For the first time, she saw the rolling white surf, and her heart lifted.

Yet when she got out at St Ives, the sea was like a lagoon. It was an unbelievable colour, a translucent jade with patches of deep purple. Minutes later, Tessa was standing on Porthminster Beach. She dropped her duffle coat onto the sand, took off her shoes and ran down to the shore in the hot sunshine. The water was crystal clear, the waves lapping at her ankles like curls of golden glass. So different from Weymouth. A world away . . .

Godrevy Lighthouse shone like a helmeted warrior guarding the pristine bay, and to her right were wooded cliffs. A place to sleep, she thought. To her left was the harbour, a crescent of cottages and boats, and a green hill, like Glastonbury Tor, with a small grey chapel at the summit.

Tessa felt like a dragonfly emerging from its chrysalis after years of being a grub in the mud. She peeled off her clothes and changed into her new sea-green bikini. *I have waited all my life for this moment*, she thought, wading into the clear water.

She swam on and on, over golden nets of sunlight that danced on the sand below. She dived and let her hair splay out like seaweed. She floated with the sun on her face. Then she sat on the hot sand and gazed out at the distant surf breaking over Godrevy Lighthouse, and wondered how she could reach it. The sea was new and mysterious. She needed to watch and learn its ways.

From the beach shop, she bought a plastic lilo, a pastie, and a Kit-Kat, and persuaded them to fill her water bottle. Then she explored a narrow cobbled street called The Warren and discovered the Lifeboat House and the harbour, fascinated by the seagulls and the coloured boats. On the far side of the harbour was a bank of soft sand leading up to some cottages, a perfect place to sleep, she thought, and went to inspect it. There was a hand-painted notice, saying *NO HIPPIES. Well, I'm not a hippie*, she thought. *Not yet.*

She'd noticed a few hippies around the station, and under the shelter of the railway bridge that spanned the coastal path. One man had been sitting there as if guarding the collection of bundles and clothes spread along the wall. Tessa had glanced sideways at him and he'd been sawing the legs off his jeans with a bread knife. She didn't feel like joining his 'hearth'. It felt hostile.

The sunset glowed above the rooftops of the town, turning the gliding bodies of seagulls to orange. The church clock struck nine, each chime resonating across the water. Tessa sat in the soft sand corner until the stars came out, her back against the warm stones of the wall. With a sudden ache, she thought of Jonti, and longed to have his friendly body there with her, his fierce little face ready to bark and defend her. She remembered him at Weymouth, how he had loved to swim with them on a hot day, and how he would always circle in front of her, turning her back if she swam out too far.

It didn't look like rain, and she was satisfied to have found a cosy corner where she could sleep under the stars. So she blew up the plastic lilo. It took forever, breath after breath, and she cried a little, thinking absurdly of her bed at home and her mother tucking her in. *Don't be stupid*, she thought, and blew even harder. She lay down on the wobbly lilo, and covered herself with her duffle coat.

'You can't sleep here. Clear off!' a loud voice shouted, and a man with an angry black fringe stood over her. 'I've lived here all me life and I won't have no bloody hippies dossing on me doorstep.'

Tessa sat up. 'I'm not a hippie – and I'm not doing any harm. I'm an art student.'

'I don't care if you're the Queen of Sheba. Buzz off. Go on, go, or I'll throw a bucket of water over you. And if that don't work, I'll take a knife to that silly plastic lilo.' His voice got louder and louder and people strolling along the harbour-side stopped to watch.

'This is a public beach,' said Tessa bravely, but she was shaking inside. Loud voices upset her at the best of times.

'Don't you get brazen with me,' he bellowed. 'Go on – take your rubbish and go.' He scooped a handful of sand and flung it over her. It stung her face and eyes, and spattered into her hair. 'D'you want another one?' he growled, putting his face close to her. He smelled of oil and fish.

'All right, all right. I'm GOING.' Tessa jumped to her feet, furious and scared. She brandished a shoe. 'Leave me alone and give me a chance to pack up my stuff, or I'll throw sand right back at you.'

'Ooh!' he jeered, but stood back, his stocky arms dangling at his sides. 'If you're not gone in five minutes, I'll have everyone in these cottages chasing you off. Bloody hippie.'

Trembling with fury, Tessa set her face and gathered up her belongings. She walked off into the twilight, dragging her duffle coat and the plastic lilo.

Freddie carried the sale board down the garden path of The Pines and hammered it into the hard red earth close to the wall. The sound rang mockingly across the rooftops of Monterose and echoed from the distant hills. When it was firm, he stood in the road looking at it from all angles, then snipped away some rosehips and tendrils of honeysuckle which were trying to obscure the black and white notice he had painted. *FOR SALE*, it said, and he'd added *LOVELY FAMILY HOME*. Then he padded back into his workshop and waited for the storm to break. Kate would be back soon, on her bike, and she'd see the notice, and so would Annie when she stood at her window.

Half-heartedly, he picked up his chisel and chopped away at a block of walnut wood. The local Catholic Church had commissioned him to carve a statue of St Joseph. A hundred pounds, he'd told them. It sounded a lot, but it was a pittance, he felt, for three months' work. It wasn't going to rescue them from the mounting debts which dated back to his illness. His Rover 90 had been traded in for a battered Morris Traveller, and his lorry stood idle. Without the work from the stone quarry, and with many more lorries on the road, his haulage business wasn't viable.

From the workshop window, Freddie watched Kate arrive and get off her bike. She had those baggy trousers on again.

He wondered why. She stood looking up at the sale board in a confrontational stance, hands on hips, leaving her bike where it had fallen. Her eyes were gleaming the way they did when she intended to get her own way. She reached up and tried to shake the post. It didn't budge. Then, to Freddie's alarm, Kate vaulted neatly onto the wall, stood up and tried to prise his carefully painted notice away from its post.

Before he could intervene, she abandoned that idea and jumped down from the wall, making her breasts bounce as she landed. Bemused, Freddie watched her march into the shed. He heard rummaging sounds and she emerged with a hessian potato sack. She shook it, smoothed it, and vaulted onto the wall again. She stretched the sack over his sale board, brushed the dust from her hands, and did a little wiggle of satisfaction at her moment of glory. With her nose in the air, she wheeled her bike up the path and disappeared inside.

Freddie smiled to himself. That was SO Kate, he thought, warrior Kate. When he went indoors for his tea, she didn't mention it, so he kept quiet. But later, Kate wanted to go into his workshop with him. She had changed out of the baggy trousers and put on a summery dress.

First she admired his woodcarvings. There were owls, swans, dolphins and a horse's head he'd done for Tessa. But Kate seemed to be searching for something else, her eyes scanning the shelves. Suddenly her face brightened, and she lifted out a bird table he'd made with a Japanese roof of tiny slats of larch. 'This is IT,' she said. 'I could sell these for you, Freddie. They're lovely. And it's what everyone is wanting now – now

that the wild birds are declining. We've got to feed them..
Susan's got a bird table in her garden, a tatty old thing, and it's
always covered in birds. I don't know what she puts on it!'

'They're easy to make,' Freddie said, 'and I could make
nest boxes as well. But I don't see how you could sell them,
Kate.'

'When I've passed my driving test, I can load the car up
with them and go round all the hardware stores and garden
centres. There are lots.'

'They won't buy 'em!'

'They will if I'm selling them,' Kate said. 'I can be VERY
persuasive.'

'Ah, you can,' Freddie found himself smiling. A chink of
light appeared in the gloom.

'Well, my test is in three weeks' time,' Kate said, 'so you
get cracking and make me a selection. Then I can take orders.
And we could put up a display by the front gate.'

'I dare say we could.'

'AND . . .' Kate's eyes had a bright, good-humoured glare.
She wagged her finger. 'We are not going to sell The Pines,
Freddie. I won't let you. That would be like giving up.'

'You can't stop me, Kate.'

'Oh yes I can. Believe me I can. There's nothing I cannot
do if I put my mind to it. Now you take that notice down or
I'll pop out at midnight and saw it off. The neighbours would
just love that.'

Freddie stood looking at her, his mouth twitching, his
mind hovering between negativity and humour. He was

aware that Kate was manipulating him, but she was also rescuing him, and inspiring him. 'I need you so much, Kate,' he said passionately, 'and I admire your guts. Don't ever leave me, will you?'

'NEVER!' she declared, giving him a hug.

Freddie thought about her idea. He strolled down to the gate and considered clearing a display area. He started to pull some of the long grass away from the wall, when he made a discovery. A row of terracotta flowerpots stood in a line at the base of the wall. His heart leapt. Growing out of each pot was a young lime tree. His seeds! They had grown. Thrilled, he disentangled the pots from the grass, stood them in wooden trays in neat rows, then he fetched a can of water and gave them a good soak.

If only Tessa was there to see them. To share his dream. For it was in that moment a dream was born. He leaned on the wall, staring down the road at the majestic hedgerow elms, some of them fifty feet high and casting bars of shadows across the tarmac. He knew that elm trees had been part of the ancient wild wood which had covered Britain centuries ago. Their bark and dense foliage was used by a cornucopia of wildlife from butterflies to woodpeckers. Granny Barcussy had told him often how elm was used for healing. If you burned elm wood like incense, it would give you confidence. The inner bark could heal eczema and rheumatism. She'd also told him that elm trees were magic, and if you stood under one, it would connect you with the afterlife.

Freddie's own childhood had been lived under and around the elm trees which stood like sentinels along every hedge and on every street corner. He couldn't imagine the land without them. It would be so bare. Yet something he'd heard on the radio haunted him. Dutch Elm Disease. Could it come to Britain? Could it destroy thousands of beautiful trees? Some said it was already here.

He crossed the road and stood under his favourite elm tree, the oldest and tallest, the one that turned the brightest gold in autumn. He looked at it carefully, and noticed a few dead branches, their leaves a dirty mustard colour. He picked some of them up from the road. It was high summer and all the leaves should have been green. Freddie stood close to the trunk and touched the bark. He closed his eyes, and listened. And then he knew. The tree was dying. There was nothing he could do.

Tessa came into his mind then. Tessa sitting at the tea table, with her hair in plaits, arguing with Annie. What Tessa said had affected Freddie deeply. 'When the earth is sick . . .'

But there was nothing he could do.

He needed Tessa to come home.

Tessa slept in a grassy hollow at the back of Porthminster Beach. At first she lay awake, listening for footsteps. The thought of someone discovering her in the night was alarming. Her mind was replaying the scene of the man shouting at her. No matter how firmly she told herself to stop, her mind wanted to recycle it over and over. She couldn't let go of the memory. She wanted Jonti so much. She regretted telling her mother she'd seen the little dog in spirit. It had caused a rift – another one. But did it matter? After all, she was free now. Theoretically.

She listened and worried, snuggled under her duffle coat which felt like her one and only friend. *But I've chosen this,* she told herself. *I could have gone home. I could have gone to London with Faye. I didn't know just how frightened I was going to feel. But I'm not going to let fear spoil my chance of freedom.*

Tired out, she eventually slept, and awoke to the dawn chorus in Cornish. Hundreds and hundreds of seagulls glided through the dawn twilight, making wild music as they circled high in the sky above the town, fading into the distance, then coming close again with a full-on chorus. Hauntingly beautiful. Different from the nightingales. A raw, unafraid, exultant cry that touched her soul in a new place, awakening something she'd spent her entire life trying to repress.

The early morning sea was aquamarine and steely. Between the cries of the seagulls, there seemed to be a ringing sound coming from the sea, from the bell buoys far away, or from all the clocks in Cornwall chiming across the water. It was more than a sound. It had resonance, and Tessa could feel it in the grains of sand, and the blades of grass, and in the ancient lichen-covered rocks. Like a silver sword hundreds of miles long, a power line she had sensed in her childhood. It was part of her as if she was a glass bead on a string.

The ringing sound disappeared with the silence of the rising sun and its flare path of golden pink across the ocean.

Even the gulls went quiet, and stood on the wet sand, their beaks to the light, in perfect stillness. Teaching the world how to greet the sun.

Tessa drank some water and ate a biscuit, then curled up under her duffle coat, and slept with the sunrise imprinted on her dreams, and with a new feeling of safety. She woke, refreshed, at mid-morning, deflated her airbed and rolled it up, stuffing it into her rucksack with the bulky coat. The waves on Porthminster Beach were still small, but surf was breaking far away over Godrevy. Maybe she'd come to the wrong place. She considered hiking along the coastal path until she reached the surf.

First she explored the cobbled streets, passing cottages with pots of bright geraniums and windows with knitted sailor dolls. The high street smelled of pasties and fresh bread. Tessa was starving and she needed to work out the cheapest possible way of eating. A huge pastie, steaming hot and crammed with well-seasoned root vegetables and minced beef seemed good value. At the last minute she changed her mind in the shop and bought a vegetarian one. It felt good. *I'm an animal lover*, she thought, *I don't EAT my friends*. She remembered the delicious vegetarian meals Starlinda had introduced her to, and the memorable comments she'd made about saving the planet. It happened in a flash. From the moment she sat on the glittering harbour-side and sank her teeth into the luscious pastie, Tessa became a vegetarian.

Satisfied, she wandered through the hot streets, wanting to swim again, but saving herself for that elusive surf. She paused, looking at a little street called The Digey. A pavement café was there, and it was crowded with long-haired, suntanned men, and girls with flowers in their hair. They were laughing and eating, some sitting in the street with their backs against the café wall, plates of food in their hand. Tessa edged her way past. She wanted to stop and look at every man to see if he was Art. But she still needed to be alone, not get involved, so she walked on, hearing a song belting out from the café.

She walked on up the street without knowing why. Something was drawing her. A new light on the cobbles. A new glaze of salt in the air. A new feeling of transition, of walking towards the edge of a cliff. Where all you had to do was trust and jump off into white space.

The hot, sweaty, pastie-smelling town was left behind and she walked towards a dazzling energy. Ahead of her, between the cottages, was a wall, and a sound like nothing else. Both a roar and a whisper. It was eternal. And it had a heartbeat. A thrum thrumming pulse, the heartbeat of the Atlantic Ocean.

She tasted the sea salt on her lips. She stared in disbelief at the towering white surf piling in, higher than the horizon, wave upon rolling wave. She wanted to dance in the street with pure excitement and awe.

There were hippies sitting carelessly on the wall, with sun-bleached manes of hair, their skin tanned a dark gold and glistening with salt. A line of Malibu surfboards were propped along the wall, and on the corner was a café with a big black footprint painted on the wall. It was called the *Man Friday*.

Tessa leaned on the wall, mesmerised by the surf. It was high tide and the waves were foaming across the sparkly shell sand of Porthmeor Beach. She ran down the steps, dumped her rucksack against the wall and quickly changed into the sea-green bikini. Then, feeling very small against the awesome sea, she waded slowly into the marbled stretches of foam, amazed to feel it sucking the sand from her ankles as the wave retreated. It had power. Power that she wanted.

At first it was glorious, feeling her body being torn between the hot sun and the cold sea. Jewel green and lace white, the waves curled and frothed around her, slapping her bare tummy, lifting her like driftwood, knocking her over, grabbing the wavy tresses of her chestnut hair and chilling her scalp. Her skin felt burning pink and alive.

Tessa was a confident swimmer, but swimming was impossible, even between waves, and she was wary of the fast surfboards that flew past with keen-eyed, wild-haired men crouched on them like Michelangelo paintings of gods flying through the heavens. She moved down the beach out of their way, and stood knee-deep, looking at the sea. Beyond the breakers the water was inky blue, the swell like green silk. That was where she wanted to be. She dived through every wave and fought her way out there until she could float and swim, and look down through clear water to the pale sand below.

She swam until she was deeply cold. It seemed part of the transformation experience. She ignored the shouting voices from the beach. She heard only the whispering roar of the sea. What made her turn back was the bright face of a small white dog circling in front her. Jonti!

The tide had turned, and it was hard to swim back. Tessa realised suddenly how far the sea had dragged her. Jagged black rocks were close, with the surf breaking over them. Why were those people on the beach waving and shouting? Who were the two men who dashed into the sea and began to swim furiously towards her? And why, suddenly, was the strength leaving her body? Her arms were weak and aching, her legs numb, her breathing laboured.

It was then that Tessa panicked and went under.

Chapter Nineteen

... OF THE AGE OF AQUARIUS

'GET OFF ME!' Tessa screamed in fury at the two men who grabbed her. She thrashed like a caught fish in the water.

'We're not attacking you, sweetheart. We're rescuing you. We're lifeguards.'

'I don't need rescuing. I can swim perfectly well. Leave me alone.'

'Listen to me, sweetheart. Listen!' They held her still in the raging sea, keeping her head up out of the water. 'We're Cornish lifeguards and we know what we're doing. You're in serious danger. You're exhausted and you're getting swept onto those sharp rocks. We're taking you back to the beach.'

Tessa felt the grip of their iron-man fingers around her arms and a primal fear caught her in its fist, emerging from her mouth as rage.

'I want to be alone. Let go of me,' she yelled, and struggled furiously, going under again, swallowing water, coughing and spluttering as some of it went into her windpipe. The coughing and the exhaustion interfered with the rage. She felt herself going limp and crying with frustration. Terrible memories surfaced. Nightmare times of being held down at the dentist. The smell of chloroform gas. The fighting. The day at the mill, and the troll-like figure of Ivor Stape forcing her back into a deep chair, holding a rag over her face with that same ominous smell of gas. 'I hate men. I hate you. Leave me alone,' she found the strength to scream, and the scream seemed to break some kind of barrier. She burst through the splinters into calmer water.

Directly in front of her was a pair of steady hazel eyes. Tessa stared into them as the two lifeguards dragged her to safety. They had put her on a Malibu surfboard and were steering it into the beach. The ink blue of deep water was changing to the white lace patterns of foam. Her feet touched the sand. She tried to stand up but her legs were quivering and she felt totally vulnerable.

'Come on – only a few yards more and we'll be on the beach,' said one of the lifeguards, and Tessa realised that he'd been talking to her quietly, all through her panic, and she hadn't listened. 'Do you want us to carry you?' he asked.

Tessa shook her head. A group of hippies were standing on the shoreline watching the rescue and they were clapping. A girl with stringy hair and a full length patchwork skirt took a moon daisy from her headband and gave it to her silently. Another woman who looked like a Native American came forward and wrapped an ethnic brown and white blanket around Tessa's shoulders. It felt strangely welcoming, and a welcome was not what she'd expected at all.

'Do you think you need an ambulance?' the lifeguard asked. 'It might be as well to get checked over.'

Tessa shook her head. She looked at him for the first time and noticed the sea water glistening on his thighs, and looked in surprise at his grey hair and wizened face. He was older than her dad! And she'd been incredibly rude. 'I'm sorry,' she said. 'I freaked out.'

He gave her a fatherly pat on the shoulder. 'No hassle,' he said. 'All in a day's work for us. Proud Cornishmen!'

He wasn't the one with the hazel eyes. She looked at the other one, and it wasn't him. She sat down on the sand and allowed her legs to shake, the moon daisy in her hand staring up at her with innocent love. 'Thank you,' she said, and the group of hippies sat down with her like a protective seed pod. They didn't ask her any questions. A feeling of trust and acceptance emanated from them.

A mug of hot coffee was put into her hands. She studied the tiny bubbles round the rim and sipped it gratefully. The magnificent sea and the surf were still there. She looked at the man who had brought the coffee, and it was him. The steady hazel eyes locked with hers. Silent thoughts took root and burst into bloom between them. It was the way it had been with Selwyn. Only this was a man, and he needed healing. He had rescued her because, in some way, he needed her.

He wasn't a Michelangelo. He was ordinary. It was the eyes that were oddly expectant, a curiously disturbing blend of neediness and confidence.

She wanted a name. 'I'm Tessa,' she said.

'Paul.'

The hazel eyes held hers for a few more moments and then he looked down. He turned away, picked up his surfboard under one arm. 'I've got to catch the waves,' he said. 'I'll see ya, Tessa. Glad you're okay.'

She watched him run down to the sea, his reflection in the wet sand a slice of bright colour from the orange surfboard.

'It hasn't put me off,' Tessa said to the two women who were still looking at her caringly. 'I've never seen the surf before, and I love it. I went out too far.'

'There's a current out there. You have to bathe between the two flags,' the elderly lifeguard explained, 'so you take care, young lady; I don't want to be fishing you out again! Now if you're sure you're okay, I'll leave you to it.' He grinned and held out his hand. 'Friends?'

'Friends.' Tessa gave his hand a squeeze, and managed to smile.

'I'm Clare, and this is Lou,' said the moon daisy girl, 'and we're camping out on the cliffs at Clodgy. Any time you want to join us, Tessa, you're welcome. Love and peace is where we're at.' She pointed at the distant rocky headland to the left of Porthmeor Beach.

'Thanks – I might,' Tessa said, 'but I'm a bit of a loner.'

'That's okay. Do your own thing.'

'I'll give you a healing drum session, any time,' Lou said, looking at her with mysterious, hooded brown eyes.

'A healing drum!' Tessa raised her eyebrows.

'I do sacred drumming, five element rhythms. It's healing the Earth through resonance and love. Stop by sometime and I'll teach you.'

'Resonance. Yeah – that means a lot to me,' Tessa said. 'I might take you up on that, Lou. And thanks for the blanket. You'd better have it back.'

'Keep it,' Lou said. 'As a token of caring love. It came from Peru.'

'Thanks – I'd love it,' Tessa said, and to her surprise Lou gave her a hug, and so did Clare. 'Group hug,' she said, and the hug went on for about a minute. Tessa could smell incense on their clothes and hair, and spicy cooking smells. For a moment she felt their three hearts beating in unison, there on the warm sand, with the mighty heartbeat of the ocean in the background.

'Love and peace. You know where we are, Tessa.' Lou and Clare walked away, their skirts flowing, and the rest of the group followed, leaving Tessa alone on the wide beach, the coffee mug still in her hand.

Wrapped in Lou's blanket from Peru, she sat against the wall at the top of the beach, thinking, and watching Paul on his orange surfboard twisting and swooping on the wild Atlantic surf.

Kate had taken to waiting for the postman, busying herself near the window or in the garden. He came at 8.45, each morning, and to Kate it felt like eternity as she watched him lean his bike on the wall, rummage through the letters in his basket and stroll up the path. There was a mini-flame of hope, then a rush of disappointment when Kate saw the letters on the mat and knew there was nothing from her girls. On the days when the postman cycled past she felt bleak and forgotten.

At night she lay awake with the curtain back, staring out at the summer stars and worrying. Letters from Lucy were rare, usually defiant diatribes about her life in a tiny bedsit in Taunton. The friends she had. The fun she had. Her wonderful boyfriend and his open-minded family who had 'moved with the times'. On occasions Lucy's letter had been so hurtful that Kate hadn't shown it to Freddie. She kept the deep hurt to herself, and told no one. But at least they knew where Lucy was.

She worried obsessively about Tessa. The idea of her daughter out there, sleeping rough, shattered the bedrock of Kate's maternal, sheltering love. She felt disempowered and helpless. Freddie loved her for her radiance and her shining optimism. Maintaining it was a struggle, creating a damaging inner conflict in Kate. A sense of failure. A sense that her life had been wasted.

A week after Tessa had gone to Cornwall, Kate caught a glimpse of a brightly coloured card in the postman's hand. She waited by the door, her heart thudding. Then, huge relief and joy as Tessa's postcard shot through the letterbox and landed on the mat like a gold brick.

Kate took it to the kitchen table and sat down. Even touching the postcard, touching Tessa's handwriting, the stamp she'd licked and stuck on, was somehow like touching Tessa. 'A little bit of treasure,' Kate mused. 'Is this all I have left of my daughter?' She hardly dared to read it, but she did, and it brought a smile to her eyes. She read it again, and scrutinised the picture of a quaint harbour town with an impossibly blue sea. Then she took it out to show Freddie.

'Look what I've got!' she beamed. 'A postcard from Tessa.'

Freddie turned round from his workbench and put down the hammer he'd been using to nail the larch wood roof slats onto a Japanese bird box. His eyes sparkled when he saw Kate's smile. 'You read it to me,' he said. 'It's such tiny writing.'

'*Dear Mum and Dad,*' Kate read, '*I'm having a groovy time. I've been swimming, and I love the wild surf. St Ives is the most beautiful place, and it's full of art galleries. The streets are so narrow that people hang their washing across them. I've made friends – Lou and Clare – and they're looking out for me. I'm very happy here, and okay, so please don't worry at all. By the way, I've met a really nice man, Paul. With love, Tessa xxx PS Put a moon daisy on Jonti's grave for me.*'

'There you are,' said Freddie. 'Will you stop worrying now? You've got shadows under your eyes, love.'

'I can't promise not to worry,' Kate said, and her eyes brightened. 'And how about that? – She's met a man! At last, Freddie.' Kate visualised Paul – a 'really nice man'. He'd be tall and wearing a good tailored suit. 'I hope he's got a sports car,' she said.

'Don't get your hopes up,' Freddie said. 'But – well at least we know where she is, don't we?'

'I can enjoy the day now,' Kate said. 'And look at these beautiful bird boxes. I can't wait to get out there and sell them, Freddie. So many different ones! Ooh, I do like that one with the little bird on it – so cute.'

Freddie basked in her encouragement. Making bird boxes wasn't what he'd dreamed of doing, but it was easy and pleasant, and maybe it would make them some money.

'I haven't seen Mother this morning,' he said. 'Will you go and show her Tessa's card?'

Suddenly the colour drained from Freddie's face. A shadow filled his eyes. Kate stared at him in concern. 'What is it? What's the matter?'

'It's Mother,' he said quietly. 'Something's wrong.'

Together they walked through Annie's garden where bees were busy on the lavender flowers, and the wistful faces of pansies lined the garden path.

'Her curtains are closed.'

'And she's locked the door.' Freddie knocked on it gently. 'Mother?'

'I'll get our key.' Kate ran into the house, still clutching the postcard, and took Annie's key from its hook. Inside Annie's apartment it was silent except for a few flies buzzing at the window. 'Hello! Annie?' she called. The kitchen was empty, and the sitting room. Annie's knitting trailed colours from Levi's chair, and a bunch of sweet peas drooped from a vase on the table. 'She can't still be in bed.'

They looked at the bedroom door, and each other. 'You go in,' Freddie said.

Kate found Annie in bed, in her flowery nightie, the sun spilling a beam of light on her silver hair. Her eyes were open, and frightened. 'I thought you were never coming,' she said in a weak voice. 'I can't move, Kate. 'Tis my heart.'

'Oh Annie!' Kate held her hand and saw that the nails were blue. She felt the pulse in her wrist. It was fluttery and erratic. 'Don't try to talk,' she said.

'I've – got to . . .' Annie whispered. 'Got – things I want – to say.'

'You need the doctor, Annie. He might send you to hospital,' Kate said.

'No – no – don't you call him. I don't want it. Let me go, Kate. It's my – time.' She stretched out a shaking hand to Freddie, and her voice faded away.

'She won't go to hospital,' Freddie said quietly to Kate. 'But you ring the doctor anyway. He might give her something.'

'No – no!' Annie cried, when Kate tried to leave. 'I want to tell you something.'

Kate went back to the bed. She listened caringly as Annie tried to speak.

'Where's Tessa?' she said. 'Is she here?'

'No, not yet.'

'I – want – to say – sorry. Sorry I've been down on her. Will you tell her? I – only – meant to help her.'

'I'll tell her,' Kate said. 'She'll understand, don't worry Annie.'

'And you,' Annie clutched her hand, 'I've criticised you – I'm sorry, Kate. You're – you're an – angel.' Tears ran down her old cheeks.

'Don't upset yourself. We know,' Freddie said, taking her other hand. 'And Tessa's all right. We've got a postcard from her here.'

Kate held up Tessa's card, but Annie couldn't seem to focus on it.

'Don't leave me,' Annie begged, and Freddie pulled up the basket chair and sat close to the bed.

Annie was quiet for a moment, her eyes searching his. 'She's going to get hurt,' she muttered.

'Who?'

'Tessa.'

In the days that followed her rescue, Tessa was increasingly drawn to the hippie commune out on the low cliffs at Clodgy. She still went back to her grassy hollow at night, and spent the nights alone there, gathering stores of joy from the moon and stars, and the dawn over the sea, exulting in her aloneness. After her 'brunch' pastie by the harbour, she headed out towards Clodgy, and walked the coastal path towards Zennor. The granite boulders got bigger and more thickly bearded with lichens in incredible colours, sage green and hot golden orange, then the burn of intensely pink heather growing in the cracks. Between the rocks were intimate bright green fairy gardens where there were ladybirds and tiny spiders, and mosses with red-gold stamens. Tessa loved it. She spent time studying it all, and did some drawings in her sketch pad. She sat for hours watching enormous waves surging into rocky coves, the beads of spray pausing high in the air before spattering down on the rocks. Later in the afternoon the rising waves glittered as the sun came round to the west. Tessa was sure there were secret angels in the sunlit waves. She felt she could manipulate the sparkles and make a magical picture happen.

She wanted nothing else.

Paul sought her out a few times, and they sat on the beach talking about poetry. When he wasn't on a surfboard, he had a book in his hand. He did a lot of energetic talking, about politics and war, about his home in London. Tessa half listened and watched his eyes. She felt the words he was using so lavishly were pelting down like a rainstorm, hiding the real Paul. She wished he would shut up.

'Aren't you lonely?' he asked her, in one of the pauses.

'No,' she said, 'I'm the opposite of lonely. I avoid people mostly.'

'Why's that?'

Tessa shrugged. 'I've always been like that.'

'So – who do you talk to?'

Tessa wanted to tell him she talked to spirits, but whenever she tried to say something like that, a crowd of frowning faces popped up before her; Miss O'Grady, the Reverend Reminsy, Lucy, her grandmother, and mostly her mother.

'You can talk to me,' Paul said eagerly, his hand on his chest. When Tessa just stared at him, he said, 'I can't figure you out, Tessa. I need to know where you're at.'

Tessa looked away. She let some of the shell sand trickle through her fingers. 'I'm an art student,' she said. 'But I'm on the brink of dropping out.'

'What's stopping you?'

'I don't want to hurt my parents.'

'Shit! You can't live your life like that,' Paul said. 'It's your life, not theirs. My parents want me to work in a bank in the city. ME! That's why I'm down here, roughing it, finding myself – who I am – they locked me away for years.'

'Locked you away? Literally?'

'No – metaphor. But they kidnapped my mind and used it as an ego trip. *My son is a genius. My son is this. My son is that.* And, at the end of the day, if I just wanted to fall in a heap and listen to music, they dragged me out to extra coaching and chess clubs and stuff like that.'

'My lot kidnapped my SOUL,' Tessa said, ignoring the sadness of being disloyal, 'and they didn't use it as an ego trip. They dumped it, like rubbish.'

'That's criminal,' Paul said, looking at her intently, his hands hovering as if he wanted to touch her.

'Well – my dad didn't,' Tessa added. 'Dad is really cool.'

Paul reached out and slipped his hand round the back of her neck, under her hair. Something came alive deep down in her body. His hand felt rough and strong on her skin. His eyes lost the steady gaze that had attracted her to him, and became hard and needy. He pulled her closer. She twisted away and glared at him. 'Oh no you don't.'

344

He jumped back. 'What's wrong with you?' he asked. 'Don't you want to be touched?'

'I don't know,' Tessa said, feeling the old defences clamping around her. She drew wild patterns in the sand with her finger, spirals and sunrays.

'That's a pity,' Paul said, ''cause I really fancy you. But – no hassle – if you don't want me. There's plenty more fish in the sea.'

Tessa studied his eyes. She liked him, as a person, but now she saw a glint of rejection, screening a wild wolf within him. She felt afraid of him. She stood up and brushed the sand from her thighs. 'Surf's up,' she said.

'Yeah – I'm going in.' Paul looked disappointed. 'See ya later, eh?'

'Maybe.'

Tessa walked off on her own. She swung her rucksack onto her back and headed along Porthmeor Beach to The Island. A strange, disturbing feeling drove her to walk faster than usual as she left the beach and climbed up between the rocks to the grassy summit where St Nicholas Chapel guarded the bay. She sat down on a wooden bench, facing the sea, watching the cormorants on the rocks, their sepia wings spread out against the light. Her father would love them. She had a sudden longing for him, an ache of homesickness. In that moment, she was home again, at The Pines, and some great event was imminent. She was standing in her granny's garden, breathing the heady fragrance of pinks and pansies. She saw Annie, vividly, standing on the path, looking at her.

The troubled frown she'd so often had was gone. Annie's brow was smooth, and a radiant smile lit her face. She held out her arms to Tessa, something she'd never done, and her aura swirled with pastel colours, like pearl.

Tessa watched the brilliance of her vision. Annie looked so peaceful, and she'd never been peaceful. Her cheeks were rosy and tiny flowers shimmered around her as if drawn into her aura. 'I'm on my way,' she said, 'on my way home.'

The vision faded and vanished. Tessa ran down the path from The Island, dodging people who were walking up there, her rucksack swinging on her back. She ran to the telephone box by the harbour and dialled 100.

'Operator. Can I help you?'

'I want to make a reverse charge call, please,' Tessa said and waited, wondering if the operator could hear the pounding of her heart. She gave her home number, and the number of the phone box. She heard her mother answer, and the operator say, 'Will you accept a reverse charge call from a pay phone in St Ives?' and her mother's voice saying, 'Yes.'

'Hello Mum. It's Tessa.'

'Hello dear! Are you all right, my love?'

Tessa struggled with the need to cry. It was the kindness in Kate's voice that triggered it.

'Tessa?'

'Mum – it's Granny – isn't it?'

There was a shocked silence.

'I saw her,' Tessa said. 'She looked – beautiful, Mum – like an angel. She – she's gone over, hasn't she?'

346

'Oh Tessa!' Kate burst into tears, and Tessa just hung on and waited. Finally, Kate managed to speak. 'Are you still there?'

'Yes.'

'I'm so sorry, dear. Your granny died about an hour ago. Peacefully in her own bed.'

It was mid-afternoon, but Tessa headed back to her grassy hollow at the top of Porthminster Beach. She needed solitude, time to think about whether she should go home or not. Kate had begged her to go, for the funeral. 'You must be there. Lucy's coming, and Uncle George – all the family must be there.' Tessa wasn't interested in a funeral. She wanted to stay in St Ives, maybe forever. It was hard, but she decided to stand firm and not go home. Kate pleaded for an address where she could send letters, and of course there wasn't one. She'd made Tessa promise to ring her every day on a reversed charge call, but in her heart Tessa didn't even want to do that. Getting sucked into what she saw as 'old family stuff' would chip away at her precious newfound freedom. Living in the now, as Paul said. Not getting dragged to and fro by the past and the future.

She spent the rest of the day swimming in the tranquil waters of Porthminster, and wandering along the wooded cliff path which followed the railway. But part of her longed to be out at Clodgy watching the sunset.

As twilight glazed the sky with violet, Tessa retraced her steps along the wooded path to her sleeping place, planning her supper which was to be a bread roll, a triangle of Dairylea cheese and an orange.

But as she approached her grassy hollow, she was shocked to see someone else in there. Two hippies, a couple, settling down for the night, spreading their blankets and camping clutter all over the place. Tessa's first reaction was territorial fury. It was HER place. HER home. HER bed. And a bed was sacred – wasn't it?

She stopped some distance away, reasoning with herself. If she stomped in there and asked them to leave, they wouldn't care about her feelings. Rights to sleeping places didn't exist. She didn't want a confrontation, especially today when she was feeling vulnerable and tired. Now she felt violated. Angry. Lost. The list could go on and on.

It was getting dark. She saw the last train pull in to the station, and people disembarking, talking and laughing, carrying luggage. 'There's our hotel, darling!' she heard a man say, and for a moment a burning jealousy clawed at Tessa's heart. She wanted a man to call HER darling. She wanted a soft, clean bed, and a bathrobe and a hot chocolate.

She considered waking over to Clodgy and sleeping with the commune. It was a long way in the dark, and she still wanted to be on her own. In the end, she trudged miserably up the cliff path again and found a little alcove in some rocks. Too exhausted to inflate the airbed, she flung her duffle coat down and lay on it, using her rucksack as a pillow, and covering herself with Lou's ethnic blanket. The ground was rocky and uncomfortable. Only then did she allow the tears to flow.

She cried herself to sleep and woke up at midnight with the sobs still in her body, and a hollow feeling in her stomach that was almost a pain.

The sky was cloudy and it was pitch dark except for the light flashing from Godrevy Lighthouse. She lay listening nervously. There were footsteps, tiny footsteps – paws! – some kind of animal hunting through the woods. A shadow darker than the dark. It crept towards her, its feet moving faster, pattering on the dry earth. The shadow came right up to her – and kissed her face – she smelled fishy breath and felt its whiskers brush her cheek.

And then it purred.

A cat! A cat had found her. A warm, silky cat who was purring and making her smile. A cat who cuddled up to her, right under her chin, stretched his velvet paws over Lou's blanket and settled down, his eyes luminous as he stared at Tessa in the dark. She touched his gloriously thick fur in utter joy. 'Darling!' she said. 'You darling.' She switched on her torch for a quick look at him, and he was all black, his fur glistening in the torchlight. 'I LOVE you,' she said, smoothing him.

She couldn't have been happier when the cat crept under Lou's blanket and made it clear he intended to stay with her. And then she remembered she'd been dreaming about her granny, and Annie had had a black cat in her arms.

A gift of love – from spirit.

Chapter Twenty

THE BRIMMING RIVER

In the morning, the cat followed Tessa down The Warren, running beside her with his tail up. She figured he must belong to someone nearby for he looked well fed and glossy. Tessa didn't want him to get lost. Once they reached the Lifeboat House, his tail was down and he looked uneasy. She picked him up. 'Thank you, darling,' she crooned as the cat rubbed his cheek against hers. 'Don't follow me and get frightened. I'll come back later.' Reluctantly she put him down and waited to see what he would do. He gave her a quizzical stare, jumped onto the wall of a cottage garden and sat beautifully, his tail coiled around his legs. Tessa walked on with her rucksack, and when she looked back the cat was still there, washing his paws in the morning sun.

Live in the now, she thought, and headed up The Digey to Porthmeor Beach. The long night of crying had made her ache all over. She wasn't hungry. On the beach she changed quickly and plunged into the brilliance of the white surf and the jewel-green water, letting it stream through her hair. She emerged into the sunshine feeling cleansed and alive.

It happened very quickly.

One minute she was wading out of the sea, shaking the drops from her hair, her face alive with the energising joy of the sea. The next minute a man was standing in front of her, his hands open like a big flower. 'Tessa?'

She gasped, and found herself staring into his intense grey eyes. 'Art!' she cried. And then it started. That deep warm tingle inside, a new fire in a new place. She felt as if her entire body, mind and soul had burst into song.

'It is you!' Art said. 'Can I give you a hug?'

He was in his swimming trunks, his body looked warm and golden, like fresh bread.

'I'm wet,' she said.

'Who cares?'

Tessa moved in to his welcoming hug a bit hesitantly. He felt amazing, the texture of his skin deeply warm against hers which was ice cold from the sea. Her wet hair tumbled over his hairy chest and she pressed her ear against his heartbeat. His hands smoothed her back as if each fingertip had an electrical charge of energy.

They hugged for an eternal moment, and Tessa sensed a change in the air around them, a shimmering light, a skirt of diamonds swirling over the two of them, a sense that ribbons of the brightest gold were binding them together.

They pulled away. Looked at each other. Laughed, and hugged again, and this time Art's hands were lower down her back, the hairs on his arms brushing her waist. The tingle deep in her body was so strong that Tessa could hardly walk as he led her up the beach to where his surfboard was propped against the wall. They sat down on the soft sand.

'It's like a miracle. Meeting you here,' Art said. 'I've done nothing but dream about you since we met, Tessa.'

'Me too,' she admitted.

'You were only fourteen, weren't you? So – what's happened to you since? Where are you at?'

Tessa beamed. 'I'm finally doing my own thing,' she said. 'I'm at art college – or I was – but I'm through with conforming to the norm. I came down here – and I ADORE it. The surf – and the light – it's – oh, I can't find words.'

'How about – phantasmagorical?' Art said, and they both laughed. 'You've got dimples in your cheeks when you laugh, and you look – just beautiful, like a mermaid. I couldn't believe it when I saw you walking out of the sea.' His eyes wandered over her suntanned body, her skin glistening with salt crystals as the sea water dried in the sun. 'So where are you sleeping?'

'Under the stars – and I love it,' Tessa said. 'Except last night when someone else got in my sleeping place – but then a fabulous black cat turned up in the middle of the night and made such a fuss of me. He stayed all night with me.'

'A lucky black cat, maybe?'

'You could be right. My granny died yesterday, and she sent him to me. I know she did.'

'Ah – I remember – you're clairvoyant, aren't you?'

'Not openly – but yes.'

'Why not openly, Tessa?'

She hesitated.

'I see the shadow – still there in your lovely eyes,' Art said, and he took both her hands in his. 'I'd like to heal it, if you let me. I'd like to truly, truly set you free. I believe we were meant to meet today, Tessa – and what a way to meet – half naked on the beach!'

She laughed again. 'I shouldn't be laughing the day after my granny has died.'

'Why not? She wants you to be happy,' Art said. 'I rolled in the sand when my Nan died. She was such a dragon – and now she's gone, even my parents are unbuttoning their shirts. I never saw my Dad's chest in my whole life, and the day Nan died he threw his ties away and let it all hang out.'

Tessa giggled. 'That's very funny.'

'As for his feet, I never saw his feet either – until he came down here and actually took his socks off on the beach and there were these ghostly white objects underneath.'

He talked on, waving his hands expressively, and Tessa listened, fascinated, noticing details of him, the way his eyebrows moved a lot, the way the skin around his eyes crinkled when he laughed. She felt at home with him. Relaxed, as if she could say or do anything, and it would be okay.

'I'm very organised, for a hippy,' he said. 'I've got an old bus parked up on The Island car park. I've kitted out the inside and now I'm painting the bodywork in psychedelic colours.'

'I could help you with the painting,' Tessa said. 'I'd love to.'

'Groovy! – How about lunch with me in the *Man Friday*? I'd like to treat you, Tessa.'

Dazed with euphoria, Tessa slipped into her jeans and padded up the steps, with Art holding her hand very firmly. A free lunch, a chance to paint swirly colours on a bus, and precious time with Art. *My dreams are coming true*, she thought happily. *It must have been a lucky black cat!*

But Lou and Clare were not impressed. When they saw Tessa painting marigolds on Art's bus that afternoon, Lou pulled her to one side. 'You be careful, Tessa – with him.'

'What do you mean?' Tessa asked, annoyed.

'He's a lovely guy,' Lou said, her hand on Tessa's arm, 'but he's a womaniser. He'll break your heart.'

'I don't believe you.' Tessa frowned at Lou.

'Suit yourself – I'm just warning you.'

'She's right,' said Clare. 'We KNOW, don't we, Lou?'

'Know what?' asked Tessa.

Clare and Lou looked at each other. 'Trust me,' Lou said, 'we're just looking out for you, Tessa.'

'Thanks – but Art is the first man I've ever trusted. I'm following my heart,' Tessa said and Lou rolled her eyes, shrugged, and walked off.

She's wrong, Tessa thought angrily. *Art is my soulmate.*

Sex education had been a bad joke in Tessa's upbringing. In her last year at the Grammar School, the school had sent a letter out to parents informing them of their intention to introduce segregated 'sex awareness' in their senior classes. Two teachers were sent on courses, and the PE teacher, who Tessa hated, was assigned to teach the girls. It was to be a six-week course, starting in January, and that was the month when Tessa had bronchitis and then mumps. She missed all but two of the 'sex awareness' classes, and the ones she did attend were no help to her at all. The PE teacher strutted around in front of the class, tight-lipped, with a flipchart, and droned on about 'the development of the foetus'. Tessa sat at the back, daydreaming and drawing horses in her jotter, and she never found out what the 'foetus' actually was. She did frown at a chart of a baby standing on its head inside a woman's womb, but didn't make the connection. As for how it had got in there, nothing was said and nobody dared ask. At Hilbegut no one seemed to have heard of sex education, and at Art College everyone else seemed to know about it, so Tessa had pretended she did too.

Kate had prepared her well for her periods starting, but again there was no connection. Periods were known as 'the curse', just something women had to endure, preferably in silence. Kate kept a stack of sanitary pads in the airing cupboard and always referred to them as 'ammunition'. Lucy had lent Tessa a dog-eared paperback which was doing the rounds at school, and she'd read bits of it by torchlight under the blankets. She dismissed it as either boring, disgusting or irrelevant. Once, she had dared to ask her mother about sex, and Kate had said haughtily, 'You don't do it until you're married, dear, and then I'll tell you about it'. The word love was never connected with sex. Love belonged to romance in books, and that was what Tessa hoped for. Romance. Not sex!

Now that Art had ignited this mysterious flame in her body, Tessa thought about romance a lot. She talked to the cat about it. Every night he was waiting for her, followed her back to her sleeping place, and slept the night with her. She gave him a name – Ferdinand, the name of the prince in her favourite Shakespeare play, *The Tempest*.

The weather held, dry and sunny; the days rolled by, blue and gold and balmy. Still she hadn't told Art where she was sleeping. Solitude was important to Tessa. It was like a place, a place of recovery and survival. Sharing it with a beautiful cat was a bonus. The cat was a good listener, and a comfort.

Running barefooted on the soft grass paths of The Island was something Tessa loved to do while Art was surfing. The Island was not actually an island but joined to the harbour by a narrow strip of land. At the summit was the small granite chapel of St Nicholas, and the views were panoramic, with the surf beach and Clodgy on one side, and the harbour, the wooded cliffs and the miles of Hayle sands stretching out to Godrevy Lighthouse. In the afternoons the sun made a great sheet of oscillating sparkles on the sea.

Now that Tessa could leave her rucksack and coat safely in Art's bus, she exulted in being able to run freely up the grass paths between the rocks. She had a favourite rock where she liked to stand and lift her arms to the sun's vast flare path of light. She felt as if the sparkles were energising every molecule of her body. She felt close to the angels. But not close enough. There was still some kind of emotional razor wire, a cruel fence separating her from her true self. She was afraid. Afraid of that self.

Art had lent her a book he loved. A slim, cream and brown paperback, dog-eared from much use. It was *WARRIORS OF THE RAINBOW (Strange and Prophetic Dreams of the Indian Peoples)*. 'It blows my mind,' he'd said. Parts of it had the same effect on Tessa. She read it avidly, rereading and absorbing it, and in its pages she found truths that were slowly setting her free. Permission to dream. Freedom to run barefoot. Freedom to reconnect with the web of life, the animals, the birds, the secret voices of wind and water.

But what she needed most wasn't there. Freedom to love. To love like a child was no longer enough. She wanted to love like a woman. To love Art. She prayed he would wait. She prayed he would help her.

As a child Tessa had visualised her future life like a shining pathway sweeping into the distance, over mountains, through the winking lights of cities, and rainforests, and oceans. But now, when she dared to look, the pathway ended abruptly. There were iron gates, and three iron grey figures guarding them. Miss O'Grady, the Reverend Reminsy, and Ivor Stape.

Art's parents now lived in Truro and he'd told Tessa she could use their address for letters. One morning he handed her a blue envelope with her father's copperplate writing on it. Inside were letters from both her parents. They wanted her to come home. They wanted her to go back to college. *What about what I want?* Tessa thought angrily, and for the first time she understood how Lucy had felt. Then some words jumped out of Freddie's letter. The lime tree seeds had grown! Tessa's heart leapt with joy.

She told Art about the woods.

'Aw – man, that's tragic,' he said. 'Those beautiful woods. I really care about issues like that, and you do too – I can tell. Let's go out on the cliffs and give those thoughts to the universe. Maybe it will have some answers.'

Tessa was happy to go with him. She knew that something was going to happen between them. She wanted it to be on the springy turf high above the rolling waves. So far, Art hadn't done anything except kiss her on the cheek, and she'd gone away with the feel of the kiss embossed on her consciousness. What he had done was a lot of quiet focused talking, telling her she was beautiful and creative. Telling her she was a rare and sensitive being. It was a new experience for Tessa, and a nurturing one. And the quieter his voice was, the more his eyes glowed into hers, the more she burned and tingled for him to touch her. When he did, she'd be ready, she'd be on fire.

She led him to one of the fairy gardens she'd found cloistered in the mighty granite outcrops, where the grass was deep and cushiony with mounds of thrift. There they sat, with a gentle breeze wafting in from the sea, the piping cries of oystercatchers down on the rocks, and the vibrating seed heads of the sea pinks adding energy to the earth. Art looked at her for a long time, his hair frizzy in the light, his soul shining into hers. She loved the slowness, the way he was letting it build, letting their auras fuse together. She loved the hunger in his eyes, and the way he kept it back, like holding a powerful horse on a thin rein, not with cruelty. With love.

Hardly breathing, she waited for him like a butterfly on a flower. Soft. Brightly coloured. Exquisitely sensitive. And when she felt his lips finding hers, she wanted to scream and writhe with excitement. She opened her mouth and let him in, let him kiss her deeply, let him draw her into a sacred eternal moment when love flowed between them. It felt like the sun's rays focused through a magnifying glass, making fire while the ice cold waves of the Atlantic rose ever higher, wilder, brighter than snow.

Art pulled away from her, and they lay with their faces close, their eyes full of wordless light. Tessa ran her hands over his broad, bare shoulders and into his sun-bleached chest hair. She kissed his throat, then took his hand and kissed his fingers, one by one, then found his lips again, found the heat and the magic rippling between them.

'Happy?' he asked as they pulled away again and gazed at each other.

'Very, very – super happy,' Tessa murmured.

'Good,' he whispered. 'That's what I want. I don't want to rush you, Tessa. I'm holding back – you know that, don't you? I want to be sure that you're ready for me – all of me. Are you?'

Tessa hesitated. She searched his eyes. 'I don't want to spoil this,' she said. 'It's so romantic.'

'Why would you spoil it?'

'I don't know – I might – panic.'

'Panic? Why? Is it your first time?'

'No,' Tessa said, and she felt her body shutting down, the magic leaving. It was like a conflict between the new, loving, alive Tessa, and the old, terrified, imprisoned Tessa. She looked at Art hopelessly.

'Where are you?' he asked. 'Where have you gone, Tessa? A minute ago you were radiant and loving. You're a natural lover, Tessa. And you want me – I can tell. So what happened? Tell me. I want to understand.'

She sat rigid, the way she had been for most of her life. Afraid. The sea had opened her up. Now Art was there, warm and alive and concerned. He wasn't forcing her. *I might never get this chance again, in my whole life*, she thought. *I have to try.*

'Please – trust me, Tessa. What is it?' Art asked. 'Talk to me.'

She stared silently at the waves. She saw Jonti's eager little face circling in front of her in the water, only the water was black, and it was the Mill Pool. Why had she never told anyone?

'I was a bad girl . . .' she began, and couldn't help smiling when Art said, 'Aw – I love bad girls!'

'Seriously,' Tessa said. 'I was a cry-baby and a trouble-maker. A teacher called Miss O'Grady, who looked like a

badly weathered clothes peg, absolutely hated me. She
rubbished everything I did, especially my dreams and my
visions. She tried to get me expelled, and she sat me in front
of the vicar, with my mum there, and they all had a go at me
– for being creative, and for talking about spirit people, and
for being hypersensitive. They threatened to send me to a
home for bad children, and I believed them. I was so terrified
that I actually collapsed – and when I came round, I felt like
a seashell.'

'A seashell?'

'Like an empty shell washed up on a beach, with the life
torn out of it. From that moment, Art, I was suicidal. That's
when it started. I tried so hard to conform, I was like a robot.
Only my Dad understood me, then I met Selwyn, and Lexi,
and YOU. You really helped me, that day – as if you'd given
me back my dreams . . .'

'I'm glad,' Art said, gently moving a tendril of her chestnut
hair from her cheek. He tucked it behind her ear.

'BUT,' Tessa said, 'all of that happened just after I'd
been . . . abused by this strange man – I don't know why I've
never EVER told anyone. I guess I thought telling them
would make me even more of a bad girl – and what he did
completely shattered my trust in men – and it's stayed with
me, like a concrete barrier – a dam across a river – so that
every time a boy wanted to kiss me, I'd freeze or push him
away. But . . . I don't want to push you away, Art – I don't.'

'Then let's break that barrier down, together,' Art said.
'Let me hold you, safe, in my arms – darling – and you can

tell me everything you want to, and we'll transmute it together, send it into the light, and let the real, beautiful Tessa emerge.'

He held her against his heart and she relaxed with a little sigh, and began to talk. 'When I was seven . . .'

'She's living with the blimin' hippies,' Freddie said, looking at Kate over the top of Tessa's letter. 'She's with some guy living in a blimin' old bus in some car park – illegally.'

'Let me read it,' Kate said and Freddie handed her the letter in disgust. He'd read the first paragraph and that was enough. Looking around at their lovely home, it hurt him unbearably to think that his daughter didn't want to live in it. Instead she'd chosen to shack up with some hippie, the lowest of the low in Freddie's opinion.

'All the years I worked and saved me money, and she does this!'

'We've got to stop her,' Kate said. 'We could make her a ward of court, couldn't we? Get her home and talk some sense into her.'

'It wouldn't work. It would just drive her away.'

'I mean – supposing she got arrested? Or took drugs? We've got to protect her, Freddie. And what about her wellbeing? It sounds as if she's living on bags of chips and biscuits.'

'All the effort we've put into giving her a good education,' said Freddie bitterly, 'and she's throwing it all away. Doesn't appreciate it.'

'But – wait a minute – have you read the second page of her letter?'

'No. The first was bad enough.'

'It's not ALL bad,' Kate said. 'Tessa keeps telling me on the phone – and she's written it here – that she's never been so happy in her whole life, Freddie. She keeps on trying to tell us that. Shouldn't we be trying to understand? We mustn't be two old fuddy-duddies, like Lucy said we were. Don't you think we should be glad she's found happiness? Ethie never did.'

'Ah – Ethie.'

'Remember when Tessa was born?' Kate said. 'How we all thought she was like Ethie? In a way, she has been just as difficult, or worse, and you've been so good with her, Freddie. You're close, you and Tessa. I wouldn't want anything to break that bond.'

'No. I wouldn't either,' agreed Freddie. He thought of the words hidden away in the sealed envelope. Not for the first time he wanted to open it up and share it with Kate, especially now that his mother was gone. 'Tessa hasn't fulfilled her potential yet. She hasn't found her life's purpose, if you know what I mean, Kate. Even art college – I'm not sure it's right for her – are you?'

'Oh, but she MUST stick to it,' Kate said. 'We can't let her throw that away as well!'

A memory fell into place in Freddie's mind. He saw himself at twelve years old, under an apple tree with his parents. The day he found out that they had planned his future for him. The day they had trodden on his dreams.

'My parents tried to force me to be a baker,' he said, 'and it was the last thing I wanted. They gambled all their money on it – for me – and I had to do it. I hated it – but in the end I broke free, and it was hard. But Mother ended up proud of me, and dependent on me too. Tessa's got dreams, Kate. Maybe we don't even know what they are. So let's not go talking about wards of court and all that. We should wait and see what happens.' He looked at Kate's beautiful eyes, and saw how much she was worrying over Tessa. 'Let it be, Kate,' he said, 'let it be.'

He needed to go for a walk and clear his mind. At times like this he missed having Jonti to go with him. 'I'm going for a walk,' he said, 'and by the way, Kate – I have dreams too, and they're not about making bird boxes all me life.'

Kate gave him a hug and a kiss. She straightened his collar a little and looked at him adoringly. 'You're wonderful,' she said.

Freddie walked down towards the station, his hands in his pockets, thinking about his dream. It was one of those times when he felt something was going to happen.

A few people were standing along the sides of the road, and the church bell was tolling. A funeral cortège was coming slowly up the hill. Freddie stopped, respectfully, to let it pass by, and noticed a coffin with no flowers on top. *How sad*, he thought.

A man from the quarry was standing next to him, watching. 'Whose funeral is it?' Freddie asked.

'Ivor Stape. From The Mill.'

★   ★   ★

The long hot summer began to break in the last week of August. The wind changed, the sea changed, and the surfers talked knowingly about 'the return of the Westerlies', and the highest tides of the year drove the sea over the harbour wall and into the town. A huge swell, from a hurricane thousands of miles across the Atlantic, sent enormous waves towering into Porthmeor Beach and surf flew high over the Clodgy rock. But the sun still shone, and the fairy gardens in the shelter of the rocks were warm from the heat of the granite and the dry earth.

Art spent a lot of time surfing the massive waves while Tessa just played and splashed around in the foam. She didn't want a surfboard, didn't feel she could balance on one, but loved being in the sea. Her body was tanned, her chestnut hair had strands of sun-bleached gold, and her face was rosy and alive. She had never felt, or looked, so good. Yet she still slept alone under the stars, with the cat nestled into her shoulder.

One morning when Art was in the sea, Paul turned up with all his stuff crammed into a huge rucksack. He swung it down from his shoulders and sat down on the sand next to Tessa. She felt awkward with him now, sensing his jealousy of her friendship with Art.

'Don't look so worried, Tessa,' he said, and his hazel eyes looked at her with resignation. 'I'm heading off – back to London.'

'You are?'

'Yeah – don't look so shocked. I've had a great summer – but I don't want to be stony broke forever. I want to build something – I've got to give it a go – work, I mean. Conforming. Going straight. Shaving my head and wearing a suit.'

'That's so sad,' Tessa said, studying the disappointment in his eyes.

'Yeah – it is, and it isn't. I want to study music – and London is the place.' Paul fixed his eyes on hers. 'But it's not over, Tessa, between us. I know you're with Art now – but if it doesn't work out, here's my London address. Look me up sometime – please?'

'Okay,' Tessa said. 'I've got a friend in London, so I might be there sometime.'

'I think you're fantastic, Tessa. Look me up – when – when he breaks your heart.'

'Oh he won't!' Tessa said, but Paul stood up, heaved the rucksack onto his shoulders and walked off without another word. She sat holding the card he'd given her, with mixed feelings. She liked him. But there was no comparison. She loved Art, blindly, unconditionally, and forever.

There was a sense of summer ending. The hippie commune was starting to disband as people drifted away, going back to university, or home, or moving inland for the winter. Tessa knew she wouldn't be able to continue sleeping out, and every night now felt like a gift.

On the last hot day, when people were talking about a storm coming in, she and Art walked the coastal path towards Zennor. 'It's now or never,' Tessa was thinking. She'd got herself on the pill, thanks to Lou who knew a doctor who didn't ask questions. Art had been fantastically patient with her. Soon she would be sleeping in the bus with him. She wanted it to happen in the place she loved, in the deep warm grass between the rocks with the glittering waves pounding at the shore.

She was terrified she would do it wrong.

'You have to trust your body, Tessa,' Art said. 'It knows exactly what to do – and yours definitely does.'

She was terrified that the image of Ivor Stape would haunt her at the last minute and turn off the magic.

'I am stronger than him,' Art said reassuringly. 'I'm alive and here for you, Tessa – darling.'

She loved it when he called her 'darling'. Spoken in his quiet voice, echoed in his eyes, 'darling' was a transformational word.

There would be fear.

But, on the other side of fear, there would be magic.

She sensed his excitement as he lowered her into the grass. She loved that he didn't hurry. Art took it slowly, kissing and touching and murmuring to her. She loved the tantalising way he paused to look into her eyes and tell her she was beautiful, the most beautiful woman on earth.

She loved the way he said, 'I'd like – to make love with you – now.'

The resonance of the 'now' seemed to open a stream of magic within her. And, once it began its tingling journey, she couldn't stop. She didn't even remember how or when her clothes had come off. She just let go, and loved the hard, hot feel of him inside her, the way he sighed and groaned with pleasure, the way she cried out with joy, again and again, until the stream of magic became, at last, the 'brimming river'.

> *'And out again I curve and flow*
> *to join the brimming river.*
> *For men may come and men may go,*
> *but I go on forever.'*
>
> 'The Brook'
> by Alfred Lord Tennyson

Epilogue

Freddie was sipping his mid-morning cuppa when he saw a man in a suit coming up the path, a long brown envelope in his hand. 'Whoever is that?' He waited for the envelope to come through the letterbox, but the man rang the doorbell. As usual, Freddie let Kate go to the door while he sat in the kitchen, listening.

'Are you Mrs Barcussy?'

'I am, yes. What can I do for you?'

'Is your husband here?'

'Yes.'

'Good – then I need to see both of you. It concerns your daughter, Tessa.'

'You'd better come in,' Kate said, and Freddie heard the fear in her voice. What had Tessa done now? He glanced uneasily at the man who stood awkwardly by the kitchen table, tapping the long brown envelope. Kate pulled out a chair. 'Do sit down.'

He's too clean, Freddie thought, looking at the man's well-scrubbed nails.

'I'm Elliot Rutherford and I'm a lawyer, from Rutherford

and Barnes, Solicitors in Monterose,' he began, and Kate reached across the table and held Freddie's hand tightly.

'It concerns your daughter, Tessa, in connection with the will of the late Mr Ivor Stape of The Mill.'

Freddie tensed. 'We don't want nothing to do with him, or his will,' he said forcefully, 'and Tessa's not here. She's – away.'

'Well – legally, I have to give you this.' Elliot Rutherford pushed the envelope across the table.

Freddie pushed it back. 'We don't want anything from Ivor Stape. You can take it away with you.'

'No – I can't do that. I am bound by law to make sure that you read it,' said Elliot Rutherford, 'and if you refuse, then I am duty bound to open it and read it to you.'

'Is it bad news?' Kate asked.

'I don't think so.'

'Then I shall read it.' Kate took the envelope and opened it. She pulled out a document on expensive, cream paper, and unfolded it. She stared at Freddie. 'It's his will. Ivor Stape's will – what's that to do with us?'

'Read clause 17, over the page,' said Elliot Rutherford. 'I've marked it in red for you.'

Freddie watched Kate's eyes scanning the text. Then she looked up at him with one of heart-stopping smiles. 'Everything's all right, Freddie. And guess what?'

'What?'

'Ivor Stape has left Tessa a plot of land! Ten acres, on the edge of the woods – oh – fancy that, Freddie!'

Elliot Rutherford smiled at Kate's enthusiasm. 'Tessa can't have it until she's twenty-one, so you are to be the custodians – hold it in trust for her.'

'Where exactly is this land?' Freddie asked. 'Have you got a map?'

'I have. There – it's shaded in red.' Elliot Rutherford unfolded the map and slid it across the table.

Freddie put his glasses on and studied it. 'Ah – I know those fields. That's good land – lovely land. Next door to Lexi's place.'

Unexpectedly, Freddie had one of his visions. He saw spirit people around the table. Granny Barcussy, Annie, his father Levi, Kate's father Bertie, all of them nodding and smiling, and little Jonti sitting at Bertie's feet. Freddie's bitter thoughts melted away, and light flooded in as he saw the last piece of his dream fall into place.

'I believe Mr Stape added a note to that clause,' said Elliot Rutherford. 'You might want to read that too.'

Kate and Freddie bent over the document, their heads close as they read the codicil attached to clause 17. 'Well!' said Kate. 'What a surprise. He's apologised – and said that Tessa told him how much she loved the stream, and that's why he left her the land.'

'That middle field has got a stream in it,' said Elliot Rutherford.

'Ah – I know,' Freddie said, and he looked at Kate. 'That's a spring. And it's the source of the Mill Stream.'

*   *   *

Kate hardly recognised the young woman who stood at the door. 'TESSA!' she gasped, and held out her arms.

'Mum!'

They hugged, and laughed, and hugged again.

'You look – so different. I can't believe it,' Kate said warmly. She stood back and looked at her daughter with pride. The light blue denim jacket and flared jeans suited Tessa, and so did the gold-blonde streaks and the crinkly ribbons and beads in her hair. Her face was suntanned and alive – and she was laughing! But what amazed Kate was the radiance in her pale blue eyes. They were full of light, the way they had been on that day so long ago when she'd been dancing in the rain.

'That's because I'm happy, Mum,' Tessa said.

'But you – you look – transformed,' Kate said. 'You look like a goddess in a painting.'

Freddie was overwhelmed when he saw Tessa. 'That's my girl!' he muttered, holding her. 'I'm glad you've come home.'

'Art is here too,' Tessa said, smiling at Art who stood back quietly, enjoying the reunion.

Kate gave Art a hug while Tessa and Freddie were gazing at each other, both smiling from ear to ear.

'You're very welcome, Art,' Kate said. 'Did you drive all the way from Cornwall in your wonderful bus?'

'Yeah – took us three days, but we had a great time. Camped on Dartmoor under the stars.'

Kate took Art's hands. 'Thank you,' she said, 'from my

heart. You've transformed our little Tessa into a shining star.'

Art grinned. 'No hassle.'

Later that day, Art and Tessa sat on the grass at the source of the Mill Stream. The water glinted in the mellow October sunlight as it gushed out of the hillside. The land smelled of apples and wood smoke, and the air had a chill of autumn. Spindleberries and sprays of rosehips hung over the spring, tendrils of old man's beard, purple elderberries and bryony.

Tessa had brought a peace rose from the garden, and they sat looking at its creamy petals, flushed with pink, a huge flower, voluptuously soft.

'It could float all the way – down to the river – and out into the Atlantic!' Art said.

'Who knows – it will have to cross the dark mill pool,' Tessa said, 'like I did. It's part of the journey.'

Together they threw the rose into the spring, and watched it go twirling away down the bright stream.

'Love and peace,' Art said. 'May it travel far.'

Author's Note

The words of Madame Eltura will be revealed in the third and final book of this family saga, which will tell the inspiring story of Tessa's struggle to fulfil her destiny.

Acknowledgements

Thank you to my agent, Judith Murdoch, for believing in me; the great team at Simon & Schuster UK, and to Beth Emanuel for her dedicated help in preparing the manuscript.